By Todd McCaffrey
Published by Ballantine Books

DRAGONHOLDER
DRAGONSBLOOD
DRAGONHEART

By Anne McCaffrey and Todd McCaffrey

DRAGON'S KIN
DRAGON'S FIRE
DRAGON HARPER

DRAGONGIRL

DRAGONGIRL

TODD McCAFFREY

BALLANTINE BOOKS • NEW YORK

Copyright © 2010 by Todd McCaffrey and Anne McCaffrey

Published in the United States by Ballantine Books, an imprint of The Random House Publishing Group, a division of Random House, Inc., New York.

DEL REY is a registered trademark and the Del Rey colophon is a trademark of Random House, Inc.

Library of Congress Cataloging-in-Publication Data

McCaffrey, Todd
Dragongirl / Todd McCaffrey.
p. cm.—(Dragonriders of Pern)
ISBN 978-0-345-49116-9
1. Dragons—Fiction. 2. Pern (Imaginary place)—Fiction. I. Title.
PS3563.A25525D68 2010
813'.54—dc22   2010014672

Printed in the United States of America

www.delreybooks.com

2 4 6 8 9 7 5 3 1

First Edition

This one is just for Ladybug.

ACKNOWLEDGMENTS

No one truly labors alone, authors in particular, and I'd like to acknowledge those who helped bring this book to fruition.

First, of course, I'd like to say thanks to my mother, Anne McCaffrey, for continuing to allow me to play in her sandbox.

Second, I'd like to thank my marvelous first readers: Angelina Adams, Margaret Johnson, Susan Martin, and Pam Bennett-Skinner. Their comments allowed me to make this book much *much* better than it otherwise would have been.

Shelly Shapiro, editor *par excellence* at Del Rey did not shy from her role of demanding the very best I could give, and Martha Trachtenberg once more performed a marvelous job of copyediting. They are definitely a great team.

Judith Welsh, my editor at Transworld, once again provided her insights and support, working seamlessly with the editors at Del Rey to allow us to produce one consistent editorial voice.

And finally, I'd like to thank Don Maass, my agent and first-first reader.

Despite everyone's efforts, there are probably some errors in this book—that's just the nature of the beast. As the guy who ultimately determines what goes into the book, those errors are all mine.

FOR READERS NEW TO PERN

Thousands of years after man first developed interstellar travel, colonists from Earth, Tau Ceti III, and many other worlds settled upon Pern, the third planet of the star Rukbat in the Sagittarius sector.

They found Pern idyllic for their purposes: a pastoral world far off the standard trade routes and perfect for those recovering from the horrors of the Nathi Wars.

Led by the hero Admiral Paul Benden, and Governor Emily Boll of war-torn Tau Ceti, the colonists quickly abandoned their star-traveling technology in favor of a simpler life. For eight years—"Turns," as they called them on Pern—the settlers spread and multiplied on Pern's lush Southern Continent, unaware that a menace was fast approaching: the Red Star.

The Red Star, as the colonists came to call it, was actually a wandering planetoid that had been captured by Rukbat millennia before. It had a highly elliptical, cometary orbit, passing through the fringes of the system's Oort Cloud before hurtling back inward toward the warmth of the sun, a cycle that took two hundred and fifty Turns.

For fifty of those Turns, the Red Star was visible in the night sky of Pern. Visible and deadly, for when the Red Star was close enough, as it was for those fifty long Turns, a space-traveling spore could cross the void from it to Pern. Once it entered the tenuous upper atmosphere, the spore would thin out into a long, narrow, streamer shape and float down to the ground below, as seemingly harmless "Threads."

Like all living things, however, Thread needed sustenance. It was highly evolved—it ate anything organic: wood or flesh, it was all the same to Thread.

The first deadly Fall of Thread caught the colonists completely unawares. They barely survived. In the aftermath they came up with a desperate plan: Having abandoned their high technology, they turned to their remaining ability in genetic engineering to create a shield against the recurrent threat. They used life-forms indigenous to Pern, six-limbed, winged, fire-lizards that were genetically modified and enhanced to produce huge, rideable fire-breathing dragons. These dragons, telepathically linked at birth to their riders, formed the mainstay of the protection of Pern. In their haste to provide protection to their new homeworld, the colonists devised many other solutions. Some were forgotten or dismissed as ineffective.

The approach of the Red Star brought not only the mindless Thread but produced tremendous additional stresses on Pern itself. The tectonically active Southern Continent heaved with volcanoes and earthquakes, providing an additional menace that proved too much for the colonists— hastily they abandoned their original settlements and moved to the smaller, stabler Northern Continent. In their haste, much was lost and much was forgotten.

Huddled in one settlement, called Fort Hold, the colonists soon discovered themselves overcrowded, particularly with the growing dragon population. So the dragons moved into their own high mountain space, which they called Fort Weyr. As time progressed and the population spread across Pern, more Holds were formed and more Weyrs were created by the dragonriders.

Given their great losses, particularly in able-bodied older folk, the people of Fort and the other Holds soon found themselves resorting to authoritarian systems under which one Lord Holder became the ultimate authority of the Hold.

The Weyrs, with their different needs, developed differently. Unable to both provide for themselves and protect the planet, the dragonriders relied upon a tithe from the Holds for their maintenance. Instead of a Lord Holder, they had a Weyrleader—the rider of whichever dragon flew the Weyr's senior queen.

And so the two populations grew separate, distant, and somewhat intolerant of each other.

The Red Star grew fainter, Thread stopped falling. Then, after a two hundred Turn "Interval," it returned again to rain death and destruction from the skies for another fifty-Turn "Pass." Again, Pern relied on fragile dragon wings and their staunch riders to keep it Thread-free. And, again, the Pass ended, and a second Interval began.

Just at the beginning of the Third Pass, a new disaster struck—dragons started dying of a strange unknown disease. With his Weyr's ranks decimated not just by injuries and losses from fighting Thread but also from the deaths caused by this new plague, Weyrleader K'lior of Fort Weyr decided upon a desperate course of action and sent his injured dragons and riders ten Turns back in time to abandoned Igen Weyr where they might heal and return in time to fight the next Threadfall.

That same night, Fiona, Fort Weyr's newest and youngest queen rider, was wondering how the convalescent riders would fare, when a strange queen rider arrived and offered to bring her and her weyrling back in time to Igen Weyr. Fiona and the other weyrlings accepted. Their desperate jump *between* time proved fabulously successful and, after spending three Turns living and growing in the past, they returned to Fort Weyr with the recovered dragons and riders—a mere three days' time after they'd left.

But the plague is still killing dragons, the Weyrs are still fighting shorthanded—and no one knows whether Pern will survive.

CHRONOLOGY OF THE
SECOND INTERVAL/THIRD PASS

DATE (AL)	EVENT	BOOK
492.4	Marriage: Terregar and Silstra	*Dragon's Kin*
493.10	Kisk Hatches	*Dragons' Kin*
494.1	Kindan to Harper Hall	*Dragon's Kin*
495.8	C'tov Impresses Sereth	*Dragon's Fire*
496.8	Plague Starts	*Dragon Harper*
497.5	Plague Ends	*Dragon Harper*
498.7.2	Fort Weyr riders arrive back in time at Igen Weyr	*Dragonsblood, Dragonheart*
501.3.18	Fort Weyr riders return from Igen Weyr	*Dragonheart*
507.11.17	Fiona Impresses Talenth	*Dragonheart*
507.12.20	Lorana Impresses Arith	*Dragonsblood*
508.1.7	Start of Third Pass	*Dragonsblood, Dragonheart*
508.1.19	Arith goes *between*	*Dragonsblood, Dragonheart*
508.1.27	Fort Weyr riders time it back ten Turns to Igen Weyr	*Dragonsblood, Dragonheart*
508.2.2	Fort Weyr riders return from Igen Weyr	*Dragonsblood,Dragonheart*

ON PERNESE TIME:

The Pernese date their time from their arrival on Pern, referring to each Turn as "After Landing" (AL).

The Pernese calendar is composed of thirteen months, each of twenty-eight days (four weeks, or sevendays) with a special "Turnover" day at the end of each Turn for a total of 365 days.

CONTENTS

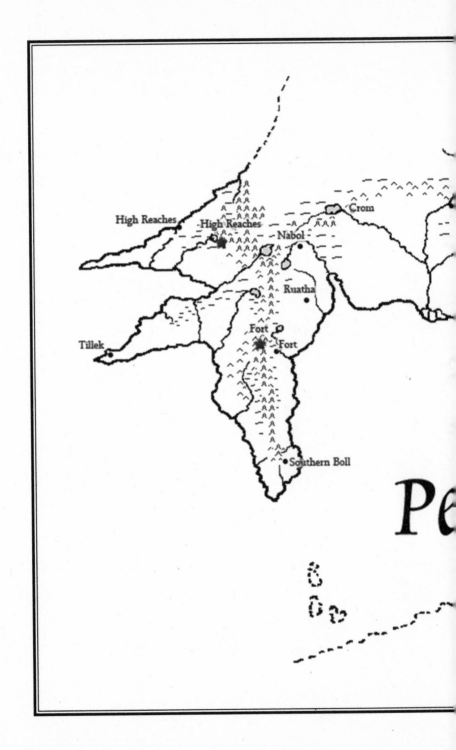

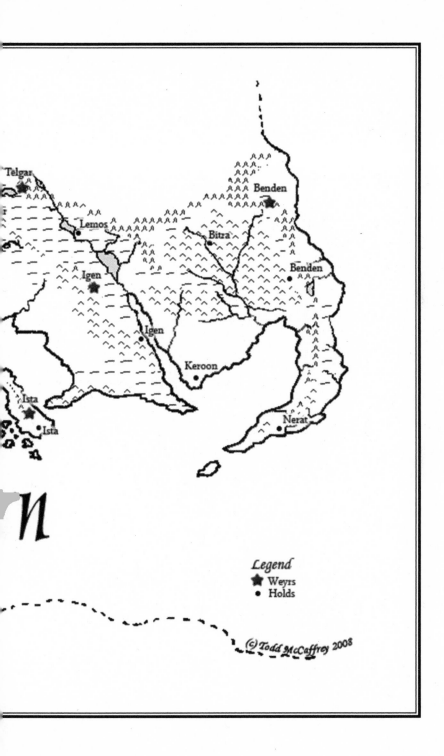

Telgar

Benden

Lemos

Bitra

Benden

Igen

Igen

Keroon

Ista

Ista

Nerat

Legend

★ Weyrs

● Holds

(c) Todd McCaffrey 2008

𝑁

DRAGONGIRL

ONE

Heart, give voice to sing
Of life on dragon wings!

Fort Weyr, AL 508.2.2

It was still snowing, and cold. Fiona shivered, wishing she hadn't out-grown her warm fur-lined leathers. Back in hot Igen, heavy clothing had been out of place, but here, at Fort Weyr, it was invaluable.

Her nose and lungs froze as she took another breath. Frantically, she pulled a portion of her thin scarf up to cover her nose; the air was easier to breathe that way, but her breath fogged her vision.

It had been an age for her since that time—only days ago here—when the strange gold rider had come:

"Get dressed," the rider had said. "We must be quick. We can't wake the others."

Fiona had had only an instant to decide: a rash plunge into the un-known. Why had she taken it?

But she had; and for three Turns she'd been Weyrwoman of Igen Weyr, which had been abandoned until she and the other Fort dragonriders had gone back ten Turns in time to use it as a place to grow and heal . . .

She'd learned to trade, learned to fly, and learned what it meant to be a Weyrwoman.

She had nearly seventeen Turns now, but here, back in her own time, they still thought her not yet fourteen. A part of her longed for that, longed to give the responsibility for decisions to others, to rest and relax and just focus on raising her queen.

Her queen. Beautiful Talenth had grown, had become a queen in all her glory, ready for her first mating flight, ready to add her hatchlings to the dragons of Pern.

When Fiona had realized that, had really understood, she had turned to T'mar. The bronze rider had been her mentor, her trainer, and the Weyrleader of the small group of injured and immature riders who had accompanied her back in time. He had been the one person who could help her take that next step in becoming a queen rider. There was a bond between them, she knew it. More than shared peril, more than shared times. He had a piece of her heart, freely given. But, she thought with a breath of the cold air, he didn't have it all.

Kindan. He was also there, on her horizon. As a child, she had loved him, while he had loved her older sister, Koriana. During her time at Igen, in the past, she had met him again, but she'd been older, and he hadn't recognized her. Now, as a grown woman, she had discovered that her feelings for him were no less than they'd been when she was a girl. Did she love him, she challenged herself, or did she just want to prove that she was as good as Koriana, whom he'd held in his arms as she died?

"Are you ready?" Terin asked, from her perch in front of Fiona.

"I'm ready," Fiona said, moving her scarf away and glancing down to the Weyr Bowl below.

The older riders had already landed. T'mar was being embraced by Weyrleader K'lior, and there, to one side, stood dark-haired, quiet Xhinna.

"Oh, please, let's land by Xhinna!" Terin said, as she spotted the weyrgirl. "Wait until she sees that I'm taller than her now!"

Three Turns. Three days. Xhinna had been her best friend before she'd left for Igen, but much had happened since, and Fiona realized that Xhinna had become a memory, nearly lost in all that time. Now Xhinna was only three days older, while Fiona had aged three Turns. Could they just pick up where they had left off? Or start anew?

Seeing Cisca, Fort's Weyrwoman, walking toward her as she leaped down from Talenth aroused further apprehension. At Igen, Fiona had been a Weyrwoman among boys and injured riders. Could she now return to her junior role under Cisca? It would be safe, she knew. It would be easy, too. But the part of her that stored and cherished the images of her father and Kindan, both so strong and determined, urged her to do more. And then Fiona wondered: Were leaders always scared?

If it was any warmer down in the Weyr Bowl, Fiona couldn't tell it from the cold·stares she received. She couldn't place the reaction at first, until she realized: They didn't recognize her.

Terin's hand slipped into hers and Fiona guessed that the younger girl was coming to the same realization. Terin waved her free hand at Xhinna. "Xhinna, it's me!"

The weyrgirl turned in their direction, her blue eyes sad and careworn.

"She looks like she lost her best friend," Terin said to Fiona.

"She has," Cisca said, having gotten close enough to overhear. Fiona looked at her, surprised that she was nearly eye level with the Weyrwoman. "Three days ago the weyrlings and—"

Even Cisca didn't know who she was. Fiona felt a lump in her throat. It was hard to speak. "Me, Weyrwoman."

"The gold rider brought us," Terin said, glancing up to Cisca and then quickly away, her eyes drifting back to Xhinna.

Cisca was staring intently at Fiona, studying her face. Then she let out a sob. "Fiona?" She grabbed Fiona and clutched her tightly, bruisingly, and Fiona felt guilty as the Weyrwoman's hot tears rained down on her. "We thought—" She pushed away from Fiona, her face clouding as anger replaced relief.

"I brought them back, Cisca," Fiona said hurriedly, waving an arm to the riders and dragons behind her, hoping to avoid the Weyrwoman's wrath. "They're ready to fight. All of them."

Cisca looked beyond her to the riders and dragons in the Weyr Bowl. "The weyrlings?"

"Trained and ready," Fiona said, letting justifiable pride creep into her voice. This much she had done. She had fought, she had succeeded, she had overcome her own fears and kept them hidden from all: She had *been* a Weyrwoman.

Fiona stirred slowly to wakefulness, feeling surprised at the warmth around her. She vaguely remembered crawling out of her bed with her blankets draped over her and curling up against Talenth, but now she felt another body lying against her, pressing her more tightly against her queen.

As tired as she'd been, she'd made her full report to Cisca and then had carefully explained to Terin that she needed to make amends with Xhinna and would it be all right if Terin found some other place to sleep that night?

Terin had been too quick to agree; Fiona suspected that her request had been used as an excuse by the strawberry-haired teen to seek out the handsome F'jian.

The other body shifted away quickly and Fiona groaned.

"I'm sorry," a voice spoke as the other person jumped to her feet. It was Xhinna.

"Don't be," Fiona replied, turning to look up at her and gesturing invitingly for Xhinna to rejoin her. "I'm certain that I was freezing until you came." She made a face. "I don't know how I'll adjust to this cold again."

Only slightly relieved, Xhinna sat back down beside her. With an irritated sigh, Fiona pulled her close. "There," she murmured, "warmer."

Xhinna remained tense beside her. Fiona opened one eye and saw that the younger girl was eyeing her with a mixture of trepidation, assessment, and fear. Fiona opened both eyes, turned, drew Xhinna's head toward hers and laid a sisterly kiss on the girl's forehead.

"I'm sorry that I couldn't bring you with us," Fiona murmured in her ear. She pulled back enough to stare Xhinna in the eyes. "I love you, you are a dear friend, and I missed you."

"But you're so old now!"

Fiona could feel the many levels on which Xhinna made the comment and nodded slightly.

"I am," Fiona agreed with a twist of her lips. "Do you still want to be friends?"

Xhinna pursed her lips but said nothing, instead closing her eyes and leaning back against Fiona. A small sound escaped her lips, perhaps a sob, perhaps a sigh of contentment . . . or acceptance.

Melanwy, the aged ex-headwoman who had gone *between* forever with Weyrwoman Tannaz only a short time ago for Xhinna, and that same short time plus three whole Turns for Fiona's time-jumping self, had scorned and loathed Xhinna because of the young girl's nature. That same nature which had made certain that she would never Impress a queen dragon. But Fiona had accepted Xhinna for who she was—just as she had accepted blue rider F'dan for who he was. Everyone had a heart; just because different things set them beating didn't mean that there wasn't something for Fiona to love in all of them.

She knew that if she were to continue to be Xhinna's friend, she had to make Xhinna comfortable in the knowledge that she would never be her lover but also make it clear that she would always accept Xhinna's love. The two things were different, something Fiona grasped at a level beneath conscious thought even though, until very recently, she had never experienced the difference between loving and having a lover.

"Friends?" Fiona repeated when Xhinna made no reply.

"Promise me this," Xhinna said. She waited for Fiona to nod before continuing, "Promise me that you'll never leave me again."

"I swear by the egg of Talenth that, if it's in my power, I'll never leave you again, Xhinna," Fiona said, hugging her tightly. She whispered into her ear, "I missed you."

"But *you* didn't think *I* was dead," Xhinna said, not entirely mollified.

"The gold rider—" Fiona began, but Xhinna cut her off.

"Wasn't it you, from the future?"

Fiona pursed her lips thoughtfully. "I don't know." She saw Xhinna's look and said, "Really, I don't know. I could have been but . . ." She broke off, shaking her head. "The gold rider said you weren't to come, and I knew that I had to go."

"How?"

"I don't know," Fiona said, shaking her head, "I just did." She paused a moment. "Maybe I was wrong."

"The weyrlings are grown, the riders healed, we've got more fighting strength than we did three days ago," Xhinna said then. "What you did was important."

"Thanks."

"Friends," Xhinna said solemnly.

"Good," Fiona replied, snuggling up against her. "I can't stand sleeping alone."

TWO

Short Fall,
Watch all.
Winds change
Dragon's bane.

Fort Weyr, AL 508.2.5

"It's time," Fiona said three days later, nudging Xhinna as she forced herself out of the bed and into the cold night air. She put on her slippers and pulled a warmer nightgown around her shoulders, allowed herself a moment's memory of the hideously hot Igen summer nights, then squared her shoulders determinedly and set off to the necessary.

Xhinna joined her not long after Fiona had dressed in her riding gear, yawning widely.

"Why are you wearing that?"

"It's warm," Fiona said feelingly. Xhinna snorted and shook her head at the weyrwoman's affectation. Feelingly, Fiona responded, "You try living in Igen for three Turns!"

Wisely, Xhinna said nothing, but her eyes danced mischievously as she waved the weyrwoman out with a promise to follow along shortly.

Fiona greeted Talenth cheerfully and her queen warbled a greeting in response. Out in the Weyr Bowl the dragonriders were already gathering, checking riding straps and firestone hooks carefully before patting their dragons and proceeding to the Kitchen Cavern for a last bit of warm food or *klah*.

Thread would fall today at Benden and over Keroon, south of Nuella's wherhold. The sun would be rising as the Thread started to fall, so the watch-whers would not be able to help.

The sun rose three hours earlier over Keroon than over Fort Weyr, which was why Fiona and the rest had woken in the still of night.

She grabbed a spare mug and poured it full of *klah,* gulping the liquid as quickly as she could in spite of the heat.

"Good morning, weyrwoman," Ellor, Fort Weyr's headwoman greeted her.

Fiona nodded. "Everything ready?"

Ellor smiled. "We'll be setting up the tables out in the Bowl as soon as it's light."

A cough, sickly and huge in the night air, reverberated around the Weyr, followed by another and another.

"We've eighteen for certain with the cough," Cisca said as she entered the Bowl and spotted Fiona.

"Didn't we have more?" Fiona asked in surprise. For three Turns back in time, Fiona had been able to forget about the sickness that had been killing the dragons. She hadn't realized until now how much of a relief that had been for her.

"We did; they went *between* or died," Cisca told her bleakly. "And more took their place."

Without the dragons, Pern would be defenseless against Thread. With nothing to flame the Thread into char before it reached the surface, the live Thread would suck the life out of everything that grew, including humans. If the sickness couldn't be cured soon, they would all die.

"I think we've got more," Tintoval, the new Weyr Healer added as she entered the Kitchen and repeated Fiona's action of grabbing a mug and filling it with steaming *klah*. She nodded to Fiona and Cisca in greeting, before continuing grimly, "I haven't been able to identify them, nor have I heard anything more from Benden about a cure."

"We're set for firestone," Fiona reported. She had directed a work party the day before in filling the sacks in preparation for the Fall. "They'll fly out with three sacks each."

Cisca nodded. "K'lior said that he'd detail a wing to bring more when needed."

"I've got Terin and some of the younger weyrfolk assigned to help with the loading."

"Good," Cisca said. She turned to the Weyr Bowl, downed her *klah*, refilled the mug, and headed out. Fiona followed her.

The dark chill air absorbed most sounds and added an eeriness to the preparations.

Cisca found K'lior and passed the mug to him. He took it with a grateful look, downed it, and continued on his way, stopping to converse with one rider, patting another on the back, checking the harness of yet a third, passing up firestone sacks to a fourth.

Without prompting, Fiona followed suit, cheerfully greeting those she knew from Igen Weyr and politely encouraging those she knew only barely.

Even with the dragons of Igen, there were so few. F'jian led a wing of his own, J'gerd and J'keran flew as wingseconds in older wings.

H'nez flew with K'rall as his wingsecond. "I can always use an experienced hand, particularly with these young hotshots," K'rall had declared when K'lior had made the announcement.

"Good luck, bronze rider," Fiona called to H'nez as she passed quickly by. She might not like him, but she didn't wish him ill; Pern needed all its riders.

H'nez was surprised by her kindness and returned with stiff awkwardness, "Thank you, weyrwoman."

"Fly safe, old man!" Fiona called more cheerfully to K'rall when she spotted him.

"I will, weyrwoman, count on it!" K'rall's bass voice boomed across the Bowl. No less loudly, he added, "I've been promising Seyorth a mating flight soon, and I wouldn't want to let him down!"

Fiona blushed and chuckled at his impiety.

"Well, you'd best make sure he's got his full strength," she replied gamely, "because Talenth is going to outfly every bronze here!"

From her weyr, Talenth bugled loudly in agreement.

K'rall boomed another laugh. "Seyorth says that she can *try*!"

With a final snort, Fiona waved and moved on to the next dragonrider.

She paused when she came to T'mar. Since their return, she hadn't had much chance to speak with him. He was briefing his wing, and she waited while he was speaking. He didn't get much further because his riders started nodding significantly in her direction, distracting him. Finally, with an irritated, "What?" he turned and saw her.

"Wingleader," Fiona said, with a polite nod.

"Well, now at least I see what all the commotion is about," T'mar said, his eyes twinkling. He nodded back to her. "Weyrwoman."

"Good flying," Fiona said, wishing they were alone and she could say more.

T'mar met her eyes frankly. "Thank you."

She turned her attention to the rest of the wing. She knew only a few of them from Igen and greeted them warmly, was polite to the others, and left them as quickly as she could.

She had almost completed her rounds when she was grabbed from behind, lifted in the air and spun in a quick circle before being placed back on the ground with a yelp of surprise.

"Hah!" F'dan said to her as he spun her on her heels to face him. "You thought I was some lovestruck bronze, I'll bet!"

"F'dan!" Fiona exclaimed, burying her head against his chest. He held her tightly for a moment, then released her. "Whose wing are you in?"

"I'm flying with the Weyrleader, of course!" F'dan boasted grandly.

"Well, be certain you keep an eye on him," Fiona said. She glanced around for K'lior and his wing. "Is P'der flying with you?"

"Of course!" F'dan replied. He wagged a finger at her. "You've done your work too well, weyrwoman—you've got one hundred and twenty-two dragonriders flying against this Fall who are beholden to you."

"I did my duty," Fiona replied with a diffident shrug.

"And did it well," P'der added as he approached, reaching out to touch Fiona on the shoulder affectionately.

"Well enough," Fiona said feeling uncomfortable with the praise. She stepped back and gestured toward the dragons behind them. "And now you can do yours."

"We certainly shall," F'dan agreed emphatically. He leaned in closer to her as he added, "And someday soon, when there are enough queens again, we'll have you flying with us, on the queens' wing."

Fiona's face lit with a huge grin. "I'll look forward to that!"

"F'dan, P'der, mount your dragons," K'lior called as he strode briskly past them to his waiting Rineth.

"Fly well, Weyrleader!" Fiona called.

K'lior turned and waved at her in acknowledgment before climbing up Rineth's foreleg and settling himself on his perch, tying himself tight against his riding straps and making one final check of his firestone sacks.

Fiona's view of him was blocked as Cisca rushed up past her and called up to K'lior. "I expect you back in one piece, dragonrider!"

"I'll do my best, Weyrwoman," K'lior called back with a chuckle.

"You'd better," Cisca replied, her voice shaking with feeling. Fiona moved forward and grabbed the hand Cisca had left trailing behind her. The Weyrwoman turned at this and smiled when she saw that it was Fiona before turning back and raising her free arm in farewell. Fiona drew alongside her and waved good-bye with her free hand as K'lior gave the signal and, wing by wing, one hundred and ninety-four dragons rose to take their positions near the Star Stones and then winked out, *between*.

"We left no watch dragon," Fiona noted in surprise as she scanned the heights.

I'll do it, Talenth replied promptly. Fiona whirled in time to see her beautiful queen rush out of her lair, leap into the air, and climb gracefully with a few sweeps of her golden wings to land daintily beside the Star Stones, her gaze set intently on the distant horizon and the rising sun.

"Well, she seems eager enough!" Cisca chuckled. She turned to Fiona as she added, "I hope she rises soon. We need a mating flight."

Fiona nodded mutely.

With the dragons gone, Fiona met with Tintoval and helped her assemble the first-aid teams.

"You'll keep an eye on me, won't you?" Tintoval murmured when she found a moment where she and Fiona were alone.

"You'll do fine," Fiona assured her.

"At this point, though, you know more about healing dragons than I," Tintoval reminded her. Her honesty compelled her to add, "And what you did with those severely injured riders—"

"That was nothing we hadn't discussed beforehand!" Fiona protested.

"Discussing and treating are two different things," Tintoval told her.

"There was no one else—"

"You did brilliantly," Tintoval said. She grimaced in Cisca's direction as she added, "I'm not quite sure you've heard that enough since your return."

Fiona grinned. "Well, we've had other things to discuss," she allowed, adding more seriously, "but Cisca is a good Weyrwoman and she does well."

"Hmm," Tintoval murmured thoughtfully. "You'd be the best judge of that." She paused, then added, "With your three Turns in Igen, you've more experience than she."

"I wouldn't have managed without her example," Fiona said.

"Perhaps."

"Come on," Fiona said, nudging the Weyr Healer. "We need to check on the others."

K'lior took in the situation the moment he and Rineth burst from *between* over Keroon.

Tell T'mar and K'rall that they are reserve and will provide firestone, K'lior said.

They are returning to the Weyr to load more firestone, Rineth reported at the same time as thirty-two dragons winked out *between.* K'lior nodded to himself in satisfaction.

They wouldn't be fighting a full Fall, as it had started first over Benden and had proceeded south toward Keroon, so he felt that a full Flight of dragons would suffice—and assigning two small wings as reserve would allow him to dismiss his worries about getting extra firestone or not providing the Weyr with some final defense in case—

He spotted the pitifully few Istan riders as they appeared and waved, closing in on J'lantir.

—in case Fort Weyr suffered as badly as Ista. He turned to look over his shoulder, casually examining the formations behind him and more carefully eyeing the Threadfall.

We'll fight as full wings, K'lior told Rineth. *M'valer and M'kury will lead the other two. Have the wings re-form now.*

In a moment six understrength wings had re-formed into three full-strength wings.

K'lior was greeted by J'lantir, the acting Istan Weyrleader who had taken over after C'rion had gone *between* in their first Fall. He gladly accepted J'lantir's offer to let him lead the Fall and quickly integrated the Istan wing with his own wings, arraying them on his left, with the other two Fort wings on his right.

Four wings abreast, they rose to fight Thread.

Talenth's challenge alerted Fiona, who glanced up from her position at the nearest aid table. Her eyes narrowed as she counted two wings of dragons circling in for a landing.

Zirenth and Seyorth, Talenth reported. *They have been sent for firestone.*

Fiona raced over to the firestone shed, calling for her helpers as she went.

"We've got time," T'mar's voice in her ear surprised her as she was opening the shed doors. "They've got at least an hour before they'll need more."

"So we should have you back in half the time," Fiona replied, pulling open the second door and gesturing for the young weyrfolk to head inside. "You've got three sacks already, how many more?"

"Five each," T'mar said after a moment's thought. "That way we'll be able to fight a full Fall, if needed."

"You think that K'lior might pull replacements directly from these wings?"

"It depends upon how the Fall goes," T'mar replied. "He could just as easily put one wing into the fight and use the other to resupply." He shrugged. "I think this will work either way."

Fiona, who saw no flaw in this logic, flagged Terin and started her on the count. "Five each!"

All too quickly, Terin reached, "One-fifty, stop!" And the dragons rose into the air again, climbed up to the Star Stones, and, with Talenth's cheerful salute, disappeared once more *between* to battle Thread.

As they disappeared, Fiona reached out and wrapped her arm around Terin's shoulders. The young girl looked up at her for a moment then buried her head against Fiona's chest.

K'lior glanced around as the massed wings of Ista and Fort charged up to greet the downpouring Thread. They had arranged themselves just behind the Benden riders until M'tal's signal for them to break off, and then with a roar, K'lior urged his men upward.

The changeover had been perfect but now, only an hour into a two-hour fight, the dragons were getting weary, particularly the Istan dragons whose riders seemed determined to handle the entire left half of the Fall on their own. K'lior understood pride and worked as best he could with it, but when the Istans took their second loss—one that looked permanent—K'lior didn't hesitate to dispatch a replacement from T'mar's wing.

Tell Lolanth that we'll thicken his wing, K'lior said, sending D'teril and S'gan to join them. The two blue riders were glad to tear away from the reserves, dropping their spare sacks, and were quickly assimilated into the left and right flanks of the Istan riders.

A sudden roar from behind caused K'lior to duck and send Rineth plummeting out of the way of a clump of Thread that had fallen dangerously close while he'd been distracted.

K'lior had the image of a blue wall in motion, flame at the forefront as F'dan and Ridorth fought to protect him—but not without cost. K'lior heard F'dan's terrible shriek and Ridorth's concerned bugle and then the pair were gone, *between.*

It was all the warning that K'lior had as remnants of the clump, only partly charred, continued to fall toward him. With a move that he later couldn't explain, he and Rineth were suddenly twenty meters lower in the sky, the great bronze climbing straight up, jaws agape with vengeful flame and an air-shattering bellow, engulfing the Thread in a ball of fire.

And then, as suddenly, they were flying level once more, K'lior trying to regain his composure and sending a silent salute to F'dan.

More Thread, Rineth warned him. K'lior turned as he caught sight of a blur of bronze wheeling beside him—H'nez had decided to join the fray.

His decision was ill-timed as scant seconds later, Ginirth bellowed in pain and disappeared, *between.*

K'rall says he did not send him, Rineth relayed. K'lior dismissed this with a grimace. There was Thread to fight, matters of discipline would come after.

T he bellow of pain from the dragon bursting into the morning sky above Fort was mortal and Fiona knew it even as the blue plummeted toward the ground.

Talenth! Fiona shrieked in her mind as she rushed toward the falling pair, even before she could register that her queen had already left her post, was diving beneath the blue, pushing up against him, slowing his fall.

The rider tumbled off and, as he fell, Fiona could see that the entire left half of his back was one giant open wound, with ribs severed and organs dripping with the heat of the Thread's voraciousness. The Thread itself was nothing more than dusty *between*-seared crusty remnants of clotted blood. The wound was fatal but Fiona rushed toward the falling rider all the same.

Just as she reached him, another dragon burst into the sky above, a bronze creeling horribly, its left wingtip shredded.

Fiona needed no words to direct Talenth to the bronze's aid; the blue was already close enough to the ground that Talenth could easily roll him off her back.

The blue rider landed in her arms facing her.

"F'dan!" Fiona cried. He was dead.

A grief-filled cry from Ridorth distracted her. *Ridorth, stay!*

Fiona reached out to Talenth and, together, they held on to the blue, forcing him to remain as Fiona cried for help, dragging F'dan toward his mate as quickly as she could. A moment later a pair of hands grabbed his feet and her movement became easier.

"Get him to Ridorth," Fiona begged through her heaving breaths.

Hold him! Fiona ordered Talenth. She was dimly aware of someone shouting at her, of another dragon crying in pain, but her whole focus was on the distance between her and blue Ridorth, who trembled wild-eyed at her approach.

It's okay, Fiona assured him, *I just want you to take F'dan with you.*

Ridorth calmed and lowered himself as close to the ground as possible.

He's hurt, Talenth said. *I don't know if he can get* between.

Fiona nodded, even as she indicated to her helper—it was Xhinna—to lay F'dan's body against Ridorth's neck. Xhinna anticipated her and climbed up the blue's side, pulling F'dan up into place on his blue's neck before hopping down once more, eyes streaming with tears.

Talenth, Fiona called and her beautiful queen settled beside her. Xhinna was looking at her, crying something with a horrified look on her face but Fiona didn't hear the words, ignored the bellowing bronze in the distance, and concentrated only on this last gift to her friend as she climbed up onto Talenth's neck.

Tell Ridorth to follow us, Fiona said, feeling a pressure behind her eyes that grew even as Talenth helped Ridorth gain his feet and leap into the sky. In a moment, they were *between.*

Take him with you, Fiona called to the blue she couldn't see, hear, or touch. *Good flying!*

And in a moment that seemed to last forever, Ridorth and F'dan were gone.

Let's get back, Talenth, there are more injured.

Their return into the daylight, the warmth, the sounds, and the sights were like a slap to Fiona as she took in the growing number of injured, the anxious look on Cisca's face, the shock on Tintoval's and—

Get me down, Fiona ordered Talenth. The great queen swooped and had barely touched before Fiona had jumped down and was rushing over to the injured bronze.

"Where were you?" Cisca shouted, rushing toward her. "We couldn't find you, we thought—"

Fiona cut her off with a grim smile, shaking her head. "I was merely honoring him."

"Honoring a dead blue while there are bronzes here injured?" a voice cried in shock. It was H'nez. Fiona turned to him, her face bone white with anger, but the bronze rider didn't notice. "Your duty is—"

Fiona didn't hear him finish, turning on her heels to walk away.

"Where do you think you are going?" H'nez bellowed after her. In the distance she could hear Ginirth's pained bellowing and it tugged at her heart. "You call yourself a weyrwoman!"

Too much. Fiona twisted on the balls of her feet even as her hand rose and she leaped across the distance between them, her hand landing with a resounding *slap* on the side of his face, sending him reeling.

In the distance Talenth cried in dismay and anger, joined by Melirth.

"Get yourself under control, bronze rider," Fiona said icily, eyeing the man who now knelt, a hand raised to his injured face in surprise. Her

own hand stung from the blow but she willed the pain from her consciousness. She reached out to Ginirth with her mind, apologetically.

"Tintoval, get the aid kit," she called, as she strode over to the injured
bronze. "We'll need sutures and the fine needle."

She was about to say something reassuring to H'nez, words of peace
and healing when she heard Talenth: *He broke ranks.*

"You broke ranks?" Fiona exclaimed, her eyes impaling H'nez with
burning ire.

"When Ridorth and F'dan went *between*," H'nez said, licking his lips, his
eyes not quite meeting hers. Fiona felt his confusion, his anger—directed
at himself, his sense of loss, and suddenly she saw the man in a different
light.

"That's for the Weyrleader," she said, her tone dismissing the issue.
She jerked her head, indicating that he should join her. She gave Ginirth's
wound a close examination, but she was certain that she already knew
enough from what she'd seen during his landing and what she'd felt in
her brief contact with the bronze. "This is ugly but it will heal. You'll be
flying next Fall."

Tintoval approached, handed the aid kit to Fiona, and, as another casualty burst out of *between*, went off, more than willing to leave the difficult rider and his injured bronze in her care.

Dowsed with numbweed, Ginirth allowed her to stitch him up. Fiona
couldn't say how long it took to finish. She waved aside H'nez's fervent
thanks, too aware of the other cries in the Bowl around them, racing off
to check on Tintoval and then help Xhinna sew up a badly burned arm
before finally checking on Cisca.

The Weyrwoman looked up from her work long enough to give Fiona
a grateful nod, then went back to the difficult job of suturing a punctured
dragon's neck. Afterward, when rider and dragon were turned over to
the care of weyrfolk, Cisca gave Fiona a longer look, flicking a lock of
brown hair away from her face irritably.

"We thought you were going with them, grief-stricken," Cisca said, referring to F'dan and Ridorth. She cocked her head toward Melirth, who
was anxiously watching the proceedings from her lair. Fiona shrugged,

at the moment too exhausted both physically and emotionally to be concerned with the past worries of others. Cisca's face hardened. "If you can't work with me, I can't have you in my Weyr."

For one brief instant, Fiona thought longingly of her days at Igen Weyr, but the moment passed and she hung her head. "I'm doing the best I can, Weyrwoman."

Cisca gave her a long thoughtful look before glancing up and over toward H'nez's weyr. "You are too much alike with that bronze rider, more willing to listen to yourself than anyone else."

Fiona lifted her head, eyes flashing angrily, but she said nothing.

"You were too long your own counsel," Cisca declared in a tone that was shaded with pity. "You carried a grown woman's burden and more."

"I did what I had to," Fiona replied.

"And now, you don't have to anymore," Cisca reminded her. "Do you think you can live with that?"

Fiona grimaced, her eyes troubled. "I don't know."

"Seven lost, eleven severely injured, and eighteen lightly injured," Tintoval reported that evening as the Weyr recovered from their fourth Fall.

"That's not all," Cisca reminded her glumly, nodding to her to tell K'lior the rest.

"And ten more feverish."

"We've one hundred and forty-eight fighting dragons," K'rall murmured from his end of the table. "That's nearly twice what we had two Falls back."

"But," K'lior objected, "as you just said, in two Falls we lost nearly half that number."

"Our next Fall isn't for another sixteen days," M'kury said. "Couldn't we send our injured back again to Igen?"

"I'm sure that Fiona could handle it," T'mar said, glancing toward the abnormally subdued weyrwoman. She stirred at his gaze, giving him a bleak, unfathomable look. Longing? Dread? He couldn't tell.

THREE

Wheel and turn
Or bleed and burn.
Flame and dodge
Or between, dislodge.

Fort Weyr, AL 508.2.6

"It's still hard for me to accept: You're three Turns older than when I last saw you," Tintoval marveled to Fiona as they started out of the Kitchen Cavern on their rounds of the sick and injured early the next morning.

"It's just as hard for me to accept that everyone here hasn't become three Turns wiser," Fiona replied. She'd let Xhinna sleep in: The youngster had been up most of the night leading the weyrfolk in their ministrations of the worst injured dragons and riders.

"Wait!" a voice called from behind them. "Wait up!"

Terin raced to them. "I thought I could help."

Fiona grinned and nodded in response.

"So," Tintoval said to Terin as they started up the stairs to the highest weyr of their convalescents, "you've thirteen Turns now?"

Terin smiled. "Nearly fourteen." She glanced at Fiona and added, "And Fiona has nearly seventeen. Did you know that she was born twelve days before me?"

"No, I didn't."

"It was funny back in Igen, celebrating our birthdays and our birthdays."

"Excuse me?"

"One for our birthdates and the other for when we Turned," Fiona explained.

"We turned in the thirteenth month," Terin said when she noticed that Tintoval looked no more enlightened.

"Because we went back in time to the summer," Fiona added.

They reached the level of their first injured pair, W'jer and Janorth, and turned right toward his weyr.

"I'll check on W'jer if you two will look at Janorth," Tintoval suggested as they approached the entrance to W'jer's quarters.

"No," Fiona said. Tintoval's eyebrows furrowed in surprise. "You'll need to learn to treat dragons, too."

"I'm still learning my craft with humans, weyrwoman," Tintoval told her reprovingly.

"Why don't you both check on him while I take a quick look at his dragon and then we'll switch?" Terin suggested diplomatically.

Fiona exchanged looks with the Weyr Healer; the compromise seemed acceptable to both of them.

W'jer was one of K'rall's wing. His right thigh had been seared through to the bone by the same Thread that had lacerated his brown Janorth through to the bones of his neck.

"Good morning, W'jer," Fiona called as they entered. "How are you this day?"

W'jer's face was grizzled, weathered from Turns of flying high and squinting into the distance. His hair was disheveled and wavy, his lips drawn in a thin tight line as he fought with the pain of his injury.

"Well enough, weyrwoman," W'jer replied, nodding to Tintoval and Terin as he spotted them behind her. He sat up in his bed, seeming a bit put back by such an invasion of younger women, and gestured to his injury. "We slept some, last night."

Tintoval moved around Fiona and gestured for permission to examine his wounds. W'jer nodded and only twitched his lips when she began to unwrap the bandage. Tintoval hissed as the wound was uncovered.

Fiona peered around her and, without changing her expression, pulled a bottle out of the sack she had slung over her shoulder, found some clean gauze, and passed it to the healer. "Sometimes the Thread leaves an infection."

"I'm going to have to clean out the wound," Tintoval apologized to the rider as she took the proferred bottle. "This will sting."

"No worse than Thread, I'm sure," W'jer said gamely. He set his jaw tight as Tintoval gently poured the peroxide solution over his leg and it foamed as it ate away the infection.

Fiona, with a tight smile of sympathy, reached into her sack again and pulled out a small jar of salve that she passed wordlessly to Tintoval before stepping around her to the service hatch. She quickly scrawled an order for fellis juice and numbweed and sent the tray rushing on its way down to the Kitchen Cavern.

"Numbweed and fellis juice are on their way," she reported to Tintoval as the healer finished her inspection of the cleaned wound and started applying the healing salve. Tintoval nodded silently. Fiona felt the woman's stern self-control and laid a hand on her shoulder assuringly.

"You're doing fine, W'jer," Fiona said to the brown rider who had noted their exchange with growing alarm. "You'll be up and about in three sevendays or sooner."

"And Janorth?"

Fiona turned to look through to the brown dragon's weyr, caught sight of Terin motioning to her urgently, and said lightly, "Let me go check."

As soon as Fiona was close enough to speak to in a voice that wouldn't carry, Terin told her, "He slept badly last night and tore off his bandages."

Fiona grimaced; there was green dragon ichor everywhere.

"You should have called," Fiona said reprovingly to the brown dragon as she cleaned away the ichor. "Talenth was ready to hear you."

I didn't realize, Janorth said apologetically.

Fiona grinned and slapped the brown affectionately on his chest. "We'd rather you say too much than too little."

I'll remember.

"See that you do," Fiona said, leaning down beside Terin to examine the base of the wound. Fortunately it was forward on the neck; if the injury had been at the join to the chest, recovery would have been much more difficult. She sighed. "The stitches have come open."

Terin nodded, absently wiping a long stream of green ichor on her tunic before wiping her forehead.

Talenth, we need some thick sutures, double dragon size, Fiona called. *See if Xhinna is awake.*

She could have called down the service hatch, but Xhinna would be quicker, if she was available.

She sleeps, Talenth replied instantly. *She is having strange dreams.*

Strange dreams? Fiona mused. She never knew that dragons could tell when people were dreaming, let alone have an insight into them.

Then check with Ellor, she said.

A moment later, Talenth responded, *The Weyrwoman will fly them up.*

Surprised, Fiona moved to the edge of the weyr and glanced out. In a moment the great queen was beside her, hovering close in while Cisca threw a sack attached to a rope. Fiona caught it on the first try and quickly undid the knot, then waved in thanks.

"We need some new weyrlings for this sort of work," Cisca called as she waved in response.

"I'll see what I can do!" Fiona shouted back, grinning.

"I'm talking with Melirth about the problem, too," Cisca replied, grinning in turn. "A mating flight—or two—would also do wonders for morale."

Fiona chuckled, then returned to the job of sewing up Janorth's gash. Once done, she rejoined Tintoval and W'jer. The healer had treated the dragonrider's wound with numbweed, rebandaged it, and dosed him with fellis juice. Between them, Fiona and Tintoval managed to get W'jer settled back into his bed for "a good long nap."

"We'll check on Janorth before we leave," Fiona said, gesturing for

Tintoval to follow her to the brown's weyr. Terin was happily scratching the brown's eye ridge and crooning to him encouragingly.

"You just rest up, you'll get better soon," Terin said to him as Janorth's multifaceted eyes whirled with the green of contentment.

Tintoval looked to Fiona for direction. Fiona smiled and raised an eyebrow, glancing challengingly at Janorth's resutured neck.

"What sort of sutures did you use?" Tintoval wondered as she knelt down and examined Fiona's deft handiwork.

"That's double dragon size," Fiona said. "Dragon size is used for most wounds; for wing-work we use regular human sutures; but *this* required the larger ones." She paused, thinking back to her time at Igen Weyr in the past, when she'd had to learn all this on her own, by doing it. "When we were at Igen, we had the hardest time getting dragon sutures until I managed to explain what we needed to the traders."

"Where did they find sutures?" Tintoval asked, her eyes narrowed worriedly.

"They didn't," Fiona said with a shake of her head. "They discovered that the Fishers use a similar rope and convinced them to produce a sterile version."

"Clever."

Fiona smiled in agreement. "I often wonder how much more we could do if we asked others to help us."

"That's a good thought," Tintoval said reflectively, her eyes falling on Terin. Fiona gave her a quizzical look but the healer merely shrugged and smiled in response, clearly not yet ready to share her thinking.

It wasn't until they were seated in the Kitchen Cavern for a late lunch that Tintoval broached her idea. Waiting until Terin had swallowed her last mouthful, the healer asked, "Terin, are there any young weyrfolk who'd like to help us?"

Terin frowned in thought before saying, "Mostly Ellor keeps them in classes or working, but I'm sure the ones whose fathers are riders would love to help."

"We didn't check on those whose families are tending them," Fiona told Tintoval. "But there aren't that many because too many of the women are working."

"In the kitchen?" Tintoval asked, glancing around at the few helpers.

"In the tanneries, on the looms, in the pastures, in the storerooms, on spinning wheels, knitting, dyeing, tailoring, leatherworking, and metal-working," Terin replied, adding, "and in the nurseries and classrooms with the children."

"It was a bit of a shock to realize how much like a Hold a Weyr really is," Fiona said with a grin. "Only there are more women than men."

Tintoval mulled on Fiona's last comment for a moment before asking, "Why is that?"

"Well, with a Weyr's strength of about five hundred dragons, you'd expect around the same number of mates," Fiona replied slowly as she examined the question. "I imagine that many of the boys who don't Im-press leave the Weyr."

Tintoval's raised eyebrows begged her to explain. "They would find themselves welcomed in every Craft and Hall." She waved a hand ex-pansively around the Kitchen Cavern. "They're well-fed and tended, trained to handle most any task so they would be a boon to any holder or crafter. And," she concluded, "there's all the prestige associated with the Weyr and being able to boast of weyrblood."

"Dragonriders are healthier than most," Tintoval mused. "The women are better-fed in the Weyr, too, so they also have a better chance of sur-viving childbirth. So it's to a woman's advantage to stay in the Weyr in-stead of leaving."

"And we'll never run out of work!" Terin exclaimed.

"So," Tintoval wondered, "are there any spare children we could draft to help us?"

"Ellor would know," Terin said. "But I can think of at least three by myself."

"Three would be a start," Tintoval allowed. "But we've fifty-seven sick and injured, I'd much prefer a dozen or more."

"Too many and you'd never train them," Fiona warned.

"Train some and have them train the rest," Terin suggested, glancing at Fiona challengingly.

Fiona grinned and said to Tintoval, "And that's why I made *her* head-woman!"

When they approached Cisca that evening at dinner with the suggestion, the Weyrwoman mused, "I wonder why we didn't think of that before?"

"Perhaps you did," Fiona said. "But you've had a lot of distractions since then, whereas I"—she gestured ruefully at herself—"have had almost three Turns now of dealing with injured dragons."

As she spoke, she realized once again that she was nearly eye level with the Weyrwoman. Cisca had little more than nineteen Turns of age; Fiona was less than three Turns younger than her now. And, in dealing with the sick, at least, she had at least a full Turn's greater experience. It was strange and difficult to remember: She was still the junior Weyrwoman, but the difference in age and experience had been nearly erased.

K'lior nodded thoughtfully. "And we haven't had a healer for so long, there was no one to do the training."

"We've all those helpers when we fight Fall," Cisca remarked, sounding perplexed. She glanced tellingly at Fiona who, after all, with Tannaz had borne the primary responsibility for dealing with the sick and injured. "Why didn't we think to use them to help afterward?"

Ellor, who had been checking on the table, heard the exchange and stepped in. "Because too many of them have regular duties during the day. We use them for first aid during the Fall, but afterward we need them elsewhere."

"How many are clothesmakers?" Tintoval wondered. "Is that why they're so good with sutures?"

"Some are tanners and good with awls," Ellor replied. "And others are midwives—"

"I should have thought of them first!" Tintoval exclaimed. To Ellor she said, "Please be sure to send them to me." When she saw the head-woman's alarmed look, she added hastily, "I want to talk with them about midwifery."

"Don't they teach that at the Healer Hall?" Ellor wondered in surprise.

"They do," Tintoval replied, "but there's much more to *doing* than can be learned from teaching." With a frown she added, "And it's very much true that for birthing, most prefer a midwife to a healer, so it's rare that the Healer Hall sees a pregnancy; they never did in the Turns I was there."

Ellor nodded, relieved that the healer wasn't planning on drafting the midwives.

"How many of them have children?" Terin asked. Ellor gave her a reproving look; it was obvious that she considered Terin's involvement in the conversation to be impudent.

"That's a good question," Fiona said purposely.

Taking the hint, Ellor replied, "A few."

"Perhaps those midwives would like to have their children watched during the day," Terin said.

"The ones who are too old to just run errands and call for help if it's needed could learn a lot with us," Tintoval said in agreement.

Ellor nodded, a speculative look on her face. After a moment, she smiled, glancing evilly at Terin. "I know just the one to start with, too!" she exclaimed.

Terin gave her a worried look, which rapidly changed to one of alarm.

"Do you remember Bekka?" Ellor asked, her eyes dancing.

Terin groaned. "The one who never sleeps?"

"That's her," Ellor agreed with a broad smile. She turned to Tintoval. "She's Merika's eldest, three months shy of thirteen Turns." She glanced at Terin, adding, "She's older than you."

"Not anymore," Fiona corrected. Ellor's expression dropped; she said nothing, but Fiona could feel the older woman's anger.

"You say she never sleeps?" Tintoval asked, glancing at Ellor.

"She takes short naps, like a fire-lizard," Ellor explained with a grin. "I was actually thinking of drafting her for late nights here in the Kitchen."

"If she's any talent with healing and she doesn't sleep," Tintoval said thoughtfully, "she might make a good recruit to the Healer Hall."

"The Healer Hall?" Ellor repeated, shaking her head uncertainly. "I don't know if they could manage with someone like her."

Tintoval smiled. "They managed with me!"

Bekka proved everything that Terin remembered. Although she had twelve Turns, she was small for her size so she looked younger. It took Tintoval and Fiona only a few moments to discover that the youngster was every bit as smart—and irrepressible—as her mother, Merika, had warned.

"She's a handful, make no mistake," Merika had said with a look that crossed affection with exasperation. "But she's got a big heart and she'll listen."

"But she won't follow orders unless she's convinced," Tintoval guessed.

"Ah," Merika had said, her eyebrows going up, "you've met the type!"

"I *am* the type!" Tintoval admitted. At Merika's look of surprise, she elaborated. "I used to keep the entire level up with my antics until Kindan arrived—and then it was just him."

Merika cast a knowing look toward Fiona as she replied, smiling, "He's been known to have that effect; I've heard he's even been able to charm young girls into behaving, on occasion."

"He certainly had it with me!" Tintoval agreed with a laugh. She continued, pressing Merika, "So, will you let Bekka train with me?"

"Train?" Merika had repeated in surprise.

"As a journeyman healer, I can take an apprentice," Tintoval told her.

"Don't you want to meet her first?"

"From what I've heard, I meet her every morning in the mirror," Tintoval told her.

Fiona, who'd had only a brief experience with the new healer before she'd gone back in time to Igen Weyr with the weyrlings and convalescents, found this exchange alarming. Tintoval must have noticed her look. "It's a good thing in a healer," she explained. "We have to be alert in a moment and awake for long periods of time."

"That'd be Bekka," Terin murmured in agreement.

Merika had summoned her most irrepressible child and, with some lingering reluctance, had entrusted her into Tintoval's care.

Fiona's concern over the age and responsibility of the child evaporated with their first visit that morning. Not only was Bekka's cheerful energy infectious, she was also genuinely concerned for the well-being of both injured rider and dragon, to the point of running up and down the stairs to the infirmary on several different errands and still finding time to give words of comfort to both dragon and rider.

"Some of the injuries are worse," Tintoval had cautioned her as they made their way to their second patient.

"They won't get better if we don't help, will they?" Bekka had asked.

"No, they won't," Tintoval admitted.

"It's like when babies are born," Bekka mused. Terin made a disagreeing noise and the young girl rounded on her. "If there's no one to help, the baby's still going to be born. Mother's there to see to it that the baby and mother live." Fiona could feel the sense of pride and vocation in the girl's tone. "If we aren't there to help, then maybe the dragons and riders would recover or maybe they wouldn't. It's our job to see to it that they live."

"Yes," Tintoval agreed, "that's it exactly!"

Bekka's exuberance faded when they visited the first of the seriously sick dragons.

"Serth is only hanging on," Tintoval cautioned them before entering the weyr.

"It's been over a fortnight," Fiona murmured, remembering her last visit to S'ban and Serth: her first time escorting Tintoval on her rounds. She remembered that S'ban had been surprised at her ready willingness to clean up the nasty green ooze that blue Serth had coughed up—that all the sick dragons coughed up. "Will he make it?"

"I don't think so," Tintoval admitted. Behind them, they heard Bekka sob, but before anyone could react, the girl had already run past them, into the dragonrider's quarters.

"Bekka!" S'ban exclaimed as he caught sight of her. "What are you doing here?"

Fiona, Tintoval, and Terin rushed to intervene—only to halt in surprise. Bekka was wrapped around S'ban, her sobs muffled against the fabric of his tunic.

S'ban looked up at the sound of their approach, demanding, "What is she doing with you?"

"Merika said she could help," Tintoval said, her brows furrowed in confusion. "Bekka was upset about Serth."

"Well, she would be," S'ban said slowly, wrapping his arms tightly around the child. "She's my daughter."

Fiona and Terin exchanged horrified looks.

S'ban frowned at them until recognition dawned. "Weyrwoman? You're back?" He gave her an appraising look. "You're bigger, older."

"I am," Fiona said, drawing herself up and mustering a smile for the stricken blue rider. "I spent three Turns back in time at Igen Weyr."

"Then perhaps there is hope," S'ban whispered to himself.

Bekka pulled away from him long enough to say, "They said that Serth is going to die."

Tintoval gave S'ban a tear-streaked, apologetic look. "I'm sorry, I didn't know."

Bekka turned from her father and stared at the three women, demanding over her shoulder, "Tell them it isn't true, Da. Tell them that Serth's going to be all right."

"Oh, darling," S'ban said, wrapping his arms around her from behind and burying his head against hers, "I wish I could."

"What about Kindan?" Bekka demanded, glaring at Fiona and then Tintoval. "And that weyrwoman, Lorana?"

"They're trying," Tintoval said. "They're trying as hard as they can."

"Kindan won't give up, I promise you," Fiona declared. She glanced at S'ban. "He saved us in the Plague, he won't give up."

"A fortnight ago, I told you that he'd have to be quick," S'ban reminded her, his tone bleak.

Fiona glanced toward Tintoval. "Has there been any news since we left?"

The Weyr Healer shook her head.

"You have to do something," Bekka said, glaring at Tintoval. "You can't just wait for those Benden riders."

"My father was a Benden rider," Tintoval told her with an eyebrow arched warningly.

"T'val," S'ban said to Bekka. "Remember, I told you about him?"

Bekka nodded mutely, then glanced sympathetically at Tintoval. "Did you feel bad when he died?"

"Yes," Tintoval said sadly.

"That's why she decided to become a healer," S'ban told his daughter. Bekka absorbed this silently.

"Bekka, why don't you and I see what we can do to make Serth more comfortable?" Fiona asked, walking over to clasp the girl by the shoulder.

At S'ban's encouraging nod, Bekka broke her embrace, slipped out from under Fiona's hand, and, with a steadying breath, squared her shoulders, forced her lips into a smile, then strutted over to Serth's weyr, calling out cheerfully, "Good morning, Serth! It's me, Bekka!"

Fiona followed, found the mop and bucket, and started to clean up all the green ooze that the sick blue dragon had coughed up during the night.

"I'll do that," Bekka said several minutes later, reaching for the mop.

"No," Fiona said, "you go ahead and talk with Serth." When Bekka looked ready to argue, she added, "I think he likes that."

Bekka gave her a tentative smile and returned to the blue, stretching on her tiptoes to reach his nearest eye ridge and scratch it.

Fiona and Bekka both turned at the sounds of approaching steps. Tintoval and S'ban entered Serth's lair. Fiona flashed a grateful look through the doorway at Terin, who had stayed behind in S'ban's quarters to tidy them up.

"So, Serth, how are you today?" Tintoval asked, slapping his jaw affectionately as she moved around in front of him. She pointed toward the nostrils, nodding to Fiona. "If you crouch down you can see how congested he is."

Fiona placed her mop against the wall and followed Tintoval's examination, gesturing for Bekka to join them.

"His nose is all full of that green stuff!" Bekka exclaimed, working hard to keep herself from crying and glancing worriedly at her father.

"I don't think he's got much time left, Bekka," S'ban told her quietly, reaching up to scratch Serth's eye ridges. He looked appealingly at Tintoval.

The healer shook her head. "I haven't heard anything more from Benden," she said. She saw Bekka ready to speak and added, "I don't think it will do them any good to ask; I'm sure they're working as hard and as fast as they can."

"What if Benden's not the right place?" Bekka asked, her face scrunched in misery. "Why shouldn't we be looking here, at Fort? Fort's the oldest Weyr, after all."

"It is," Fiona agreed, "but Kindan and Lorana came here already and Cisca and K'lior helped them search the Records. The Records here clearly state that special rooms were built at Benden. That's why they went back."

"And why we aren't looking here," S'ban said, reaching a hand out to Bekka. She took it and he pulled her against his side as he turned back to scratch Serth's eye ridge some more. "We have to trust that they're doing everything they can."

"But what if they don't find a cure?" Bekka asked, drawing away from her father. "What if they don't find it in time for Serth?"

S'ban drew a deep, steadying breath and then knelt slowly beside his daughter so that he was at eye level. "If they don't find it soon, Serth will die."

Bekka was quiet for a long moment, her chest heaving in silent sobs. Finally, after a false start, she whispered the worry that had overwhelmed her: "Will you go with him, like Tannaz?"

"No," S'ban told her, grabbing her tight against him and burying his face in her chest. He pushed back, his eyes streaming even as he forced a smile, "I couldn't leave my best girl!"

"You mean me?" Bekka whispered, glancing up at Serth in complete amazement that her father, who had been bonded with the blue dragon for tens of Turns before she was born, would ever for a moment consider her more important. "You'd stay for me?"

"That's what we do," S'ban assured her, "when we're parents."

Bekka stood up, pulling back from her father just enough that she could look him squarely in the eye, her hands still resting on his shoulders.

"Then you'd have to come with me to the Healer Hall, because I'm going to be a healer." She glanced over her shoulder challengingly to Tintoval, who nodded in fierce agreement. "And if they don't find the cure at Benden, *I* will!"

S'ban's face worked for a moment as he battled his emotions. It was Serth, however, who finally said it, as he lifted his head from Tintoval's inspection and curled his neck around so that he could look directly at Bekka and S'ban.

She is your child, he said, so forcefully that Fiona could hear him easily. She saw that Bekka, Tintoval, and Terin could all hear him, too. *She will do what she says.*

The blue paused for a moment, quickly turning his head aside to cough, then turning back again. *You must stay for her. Promise me.*

"I promise," S'ban said quietly, tears leaking down his cheeks.

Again Serth twitched away to avoid spraying them with flecks of green ooze as he coughed, and again he came back, his head level with Bekka's, his gaze steady on his rider.

You will be proud of her, Serth said. *She is special, this one.*

After that, Serth turned his head back straight ahead and closed his eyes, his breathing labored but steady.

"I'll stay with you tonight," Bekka said, moving to wrap herself around her father as tightly as she could. S'ban nodded his head against hers and clutched her close.

Tintoval glanced at Fiona, seeming both embarrassed to be sharing the intimate father-daughter moment and at the same time accepting of the gift that was given them. She made to leave, but Bekka glanced up at her.

"I've got to go now, Father," Bekka said, stepping out of her father's arms.

"No," Tintoval said instantly, shaking her head. "You can stay."

"I've got to go," Bekka repeated with a defiant look. "I'll help the healer and learn. Maybe we'll come up with something that'll help Serth."

"Yes," S'ban agreed. He made a shooing gesture. "Go! Serth and I will be fine."

"I'll be back as soon as we're done," Bekka promised. She turned then and walked resolutely out of the weyr, pausing only once to turn and say, "I love you, Daddy!"

S'ban looked up from his communion with Serth and found a smile. "I love you, too, Bekka."

They hadn't gone three steps outside of S'ban's quarters when Bekka grabbed Tintoval's hand and jerked her to a halt. The healer looked down at her in surprise.

"How long?" Bekka demanded.

"How long for what?" Tintoval asked.

"How long for me to become a healer?"

"It can take as little as four Turns and as many as eight," Tintoval replied. She guessed the girl's next question, adding, "I went when I had thirteen Turns, and I've nineteen now."

"Would they take me now?"

"Why don't we see how you handle the others, first?" Fiona suggested calmly. Bekka shot her an angry look, then dropped her eyes, saying, "Sorry, weyrwoman."

"No, you're not," Fiona declared, chuckling. "You're angry but you don't want to upset me and ruin your chances."

Bekka's lips quivered as she acknowledged the truth in the observation.

"I'd hate for you to set your heart on something only to discover that your stomach betrays you," Fiona told her. She gestured for her to continue moving. "If you are all right when we've seen to all the injured riders and dragons, then I'd say you've a good chance."

"She's awfully young," Terin said worriedly, glancing at Fiona. "It hardly seems fair."

"It's not fair," Fiona agreed. She smiled at Terin. "But you did the same when we were in Igen and you weren't any older."

"I'm older than I look," Bekka told Terin stoutly.

"I know exactly how old you are," Terin told her. "You used to be two Turns and two months older than me, but now I've nearly fourteen Turns; I'm a Turn less two months older *than* you!"

"Oh," Bekka said, deflated. "I'd forgotten." A thought crossed her mind. "You don't suppose I could go back in time like you to the Healer Hall?"

"You didn't," Tintoval told her. The young girl gave her a perplexed look. "If you had," the healer explained, "then you and I would have studied together."

Bekka made a big "O" with her mouth, her eyes going wide.

"Going *between* times is confusing," Fiona told her with a chuckle.

Bekka shook off the problem, instead asking Tintoval, "So if I do all right today, when will I go to the Healer Hall?"

Tintoval sent a bemused and somewhat desperate glance in Fiona's direction.

"You'll have to get permission," Fiona told her. "I imagine you'd need your parents' and the Weyrwoman's, and I suspect you'd need a recommendation from Tintoval."

"And the Masterhealer would have to accept you," Tintoval added. "Learning to be a healer takes a lot of study. Only the very best can manage—"

"I'll manage!" Bekka declared. "I'll study!"

"She will," Terin vouched, earning a surprised and grateful look from the younger girl. "She always finishes what she starts."

"Well," Fiona said with a tone of finality, "for now we need to finish our rounds."

▼ ▼ ▼

By evening, Tintoval's opinion of Bekka was firm. She made sure that the child had had a quick bite to eat before sending her off to her father, then dispatched Terin to let Merika know of the arrangement.

"Talenth could have told her," Fiona said as she watched Terin race out of the Dining Cavern.

"I know," Tintoval said with a grin. "But this gives us a chance to talk with the Weyrwoman without either nearby." She gave Fiona a questioning look. "What do you think?"

"Of Bekka?" Fiona asked. When Tintoval nodded, Fiona said, "She does what she says, she watches, she listens, she learns." She paused as she reflected on the rest of the day. "She's a bit impetuous and she's opinionated—" She held up a hand as Tintoval started to interject, continuing with a smile, "As am I." Tintoval looked relieved at the admission but quirked an eyebrow up, looking for Fiona's summation.

"I think we should see how she can cope with Serth's loss before we go any further," Fiona told her softly.

Tintoval's face drained of color. She opened her mouth to ask a question but Fiona guessed it from her expression and answered, "I think S'ban will survive. I think he'll go with her to the Healer Hall."

"Why?" Tintoval asked. Fiona could feel some bitterness in the healer's question: Why would this blue rider choose life when her own father hadn't?

"Because Serth said so," Fiona replied. Tintoval's eyes widened in surprise. "Your father didn't have that chance to learn his dragon's wishes, but S'ban did." Then she grinned. "And I'll bet that S'ban wants to know what Serth meant about her being special."

"I think he just means because she doesn't sleep," Terin, who had crept up behind them stealthily, said sourly.

Fiona and Tintoval started at her words. Fiona frowned at her. "How much did you hear?"

"Just the bit about Serth saying so," Terin admitted, not the slightest bit apologetic. Fiona got the impression that Terin was trying to hide her feelings, that she was both impressed with Bekka and a little bit jealous—and not at all happy with her jealousy.

She reached over Fiona's shoulder and grabbed a couple of rolls from the basket, only to have Fiona intercept her hands and shake the rolls loose.

"Take these, I made them for you," Fiona told her, handing her a napkin-wrapped packet. "There's some dessert there, too." She smiled at Terin and made a shooing gesture. "Now go and sit up with Bekka."

"How did you know?" Terin asked in amazement.

"I know you," Fiona told her. "You have a good heart and good instincts." She made another brush-away motion, adding, "Call Talenth when the time comes."

Terin's face drained and she nodded, departing at a deliberate pace, her head hung down.

"The time comes?" Tintoval repeated, eyeing Fiona expectantly.

"Serth is going *between* tonight," Fiona told her.

FOUR

Eyes whirling red:
Anger or dread.
Eyes whirling green:
A happy scene!

Fort Weyr, early morning, AL 508.2.7

"Xhinna, come on," Fiona called as she rolled out of bed at Talenth's warning. She reached to the head of her bed and turned over the glow, its eerie luminance only shadowing the dark of night. Xhinna grumbled irritably, her eyes just gleaming under her eyelashes. "It's time."

"Time?" Xhinna repeated, pushing herself up and out from under the blankets in one swift movement. "Serth?"

Fiona nodded grimly. "We have to get moving."

Talenth, tell Melirth, Fiona thought to her dragon, not certain if the Weyrwoman would want to say farewell.

She sleeps, Talenth replied, obviously reluctant to wake her.

Cisca had said nothing but looked both distracted and unhappy when Fiona had shared her observations on the sick and injured that evening. Fiona had turned to K'lior for guidance, but the Weyrleader looked just as surprised at his mate's reaction and shook his head minutely, so she didn't press the matter.

Talenth? Fiona said more in warning than as a question as she and Xhinna rushed from her quarters into the queen's lair. Talenth was already up and moving. Effortlessly she dropped over the queens' ledge and sidled back so that Fiona and Xhinna could quickly mount by jumping directly onto her neck.

Before Fiona could say anything, the young queen had leaped up and was beating the foggy air with her huge wings, climbing swiftly, unerringly toward the landing ledge of the fifth level. Fiona had a moment's irrelevant thought about how T'mar would react if he knew that she and Xhinna were flying without any straps whatsoever before they were at their destination.

Jump down, Talenth told her, shifting her weight so that they could follow her near foreleg to the landing. Fiona flung herself feetfirst off her dragon's neck, expecting and meeting the guiding leg before landing lightly on her feet on the ledge. She helped Xhinna down and then the two were off, running toward S'ban's quarters and Serth's lair even as Talenth quietly beat upward in the dark to take station with the watch dragon at the Star Stones.

"Bekka? S'ban?" Fiona called at the entrance to the blue rider's quarters. She heard someone call back and quickly entered, passing through S'ban's rooms, her brows furrowing as she noticed his rumpled, lumpy bed, and into Serth's lair.

S'ban looked up bleakly from his position beside Serth's head. Bekka gave them a quick, grateful smile, and then turned back to her father. Terin stood close by, looking desperate to do something useful.

There were others in the room, too. Fiona recognized Merika and suddenly realized that the odd lumps she'd dismissed in S'ban's bed were probably the younger children. She nodded toward Xhinna, who gave her a quick look of comprehension and headed back into S'ban's quarters. Shortly she could be heard quietly waking the children and bringing them into Serth's weyr.

Tajen was there, too, and rose from the sandy floor when Fiona entered. Old L'rian was there, seated with his back against the wall on a chair brought in from S'ban's room. Fiona waved him back down as he started to rise. Another green rider and—to Fiona's surprise—H'nez were in attendance.

"S'ban flew in my wing," H'nez told her quietly as he approached. Fiona could see that he was clearly moved even though he tried to hide it. He turned back to the blue rider and spared a smile for Bekka. "She says that she's going to be a healer."

"I expect she will," Fiona said as she followed his gaze and wondered how it was that someone so young could shoulder such a heavy burden. Xhinna, who had managed to cajole the youngsters into the room and settle them, heard the comment as she rejoined Fiona and followed her gaze, remarking, "She was always bossy."

Fiona snorted. The irony of the comment was lost on neither of them.

"The Weyrs raise strong women," H'nez said, his lips pursed tightly at some hidden memory. Mother or lover? Fiona wondered, looking at the prickly, difficult, taciturn bronze rider in a new light.

Serth coughed, a long burble that devolved into a wracking wheeze that brought up more and more of the green mucus.

"We're all here, S'ban," Fiona murmured quietly as the blue's fit passed miserably. As if her words were a signal, all the riders and weyr-folk in the room closed in around them, arms wrapped, hugging.

From his position behind S'ban, H'nez shot Fiona a look, but she shook her head, steeling herself for what she knew she must say to Serth. She shivered in fear until she felt a head rest on her shoulder and another arm wrap around her.

"You can do this," Xhinna murmured.

"Weyrwoman," L'rian said from her other side. "It's time."

Fiona took a deep, steadying sigh.

Serth, if you're ready, you can go, she called. From on high, Talenth bugled encouragingly, the sound of her voice echoing around the Weyr before other, quieter voices responded.

With an unsteady heave, Serth found his legs, stumbled forward to the ledge outside, and fell into the air. For a moment his wings cupped the night sky, and then he was gone, *between.*

"No!" S'ban wailed desperately, trying to follow his blue but being restrained by all those who surrounded him. "No, no, no . . ." His voice faded into silence broken only by the sobs of those who surrounded him, enfolding him in all the love they could muster.

He is gone, Talenth said, her keen complete.

"Fiona!" Cisca's angry shout echoed around the Weyr Bowl at first light that morning.

Fiona rose quickly—but still quietly enough not to alarm Xhinna. The two had just barely returned from the wake that had started with the loss of Serth and had ended when S'ban—Seban, now—had collapsed, drunk beyond his pain, to be carried by H'nez and L'rian to his bed, where he was tucked in with his current partner and surrounded by piles of small children.

"He'll make it," L'rian had declared as he leaned on Xhinna's strong shoulders. He glanced at Fiona and gave her an approving nod. "Thank you, Weyrwoman. I know how hard it is for you."

Fiona had found no words for a reply, but L'rian hadn't expected any. Talenth picked them up at the ledge and flew them back to the queens' ledge, let them dismount, and clambered up to her bed, to curl up and fall immediately into a deep sleep.

Now, heading out to Talenth's weyr, she found the gold dragon awake, her eyes whirling a troubled red. Before Fiona could ask what was wrong, Weyrwoman Cisca barged in.

"You should have told me!" Cisca bellowed, her brown eyes flashing. "How dare you tell a dragon of my Weyr—" She cut off abruptly, her eyes going wide as Melirth bellowed from the Weyr beyond.

"What is it?" Fiona asked, suddenly more alarmed by Cisca's silence than her rage.

The bronzes are blooding their kills, Talenth replied, her tone sounding eager, excited, passionate in a way that Fiona had never heard from her before.

"Go!" Cisca cried. "Take Talenth!" And with that, she turned on her heel and rushed out of the room.

"Talenth?" Fiona repeated in confusion.

Xhinna appeared in the doorway, looking bleary-eyed and disheveled. "What's going on?"

"The bronzes are blooding their kills," Fiona reported.

"Talenth?" Xhinna asked, rising and glancing to the weyr beyond. There was a bellow from Melirth, as the gold soared by outside, heading for the cattle pens. Xhinna gave Fiona a shove. "Take Talenth and go!"

"Go?" Fiona repeated. Talenth was already moving, her eyes whirling excitedly; she was more alive, more alert, even more sleek-looking than Fiona remembered ever seeing. "Where?"

"Anywhere! Melirth is rising to mate!"

As soon as the words penetrated Fiona's brain she raced over to Talenth and forced the queen out and over the ledge, jumping onto her back and urging her into the air. Cisca's bizarre rage made sense now: The Weyr-woman had been responding unconsciously to her dragon's emotions.

But I want to stay! Talenth protested, seeming ready to fight with Fiona over the issue.

No! Fiona snapped, urging Talenth up and up until they were over the Star Stones. Where to go? Fort Hold was too close. Igen Weyr was— she checked herself and brought up the image of Igen Weyr, remembered the time, pictured the sun bright in the sky, and gave Talenth the image. The gold was still reluctant, becoming more excited as she heard the bronzes bugling and Melirth's taunting responses, but Fiona persisted and then—they were *between.*

Talenth grumbled irritably as they emerged from *between* into the early morning heat of Igen. Fiona could hardly blame her; the heat was so great it felt like a physical blow and she wasn't straining her wings to keep them airborne.

Just land at the Star Stones, she instructed soothingly. Talenth complied, altering her flight into a slightly turning glide that brought them to a perfect stop beside the Star Stones.

As she'd hoped, there was a breeze flowing up there. Down in the Weyr Bowl, she knew, it would be stifling even at this time of year. By night it would be as cold as it was at Fort Weyr, but night was eight or nine hours away and the hottest part of the day was still to come.

Fiona slid off Talenth's neck and clambered down her foreleg to wander over to the Star Stones and leave her gold a moment to stretch.

I like it here, Talenth's thought came so closely on Fiona's that for a moment the weyrwoman wasn't sure who had spoken. Fiona nodded, silent, and padded over to the edge of the Weyr Bowl to peer inward.

Dust swirled as a light wind fanned it, then settled again. Fiona could almost imagine the dust as the result of invisible dragons and riders preparing for a Fall. She smiled to herself. She wondered what F'dan would say about the mating flight and where she had chosen to flee. Then, with a pang of regret, she realized that she would never be able to ask him.

So many ghosts!

She felt Talenth reach out worriedly in her direction, a tendril of comfort in the morning heat, and allowed herself to lean against it, almost as though it were something physical and she could caress herself with it.

Talenth ruffled her wings, offering, *Maybe we would be cooler in our weyr.*

It's not our weyr anymore, Fiona reminded her sadly. Who might have occupied it in the seven Turns since their departure? Had any queen dragons been sent back with the injured of the other Weyrs?

Why would they send queen dragons? Talenth asked, picking up Fiona's unvoiced thought.

Why, indeed? Fiona mused, trying to keep her thoughts more quiet, more to herself. It wasn't as though there were any injured queens and, as far as she knew, only a handful were as young as Talenth. Fewer now, with the loss of Lorana's Arith.

But even if all the queens were mature and ready to mate, would the

Weyrs be able to recover the losses caused by the sickness? Was that why she had been led back in time here by the mysterious queen rider?

I need to check the Records, Fiona told Talenth. The queen rumbled in annoyance, making it clear that if they weren't going to their old weyr, then she'd just as soon stay where she was, but Fiona reinforced her request, making it an order, and Talenth irritably unfurled her wings and extended her foreleg for Fiona to climb.

Melirth was rising, Fiona thought to herself in the deepest part of her mind. The bronzes—all of them—would be chasing her. The bronze riders would have only one thought: to catch the queen. Their emotions would be strong, their thoughts concentrated on the passions that emanated from their beasts—

Talenth bugled loudly and Fiona shook herself. It seemed that even when she tried hard to keep her emotions to herself, her dragon could sense them. And, she realized with a mixture of dread and elation, she was feeling her dragon's arousal. She took a deep, calming breath as she forced images of T'mar, H'nez, K'lior, M'kury and, most of all, Kindan from her mind.

Our time will come, Fiona promised Talenth fiercely.

The sound her queen made in response had no irritation in it at all.

The heat in the Records Room was stifling, the air still, and Fiona was soon sweating profusely as she dragged Record after Record into and out of the range of the thin beam of light she'd managed to coax from the outside by dull mirrors.

She calmed herself first by locating the old Records of the last Fall and was pleased to see that they were exactly where she'd remembered them. If anyone else had bothered with them, they'd clearly put them back carefully, but judging by the layers of dust, Fiona was pretty certain that hers were the last hands to touch them.

She moved slowly, partly to defeat the heat but more to keep her thoughts from intruding into Talenth's awareness. The queen was drowsing back at the Star Stones, happy with the light breeze even as it tapered off with noonday sun.

She had to keep her notes in her head and found it difficult, especially as the dust made her more parched. She promised herself that she'd stop in at the wherhold later before heading back. It would be good to see Nuella and Zenor again.

She made herself focus on the issue that had driven her here. How often did queens rise when Thread fell? How many eggs were in each clutch? And how long did it take from mating to clutching? Clutching to Hatching? Hatching to being able to go *between*?

The information was not as difficult to find as it was to pin down. Fiona found herself going through Turns and Turns of Records.

She would get some inkling, and then another mating flight or Hatching would throw her numbers off: Was a clutch twenty-one or thirty-one eggs? Was one gold egg or two gold eggs common? Was it twelve weeks or fifteen weeks from mating flight to Hatching? Whenever she thought she'd got it sorted, nailed down with the certainty of someone like Verilan, the meticulous Master Archivist—or someone worried about exactly how many fighting dragons a Weyr would have by when—she would find some new entry that disagreed with her carefully deduced findings. Worse, the newest Records had been written in the Interval, which was less important to her than the Records of the Second Pass, which had deteriorated and were harder to read.

One item in the newer Records alarmed her more than any other: the recurring mention of few mating flights, right up to the time when Tannaz, the last junior Weyrwoman at Igen, elected to go to Fort Weyr, causing depleted Igen to finally merge with Telgar. Were there supposed to be more mating flights? The Records in the Interval showed no such alarm, and the Records from the Second Pass made no more than passing mention, small gloating entries amid reports of Thread injuries and lost riders and dragons.

Something told her that Talenth had fallen asleep, and Fiona realized with a start that the arousal that had kept her so tense had drained away.

Melirth had been flown by Rineth—she could feel it. It was a good thing, she decided even as she got the feeling that H'nez was angrier than ever, up in his weyr, drinking himself into a dazed stupor. She could go back now; she probably should.

Rebelliously, she bent back over the Records. She paused when she came upon a harper's ballad, part of the Teaching Songs:

> *Count three months and more,*
> *And five heated weeks,*
> *A day of glory and*
> *In a month, who seeks?*

That sounded like mating. But "a day of glory"—was that the mating flight or Hatching?

She frowned, picking up another Record she'd placed close by and bringing it into the light. Her frown deepened.

"Three months and more"—that was the time from mating to clutching. Five heated weeks was easy to guess: the time from clutching to Hatching—the "day of glory." So what did "in a month, who seeks" mean?

In a month, weyrlings could go *between*? Seek?

Fiona sat back in her chair, out of the light and the heat, her face set sourly as she thought back, trying to remember what Talenth had been like at the end of her first month out of the shell. She shook her head irritably; she couldn't imagine Talenth going *between* then.

But you didn't try.

Fiona raised her head, glancing toward where Talenth was sleeping as she tried to identify the source of the thought. Was it her? Was it Talenth? Was it someone else?

She rose from her chair and carefully piled the Records together, placing them back in their correct locations with all the care she'd take to oil her dragon or run her Weyr.

Run her Weyr. The thought staggered Fiona. She stopped dead in her tracks.

She had been back at Fort Weyr for less than five days before she had returned *here*. Was she so used to being in charge that she could no longer cooperate with others, could only be *the* Weyrwoman?

There was only one way to find out: by trying. Igen Weyr was empty now; there was no one here who needed her.

Talenth, Fiona called loudly, rousing the dozing dragon. *Let's go.*

Are we going to see Nuellask? Talenth wondered even as she launched herself from her perch and glided down toward their old quarters.

No, we're going back to the Weyr, Fiona said. *They'll need us there.*

One thing she had read over and over in her perusing of the Records was how useful the other queen riders proved on the day of a mating flight—they were the only ones not present during the emotional turmoil of the union and so still able to manage the needs of the Weyr.

Aside from disconsolate bronze riders, there was a Weyr still occupied by sick dragons, injured riders, injured dragons, and worried weyrfolk. They needed Fiona.

She mounted Talenth and built the image of Fort Weyr in her mind even as her great dragon labored to gain altitude.

Cisca will expect us to help out, Fiona told her dragon as she instructed her to go *between*.

The cold of *between* was a tonic for her, washing away the numbing heat of hot Igen and revitalizing her in a way that she'd never noticed previously.

She burst into the air above Fort Weyr and was not surprised to find that the watch dragon was slow in challenging her.

He says that Rineth flew her, Talenth reported as she overflew the dragonpair and Fiona waved down in greeting at the rider. The gold's tone was disgruntled—not just because she already knew that, but also, Fiona discovered, because Talenth felt let down by the whole affair, almost as though she'd had to leave a party that she wanted to join.

You can't be jealous of your mother, Fiona chided her with a humorous tone. She felt Talenth's muted response and realized that her queen had already recognized her own feelings and regretted them. *Your turn will come soon enough.*

Again, she felt Talenth's mixed emotions. This time she got a good enough distinction that she could soothe her fears. *I'll be fine!* Fiona told her with all the confidence she could muster. *Remember, I've already practiced.*

Fiona found that, even though she'd "practiced," the memory still had her blushing. She knew enough from the mating flights of greens to expect that she would find her emotions tied to her dragon's desires, and she was certain—no, she corrected herself, she *hoped*—that she would be able to handle the mating flight.

There were Records of what happened to those riders who couldn't control their dragons. Fiona took a steadying breath; some of those Records made grim reading.

Where's Terin? Fiona asked Talenth as they glided toward her quarters.

She's with F'jian, Talenth responded.

All right, where's Bekka? Fiona asked, guessing that the younger weyrfolk would be quickest to recover.

She's with Xhinna, Talenth replied. Of course. Xhinna would be guarding and protecting the youngsters no matter how much passion beat about her; she was a natural parent.

Take me to them, Fiona said.

They're in Seban's quarters, Talenth responded, changing the angle of her flight.

Tell them I'm coming, Fiona said as she leaped down from her dragon and onto the landing ledge.

Seban was sleeping in his bed when Fiona entered the room. Xhinna was seated on a chair beside the bed, with Bekka on her lap. Bekka had a faded smile on her face, the sort of love-everyone look that Fiona recalled from her own experiences of children and mating flights. Xhinna looked very much like a mother or big sister caring for a little one.

"She made the feelings okay," Bekka murmured, surprising them all. She sat up with the barest hint of an impish grin on her face, rubbed her eyes, and looked at Fiona. "You missed it. Melirth flew Rineth. It was great."

"Yes," Fiona agreed. She glanced at Seban. "I just wanted to make sure . . ." She faltered, not wanting to remind Seban of his loss. "I should go check on the others."

"By all means, weyrwoman," Seban said, sitting up in his bed while at the same time carefully plucking Bekka from Xhinna's lap and setting her on her feet. "Why don't you take Bekka? She seems to be all recovered now."

Fiona nodded and glanced at Xhinna. The girl yawned and said to Seban, "Can I stay here a bit?"

"I'd appreciate the company," Seban told her, then turned to Fiona. "Weyrwoman?"

"Of course," Fiona said, reaching a hand for Bekka. "Come on, Bekka, we'll have Talenth take us down to the Kitchen Cavern and see what we can cook up, shall we?"

Bekka's eyes bugged out. "I can ride your queen?"

"If your father doesn't mind that I don't have straps," Fiona said, glancing at Seban and adding ruefully, "We left in rather a hurry this morning."

"Please, Daddy?" Bekka begged, making her blue eyes as big as she could, thrilled at the prospect of riding on a queen dragon.

"I'll be extra careful," Fiona said, "I promise."

"I'm sure she's safe with you, weyrwoman," Seban said.

"Okay," Fiona said as she set Bekka down on the ground of the Weyr Bowl, "first we need to see if fires are lit, and if they are . . ." She raised an eyebrow, inviting the young girl to finish the thought for her.

"*Klah!*" Bekka declared. "We should make lots of *klah!*"

"And?"

"Tea."

"Yes," Fiona agreed. "Tea would be good. I expect people will be hungry, too. And we'll probably want to get help."

"What about the headwoman?"

"What if she needs to rest?" Fiona asked, forcing any hint of a leer out of her expression.

"I'm sure I know some youngsters who'll help," Bekka said. She made a slight face as she added, "They're not all as quick as I am, but they'll do."

"Then we should get them," Fiona agreed as they entered the Kitchen Cavern. "And when we've got *klah* and tea and hot rolls and we're ready, why don't *you* take some to the Weyrleader and Weyrwoman?"

Bekka's eyes widened and she shook her head.

"You'll do fine," Fiona assured her. She gestured toward the hearth. "First, the *klah.*"

Fifteen short minutes later, Bekka walked slowly out of the Kitchen Cavern, balancing a tray in her hands with exaggerated care. Fiona watched her out of the corner of her eye and then turned her attention to the recovering weyrfolk.

"It was a good flight," Ellor declared as she bustled in to the Kitchen Cavern and nodded in thanks to Fiona. "Melirth blooded four kills before she took off, and in the instant, all the bronzes were after her." She paused long enough to shake her head in surprise before adding, "And some browns, too."

Fiona gave her an encouraging look, so Ellor, after pouring herself a full mug of *klah,* perched near the hearth and continued. "It seemed forever before the first suitor dropped out, one of the browns. Then a bronze, another bronze, and finally a brown.

"Well, I can tell you, we were all in a state," Ellor said. "Particularly when someone shouted that H'nez's Ginirth was closest." She paused dramatically. "But Melirth just bugled another challenge and rose higher and flew faster.

"F'jian's Ladirth was the next to drop out," she said. She shook her head again. "I don't know what the boy was thinking." Then she smirked, saying, "Probably *wasn't* thinking, was he?"

Fiona nodded in agreement.

"Ginirth dropped out a moment later, and then it was down to M'valer's Linth, M'kury's Burinth, and, of course, K'lior's Rineth."

"Rineth flew her," Fiona said, hoping to hasten Ellor in her story, but the headwoman was not to be rushed.

"He did, but it's how he did it that's worth the telling," Ellor replied, pausing once more, eyes shining brightly as she realized that she'd kept her audience still ensnared. She paused dramatically, then said: "It was M'kury's Burinth who caught her first!"

"Really?" Fiona asked, surprised.

"Yes, and then Linth," Ellor continued. "Rineth was a distant third." Fiona gestured for her to speed up. "Well, Melirth—clever lass—just folded her wings and let the other two try to hold her. They couldn't, and they had to let go or risk tearing open her belly. So, with a cry of triumph, she fell through them and prepared to soar away when—"

"Rineth caught her," Fiona guessed.

"Exactly," Ellor said, not pleased that the weyrwoman had guessed the climax. "Only she tried the same trick, going all limp—"

"But Rineth was strong enough for both of them," Fiona said.

"No!" Ellor said, her voice a mixture of glee and admiration. "*He* was smarter than the others! He went limp with her and they plummeted together."

"Hmm!" Fiona murmured in admiration.

"So finally, just as they were almost too low, Melirth relented and spread her wings and then—"

"They mated," Fiona concluded.

"It was a brilliant flight," Ellor agreed with a firm nod. She drained her *klah* and gave Fiona a sly look, saying, "Of course, we all celebrated."

"Celebrated!"

"Well, you know what I mean," Ellor replied.

"A good flight."

Ellor nodded.

"And much needed."

Ellor's responding nod was emphatic. "With all those sick and our casualties, it's been the only glimmer of hope since before the fire-lizards were banished."

"Thread falls at Nerat and Upper Crom tomorrow," M'kury remarked conversationally as the wingleaders sat at dinner that night.

"Benden and Telgar," H'nez said dismissively.

"I thought Benden was understrength," M'kury persisted, glancing at K'lior. The Weyrleader made no response, his attention focused fondly on Cisca; they were holding hands.

"Benden's injured and older weyrlings timed it," M'valer reported. When the others looked at him in surprise, he added, nonplussed, "M'tal contacted me with the news. They have thirty-two healed dragons and riders, twenty-five weyrlings now old enough to fight, and—" He paused dramatically, shifting his gaze to catch K'lior's eyes. "—ten recovered from the sickness."

"Ten?"

"Recovered?" Fiona and Tintoval echoed in unison.

"That's what he said," M'valer affirmed.

"But that—"

"That's the first we've heard of recoveries," K'lior said, glancing hopefully at Cisca.

"They lost over sixty and they've got more still sick—at least forty," Cisca replied grimly.

"Ten out of a hundred isn't so good," M'kury observed.

"It's better than none," H'nez and Fiona objected at the same time. Fiona shot a glance at the bronze rider; he seemed as dismayed by their unified response as she was.

"They've nearly four wings for their Threadfall," M'valer said, sounding hopeful.

"And Telgar's strength is more than enough," M'kury said by way of agreement.

"We've nearly two weeks before our next Fall," H'nez remarked.

Fiona couldn't decipher his tone—was he pleased or upset? Maybe both, she decided, glancing at him thoughtfully.

Fiona noticed Cisca absently chewing on the edge of her finger, a sure sign that the Weyrwoman was worried about something.

"Weyrwoman?" Fiona said, raising an eyebrow inquiringly.

"What is it, Cisca?" K'lior asked with a nod toward Fiona—grateful that she'd commented on the Weyrwoman's mood.

"It's not our place, I know," Cisca said, forcing her hands under her thighs, "but I'm worried about Telgar."

"Worried, why?" M'kury asked.

"They've got the strength; they even sent their injured back in time to Igen," H'nez said.

"They've still got sick dragons, don't they?" Cisca said, nodding toward K'lior.

"They do," K'lior said slowly, his expression grim.

"They're not going to fly with them, are they?" Fiona asked, turning to Tintoval for confirmation. When the healer shrugged, Fiona turned her questioning look to Cisca. "Isn't that dangerous?"

"It is," Cisca agreed. "M'tal tried it once . . ."

"And it was a disaster," K'lior finished. He shook himself.

"The Weyrs are autonomous, they rule themselves," H'nez said.

"Maybe . . ." Cisca began tentatively. All eyes turned toward her and she flushed. "Well, it would be awkward, but perhaps we could offer to help them."

"Help?" H'nez exclaimed, eyebrows arched in surprise. "Help a full-strength Weyr?"

"I doubt D'gan at Telgar would appreciate such an offer," M'kury said with a sideways glance toward H'nez.

"I'm not sure I'd appreciate such an offer in similar circumstances," K'lior said. Cisca gave him a shocked look. "Coordinating different riders from other Weyrs can be difficult, can even cause greater injuries."

"So we're to say nothing to Telgar?" Cisca asked, glancing at the wingleaders, including K'lior. K'lior pursed his lips in a grimace and then nodded. "Even though his dragon is among the sick?"

The others looked at her in surprise, so she added, "Didn't you hear the drum message to Kentai this morning?"

"I did," Fiona said. She flushed as she confessed, "But I didn't think about what it might mean."

H'nez glanced at her, then said to Cisca: "You can't ask a man like D'gan to—"

"See reason?" Cisca asked.

"Stand down in the face of his duty," K'lior corrected her.

"No," Cisca said with a sigh, "I suppose not."

Fiona reached over and patted the Weyrwoman on the shoulder. "It will be all right."

Cisca glanced up at her and shook her head. "You can't say for certain."

"No," Fiona agreed, "but we can hope."

Tintoval caught her eye. "Could you help me with the last of the rounds?"

"Of course," Fiona said. Immediately, she summoned Talenth, who carried them up to the first level on which they had patients.

"You seem to have read my mind," Tintoval said as Fiona helped her dismount. "I was hoping we'd avoid the stairs this time."

"Actually, I wasn't really thinking," Fiona admitted.

"What did you do during the mating flight?"

"I went to Igen," Fiona said. "I thought reading Records might distract me."

"And did your search of the Records give you any hints on how to deal with Weyrwomen?"

Fiona shook her head.

"I would have thought as much myself," Tintoval said to Fiona's surprise. With a laugh, the healer explained, "They were written by the Weyrwomen, mostly."

"Oh," Fiona said, "I missed that."

"So what would have helped were Records of how they dealt

with their terrible, upstart, snappish, recalcitrant junior weyrwomen," Tintoval said, smiling. "Take that and just reverse it for how to deal with Weyrwomen."

Fiona frowned. The topic was not something she wished to pursue at the moment. The healer seemed to notice, for she merely gestured with a nod for Fiona to precede her as they made their way to their first patient.

It was late when Fiona finally settled back in her bed, exhausted by the day's events and her efforts, but also strangely nervous, anticipatory, strung out. Xhinna had decided to stay at Seban's that night, along with Bekka, to keep the ex-dragonrider company.

Fiona slept fitfully, as she always did when she had to spend the night by herself. Even so, she still slept better than she'd ever slept in her old home at Fort Hold: Here, she always had Talenth's comforting presence in the back of her mind, a constant reassurance that she was never *truly* alone.

She arose shortly before dawn, cold and anxious. She heard Talenth in the weyr beyond, shaking and making strange noises in her sleep. Perplexed, Fiona sat up, pulled on her nightgown, found her slippers, and paced over to her queen.

She slipped her mind close to Talenth's, resting a hand on the great queen's neck, trying to ease her fears. The queen wouldn't quiet, her twitches and noises abating only slightly. Fiona stiffened, feeling some of the pain and worry that was troubling Talenth.

Something bad was about to happen.

Something terrible.

Alarmed, Fiona shook Talenth. *Wake up!*

The gold dragon startled awake, turning her head to gaze at Fiona in surprise.

What is it? she asked worriedly.

Do you feel anything? Fiona asked, sending a tendril of memory toward her, reminding her of how she'd slept.

Something is coming, something soon, Talenth responded, trembling.

Fiona moved beside her, her hand raised to an eye ridge in an attempt to soothe the great queen, but Talenth turned away, her head craning toward the weyr's entrance, her nostrils flaring.

Fiona moved up beside her, onto the queens' ledge. The Weyr Bowl was silent and still.

Suddenly fear gripped Fiona as Talenth bugled loudly in the dawn, her cry alerting the watch dragon, who echoed it and—

Fiona was lost, stricken.

"D'gan, *no!*" The words that tore out of her mouth were not hers. In that moment she felt a wave of horror and wrenching loss. *The Weyrs! They must be warned!*

The voice wasn't hers; it came to her from elsewhere, like a horrified echo that raked her mind.

"Fiona! Fiona!" Someone was shaking her. She opened her eyes and looked up, only barely recognizing Cisca. "What is it? What happened?"

"The Weyrs," Fiona said aloud, tears streaming down her cheeks as panic, fear, and an unbearable sorrow tore through her, "they must be warned." Her eyes went wide. "D'gan's Kaloth is too confused by the sickness. D'gan—Telgar—they went to fight Thread but they're lost. Lost *between.*"

"Rouse the Weyr!" K'lior's voice shouted. "Rineth!"

In moments all of Fort Weyr was awake, dragons soaring from their weyrs down to the foggy Weyr Bowl, their cries deafening, wave after wave of sound that beat through Fiona's chest and reverberated with her heartbeat. Talenth was beside her, reaching for her protectively, grabbing her with her talons, jostling Cisca and K'lior aside as she placed her rider firmly on her back and launched herself into the sky with one blaring scream.

Fiona had only an instant to marvel at Talenth's behavior before she was struck again from the inside out as though she were being blown open by a force not her own—and then, suddenly, she knew. She felt Rineth and Melirth beside her, T'mar's Zirenth, felt all the bronzes, all the browns, all the blues, all the greens of Fort Weyr.

Felt them as though they were inside her and she screamed. She screamed with pain, she screamed with awe, and she screamed with power. In desperation, she spread the power to Cisca and then K'lior, and the two stood below her on the queens' ledge transfixed. The power grew even more and she felt it—thankfully—shift from her.

No longer the sole focus, Fiona found that she could still breathe, that her chest was heaving, her ears were smarting from all the sounds, her eyes were cried out, and her panic was still overwhelming.

The power had gone to Benden. To one person. How could one person hold such power? She felt an echo, the slightest of contacts—was this the person who had brought her back in time to Igen? The sensation felt similar . . . but not quite the same.

The power was searching, searching, seeking frantically—and not finding. Its desperation grew, and Fiona found herself gasping again as more power surged up through her from the dragons and riders of Fort Weyr to join with Cisca before flowing to Benden . . . and still failing to find what it sought.

Finally, a lone dragon was found, clasped, recovered. And even as the power triumphed, it felt something that caused it to pause.

And then Fiona was herself once more, gasping and crying out in relief as Talenth stopped bugling, as the dragons settled, as the power faded, and she felt only like someone who had been burned from the inside out.

The pain and suffering, the loss of all those Telgar dragons, felt like a hole inside her, tugging at her with a desperate urgency.

"We need to go," Fiona whispered to herself. "We need to go to Telgar."

Talenth rumbled in assent but, exhausted, could only glide back to the ground near their weyr.

"Telgar is no more," Cisca said. She helped Fiona down from her dragon and wrapped comforting arms around the younger woman. Fiona let herself fall into the embrace and could only make the smallest of sounds when K'lior joined them and the three, Weyrleaders all, silently commiserated over their pain.

FIVE

Weyrwoman, your duty is clear—
To the needs of the Weyr adhere.
Choose your mate with greatest care
So all the weyrfolk will best fare.

Fort Weyr, later, AL 508.2.8

Fiona was the first to break the embrace. She gave Cisca and K'lior a look that made it clear that she was doing it reluctantly, that nothing would have pleased her more than to stay in their warmth much, much longer. She was not surprised to see Cisca nod in understanding; they had shared too much in the horrifying moments when they had felt the death of all the dragons and riders of Telgar Weyr—and the amazing display of power from Benden.

"I should go," Fiona said, wiping tears from her eyes. "Talenth is the oldest queen not leading a Weyr; they'll need us."

Cisca nodded.

Fiona continued, "Melirth will be sure to lay a gold and ..." She trailed off, not certain which words to use.

"We can't leave Telgar empty with Igen empty, too," Cisca agreed. "But are you certain you're up for it?"

Fiona wanted to tell her no, she wasn't, but her duty was clear. Fort was in good hands; Telgar in none. She didn't trust her voice, so she forced herself to nod.

K'lior glanced at Cisca in a wordless communion before saying to Fiona, "I'll send T'mar and a wing with you."

"We'll help with the Falls," Cisca added, glancing to K'lior.

She shook her head, still in shock. "A whole Weyr! Lost in a moment."

"D'gan's Kaloth was too confused by the illness," K'lior reminded her. "They jumped *between* without proper coordinates."

"All of them?" Cisca asked, looking to Fiona, even though she knew the answer.

"I think so," Fiona said. She made a face. "I was only part of it—you felt it—it was like all of me—of us—was grabbed and directed from Benden."

"Lorana," Cisca said. "She tried to find D'gan and the others." She shook her head. "I don't know how she did it, let alone why she chose you."

"I've never met her," Fiona said.

Cisca shrugged the issue off. "What do you need for Telgar?"

"I'd like Terin and Xhinna to come," Fiona said. "I'll need their help."

"We'll send them on with T'mar," Cisca promised. She looked at K'lior. "Should we send anyone else?"

"Their healer was a dragonrider," K'lior said with a frown. Whatever else he was going to say was lost as he glanced out toward the Weyr Bowl and saw the growing clusters of dragonriders and weyrfolk approaching.

"I should go *now*," Fiona declared. "They'll be grief-stricken at Telgar." She clambered back onto Talenth's neck. "I'll send word as soon as I can."

"I understand," Cisca said, gesturing Fiona skyward. "Go now, we'll send others along as soon as we can."

Fiona was just urging Talenth into the air when a voice cried out, "Wait!"

Xhinna was running toward her, her face wet with tears, her look determined. "You're not going without me!"

Gladly, Fiona reached down for her. Dragonriders boosted Xhinna up to her and the young weyrgirl clambered up the rest of the way.

"You left me once—you're not leaving me again!"

Talenth had nearly reached the heights and the Star Stones when Xhinna jerked her head around and pointed, shouting over her shoulder to Fiona, "Look!"

As they drew closer, Fiona saw Seban and Bekka hurrying toward them. Seban was carrying a large carisak and had a coil of something on his shoulder, and Bekka toted a large, lumpy bundle.

"We're coming with you, Weyrwoman," Seban announced as Talenth steadied into a hover beside the Weyr's edge.

"What about the Healer Hall?" Fiona called back in surprise, glancing from Bekka to Seban and back again.

Bekka merely shook her head. "We're coming with you!"

Fiona smiled at the youngster's spirit. With an abundance of energy and no lack of courage, Bekka leaped toward Fiona, whose surprised squeak was enough to alert Xhinna; between the two of them, they managed to haul the youngster into position on Talenth's back. Seban, with a wry look for his daughter, managed a more practiced transition and was soon mounted in front of Xhinna, with Bekka placed carefully between them.

"We've got no straps!" Fiona cried, annoyed with herself and chagrined for the time, now Turns past, when she'd berated T'mar for a much milder stunt.

"We've straps," Seban called, whipping a line of leather from around his shoulder and deftly looping it under Talenth's chest. Catching the far end as it whipped up, he smiled at Fiona and said, "We've cargo too precious to lose!"

Even so, Fiona impressed upon Talenth the delicacy of their passengers, but she needn't have worried: Talenth pumped her great wings smoothly and lifted the four of them effortlessly toward the Star Stones, where the watch dragon bugled in honor and his rider saluted them.

Fiona took a deep, steadying breath and pulled the image of Telgar into her mind, corrected it for the later time of day, and said to Talenth, *Let's go.*

It looks abandoned, Fiona thought sadly as Talenth wheeled once more over the heights of Telgar Weyr. No dragon challenged them. Below, no one moved.

The air was cold, full of winter, with less of the dampness that she always felt at Fort Weyr.

There is so much to guard here, Fiona thought as she scanned past the Weyr Bowl and southward beyond to the great wheat plains of Telgar and then westward toward Crom and the coal mountains to its north.

She felt Xhinna's hand grip her thigh tightly and realized that she wasn't the only one who felt the pall that had fallen on the Weyr below them. She wondered if Xhinna also recognized the great importance of this Weyr. Without Telgar, the center of Pern could not survive against Thread.

Who, she wondered suddenly, was flying the Fall now raining at Upper Crom?

Talenth, check with Lyrinth; there's a Fall at Crom, Fiona said.

Lyrinth says that it is all right and asks you to stay at Telgar, Talenth responded a moment later.

"We'll land," Fiona announced to the others.

"This must be the very worst for them," Bekka said sympathetically. She glanced up at her father's back, then turned back to Fiona, sharing her feelings with her eyes. Fiona had no trouble interpreting the look: The very worst was even worse than Seban losing his dragon.

"Yes, it must be," Fiona agreed. "Our job is to make it better."

Talenth descended smoothly into the Weyr Bowl. Just as she was ready to pull up and land, she let out a great bellow that echoed once around the Weyr, and then she repeated it, modulating her tone to a keen, a warble of pain and anguish.

Fiona was surprised at Talenth's behavior, but quickly comprehended her purpose: The queen had returned, the Weyr would live, it would prosper—*she* declared it.

My beautiful, beautiful love! Fiona cried in praise.

This is our Weyr now, we will do well here, Talenth told her.

"Talenth has declared this to be her Weyr," Fiona told the others as she threw her right leg over her queen's neck and slid full-tilt toward the ground, certain that Talenth would cushion her fall with a well-placed leg. And so she did.

Xhinna was next, then Bekka, lowered down gingerly by Seban, who followed her with their baggage and then leaped nimbly down himself.

Fiona looked around, trying to decide what to do next. Talenth decided for her. With another loud bugle, the gold dragon took to the air, climbed steadily, passing by each and every opening until she arrived at the Star Stones, and with a sorrowful cry, took station: watch dragon for a mourning Weyr.

"We'll need some *klah,*" Fiona said, spotting the Kitchen Cavern and setting off toward it. "And then some food and then—"

"A fitting ballad," a grim voice spoke up from the distance. Fiona and the others turned to see a middle-aged man, stooped and stricken, dressed in harper's blue, approaching from near the Hatching Grounds.

Fiona nodded to her companions, and Seban and Bekka continued on toward the Kitchen Cavern, intent on providing sustenance for the doubtless weary weyrfolk. Xhinna elected to wait for the harper, who said as he approached, "Norik, Weyr Harper."

"Xhinna of Fort Weyr," Xhinna replied. Then she shook her head. "Of Telgar now."

"There is no Telgar," Norik said.

"By the First Egg, there is!" Fiona exclaimed. She hadn't meant to yell, but she heard her voice echoing off the Bowl walls. From on high, Talenth cried in loud agreement.

"Who says so?" Norik demanded, sweeping a hand around the empty Weyr. "Who will fly the Thread that falls even now at Upper Crom?"

"*I* say so," Fiona roared back, turning to stare down the weary man. "I,

Fiona of Igen, Talenth's rider, say that there is a Telgar Weyr and that we will fight Thread whenever and wherever it falls!"

As if in answer, Talenth bugled once more, this time in challenge.

Fiona only had a moment to marvel at her actions: How much of her outburst had been her and how much her dragon? She didn't know if what she was doing was right; to her knowledge, no one had ever done it before. But, just as she felt Talenth's stalwart declaration, she felt that it was the right thing to tell those who survived at Telgar that there was a queen dragon who was theirs—and a Weyrwoman who would stand for them.

Her call was answered loudly by bronze Zirenth, bronze Ladirth, bronze Ginirth, and more than twenty browns, greens, and blues.

"Igen?" Norik repeated numbly, his gaze stuck on the approaching wing of dragons like a dying man offered a final glimmer of hope. "You come from Igen?"

"I was there, Turns back," Fiona said, surprised by her own words. She raised her voice as she continued, "High Reaches flies for Telgar today, and Fort has sent its wings."

"That is good," Norik said, shaking his head. "But there is still no Telgar."

"There will always be a Telgar," Fiona said firmly.

Norik looked doubtful as he glanced toward the Bowl and the dragons and riders dispersing within it. "This is a sad day."

"You were right: We will need a ballad," Fiona told him, nodding consolingly. "And I would like you to write it, if you can." She held his eyes. "Honor is due this day."

"For the living or the dead?" Norik wondered.

"Both," T'mar said as he approached. "You are Norik, the harper."

The harper looked at him, straining as he examined T'mar, his eyes going wider as he recognized him. "You look like T'mar, but you seem older."

"Three Turns at Igen," T'mar agreed calmly. Norik mouthed the word "Igen" with something like hope. T'mar held out his hands to the anguished man, saying, "I grieve for your loss."

▼ ▼ ▼

"What's *he* doing here?" Fiona asked, pointing toward H'nez, as they settled themselves at the nearest table in the Kitchen Cavern and she had a chance to survey the riders K'lior had dispatched.

"He claimed the right," T'mar told her quietly. "He'd argued for the first available transfer and this was it."

Fiona frowned. She'd forgotten H'nez's argument with K'lior, so many Turns ago for her and those who had come back in time from Igen Weyr, so recently for the bronze rider. H'nez had demanded the right to transfer to the first available Weyr.

"We need all the riders we can get," T'mar reminded her. "We've only forty in all."

"More would have come," F'jian added with a nod toward her. "When K'lior asked for volunteers, nearly every man in the Weyr stepped forward." He grinned as he told her, "All those who'd been with us in Igen, of course, but even those who hadn't were eager."

"Well, K'lior has his own Falls to fight," Fiona said agreeably. Her expression fell as she glanced at H'nez once more.

"Don't be fooled by him," Seban spoke up from where he sat, nodding toward H'nez, as he helped Bekka tend a pot near the hearth. Fiona shot him a surprised look and the ex-dragonrider explained, "He's a good leader, he looks after his riders and makes them look after his dragons."

"You were in his wing."

"And proud of it, weyrwoman," Seban declared. She noticed that he hadn't stressed her title and took it for the reproof it was.

"He needs a smaller head," she muttered.

"Unlike some," Seban teased in response, surprising her at his hearing.

Fiona dimpled, then made a dismissive gesture with her hand and turned back to T'mar, who gave her a worried look.

"What?"

"Until your Talenth rises, the question of who is senior wingleader is a problem," T'mar told her.

"It's not a problem at all," Seban declared, jerking his head toward H'nez. "He Impressed Ginirth Turns before any bronze here."

"Shards!" Fiona said.

If H'nez noticed that he was the topic of conversation, he didn't show it. In fact, Fiona realized, he was busy playing with some of the younger weyrfolk; he'd coaxed them out of hiding with the promise of sweets in return for work and information. He was, she admitted sourly, doing exactly what she was supposed to be doing.

"We'll have a hot lunch soon," Terin said as she plopped down next to F'jian. The bronze rider smiled at her and tousled her hair affectionately. She batted his hand away, snarling, "Not now or I'll have you scrubbing up." She glanced toward Fiona. "So what now, weyrwoman?"

"Seban?" Fiona called over to the ex-dragonrider. "Do you think you and Bekka are up for a tour?"

The young girl looked up from the boiling pot, her eyes alight.

Fiona stepped over to them, gesturing for the cooking glove. "Terin and I can handle the cooking, I need you two to get to know people here." She glanced challengingly at Bekka. "How many people do you think you can meet in the next two hours?"

"Two hours?" Bekka repeated thoughtfully, before breaking into a huge grin. "Why *all* of them, Weyrwoman!"

"As many as you can would be fine by me," Fiona told her with a smile and a glance at Seban, who gave her a somber nod of assurance. As the two started out into the Weyr Bowl, Fiona called after them, "Don't forget, we'll be having lunch in the Dining Cavern, let everyone know!"

"The Dining Cavern hasn't enough tables set out for that many people," Terin observed quietly.

"Well then, get some riders to pull out the extra tables," Fiona replied. "Besides, it's not so much the eating they'll need as the assurance."

"I'd say you're right there, Weyrwoman," Norik agreed from his place nearby. He was hovering over a small slate, a stick of chalk hanging limply in one hand. He still hadn't written a single word.

F'jian noticed and walked over to him. "Would this do," he asked respectfully, opening his mouth and singing quietly in a soft tenor voice:

They flew for their Weyr
They flew for their Hold
They flew who knows where
They're lost, those so bold.

"It's a start," Norik agreed after a moment of awestruck silence. He bent to the slate. "What were the first words again, bronze rider?"

Fiona forced herself out of her chair rather than let the writing of Telgar's dirge to be a further reason to put off her conversation with H'nez.

H'nez glanced up at her approach and carefully worked her in to the conversation he was having with the youngsters, nodding toward her and saying, "And this is Weyrwoman Fiona. She was holder bred, her father was the Lord Holder of Fort Hold. Does anyone remember his name from the Teaching Ballads?"

A number of hands shot up and H'nez pointed to an older boy.

"Lord Holder Bemin," the boy replied promptly.

"Very good," H'nez said. "And what's your name?"

"Belivan," the boy replied proudly. "My father is—was—" his eyes fell "—a brown rider."

"My father rode a blue," a younger girl piped up.

"And mine a green," another sobbed.

"They must have been great riders," Fiona said.

The children nodded in agreement.

"And they did their duty to Weyr, Hold, and Craft," H'nez added smoothly. They all nodded once again. "And so, tonight, we will honor them."

It didn't take much coaxing from Terin to get some of the older children to start helping her around the Kitchen even if they were, at first, more nuisance than aid. Some knew where the stores were and others knew where the cooking pots were kept and still another group knew where the spices were placed.

Satisfied that Terin had them well in hand, Fiona made her way to the back corridor to search out the holders of the lower level. Before she did, however, she found a few moments alone with H'nez.

"Seban has reminded me that you are the senior rider here," Fiona said. H'nez nodded, his expression blank. "So, until Talenth rises, you have the duties of the Weyrleader."

Again, the tall, lanky bronze rider nodded.

"There's a Fall in three days' time," H'nez said. "Lower Telgar."

"I'm sure that we can get help."

"We'll need to visit the Holds and Crafts before then," H'nez observed. "To let them know that they are protected."

"We should go to the Smithcrafthall and see if we can get some of those new flamethrowers," Fiona said.

H'nez nodded in agreement.

"But our most immediate concern is housing our dragons and riders," he said.

"They could stay in the Hatching Grounds," Fiona suggested.

H'nez shook his head. "That would make their stay here seem temporary, and it would probably upset the weyrfolk."

"What are you suggesting?"

"It is a custom of Fort Weyr," H'nez began slowly, "to settle the remains of a lost dragon and rider as quickly as possible, then reallocate their weyr."

"But they've just lost so many!" Fiona cried in horror at the thought.

"I don't know what the tradition is here," H'nez told her. "We should find out and honor it."

"I could look in the Records . . ." Fiona trailed off as she realized what that would entail: entering the Weyrwoman's quarters.

"I could come with you, if you'd like," H'nez offered.

Fiona shook her head reflexively. "It's my job."

"Then, I'll leave you to it," H'nez said, turning back to the Kitchen Cavern. He paused just a moment, before turning back and asking, "You'll inform the other bronzes?"

He meant their riders. Fiona nodded, sent a quick message to Talenth who sent it on to the Zirenth and Ladirth.

"I've told them."

H'nez paused a moment longer, seeming about to say something, then turned and strode away purposefully on his long, lanky legs.

As she made her way farther into the dark corridors behind the Kitchen Cavern, she heard a gitar being strummed in a slow mournful tune: Norik practicing his ballad.

She turned to where, at Fort Weyr, there were the larger teaching and play rooms. She was rewarded with the sound of voices in the distance and increased her pace, thinking back to when she had met Xhinna Turns past and yet not so long ago.

As she saw the dim light of glows softly filling the corridor, she drew herself up, prepared to make a grand entrance, in the tradition impressed upon her by her father.

She took a step, and stopped. These people are hurting, she thought, letting her shoulders settle. They want words of comfort, not grand displays.

She took a deep breath to settle her nerves, then walked into the room. Silence fell but Fiona pretended not to notice, her father's words echoing in her head, "Leaders lead."

She spoke quickly to the women inside, who were clustered about in small groups, some working at tables, some dandling babies, others just sitting quietly, bereft. She told them who she was, assured them that Telgar would recover, that she rode a queen who would rise soon, and that they should be prepared for the noon meal and a wake in the evening.

"My man, L'rat, what's to become of his things?" a woman asked quietly from the far corner. She was dark-haired, with dark, shiny eyes and brilliant teeth. To Fiona, she seemed like one with trader blood.

"They'll be handled in the usual way, when a rider is lost," Fiona assured her.

"How soon will your riders want to move in?" another woman demanded.

"*Your* riders," Fiona replied, "are here already and need quarters now."

"So who'll clean out near five hundred weyrs?" the short, dark-haired woman demanded.

"Hush, Shaneese, that's no way to talk!" the other woman chided her.

"You've quarters of your own, Vikka, so you've no concern," Shaneese retorted, "but others lived with their mates and it'll take more than one afternoon to find new quarters."

"I'm not throwing anyone out," Fiona declared sternly. "Shaneese, can you get me a list of those who live in the weyrs?"

The short woman eyed her warily for a moment before giving her a stiff nod.

"Good," Fiona said. "There are only forty riders now, so it should be possible to find them accommodations without displacing any families." She glanced toward the woman named Vikka. "You have quarters of your own?"

"Aye, Weyrwoman," Vikka said with a curt nod. "I'm storeswoman and need to be close to the main gates."

"How are we for stores?"

"Oh, we'll not run out for a long time, Weyrwoman!" Vikka declared, with a hard to read expression on her face. "D'gan was good at providing for the Weyr."

Someone snorted derisively and Fiona glanced in the direction of the noise to spot a tall, blond woman who looked back furtively.

"Weyrleader D'gan believed in the rights of the Weyr," Vikka explained to Fiona. She jerked her head toward the blond woman. "Tevora was a crafter's daughter before . . ."

Fiona felt a moment of revulsion for the dead Weyrleader. She glanced at Tevora with renewed interest.

"Which craft?" she asked her quietly.

"Smith," Tevora said with a snivel. "I was taken—"

"It's an honor to be brought to the Weyr!" Shaneese snarled.

"It's an honor when you want to go!" Tevora snapped back, advancing on the smaller woman angrily.

"No one stays at the Weyr against their will," Fiona said, glancing around the room for any signs of similarly mistreated women.

"So you say!" Tevora shot back angrily.

"Yes," Fiona told her calmly. "So I say." She glanced around the room. "We're cooking lunch, and we'll have a proper mourning this evening, please tell everyone."

Some of the quieter women looked up hopefully at that.

"It will take time to heal, I know," Fiona told them. "And things will change, as they do whenever there's a new Weyrleader."

"And who would our Weyrleader be?" Shaneese asked, none too politely.

"For the time being, the senior bronze rider is H'nez of Fort Weyr," Fiona replied. She cocked her head toward the Weyr Bowl. "My Talenth has reached three Turns—"

"Three Turns!" Vikka exclaimed, brows furrowed. "I don't recall a Talenth in the Ballads for Fort."

"She was of Melirth's last clutch," Fiona explained. "We went back in time to Igen, and remained there for three Turns to allow our weyrlings time to mature."

"So she'll rise any day now," Vikka said with a knowing nod.

"And then what?" Shaneese demanded. The other women in the room looked at her with various displays of anger or irritation but she brushed them off, continuing, "The sickness, has a cure been found?"

Fiona shook her head.

"So how long before your dragons start coughing?" Shaneese persisted. "How long before they die?" Her gaze bore into Fiona as she added, "Will your queen even last long enough to clutch?"

"Shaneese!" Vikka exclaimed, bearing down angrily on the smaller woman. To Fiona she said, "You must forgive her, Weyrwoman, she so loved her L'rat."

"There's no forgiveness necessary," Fiona said, forcing herself to remain calm despite the black-haired woman's onslaught. She glanced at Shaneese. "Kindan and Lorana at Benden Weyr have been working on a cure."

"Lorana?" Shaneese repeated. "The one who lost her queen?" She snorted in derision. "Why should she want to help others?"

"Kindan lost Koriana and still he found a cure during the Plague," Vikka replied. She glanced back to Fiona in dawning recognition. "You're Koriana's sister, aren't you?"

"I am," Fiona said, forcing herself to speak over the lump in her throat. "So I know something of Kindan and I tell you, he won't let us down."

Something changed in Shaneese's manner as she absorbed this. "I see," she said. "Well, I hope he's quick because I'm not sure I can handle another dragon dying."

"Where can I find the headwoman?" Fiona asked, deciding that she had said enough here and it was time to continue her tour.

"That'd be me," Shaneese said. "At least it was until this morning."

"If you want to step down, I understand," Fiona said, recovering quickly from her surprise. She glanced over to Tevora. "When I go to the Smithcrafthall, I can bring you, if you'd like."

Tevora glanced up nervously, then shook her head. "They probably think I'm dead."

A mousy-haired woman reached over and patted her on the shoulder. "You are good with metal, Tevora, we could certainly use you here."

"Dedelia, keep an eye on her," Shaneese said to the mousy-haired woman. She glanced around the room and started calling out names. "Go help in the kitchen."

To Fiona she said, "Come on, Weyrwoman." As she bustled out, she glanced over her shoulder and said to Dedelia, "And get them back to work, there's clothes to be washed and mended, not to mention the weaving that's been let go this morning."

"And, finally, here's the medicinal storeroom," Shaneese said as she completed their tour of the first level of the Weyr. She glanced inside and nodded to herself as she spotted two women working, bent over jars and measuring sets. "The stocks are complete, we want for nothing."

"We want for nothing" seemed to be a catchphrase for Shaneese and Telgar Weyr. Fiona was amazed at the amount of goods amassed in the storage rooms, at the quality of fabrics, hides, and metals that were on hand for the Weyr's use.

"Say what you want about D'gan, he never let the Weyr be shorted," Shaneese said as she took in Fiona's expression. She called to the two women, "This is Fiona, she's the new Weyrwoman."

"If a small girl comes running in here all out of breath asking for any herbals or medicinals, give them to her," Fiona told the two older women. One of them gave her a surprised look. "Her name's Bekka and she doesn't sleep. Her father is Seban, who until recently rode blue Serth. She's agreed to come here as healer in training."

"Healer in training?" Shaneese looked at Fiona in surprise. "She'll either learn quick or we'll all be for it."

"She doesn't sleep," Fiona repeated with a smile. "She reads, she'll learn."

"How many Turns has she, then?" Shaneese asked.

"She has twelve Turns," Fiona said. At Shaneese's skeptical look she added, "My headwoman at Igen had ten Turns."

"That's starting them young!" one of the herbal women exclaimed.

"'Needs must when Thread Falls,'" Fiona replied, quoting the old saying. "My 'old' headwoman, Terin, came with me; she's cooking our lunch."

"I'm looking forward to meeting her," said Shaneese, adding with a wink to the storeswomen, "especially if she makes a good meal."

"Well, we're done here, we should probably see if she needs any more help," Fiona decided, nodding to the two women in farewell and turning back toward the Kitchen Cavern.

Shaneese examined the kitchen dubiously when she entered, clearly expecting the worst. Her eyebrows rose slowly but steadily as she saw the organized and purposeful bustling of the cooks, the cheerfully helping youngsters setting table, the soft croon of Norik as he strummed on his gitar. Her eyes narrowed as she spotted Terin.

"I thought you said she had ten Turns."

"She had, when we first came to Igen," Fiona said. "We were there for three Turns, so she's nearly fourteen Turns now, even if her birth was just over ten Turns ago."

"Well, ten or fourteen," Shaneese said, "she carries herself well."

Terin smiled as she spotted Fiona and pranced over to her, gesticulating wildly around the room.

"I don't know where they all came from but they saved the day!" Terin said as she sketched a salute toward Fiona. Her smile dropped a bit as she added in an undertone, "They're all so quiet, though."

"I don't like noise in my kitchen," Shaneese said. Terin glanced at her inquiringly and the older woman unbent enough to extend a hand, saying, "Shaneese, headwoman of Telgar Weyr."

"Oh, by the First Egg, that's a relief!" Terin said, shaking the woman's hand gladly. She gave Fiona a frank look as she said, "I was afraid I'd never manage all these people by myself."

"The Weyrwoman says you managed a whole Weyr by yourself for three Turns," Shaneese said, nodding in Fiona's direction.

"I did," Terin agreed, "but I had only dragons and their riders to handle, not thousands of women."

Shaneese looked at Fiona questioningly.

"We were the only women to go back in time to Igen," she explained.

"If it weren't for Mother Karina and the traders—"

"You knew Mother Karina?" Shaneese demanded, her brows bristling.

"Of course!" Terin exclaimed. "She had the most marvelous recipes for hot weather foods." Terin smiled in memory as she added, "Of course, as time went on, I managed to come up with a few of my own."

Her expression faded to one of surprise as Shaneese spun on her heels and left the cavern.

"What did I say?" Terin asked, looking crushed. Fiona could only shake her head. She'd sensed a feeling of pity and sadness from Shaneese just before the Telgar headwoman had rushed off, but couldn't comprehend the reason behind it.

They stood there, perplexed, for only a few moments before Shaneese returned, carrying a small box in her arms.

"I was asked to hold this for you," Shaneese told them in a small voice as she placed the box down on a nearby table and gestured for them to come over. "She said I'd know when the time was right," Shaneese continued, shaking her head sadly, "but I never expected—" she broke off and nodded toward the box. "You're to open it."

Terin stared at her, open-mouthed.

"Both of you," Shaneese said, gesturing to Fiona impatiently.

Together, Terin and Fiona lifted the lid of the box. Inside were two small envelopes made of embroidered fabric. One was marked "Terin," the other "Fiona."

Shaneese saw the labels. "I guessed right," she said with some relief in her voice. Fiona glanced at her and Shaneese explained, "I never looked inside."

Fiona handed the first to Terin and slowly picked up the second. The scent off the envelope was instantly recognizable.

"Mother Karina?" Fiona asked, glancing toward Shaneese. Shaneese nodded. "She used to trade with us. When—just before she passed, she asked me to keep this. She said I would know who to give it to and when."

Fiona snorted. "She always liked being secretive."

"She was my grandmother."

"Mother Karina was your grandmother?"

"Yes."

"So you knew Tenniz?" Terin asked.

"He's the reason I came here," Shaneese said with a tone of resentment in her voice.

"Tenniz, is he still—?"

Fiona's question was cut off by Shaneese's curt headshake. She gestured brusquely toward Fiona's envelope. "Open it."

Fumbled-fingered, Fiona undid the string that was looped around the button that held the envelope closed. Inside she found a small parchment and a gold brooch. It was shaped like a harp.

She eyed it critically for a moment: The workmanship was both brilliant and unmistakable—Zenor had made it.

She glanced at the note and her breath caught.

I am sorry I cannot give this to you in person, the note read. *But I knew that we would not meet again. Tenniz saw it. He said to tell you that it will all turn out right. Love, Mother.*

Beside her, Terin sobbed and clasped something to her breast. As Fiona's eyes fell on her, she turned and extended her hand to her. "I don't understand," Terin said with a sob, as she indicated the small gold trinket, "this should be yours."

It was a gold fitting for a riding harness, in the shape of a queen dragon soaring upward.

"What does the note say?" Fiona asked, wondering if perhaps the labels had been switched and showing Terin her harper's brooch.

Terin gestured to the note that lay on the table. Fiona looked down and read, "*'This is yours and no other's.'*"

Fiona felt a shiver as she read the note—a shiver of excitement and hope. Mother Karina had sent her a message with the two notes: The message was one of hope.

"What?" Terin demanded, taking in the look on Fiona's face.

"I think you should keep it," Fiona told her. She glanced toward Shaneese. "And I'm proud to meet Mother Karina's granddaughter."

"She spoke of you," Shaneese said, her voice a whisper, her eyes filled with tears. Fiona gave her an inquiring look. "She said that when it seemed the darkest, hope would come and that it would be borne by someone she knew and loved." She met Fiona's eyes as she added, "Tenniz told her."

Fiona was still absorbing that when Terin piped up. "There's another envelope here."

Both Shaneese and Fiona glanced over at the small box in surprise. At Shaneese's insistence, Fiona retrieved the envelope. It was labeled: Lorana.

SIX

Mourn and grieve,
Wail and cry.
Remember those
Who no more fly.

Telgar Weyr, later, AL 508.2.8

"There must be some mistake," Terin said as she eyed the envelope suspiciously.

"Or perhaps Mother Karina hoped that we would bring it to her," Fiona suggested. She looked at Shaneese. "Would you keep this for us?"

Shaneese shook her head. "No, I was told to give it to you as soon as I knew."

"How did you know?"

"The time was right," Shaneese said with a shrug. She nodded toward the two envelopes. "Besides, I was clearly right. They had your names on them."

There was no arguing with that. Shaneese stood, silent, for a moment longer before she shook herself back into action.

"You'll be needing a place to store that," she said, nodding toward the box. "And you'll be needing your quarters, too, Weyrwoman."

Fiona shook her head, not up to the task of cleaning out the old Weyr-woman's quarters, but Shaneese ignored her. She called out the names of two women who bustled over immediately and told them, "Weyrwoman Fiona needs to have quarters."

"I'll go with them," Terin said after a quick glance to Shaneese.

"You'll do nothing of the sort," Shaneese told her. "You stay here and see to the cooking." She motioned for Fiona to precede her. "The Weyr-woman and I can manage well enough, I'm sure."

Fiona gave Terin a rueful look and shook her head in resignation.

"She's like her gran," Terin murmured as she motioned for Fiona to go. "All bustle and no talk."

Shaneese snorted a laugh and turned back to Terin with a happy gleam in her eyes. "Child, that's the first time I've laughed this day!"

Outside, as they crossed the Weyr Bowl, Shaneese told Fiona reflectively, "Weyrwoman Lina was a gentle woman." She shook her head. "I never understood quite why her Garoth let D'gan's Kaloth fly her so often."

"Sometimes what is good for the Weyr is not what is expected," Fiona remarked.

Shaneese nodded in agreement. "This is a sad day," she said. "But it's best if we get it—and our grieving—done with at once."

"What of those who shared quarters?"

Shaneese shook her head. "That's a different thing." She frowned. "Today what we can do is start things fresh, with a new Weyrwoman, her new quarters, and proper grieving." She paused, gesturing for the two women to precede them before adding, "As time goes on, we'll make adjustments in who lives where."

Shaneese held Fiona up until one of the women came out of the weyr again carrying a bundle wrapped in sheets.

"Make sure you bring back new sheets," Shaneese ordered. The other woman nodded and hurried along. Shaneese gestured to Fiona, "I think we can go in now."

The other woman was still bustling about, cleaning the room and moving things into the far corridor that linked into the Weyr's main caves.

"We can get you new tapestries," Shaneese said, gesturing to the gaudy hangings on the walls. Fiona began to shake her head demurely but Shaneese forestalled her, saying, "Much as I loved her—she was good in many ways—the Weyrwoman had terrible taste and D'gan's was worse." She cocked her head toward Fiona. "What sort of colors do you prefer?"

"I grew up with brown and gold," Fiona said, recalling Fort Hold's colors vividly. She glanced around the room. Underneath the hangings, the walls were a bright off-white that livened the room. Fiona stepped over to the shutters and opened them, peering out over the Weyr Bowl. A chill wind blew in and she closed them again, regretfully.

"They had mirrors at Igen," Fiona began only to halt at the sight of Shaneese's face, "to bring light into the rooms."

"I know what you're talking about but we haven't been able to get them from the Smithcrafthall," Shaneese told her. Fiona gave her a look of surprise. Shaneese shrugged. "You may have noticed that the Weyr doesn't lack for bright, shiny things: gaudy gold and bright jewelry; baubles, mostly."

Fiona raised a hand, prompting her to continue.

"D'gan was a demanding Weyrleader," Shaneese said, glancing around the quarters with a frown. "He had no trouble taking what he felt was the Weyr's due."

"I'd heard," Fiona said. "At Igen, we preferred to trade for goods."

"That was before Thread," Shaneese reminded her. She waved a hand, dismissing the issue. "Anyway, what D'gan didn't want, the Weyr couldn't get."

"I see," Fiona replied, wondering how much Telgar's weyrfolk had suffered for their Weyrleader's whims. She brightened. "I think I prefer our Igen ways."

"'Our Igen ways,'" Shaneese repeated to herself, eyeing Fiona critically. "And now, with Thread falling, Weyrwoman, what would those ways be?"

"Fair trade when possible," Fiona said. "I'm holder bred: I know of the demands of the Weyr. If the Weyr can't live by the tithe then perhaps we can trade for our extra needs."

"We could profit from trade," Shaneese agreed. She shook her head, alerted by the noise of a bell ringing in the kitchen. "It's lunchtime."

Shaneese was impressed with Terin's command of the kitchen and happy to see so many of the weyrfolk gathered. H'nez greeted as many as he could, paying particular attention to those sent by Bekka and Seban.

Fiona invited Shaneese and Norik to sit with her at the head table. At H'nez's subtle direction, the rest of the dragonriders spread themselves out among the other tables.

F'jian proved very popular with the younger women, causing Terin to hover around his table protectively.

Xhinna appeared at Fiona's table for a moment, then drifted off. Fiona next noticed her seated with Tevora and then at a table with Vikka, talking animatedly.

H'nez caught Fiona's eyes as she scanned the crowd and nodded toward her emphatically.

Ginirth asks if you would say some words to the weyrfolk, Talenth told her.

Fiona nodded toward H'nez and rose to her feet, tapping the side of her mug with a spoon. To add to her effort, Talenth bugled from outside.

The huge room was instantly silent.

"For those of you whom I haven't yet met," Fiona began, "I am Fiona, formerly of Fort Weyr." She paused for a moment, scanning the new faces in front of her. "Tonight we will grieve those lost." She paused again to let the weyrfolk digest her words. She caught H'nez's eyes, then F'jian's and T'mar's and all the other dragonriders as she continued. "Tomorrow, Telgar Weyr begins anew. In three days' time, Thread falls over lower Telgar and Telgar Weyr will fight Thread once more."

The dragonriders all rose and cheered.

Fiona waited for them to finish, then continued, "My Talenth has more than three Turns and she'll mate soon." She found herself blushing as she added, "Soon we'll have eggs on the Hatching Grounds and we shall start seeking out Candidates, with first choice going to those here." Her eyes fell on Xhinna and Terin. Terin grinned in response; Xhinna's expression was unreadable.

Fiona glanced at H'nez, feeling that her words had failed to sway the mood of the weyrfolk.

H'nez took the hint and rose. "I am H'nez, rider of bronze Ginirth," he said, "and the senior rider here. If you have any questions regarding the weyrs and their dispositions, you may bring them to either me or the Weyrwoman."

H'nez scanned the quiet room expectantly and sat down again a moment later, with a stony expression.

"This is a hard day for us," Norik spoke up from his place at the high table, addressing Fiona.

"There is time to grieve," Fiona said, glancing around at the somber faces of the weyrfolk. Fiona sought out Terin and pointed a hand toward her. "Among those you may not have met yet," she said, "is Terin who was headwoman with me at Igen."

"Igen?" a voice called out.

"You were at Igen?"

"We went back ten Turns in time with our injured dragons and riders," Fiona explained.

"I'd heard a rumor," someone muttered.

"Many of us remember Igen," Norik told Fiona. "And those who don't are curious."

"By the First Egg, it was hot!" Terin exclaimed from her place near F'jian.

A general chuckle ran around the room. "It always is!"

"And the sandstorms were amazing," F'jian added, his remark echoed by several of the younger riders.

"You were at Igen, too, bronze rider?" a voice called out.

"And T'mar," F'jian said, rising and pointing toward the older bronze rider. "Many of us were," F'jian added as heads craned back from T'mar to him. "When K'lior asked for volunteers to come here"—he paused, worried that he might be upsetting the weyrfolk, then continued unabashed—"the whole Weyr volunteered to follow Fiona."

"The whole Weyr?" one of the weyrfolk asked, cocking her head toward Fiona speculatively.

"The whole Weyr," T'mar agreed. He pointed toward Seban. "Even those who lost a dragon a short time before demanded a chance to be here."

Fiona sensed a change in the room, a sense of curiosity, excitement, honor.

"It was an honor to serve at Igen," Fiona said, feeling the focus of the room shift back toward her. "It will be an honor to be your Weyrwoman and see Telgar fly high."

She nodded once to the faces peering up at her and then sat back down, turning toward Shaneese.

"They need time," the headwoman told her kindly.

"There isn't much," Norik said.

"Have we enough wine for tonight?" Fiona asked, glancing at Shaneese. "And have we got sitters for the smallest ones?"

"Yes," Shaneese replied. "We'll have that by this evening."

At Norik's suggestion and H'nez's concurrence, the weyrfolk constructed a huge pile of logs at the east end of the Weyr, not too near the lake and the easily stampeded herdbeasts but close enough that fresh water would be easily at hand.

"It's a long roll," Norik said warningly to Fiona when they met in the Dining Cavern near dusk that evening.

"We'll skip no one," H'nez replied, glancing at his assembled riders. Each had a large sack perched on their shoulders. "We will honor all who flew from Telgar."

"There are only forty of you," Norik said, the concern in his voice obvious.

"Forty-one," Fiona said, pointing to herself.

"Each rider will stand for nine," H'nez declared. "T'mar, F'jian, and I will stand for eleven, the weyrwoman for ten."

Norik considered this for a moment, then nodded, sitting at the table and revising his lists hurriedly. He glanced at H'nez and Fiona as he said, "I'm not sure who should stand for D'gan."

"I'll stand for D'gan," H'nez said with a quick look toward Fiona.

"You are the senior," Fiona agreed. "But not Weyrleader." She looked at Norik. "Will that be a problem?"

"To dishonor a Weyrleader . . ." Norik paused as he considered the implications. It was a common practice in the Weyrs to hold a gathering to honor those fallen. The greater the rank, the greater honor due. By tradition, the senior flightleader could honor his fallen Weyrleader . . . but the situation here was more complex because the tragedy was so great—never before had a whole Weyr been lost like this.

"Fine," H'nez said sharply to Fiona, "you stand for him; I'll stand for his son, D'lin."

"I think that's an excellent compromise," Norik said. "D'lin was well-respected within the Weyr."

"I'll have the men form up," H'nez told Fiona.

Events moved quickly as dragons deposited riders by H'nez who, after having them form up, handed out the lists that Norik had prepared.

Fiona sidled over to them, gauging their mood.

"Most of you have seen or done this before," H'nez told the assembled riders, "but never on this scale."

"I haven't," F'jian spoke up. "What do we do?" In a lower voice, he added, "I don't want to get it wrong."

"Tonight we will take roll for the Weyr," H'nez replied, directing a tight, intense look at the youngest bronze rider. "When any of the names on your list are called, you're to stand for them."

"The light's bad," F'jian said.

"You'll have to memorize your list," T'mar spoke up. "It's tradition."

"It's considered an honor to answer for those who can't," a voice spoke up from the dark. It was Seban. His tone was shaky as he continued,

"Among other things, it signifies that you are a rider and that you take on the mantle of the rider you stand for." He paused. "You stand for him."

"So you'd best memorize that list well," H'nez continued with a thankful nod toward the ex-dragonrider. "Because you answer for those men and anything they did."

Fiona had a sudden insight and spoke up, "Think carefully before you agree to this."

H'nez looked toward her, gesturing expectantly. All eyes were on her.

"If you do this, you are no longer of Fort," she told them. "For by standing for these riders, you stand for Telgar."

There was a long moment's silence broken by F'jian's voice. "We stand for you, Weyrwoman."

Fiona smiled and nodded low in gratitude. "Then you stand for Telgar."

With an acknowledging look, H'nez stood back in front of his men. He said one word, loudly, clearly in the night, "Telgar!"

"Telgar!" the riders shouted back, their voices echoing resoundingly around the Weyr.

As if in answer, a slow, steady beat began from the harper's big drum.

"Memorize your lists," H'nez told the riders. Fiona took a long moment to examine her list, reciting it to Talenth and repeating it to herself until she had mastered it.

Drawn by the mournful, slow, steady sound of the bass drum, Telgar's weyrfolk slowly began gathering. Seban marched forward to the dragonriders and collected the lists.

"Are you ready, Weyrwoman?" H'nez asked politely as he placed his list on top of Seban's pile.

"Yes."

"Riders of Telgar," H'nez spoke, his voice low but firm, with a strength Fiona had never heard emanate from him before.

In response, the thirty-nine dragonriders formed into three ranks, each behind a wingleader.

H'nez raised his hand, held it there a moment, then lowered it.

Slowly, steadily, in time to the beating of the drum, the riders of Telgar Weyr moved forward to honor the fallen.

The drummer must have kept a good eye on their movements, for as they entered the end of the ring formed by Telgar's weyrfolk, he beat a quick double-beat, then stopped.

Norik's voice came out of the dark, full, rich, drenched in pain and sorrow as he intoned rather than sang the ancient words:

> *Drummer, beat, and piper, blow,*
> *Soldier strike, healer go.*
> *Guard the keep and sear the passes,*
> *'Til the dawning Red Star passes.*

The drummer punctuated each phrase with an appropriate drumbeat. The drums fell silent as Norik finished, letting the silence build up in the evening sky.

Fiona began to worry; the lull seemed too long. As if in response, Seban moved forward to the center of the circle.

"I call the roll," his voice echoed in the night air.

"Riders of Telgar, you are called," Norik intoned. "I call for K'lur, rider of Koth the green."

Silence filled the air and then, slowly, the drumbeat began again, slow, steady: a heartbeat.

From the ranks of riders, M'rorin strode forward.

"I stand for K'lur," M'rorin called loudly, his voice catching as he spoke the words. "I stand for him for he has passed *between*."

"Who stands with K'lur?" Norik called, his eyes searching the weyrfolk. Slowly from the group a woman, carrying a baby and leading two small children, moved forward.

"I stand with K'lur," the woman said. "For he did his duty, was a good father to his children, fair and kind to all."

She crossed to M'rorin's side and together they waited while the slow, steady, heartbeat drum beat four times. Then M'rorin stood forward.

"K'lur is no more. I stand for him, a father to his children, his mate. Fair and kind to all."

The drum started again, slow, steady heartbeat. M'rorin and K'lur's family moved with him, then stayed as he bowed and moved back to the ranks of dragonriders.

"I call for M'rit, rider of Jalith the blue," Norik called and the ritual continued, each rider standing forward in stead of the lost rider, weyrmates and weyrchildren standing forward with them, and moving off once more to the slow heartbeat of the drum.

"I call for D'gan, Weyrleader, rider of Kaloth the bronze," Norik called out in the end.

Fiona moved forward. "I stand for D'gan," she called loudly, her voice filling the air, her shoulders and head lifted high. She heard some harsh intakes of surprise from the weyrfolk and murmurs of approval. "I stand for him, for he has passed *between*."

Norik nodded approvingly and held a long, expectant silence, before calling out, "Who stands with D'gan?"

No one moved. The silence grew. Tension filled the air. Finally, someone moved, a small girl separated from the crowd and moved to join Fiona. It was Bekka.

"I stand with D'gan," she spoke up, her chin raised high, eyes defiantly searching the faces of the shamed weyrfolk. "I stand with D'gan," she said again, "Telgar's Weyrleader, the man who did his duty, no matter the cost."

A sudden noise burst faintly in the evening sky and the watch dragon bugled in amazement as, overhead, a huge phalanx of dragons descended steeply in the night air, their riders dismounting quickly and marching at speed toward Fiona.

At the edge of the ring they paused. One stepped forward.

"I stand with D'gan," the rider called out. It was K'lior, Weyrleader of Fort Weyr. "He was a demanding man, he expected nothing less than the best of his riders. Fort stands with Telgar."

Another rider strode forward, wearing Istan colors.

"I stand with D'gan," the man said. Fiona didn't recognize him. "He showed us the meaning of duty. Ista stands with Telgar."

"I stand with D'gan," a strong-featured man said as he strode forward. "He set high standards. High Reaches stands with Telgar."

"I stand with D'gan," B'nik, Benden's Weyrleader declared as he stepped toward the center. "He showed me the meaning of valor. Benden stands with Telgar."

A fifth man joined the others with a woman at his side; they were holding hands.

"We stand for D'gan," the man said, raising their clasped hands high. "His last thoughts were for the Weyrs, his last warning was to all the Weyrs of Pern."

The woman moved forward, turning challengingly toward Fiona. "Who stands for Telgar?"

"I do," Fiona responded immediately, controlling her surprise at the woman's unexpected behavior.

"I do," the woman echoed then, meeting her eyes.

"I do," the man at her side added.

"I do," the High Reaches Weyrleader declared.

"I do," B'nik, Benden's Weyrleader affirmed.

"I do!" called Ista Weyr's leader.

"I do!" K'lior said loudly, proudly, for Fort Weyr.

"I do!" H'nez's voice rang in the night, joined almost immediately by T'mar, F'jian, and the rest of the riders.

"Telgar?" Norik's voice rose above all the others. "Who stands?"

"*I do!*" The riders and weyrfolk shouted back.

"Telgar!" Norik shouted, striding forward with a torch in his hand and lighting the bonfire that had been laid at the lakeside.

Overhead, watch-whers streamed by, bearing glows in their paws, lighting the night. Dragons roared in challenge.

"Telgar!" Norik shouted again.

"Telgar, Telgar, Telgar!" the gathering shouted back, filling the Bowl with a wave of sound that drowned out all echoes.

"*Telgar!*" shouted all those gathered in the Weyr reborn.

SEVEN

Heart and mind together
Impressed, bound forever.

Telgar Weyr, early morning, AL 508.2.9

Fiona was glad to be warm and realized that it was because she'd managed to amass a large group of people to share her bed. She opened one bleary eye and spied Xhinna, then the top of a smaller blond head— Bekka; another body lying against her other side felt like Terin, and she wondered how she'd managed to pry her away from F'jian when she heard a male snore from the other side of Terin. Anchoring the far side of the bed beyond Bekka was Seban, with an arm wrapped possessively around his daughter.

Fiona closed her eye and smiled as she snuggled further into the warmth of all those bodies.

She was glad to have her friends from Fort Weyr and from her sojourn back in time at Igen Weyr, just as she was glad to learn that many of the Fort Weyr weyrfolk had joined their riders, even whole families. The youngest had immediately found friends among the Telgar children, and Fiona planned to emulate them immediately.

She would have no factions in *her* Weyr.

A cough caused her to open her eye again as she glanced around, wondering if someone else had heard it. Bekka stirred in her sleep, moaning, then settling as Seban moved sleepily to comfort her. Terin made a slight whimpering sound that was answered by a half-formed murmur from F'jian, echoed by Xhinna.

Fiona closed her eyes, wishing her head weren't pounding quite so badly. She wasn't willing to admit it was the wine she'd drank—perhaps it was the noise or cheering or the intense emotions of the night before. Perhaps it was the muzziness that still seemed to cling to her, T'mar, and the others, though they managed to ignore it most of the time. Perhaps—

The cough came again.

Fiona was instantly out of bed and rushing toward Talenth, an inchoate scream filling the room, waking all the others.

I don't feel well, Telgar's only queen dragon informed her.

F'jian and Terin arranged breakfast and forced Fiona to eat, setting up a table and chair next to Talenth in her lair.

"You've got to keep your strength up," Terin said.

"I'll get Norik," Xhinna said, rushing off.

F'jian and Terin excused themselves, moving back to Fiona's quarters to wash and prepare for the day.

"She'll be all right," Bekka said, looking from the gold dragon to her rider, her face sketching a quick smile. "You'll see."

Fiona nodded in acceptance of the calm words; her expression remained bleak. The sickness that had taken so many dragons—starting with Salina's Breth, Lorana's Arith, through to Seban's Serth, had come upon her dragon. Her queen. Her life, her breath, her hopes, her love—the very center of her being. How could she survive without Talenth?

"What will you do?" Seban asked her quietly from his position near Talenth's head. He'd scratched her eye ridges until she'd closed her eyes and lowered her head to go back to sleep.

"I told her that I wouldn't let her go without me," Fiona said, glancing with troubled eyes toward her queen. She frowned at Seban. "But I promised Telgar that I'd stay."

"Nothing's going to happen to her," Bekka declared once more, turning to her father for support. "Tell her, Da! Tell her that her queen's going to be all right!"

Seban gave his daughter a troubled look, shaking his head sadly.

"You can't give in!" Bekka said, glancing from Fiona to Seban and back.

"I'm not," Fiona assured her. "She only started coughing this morning—"

"Maybe you should move weyrs," Bekka suggested suddenly. "Maybe this weyr has bad air and if you moved—"

"We should have done that first," Seban interrupted her gently. "Once she's got the illness, it makes no sense to move." He paused, his lips tightening before he added, "It'd be more of a hurt to her than a help."

Bekka sought wildly for another solution. "Tintoval! We should tell her," she said suddenly. "Maybe she'll know something. Maybe they've learned something new."

"That's a good idea," Fiona agreed with a glance toward Seban. "Why don't you go ask H'nez if Ginirth can send a message?" She nodded toward Talenth. "I'd ask her but she's sleeping."

Relieved at finding something to do, Bekka agreed immediately and raced out of the weyr, jumping off the queens' ledge and shouting, "H'nez!" at the top of her lungs.

Fiona managed a quick smile before she turned her eyes back to Seban and Talenth. Quietly, she said, "How long have we got?"

"She's not bad yet. Two sevendays, maybe more," Seban said judiciously. Then, in an attempt to lift Fiona's spirits, he added, "She's a queen, so she may be stronger—"

"Salina's Breth was the first to go," Fiona reminded him, her tone devoid of any emotion.

Seban was silent for a long time, so long that Fiona was startled when he spoke again, "Whatever you do, Fiona, I'll support you."

Fiona nodded in relieved acceptance and gestured with a hand out toward the Weyr. "They've only just started to hope again, it seems terrible to steal it from them so quickly."

"Yes," Seban agreed, eyeing her with renewed respect. "It does, indeed, Weyrwoman!"

"Help me keep my hope," Fiona begged him in a small voice.

Seban gave Talenth a final pat and walked over to her, placing his arms in a circle around her shoulders sympathetically. Fiona allowed herself to lean back until her head was on his chest and closed her eyes in silent communion with the ex-dragonrider.

H'nez found them that way several minutes later when he came striding briskly into the weyr.

"Weyrwoman," he called, glancing over to the sleeping queen. "I came as soon as I heard."

"Thank you," Fiona said. "Did they have any news at Fort?"

H'nez shook his head. "They've more ill there, too."

At noon, the Dining Cavern was not as full as it had been the day before; still Fiona was glad to see that many of the weyrfolk had gathered there. She acknowledged their looks in her direction with a smile or a nod as appropriate and went over to the hearth to see what was cooking.

"Sit down, Weyrwoman, sit down!" one of the cooks called. "We'll bring you something in a trice."

"It's no problem," Fiona said. "I was used to shifting for myself at Igen."

"And now, Weyrwoman," Shaneese spoke up from her side, "you're here at Telgar."

Fiona recognized the peremptory tone and, with a quirk of her lips toward the headwoman, demurely took her seat at the head table.

Terin rushed up with a full tray, giving Fiona a stern look.

"This is *not* Igen," Terin scolded her as she set the plates out. "There are people here to care for you; it's their duty."

"I was just—"

"I know," Terin said, her tone softening. She leaned in closer to Fiona. "They need to know they're needed, you can't change them too quickly."

Fiona ducked her head meekly and Terin, who knew her too well, snorted. "Just give them a sevenday before you put everything on its ear."

"I'm afraid that's too late," Seban murmured as he approached them. He smiled at Fiona and nodded to Terin as he continued, "Word about Bekka's efforts has already caused quite a stir."

"Besides," Fiona admitted sadly, "I may not have that much time myself."

She caught Terin's and Seban's worried looks and explained, "At least until Talenth . . ." Her voice trailed off and she let out a deep sigh to hide her worry.

Terin set the tray on the table and quickly wrapped her arms around Fiona's shoulders. "Whatever you decide will be all right with me."

"I'm not giving up!" Fiona told her forcefully. She forced a smile for Seban. "Kindan never gave up, and I won't give up."

Terin sniffed, patted Fiona on the shoulders once more, then picked up her tray, repeating before she bustled off, "Whatever you decide."

From above her someone cleared his throat. It was H'nez. "Do you mind if I join you?"

Fiona shook her head, gesturing to a seat with her free hand. He smelled of firestone and of the cold *between:* He'd been drilling the wings. Fiona approved of his thoroughness even in these trying times. "I was expecting it."

"Normally, I'd insist," H'nez said by way of agreement. He gave her a brittle smile. "But with things the way they are, I'd prefer meeting as many of the weyrfolk as I can."

Fiona nodded in understanding.

H'nez reached to grab the mug at his place setting and poured it full of *klah*. He took a quick drink. "Normally, before a Fall, the Weyr sends out a watch rider but—" He paused, shaking his head in consternation.

"We're shorthanded," Fiona agreed. "Perhaps I should visit Nerra first."

H'nez pursed his lips tightly.

"You're not one of those who thinks women shouldn't be Lord Holders, are you?" Fiona asked, glancing at him sharply. She was willing to bet that he was; H'nez had always struck her as a stickler for tradition.

"If I ever were," H'nez replied slowly, his eyes dark, "my experience with Weyrwoman Cisca—and with you—would have cured me." He paused. "No, I was worried about your queen. Is she up to it?"

Fiona checked with Talenth who, having had a good, long sleep only occasionally interrupted by coughing, informed her that she would love to go flying. "She is," Fiona told him. "Why?"

"I think that given what we've heard of D'gan's dealings, it might make more sense if you and your queen met with the Lord Holders," H'nez said regretfully. Fiona could easily imagine how much he'd prefer cementing alliances with the Lord Holders himself rather than relinquishing the duty to her.

"I suspect you're right," Fiona agreed after she swallowed. The food was good. She detected some subtle seasoning in the vegetable that she associated with Terin's cooking, but she had no problem with the flavors of the spiced roast or the other dishes that clearly hadn't felt Terin's hand.

T'mar joined them at that moment and the conversation turned to matters of the fighting wings.

"I'm worried about the firestone," T'mar began without preamble.

H'nez nodded sourly in agreement.

"I'd prefer not to burden K'lior, if possible," he allowed.

"Where else could we get firestone in time?" T'mar wondered.

The rangy bronze rider twitched a shrug of agreement.

"If we had the hands, we could go back in time to Igen and mine it ourselves," Fiona said.

T'mar appraised the notion for a moment before shaking his head. "We've neither the hands nor the dragons for that."

"And wouldn't they be too tired timing it?" H'nez wondered, glancing reflectively at T'mar. "You were certainly exhausted after your time there."

T'mar's lips flickered in a frown. "It wasn't so much going back in time in itself but that we were there for so long."

"Explain."

"I noticed it more after the time passed that I'd Impressed Zirenth," T'mar said. "Up until then, I felt like I'd been in a room with bad air but after that I felt like I was always just too far away to listen on a conversation that I was straining to hear."

"Yes," Fiona said in agreement. "It was as though someone was calling to me but I could never find them."

"It strained the nerves," H'nez surmised.

"More than that," T'mar said. "It was like a fingernail running down a slate—every moment of every day."

H'nez winced appreciatively. "Not a pleasant experience," he decided. "And not something we'd like to recover from just before a Fall."

"Which leaves us with the issue of firestone," T'mar agreed.

A dragon's sudden warble from outside the Weyr Bowl caused Fiona to turn her head sharply, first surprised, then amused.

"Bekka has decided that Talenth needs to eat," she informed the concerned wingleaders with a grin.

"Seban was a good rider," H'nez said as if in consolation. "I'm sure that Bekka has Talenth's best interests at heart."

"I've no doubt," Fiona agreed. "Apparently Talenth was surprised at just how much she's learned from her father."

A distant cough caused Fiona's grin to slip and she turned, stricken, toward F'jian.

"That wasn't yours," Shaneese said to Fiona as she approached; following the Weyrwoman's gaze, she groaned, "Oh, no!"

"It's spreading," Fiona said grimly, watching as Terin wrapped her arms around the young bronze rider who sat, stunned with fear.

Norik strode over quickly from the entrance at the far side of the Cavern leading from the storerooms and dormitories.

"That's two in as many days," he said as he approached. He looked consolingly toward Fiona. "As near as I can tell—with Bekka's help—Healer V'gin recorded that there was no pattern in the spread of the disease."

He pursed his lips sourly as he glanced toward Fiona. "But we did discover that the longest a dragon lasted from the onset of the illness was no more than three sevendays."

"That agrees with what we've seen at Fort," H'nez said. He grimaced as he added, "Two sevendays is the average."

"Then our time is set," Fiona said, rising from her chair, anxious to be doing something. "Either we find a cure in the next twelve days or Telgar will lose her queen."

Shaneese put out a hand toward her, gesturing for her to sit again. "You haven't finished eating and from what I've heard, neither has your dragon."

Fiona opened her mouth, ready to argue, but Shaneese gave her an imperious look that was so reminiscent of her late grandmother, Mother Karina, that Fiona found herself obeying automatically.

"You can't handle the work you put on your plate until you've finished the food you've put there first," Shaneese told her sternly, before turning back to H'nez, saying, "I understand that there's an issue with the firestone?"

Fiona swallowed hard, crying in surprise, "How did you know?"

"I'm headwoman, it's my duty," Shaneese said, waving Fiona back to her meal, adding to H'nez, "Besides, it was obvious from the Weyrwoman's surprise and your sudden return."

Fiona felt Talenth pounce on a small sheep out in the pens at the same moment that she heard the queen's triumphant whistling. She got the distinct impression that her queen was not all that hungry but had dispatched the sheep merely to placate Bekka.

Eating is important, Fiona chided her dragon and was chagrined to hear Talenth's sardonic agreement, *As you say.*

After that, the Weyrwoman concentrated on her food.

She kept a half ear on the conversation and was relieved to discover that Shaneese and her assistants had already devised a plan to dispose of the old firestone. And, Shaneese assured them, there were plenty of hands ready to do the work.

"After all, there are nearly fifteen hundred weyrfolk," Shaneese pointed out with a sense of pride. She raised a hand and made another one of her now all-too-familiar peremptory gestures, which was met with the prompt appearance of another woman, several Turns Shaneese's senior who was introduced as Bevorra, Shaneese's other assistant headwoman.

"She and the storemaster will arrange everything," Shaneese said as Bevorra hustled off toward another group of women. She turned to Fiona. "So you only have to meet with the Lord Holders.

"You should probably visit Crom first: From what I've heard, Nerra's more likely to listen to you than Lord Valpinar at Telgar."

"You shouldn't go alone," Norik spoke up from where he'd been standing, near Fiona. She glanced up toward him. "Given the history between D'gan and Lady Nerra, I can't imagine how you'll be received in Crom."

"D'gan was demanding," Shaneese allowed, clearly reluctant to say more.

"He demanded that his dragon and his Weyr die for his arrogance," Norik observed icily.

"As you say," H'nez interposed smoothly, "he paid with his life. His deeds are done; you've written his eulogy and his dirge."

"I have," Norik said flatly, directing a look of challenge and appraisal toward H'nez. The bronze rider met his eyes unflinchingly until Norik lowered them and sighed wearily. "I've written too many sad songs. Perhaps it is time I found different lodgings."

"No one is asking you to leave!" Fiona declared with an angry look toward H'nez. Suddenly she recalled the stories of H'nez's long-ago feud with a different harper, a feud that had led to the death and the decline of Fort's Weyrwoman. Would he, she wondered fleetingly, never stop bickering with harpers?

Apparently H'nez must have guessed some of her thinking for he told Norik contritely, "My apologies, harper. Tempers are short, hearts chaffed."

"D'gan never would have apologized," Norik said, obliquely accepting H'nez's offering. He glanced at Fiona and said in an apparent decision, "Perhaps I could accompany you?"

Fiona started to reply but Norik continued, with a gesture toward Seban, "I believe that Seban and Bekka should accompany us, as we've identified several gaps in our medicinal stores."

Seban smiled at the Weyrwoman. "That is, if your Talenth is up to four."

Are you up for a journey with four on your back? Fiona asked her dragon who she discovered was trundling back toward her weyr, obediently following Bekka. Fiona got the distinct impression that Talenth found the tiny girl amusing.

Are we taking Bekka? Talenth asked. Fiona was surprised but not shocked to hear such a direct reference to another person. What shocked her was Talenth's ready agreement, how eager she was to fly; Fiona had expected the queen to want to rest, not to risk exacerbating her cough. For a moment, Fiona felt torn between her need to protect her queen and her desire to enjoy the time they could together. She sensed the deep wistfulness in Talenth's underlying emotions and knew there was only one answer:

Of course!

"Your little one weighs nothing," Norik observed twenty minutes later as he hefted Bekka up toward Seban.

"If you can get her to eat, perhaps she'll get heavier," Seban answered easily, settling Bekka and reaching a hand down for the harper. Norik took it and flexed his legs to hop up from his position on the top of Talenth's foreleg and climb up to the gold dragon's neck. Fiona followed quickly, her enthusiasm for her beautiful, marvelous, huge dragon undimmed by her fear for her health.

Talenth made a pleased noise as she rose to her full height, took a few quick steps forward to gain momentum and leaped on her back legs into the air.

Fiona let out a shout of pure glee as Talenth climbed as strongly as ever toward the watch heights, circled the Star Stones, returned the watch dragon's greeting, and took them smoothly *between* to the distant Crom Hold.

"**D**'gan was a difficult man," Norik said as they circled above the watch heights of Crom Hold scant moments later. "He used Lord Fenner harshly and provided no aid when the Plague struck."

"He supported Fenner's son, Fenril, didn't he?" Fiona asked.

"He did," Norik agreed blandly. "His concerns were the Weyr and its proper tithe. He felt that Fenril would provide that."

"Was Fenril the man who let his people starve while he drank his cellar?" Bekka asked Seban.

"He was," Norik said.

"*I* wouldn't have done that," Bekka said. "If I were Lord Holder, I'd make certain to take care of my people first."

Seban hugged her tightly.

"So, Lady Nerra has no call to love our Weyr," Fiona said in surmise.

"No, my lady, she does not," Norik agreed.

Fiona felt the loathing emanating from the sullen holders around her the moment Talenth settled on the ground, long before she set foot on the clean cobblestones of the courtyard and had a moment to scan the surrounding walls.

Seban, who had been concerned with getting Bekka off Talenth's neck without injury to child or dragon, noticed only when his daughter found herself pressed tight against him in unfocused fear.

Norik joined them, caught their feeling, and quickly noted the stance of the guards on the walls above.

"Crom hospitality leaves much to be desired if those are arrows I see pointing toward us!" the harper declared in a booming, angry voice.

"Go back to your Weyr!" a voice growled back, echoing around the walls, ominously.

"I am Fiona, formerly of Fort Weyr, now of Telgar Weyr," Fiona called. "I have news for the Lord of this Hold."

A huge burly man confronted her as Fiona stepped over the threshold, his arms crossed with his shield raised in front.

Fiona glanced up at him once and immediately had his measure: He was one of the faithful guards who had stood with Nerra against Fenril after the Plague.

"You must be Jefric," she declared. She felt the man's surprise. "We heard about you at Fort Hold."

"You are holder bred?" a woman's voice called from the far end of the hall.

"Yes, Lady Nerra," Fiona replied. "My father is Lord Bemin. I am Fiona, last of his line."

"You ride a Telgar queen?" Nerra asked in surprise, rising from her chair and moving down the hall toward Fiona.

"The only queen now at Telgar," Norik called out from his position beyond the guard Jefric. Nerra jerked her head toward him in surprise. Sensing her wishes, Jefric stood to one side, allowing her to look directly at the rest of the group. Norik started forward, stopping to bow on one knee in front of Nerra.

"My Lady," he said, his voice full of sorrow. "I am Norik, the last harper of Telgar Weyr." He glanced up at her, then down again in shame. "Lord D'gan is no more."

"He died fighting to save Pern," Fiona said, glancing down sympathetically toward the harper. "He and all the riders and dragons of Telgar Weyr."

Nerra's face drained of color and she raised a hand to her eyes. "All?"

"K'lior dispatched myself and forty dragons—all we could spare," Fiona explained. "High Reaches Weyr flew the last Fall."

"The illness took them," Seban said, stepping forward and sketching a quick nod toward Nerra. "I am Seban, once rider of blue Serth."

"Jefric," Nerra called softly, "have the men stand down."

As if the words released her as well, Nerra suddenly seemed to shed her tension and she gestured gracefully to Fiona and her party, indicating the head table.

"Please," she said, as she moved toward it, "join me."

Nerra insisted upon accompanying Fiona when she went to Lord Valpinar at Telgar, while offering Seban and Bekka free run of her herbal stores.

"I'm told he is not well-disposed to dragonriders at the moment," the Lady Holder said by way of explanation.

"Dragonriders? All of them?"

"His experience has only been with D'gan's old riders," Nerra replied, "but . . ."

"Once bitten, twice shy."

"Exactly," Nerra agreed. She craned her neck up toward Talenth's shoulders and gulped at the distance. The sky above was partly cloudy, the weather cool. Nerra had on her warmest clothes.

"Let me help you up," Fiona offered, bending down and cupping her fingers together to provide a lift. The courtesy seemed to surprise Nerra, which caused Fiona a moment's anger at the old Telgar riders: Had they not shown such simple courtesies to their Holders?

Once Nerra was safely perched, Fiona scrambled up behind her and strapped them both in safely.

"Are you ready to fly, my lady?"

Nerra hesitated, then nodded.

Talenth, take us up, Fiona said. The queen rose easily into the air, her upward spiral marred only by a cough just before they reached the cliff heights.

"Is she okay?" Nerra asked in concern.

"She's got the sickness," Fiona told her. "But she insisted on coming."

"The same sickness that took Telgar?"

"The same."

"Does that worry you?"

"Very much," Fiona said, fighting back a sob.

"What will happen if she succumbs?"

"I don't know," Fiona said. "For now, though, we'll do what we have to do."

"Well, I can see why you came rather than your H'nez," Nerra said.

"You can?"

"And brought your entourage," Nerra added, turning back to show Fiona her smile. "A Weyrwoman must know how to be charming and diplomatic; a Weyrleader need only know how to lead."

"Weyrleaders can be diplomatic."

"Queens command respect," Nerra said. She glanced down at the scenery below and quickly up again. A moment later she looked down, scanning the fields of her Hold with interest.

"Are you ready to go *between*, my Lady?"

"Yes," Nerra said with a firm nod. "I don't want to tire your queen too much."

Fiona gave Talenth the image and they went *between* to Telgar Hold.

EIGHT

My heart is a dragon
Soaring in the sky;
My heart is a dragon
Flaming from on high.
My heart is a dragon
Filling all with love;
My heart is a dragon
Protecting from above.

Telgar Weyr, late evening, AL 508.2.9

At dinner that evening, Fiona relayed the results of her meetings with Lord Valpinar and Lady Nerra to H'nez and the other wingleaders.

"Apparently," she recounted, "D'gan had once gone so far as to tell Valpinar that his attitude would buy him grief from the skies."

"He wasn't threatening to let Thread burrow, was he?" H'nez asked in shock.

"Lord Valpinar was left to draw his own conclusions," Fiona said, her fury abated by the bronze rider's appalled reaction.

"You assured him—"

"I told him that we would do our duty to Hold and Hall as long as we had breath to draw," Fiona said. H'nez nodded approvingly and the other bronze riders added their fervent agreement. She smiled, adding, "And I've arranged that Tevora can go back to the Smithcrafthall."

Fiona's attention was distracted when she saw Xhinna herding a group of small children toward a table, aided by a beautiful dark-skinned, dark-haired, aquiline-nosed girl near her age. Xhinna noticed her look and gave her a tremulous smile, carefully seating the children and getting them settled with their dinner before dragging the girl, who appeared quite reluctant, over to Fiona.

Xhinna looked radiant, her eyes glowing, her whole being transformed. Her grip on the other girl's hand was both shy and possessive.

"Weyrwoman, this is Taria."

Fiona nodded toward the other girl. Taria was half a head shorter than Xhinna. They made a beautiful pair and Fiona beamed at her friend.

"They've put you in charge of the nursery?"

Xhinna shook her head. "Taria's been handling the older children for two Turns now." She bent in close to Fiona's ear. "She's all on her own and she needs someone to help."

"You must be very good at your duties," Fiona said to Taria. The girl nodded mutely, her eyes wide with fright. Fiona pulled Xhinna closer to her and whispered in her ear, "Tell her I don't bite."

Xhinna smiled, her eyes dancing as she glanced back to Taria.

"Does this mean that you'll be in the dormitory from now on?" Fiona asked, adding hastily, "You're still welcome with me—both of you—particularly on the colder nights."

"I told you, she uses her friends for blankets," Xhinna murmured triumphantly.

Taria spoke for the first time, just above a whisper. Her voice was deeper than Xhinna's and richer, with husky overtones. Fiona wondered if she sang at all, thinking that her singing voice would be a treat to the ears. "I think it's best if we stay with the children, my lady."

Fiona was pretty sure there was more to it than the girl's words conveyed.

"I suppose that's so," she said. "You could bring them along." She saw Taria's hesitation, her worried glance toward Xhinna and added, "The offer is always open."

Taria managed a nervous nod and glanced imploringly toward Xhinna. Fiona gave her friend a nod, which Xhinna returned with a smile before happily tugging Taria away with her back to the children's table.

So now it was just her and Terin. Fiona shivered, thinking that the nights at Telgar seemed colder than those at Fort even while she knew that wasn't so; she was just spoiled by her time in hot, dry Igen.

Back in her quarters, she had just changed into her nightgown when she heard the alarming sound of a dragon coughing. Her immediate relief that it wasn't Talenth again was dashed when her own queen coughed not a moment later.

Bekka rushed in just as Terin rushed out of the bathroom, her eyes wide with fright.

"Is she okay?" Bekka asked.

The other dragon coughed again, the echoes confirming Fiona's first worried conclusion: It was Ladirth.

Fiona sent Bekka off with Terin, who was clearly so upset by Ladirth's illness that Fiona feared her worry alone would keep both rider and dragon awake all night.

With an impulsive burst of energy, Fiona grabbed all her blankets and bedsheets, twisted around to pull them over her shoulder, and strode into Talenth's quarters.

"I think it's just you and me, love," she said as she arranged thick blankets on the floor so that she could lie against Talenth's chest.

She was just dozing when a voice surprised her: "May I join you?"

It was Seban. He didn't wait for an answer, carefully moving to her side and encouraging her to prop herself against him. The warmth of his body, his arms wrapped comfortably around her, the father-ness of him, was all just too much and she buried her face against the hollow of his neck, biting her lips firmly to keep from bawling.

"There's no shame in crying, my lady," Seban told her softly, his free hand stroking her hair. "There's no one here but you, me, and your queen." Fiona felt herself shudder but could not let herself go: She was the Weyrwoman, she was the strength of the Weyr, the people depended on her, the people looked to her.

"No one's looking," Seban assured her, almost as if he'd read her mind. "And if they were, what would be the harm in that?"

As if his words were the key to unlock her grief, Fiona suddenly found her tears flowing down her cheeks, her sobs uncontrollable, her nose running, and her whole body shaking with grief.

"You take so much on such young shoulders," Seban was saying softly. "You have the right to let some of it out."

The words eased her and slowly, very slowly, her sobbing slackened, her tears dried up. With a deep sigh, she buried her head further against Seban's, seeking the comfort of a child with a parent and knowing that it was hers no longer.

"Shh!" Seban breathed quietly. "Shh, now, it's all right. It's all right."

Too tired and worn out to argue, Fiona lay there, feeling the rise and fall of Talenth's chest, the steady beat of Seban's heart—the warmth of two bodies surrounding her, two loving souls comforting her.

A long time later, she opened her eyes and turned her head toward the weyr's entrance to the Bowl. Seban did not move, seemingly asleep himself. She closed her eyes again, then opened them and was surprised to see small bright eyes gleaming in the distance. They were joined by another pair, then another, and then a larger pair, higher up.

Xhinna strode into view and the eyes swiveled nervously toward her.

"Is it all right, Weyrwoman?" Xhinna asked, her voice soft and husky in the cold evening air. "They were cold in the dormitories and couldn't sleep and I remembered . . ."

Fiona saw her friend—Taria, wasn't it?—reach forward to grab for Xhinna's arm protectively and suppressed a smile, instead nodding and raising an arm to beckon them forward.

"Talenth is large enough now for the whole Weyr," Fiona called back softly. "And we'd like the company."

She gestured toward her quarters. "I'm sure there are more blankets and sheets there."

"We wouldn't—we couldn't—" Taria began nervously, clearly alarmed at the thought of sleeping on the Weyrwoman's bedsheets.

"Taria," Xhinna cut her off with a kindly shake of her head. "This is Fiona, my friend. If she says she doesn't mind, she's not lying, she means it."

Xhinna tapped a couple of the children on the shoulders and gestured for them to follow her while telling Taria, "Start getting them settled; we'll be back."

With all the grace her growing adolescence would permit, Xhinna strode into the Weyrwoman's quarters, followed by a small cluster of eager, excited girls who alternately squeaked in delight and shushed each other.

Beside her, Fiona felt Seban move and realized that the man had been feigning sleep.

"They'll settle down soon enough," she told him.

"What I cannot figure, my lady, is your ability to surround yourself so easily with love," Seban replied, his voice mixed with awe, affection, and a sense of rightness.

Fiona couldn't think how to answer him; for her, having friends was as natural as breathing.

Xhinna brusquely arranged the sheets, blankets, pillows, and youngsters and had them settled down as quickly as she could. She gave Fiona an apologetic look before she clasped Taria's arm and tugged the other girl off to a corner at the far end of Talenth's stomach.

Fiona felt the great gold dragon stir in her sleep.

Talenth, she said softly in a tone meant to reassure, *we have company.*

Fiona received a dim feeling from Talenth that she knew and was pleased.

Please tell Xhinna that I love her, Fiona said. She felt Talenth groggily relay the message, felt Xhinna's love return in response and then relaxed against Seban, making room for the small warm bodies that were curling up against her.

Sometime in the middle of the night, Fiona came starkly awake.

"Eww, it's coming out her nose!" a small girl's voice exclaimed from near Talenth's head.

"Come on back, Aryar, you'll wake everyone," another girl whispered urgently, fearfully.

"But Rhemy, what'll happen if she dies?" Aryar persisted, her voice coming toward Fiona, who kept her eyes closed, not wishing to alarm them further and possibly wake up the whole group. Fiona could hear the young girl—she couldn't have more than seven Turns at the most—pausing in front of Fiona, probably peering at her, as she continued, "They say that when a dragon dies, the rider loses half her heart with it." Aryar sniffed. "How can the Weyrwoman live with only half a heart?"

"Her heart is big enough, even just half, and with our love, it'll grow back," Xhinna's voice came quietly out of the darkness. She scooped up the youngster in her arms, prepared to carry her back to the others.

As Xhinna's steps receded into the distance, Fiona heard Aryar declare, "You have my love, Weyrwoman! I'll help you grow your heart back!"

NINE

Weyrwoman, mind the Weyr:
For all things prepare
And set the best fare
Lest all should despair.

Telgar Weyr, early morning, AL 508.2.10

Silence settled upon the group only for a short while. Fiona managed to nod off for a bit and was surprised to be woken by the sound of Talenth. This time her coughing fit lasted a long while, disturbing many of the youngsters who slept scattered around her.

"It's all right," Fiona said. "Try to get back to sleep."

She herself in contradiction of her advice rose and went to check on Talenth's head. There was a small pile of green ooze in front of it.

"It's only a little," she said to herself, remembering the bucket and mop she'd used for blue Serth.

"Come back to sleep," Seban said, grabbing her shoulders in his hands and gently guiding her back. "Your rest is important to her."

Fiona had barely gotten settled when the sound of feet coming up the path of the queens' ledge disturbed her. The noise redoubled with the sound of startled children.

"She has the Weyrwoman's permission!" Fiona heard Taria declare stoutly in Xhinna's defense.

"Yes, she does," Fiona said, opening one eye to peer at the scene in front of her. Several women, their lips tight with disapproval, were shepherding children out of the weyr. "Talenth enjoys the company."

"It's not normal!" one of the older women complained, dragging two children in tow behind her.

"Really, they shouldn't be disturbing you," another woman declared. "And with your poor dragon . . ."

"Talenth likes them," Fiona retorted. She gestured vaguely to the women. "She likes company; you could join us if you'd like."

Several of the women looked positively affronted by the suggestion and hurried out of the weyr even faster, but some paused, looking wistfully at Talenth.

"I'm sorry, Weyrwoman," Taria apologized as she gathered the rest of the children, preparing to depart. She cast an accusing look toward Xhinna. "I should have known."

"Taria, settle these children back down," Fiona ordered firmly. "If their mothers or fathers want to take them away, they will. Otherwise, they are welcome to stay." Taria opened her mouth once more, but Fiona cut her off peremptorily, jabbing her thumb toward the floor. "Here. In this weyr. With their Weyrwoman."

Taria's mouth gaped in surprise as Fiona's words registered with her.

"And you wouldn't want to disobey the Weyrwoman, would you?" Seban asked in a tone that mixed reasonableness with warning.

"Come on, Taria," Xhinna called softly, grabbing her friend's hand, "I told you that you can't gainsay this Weyrwoman, didn't I?"

"Well . . ." Taria began, clearly worried over the frowning looks of the remaining women.

"May I join you?" Shaneese called softly as she climbed up to Talenth's weyr. She smiled at Fiona. "I'd heard you were accepting sleepovers."

Several of the disapproving women gaped at Shaneese in surprise and anger, but she dismissed them curtly. "If you don't want to be here, with your Weyrwoman, then leave."

She eyed them carefully as she added, "But if you don't want to be with your Weyrwoman now, when she stands by you, you might ask yourself whether you want to remain in this Weyr?" She smiled grimly at them. "There are plenty of small holds lying fallow—you'll not lack for a roof or food."

"Where's the best place to sleep?" Vikka asked, two children waiting eagerly behind her. She nodded to Shaneese, then to Fiona, saying, "My lady, I only just found out about your kind offer." She released the children, gently shooing them toward Taria and the others. "There are many of us here who have slept with dragons but none with a queen."

"You are welcome," Fiona said, gesturing toward a spot nearby. To the women who still remained standing, undecided, Fiona said, "F'jian's Ladirth is also suffering and could use company tonight, if you'd consider it."

"That Bekka will keep everyone up all night!" a voice exclaimed out of the dark.

Seban's chuckle broke the tension that rose with those words. "It's true that Bekka rarely sleeps, but she's learned silence from an early age—her mother is a midwife and Bekka was warned that any baby she woke was hers to get back to bed."

Some of the reluctant women chuckled.

"However, some here should be sleeping, I think," Fiona said with a glance toward Taria's charges. "I know some may prefer soft beds to hard rock, and their own quarters to a stranger's."

She closed her eyes, wishing the disgruntled would either relent or leave. After a while, the sounds of movement died away. Fiona felt the warmth of some more bodies near her and the sounds of older sleepers and drifted off, content to see the morning.

"Good morning Talenth." Aryar's small piping voice, kept hushed, was the first thing that woke Fiona that morning.

"Good morning Talenth," Rhemy added in a whisper a moment later. "I hope you're feeling better."

Fiona opened an eye, only to see Seban wink at her and close his eyes again suggestively. Suppressing a smile, she followed suit.

One by one, the young weyr girls and boys filed past the queen dragon and wished her a good morning and good health.

"I've never heard the like before," Seban murmured as Taria added her voice, in heartfelt tones, to the others.

"I know you're pretending," Xhinna said right beside Fiona. "You snore when you're really sleeping."

"I do not!" Fiona replied, eyes snapping open. Xhinna smiled at her, leaned forward, and gave her a quick kiss on the forehead.

"Of course not, Weyrwoman," she agreed cheerfully. "Did you sleep well?"

Fiona stretched, careful not to hit Xhinna or Seban, and considered the question. "Well enough, thank you."

"We're heading back to the dorms to get them washed and dressed— there are far too many for your rooms," Xhinna explained. "Shall we bring your breakfast here?" When Fiona made to protest, Xhinna told her, "You know they'd be ecstatic to serve you. You can't imagine how they'd feel: 'I served the Weyrwoman!'"

Fiona smiled but shook her head. "Perhaps another day."

Xhinna accepted this with a phlegmatic shrug. "It's probably just as well—they'd spill all over you."

"Come on, Xhinna," Taria called from the entrance. She nodded to Fiona and gave the Weyrwoman a tentative smile. "Thank you, Weyrwoman."

"My pleasure."

As they departed, Fiona took her Weyrwoman's privilege and stole into her bathroom before Seban. She was out again in a moment, offering him its use before taking a more relaxed bath and getting dressed for the day.

When she was done, she went to clean up Talenth's weyr and check her over thoroughly, insisting upon going over the great gold body with her hands, searching for the smallest signs of patchiness. She was delighted to find one and oiled it promptly, to Talenth's great pleasure.

Really, though, she was saying good-bye. She wanted to savor every moment with her brilliant queen, to build a treasury of memories that would last all her days, to—

I will be all right, Talenth assured her. *You'll see. We have Turns yet.*

Fiona's sob brought Seban rushing to her side, his face full of concern.

"Do you think dragons could have the Sight, like Tenniz?" Fiona asked in response to his questioning look. She realized belatedly that he had never met Tenniz. "Tannaz was his sister."

"She was a great lady," Seban said respectfully. "By the Sight, do you mean to see what will happen?"

Fiona nodded. Quickly she told him of the gifts that Tenniz had left for her, Terin, and Lorana.

"Lorana of Benden?" Seban repeated, surprised. "I wonder why he didn't have it delivered to her there."

Fiona shook her head. "She," she said, nodding toward Talenth, "told me that she would be all right. That we will have Turns together."

"Weyrwoman," Seban began hesitantly, "dragons have very poor memories."

"I know," Fiona said, running a hand briskly over Talenth's chest. Her lips quirked as she continued softly, "I think she was trying to cheer me up."

"Like her mate, she puts her concerns for others first," Seban agreed, patting the queen respectfully.

"Perhaps dragons are more like their riders than we think," Fiona mused. "Didn't you say that if a rider wants to know how injured he is, he asks about his dragon?"

Seban chuckled. "So your gold thinks that if you feel all right, she'll be all right?"

"A view that's not without its merits," T'mar spoke up and they turned to see him standing at the entrance to Talenth's lair. He nodded respectfully toward the queen, then came to Fiona. "I don't know if you heard but F'jian's Ladirth—"

"What?" Fiona broke in anxiously, turning toward the entrance, ready to sprint away.

T'mar raised a hand in reassurance. "No, he is in no greater danger," he said. "I came to tell you that he slept well and was thrilled with all the company he had."

"Did F'jian sleep at all?" Fiona asked, relieved enough to allow herself to feel amusement.

T'mar's brows rose and he grinned mischievously. "I believe that he and Terin managed to find some distraction from their cares, with Bekka and at least a score of others devoted to the bronze's every whim." He snorted. "I wonder if we'll have to worry about our dragons being too pampered."

"Not as long as this illness lasts," Seban said bleakly and the light mood vanished. T'mar gave the ex-dragonrider a sympathic look in apology.

"We were just going to break our fast," Fiona said to get past the awkward moment. She gestured. "If you'd care to join us?"

T'mar shook his head. "No, thank you, Weyrwoman," he said, "I've duties to attend."

"Oh, come on, T'mar!" Fiona snapped at him. "Seban's man enough to let your gaffe pass—join us and tell us how the training is going."

Seban gave the bronze rider an encouraging nod and the two headed out toward the Kitchen Cavern together. "How has Ladirth's illness affected the wings?"

Fiona followed a moment later, distracted from their conversation by her worries.

She forced herself to be cheerful throughout breakfast and teased Xhinna, Terin, and Taria for their hollow-eyed cheeks and evident fatigue, but she knew she was just putting up a front, a trick she'd learned Turns before when she was still a toddler at her father's Hold.

"A Holder is the hope of all," Lord Bemin, her father, had told her solemnly once when Fiona had been having a tantrum. "When you laugh, they are happy." He lowered his chin as he asked her, "And when you misbehave, how do you think they feel?"

She'd understood, even then, what he meant, though it was Turns before she truly grasped the concept of leading by example. It was a strange thing: Even if she was feeling sad herself, just displaying cheer to others would inevitably cause her to cheer up, as well.

She wondered if she would still be able to do that if she lost Talenth. Little Aryar's question echoed in her mind: "How can the Weyrwoman live with only half a heart?"

She glanced around, spotted Xhinna, rose, and went over to her, grabbing her around the shoulders in a great hug.

"What?" Xhinna asked, turning to face her, surprised by the embrace and the emotions behind it.

"I just wanted to say that I love you," Fiona told her, ignoring Taria's concerned look from her nearby seat. Xhinna gave her a wide-eyed look and Fiona's lips quirked upward as she quoted: "'Her heart is big enough, even just half, and with our love, it'll grow back.'"

"Oh," Xhinna said in a quiet voice. "I didn't think you'd heard."

Taria had risen just in time to hear Fiona's words and gave her friend a look of admiration. Fiona shared a smile with her.

"Weyrwoman!" Shaneese bustled over quickly, suppressing a yawn with irritation. "I'd been hoping to find you."

"Yes?" Fiona asked, steeling herself for another daunting problem.

Shaneese noticed and smiled. "I wanted to introduce you to one of our treasures."

"Treasures?" Xhinna repeated blankly, turning to Taria with raised eyebrows. Taria met her look with a shrug and then turned back to deal with some rising conflict among the children.

"At Fort Weyr, we treasured our people," Fiona said, careful to keep any tone of criticism from her voice.

Shaneese smiled and turned, gesturing for Fiona to follow her as she made her way to a far corner of the Dining Cavern.

"I'm not surprised," she called over her shoulder, halting near an old man who was hunched over a strange table. "So do we."

Fiona managed to glance over the old man's shoulder and frowned. Something was odd about the table: There was something on it and it was spinning. She shifted her gaze and noticed that one of the man's legs was rising up and down rhythmically as though pumping something.

Shaneese waved a hand toward the old man, her expression respectful. "This is Mekiar, our pottery master."

Alerted by the sound of his name, the white-haired old man glanced behind him. "Oh, you're here!"

He rose fluidly from his perch and gestured for Fiona to take his place, his leg still pumping up and down. Now that he was up, she could see that he was pumping a spindle that spun the table. "Sit, sit, Weyr-woman!"

With a quick glance toward Shaneese, who nodded in encouragement, and a tolerant sigh, Fiona sat at the proffered seat. From behind, Shaneese slipped an apron over her neck and pushed up her sleeves.

"Put your leg where mine is and raise your hands," Mekiar ordered. "Keep the wheel turning."

Fiona realized that the table was a thin wheel of stone and on it was perched a gray mass. Awkwardly at first, Fiona mimicked the pumping motion she'd seen Mekiar use, adjusted her timing, and grew more absorbed and relaxed as she mastered it.

"Good," Mekiar said, leaning over her from behind. His hands reached for hers and raised them to the clump on the table. "Cup your hands like so."

She fumbled to match his grasp, perplexed. Mekiar grunted in satisfaction and quickly moved one hand from hers, dipped it in a small bowl that she hadn't noticed before and pulled out a wet hand. Deftly he sprinkled the water on the lump and grasped her hands again, pressing them into the wet coolness.

"That's clay," Shaneese explained, sensing Fiona's confusion. "I thought you could use some distraction."

Mekiar grunted in a tone that Fiona took to mean that he didn't want the headwoman distracting her, so she turned her gaze back to the lump that was changing shape under her fingers.

"What are we shaping?"

"What would you like?" Mekiar asked, guiding her fingers upward so that the clay rose toweringly. "A vase?"

He guided her fingers outward, then down with an outward pressure and the clay moved out, took on a different shape. "A bowl?"

He pressed her hands down once more and out farther and the bowl stretched out, got lower. "A plate?"

He dipped his hand into the water bowl and let the liquid flow over her hands, wetting the clay once more.

"What takes your fancy, Weyrwoman?"

Instead of replying, Fiona shot Shaneese a reproving look. The head-woman met it stubbornly.

"Don't look at her, she knows nothing," Mekiar said. His hand closed around her fingers gently. "Let yourself feel the clay, Weyrwoman, see how you can change it—"

"Relax!" Shaneese suggested.

"Go away, master your kitchen," Mekiar snapped in response, turning his attention once more to Fiona as he muttered, "She's good at bossing, not at feeling."

Something in the old man's tone soothed her and Fiona found herself nodding, ignoring Shaneese's contentious snort, and returning her gaze to the clay under her hands. She moved her left hand in symmetry with her right, increasing the curve once more before gently easing out the edges of the soup bowl—yes, it was a soup bowl, she decided with a sense of rightness that she'd only felt a few times before.

"Good choice," Mekiar said. "Let the clay decide when you are done with it, and then let your hands free and stop your leg on the wheel—" Fiona had completely forgotten about the comforting rhythmic motion she was keeping with her right leg "—and we'll see what we've got."

Fiona kept her hands working a few moments more and then pulled them away, removing her foot from the pedal and watching as the wheel slowed gently to a stop.

She looked back at the pottery master, noted his dark brows and crinkled bright brown eyes for the first time, and realized from his weathered, weary face that this man had once, Turns before, ridden a dragon.

"What do we do now?"

"If you like it, we take it off the wheel and let it dry," Mekiar told her.

"If I don't?"

"You can ball it up and throw it back in the tub with the rest of the clay, pull out some more, and start over, if you like," Mekiar said. "As long as it's wet, you can do what you want with it."

"And after it's dry?"

"You're still not done," Mekiar told her. "We fire it in the ovens, and if it survives, then you can paint it with glaze, fire it once more, and produce a finished piece." He smiled as he concluded, "And if it's a soup bowl, you can eat out of it, if you like."

"A soup bowl it is," Fiona declared, adding, "I've learned some good recipes."

"Then a soup bowl it shall be!" Mekiar agreed. Fiona watched in awe as he quickly but carefully undercut the bowl with a thin, taut wire and lifted if off the wheel to nimbly place it on a nearby drying table. He came back to her and eyed it mournfully.

"What?" she asked, wondering at his disappointment.

"Nothing!" Mekiar replied. "Only it seems rather lonely there by itself." He looked at her, his lips quirked upward. "Have you decided what you'll do with it?"

Fiona thought for a moment. "Could I make more?"

Mekiar nodded, his eyes twinkling. "I believe that you've made it rather clear that *you* are the Weyrwoman here," he said drolly.

His emphasis and his tone made her realize that perhaps, if she'd behaved otherwise, she would never have met him and certainly would not have been offered such tutelage.

"My father will be getting married soon," Fiona began. "Would it be very difficult to make more?"

"More?"

"Say, twenty?" Fiona asked, wondering at the effort required.

"I'd make twenty-three then," Mekiar said. "Two spares to allow for accidents and one just in case."

He stood and went to the large, covered barrel that held the wet clay, clumped up some more, and brought it back to the pottery table.

"First, though," he said, as he began to knead the lump of clay on the table like bread dough, "it might be a help if you tried something different."

"Like what?" Fiona asked.

"How about a mug?" Mekiar offered, gesturing for her to start pumping the wheel. "Or whatever the clay says to you."

The clay seemed to say mug. When it was shaped, Fiona was frustrated to learn that she couldn't form and attach a handle until the mug had dried somewhat. She looked at it sitting by her bowl on the drying table and tried to imagine different handle designs for it.

"Are you ready for a rest?"

"Am I keeping you from your work?" Fiona asked.

"No, my lady," Mekiar said with a small smile. "Teaching is part of my work." He gestured toward the rest of the cavern, which had been shut out of Fiona's perceptions in all her concentration. "But perhaps some food would help. It is past noon."

"Is it that late?" Fiona asked in surprise, glancing around and realizing that the Dining Cavern was filling rapidly. "Master Mekiar, I'm so sorry, I didn't realize—"

"No need to apologize, my lady," Mekiar said with obvious pleasure. "I find the clay keeps my mind from things for whole days sometimes."

Things like the loss of a dragon, Fiona mused to herself. The smile she gave him in reply was halfhearted until she remembered her manners. "Would you like to join me?"

"No," Mekiar said slowly, "I think I'd prefer to eat here and watch your clay." He winked at her. "Make sure that it gets no foolish ideas while it is drying."

Fiona smiled at that and was about to reply when Talenth interrupted her excitedly.

She comes!

Who?

The watch dragon bugled a challenge that was answered by the deep voice of a bronze. The sound was strangely familiar.

"Excuse me," Fiona said hastily to Mekiar and rushed out to the Weyr Bowl.

A large bronze had just landed near the entrance to the Dining Cavern. It bellowed commandingly.

Come to me, Fiona heard. The voice was not Talenth's. Dragons roared in response and she heard Talenth rushing from her weyr and, from the opposite side of the Bowl, Ladirth leaped into the air to glide down toward the waiting bronze. *All of you.*

There was a tone of exasperated humor. Fiona rushed toward the bronze as she realized that there were three people clambering down, one carefully passing a carisak to the lower one.

I told you I would be all right! Talenth proclaimed cheerfully as she warbled a greeting to the bronze. *Lorana has the cure.*

"A cure?" Fiona said, stopping dead in her tracks. She turned toward the figures now assembled at the base of the bronze. "You've got a cure?"

One of the men looked over at her sharply, his eyes wide in shock. "Koriana?"

He rushed toward her and grabbed her in his arms, hugging her tight to him.

"I thought—" And then he broke off and pushed himself away from her, confusion and grief distorting his face.

"An honest mistake," the other man said as he strode over, a woman— Lorana—close behind him.

"M'tal?" Fiona cried in surprise.

"We came as soon as we could," Lorana said, pausing to kneel and carefully open the carisak. She pulled out a strange-looking object and Fiona frowned as she tried to identify it. Lorana must have sensed her confusion for she glanced up at Fiona and smiled awkwardly. "It's a syringe from Ancient Times."

An eruption of noise overhead heralded the arrival of another dragon. It was a queen, far larger than Talenth.

"Tolarth is here in case we run out of serum," Lorana explained as she carefully filled the syringe. "The serum is dragon's blood: It contains the necessary protection."

"Ladirth first," Fiona said, still recovering from her shock. "Then the others."

"Your queen is sick, Cisca told me," Lorana said in disagreement. "Her first, then the others."

"All right, her, then Ladirth—he's sick as well," Fiona said. She looked at Kindan again, then at the woman in front of her, this time more carefully. Her dark hair was straight, her skin not as pale as Fiona's, her dark eyes bright and set slightly slanted in her face. She had a beauty that was born of motion and grace.

"Are you the one?" Fiona asked, trying to match Lorana's voice with the one she'd heard so often in her head during the past four Turns of her life.

"She's the one who paid with dragon gold," Kindan said, misunderstanding her question and glancing sympathetically toward Lorana. He glanced back to Fiona and dropped his eyes, ashamed of his words.

Her eyes were attracted to a shiny brooch worn on his breast—it was a gold harp! Her brooch made real and delivered.

M'tal followed her gaze. His face was more lined than she remembered.

"Now, perhaps, Kindan," he said with a gleam in his eyes, "I should explain to you why I asked you to wear that brooch today."

"You look so like her," Kindan said half in apology, half in sorrow.

"I'm glad to hear that," Fiona said. "She was my sister."

"You look so old," Kindan persisted, then M'tal's words registered and he looked down at the brooch. "The brooch?"

M'tal smiled. "This young lady found the gold that went into it," he explained. "Although it was not until much later that I realized who she really was."

Kindan frowned in thought for a moment then looked up at Fiona accusingly. "You timed it to Igen?"

"I did," Fiona said, turning her attention back to Lorana. The ex-dragonrider looked tired.

A young woman leaped down from the large queen—she looked about Fiona's age—and rushed over to the group. Her skin was darker than Lorana's; she looked to have trader blood like Shaneese, she had the same bright, dark eyes, the same white teeth, and the same light air of cultivated assurance.

"Jeila, Tolarth's rider," the girl said by way of introduction. She glanced toward Kindan, then Fiona. "Did you say you timed it to Igen?"

Fiona held up a hand. "Later, please," she said, moving toward Lorana. "Let's see to the dragons."

"They all need the serum," M'tal said as he followed. "It will not only cure the illness but prevent it."

"Lorana developed it," Kindan added, with pride in his tone.

Lorana was preparing a third syringe.

"What do I do?" Fiona asked.

"Jab it in your dragon's hide, then plunge the liquid in," Lorana said. She gave Fiona a half-smile as she added, "It won't hurt—"

"Dragon hide is thick," Fiona joined in to finish in unison. Lorana's smile widened but did not quite reach her eyes.

Fiona wanted to ask her all sorts of questions, but she felt Lorana's detachment and determination and settled for a quick, light touch of thanks on the older woman's shoulder before rushing off to Talenth.

Didn't I tell you? Talenth said cheerfully, not even reacting as Fiona jabbed her and plunged the life-saving dragon ichor into her neck.

How did you know?

You told me.

Before Fiona could overcome her shock at Talenth's declaration, Terin rushed up to her, breathless, eyes huge. "There's a cure?"

Fiona nodded.

"That's it?"

Fiona nodded again. She gestured toward the others. "Lorana discovered it."

"And Ladirth?"

"As cured as Talenth," Fiona assured her.

"Oh, thank goodness!" Terin said, bursting into tears and burying herself against Fiona, who, unbalanced, fell against Talenth before she could wrap an arm around her friend.

As if Terin's relief was a signal, Fiona felt tears flood down her own cheeks.

What is it? Talenth asked in concern. *Why are you crying?*

Because you're safe! Fiona told her. *Because you're not going to die without me.*

Talenth rumbled happily as she reminded her rider, *Didn't I tell you?*

Fiona clung tighter to Terin, letting relief wash over her until they were both cried out. Terin pulled away long enough to wipe her eyes on her sleeve, disregarding Fiona's scowl, and laughing when the Weyrwoman ruefully realized she was no better placed to clean her face and, in chagrin, wiped her own eyes the same way.

"How did Tenniz know?" Terin wondered as she stood up. Fiona raised an eyebrow in confusion. "That Lorana would come here?" Terin elaborated.

Fiona felt her face drain of color and she shook her head, suddenly feeling full of dread. Knowing that Lorana would come here, what message had Tenniz sent her?

Surely it would be a note of congratulations, she told herself. After all, what more could be asked of the woman who'd sacrificed her queen to save Pern?

She shoved her thoughts aside. "We need to inject the others," Fiona declared, putting her words into action and returning to Lorana, who directed her in refilling the syringe.

There were only three syringes so Fiona, Terin, and Jeila were kept very busy injecting all the remaining dragons.

"They'll probably feel tired," M'tal warned.

"You don't look so good yourself," Kindan said just as Fiona opened her mouth to make the same comment. She gave the harper a rueful look before gesturing M'tal toward the Dining Cavern. "Perhaps you'd care for something to eat or some *klah*?" she offered.

"Both," Kindan said decisively with a humorous glance at the older man. "I don't think he's eaten since . . . when *was* the last time you ate?"

"When was the last time *you* ate?" M'tal retorted.

Fiona scrutinized all the Benden riders appraisingly. "Terin!" she called. The younger woman glanced up from where she was helping Lorana, quickly followed Fiona's gaze, looked consideringly at Lorana, then rose to her feet, calling over her shoulder as she trotted toward the Dining Cavern, "I know! Food for foolish riders!"

M'tal chuckled at her words, saying to Fiona, "She was with you at Igen."

"Yes," Fiona said shortly. "She's well-versed in the ways of foolish riders."

A sudden noise from nearby distracted them, and Fiona moved just in time to prevent Jeila from collapsing onto the ground.

"She's exhausted," Fiona said. She glanced at the riders and weyrfolk clustered around, then shook her head, saying to M'tal, "Help me get her to my quarters."

"We're done here," Lorana called as she packed up.

"You're welcome to join us."

"Your dragons should rest," Lorana said as she and Kindan fell in behind her.

Talenth, Fiona said, *tell Terin that we are in my rooms.*

She knows, Talenth replied.

You should get some rest, Fiona told her queen. *You need to recover.*

She heard Talenth rumble in agreement and start ambling along behind them. Another set of footsteps caused her to turn. It was H'nez. He appeared worried. With a look, she invited him to follow them.

They climbed the incline of the queens' ledge and entered Fiona's weyr. She and M'tal gently laid Jeila down in her bed and then she gestured for the others to take seats around her day table.

"Terin will be along with food and *klah,*" she told them.

H'nez cleared his throat, then asked Lorana, "Did I hear you say that the dragons will be tired—even the healthy ones?"

Lorana glanced warily at M'tal.

"The cure usually makes them very tired for a day or so," the bronze rider responded. He saw H'nez's troubled look and was startled by it until, with a groan, he realized, "You've Threadfall tomorrow!"

"Yes," H'nez replied shortly.

Fiona looked at Lorana. "Will we be able to fly tomorrow?"

"We'll have to be," H'nez declared. He stood, his thoughts surrounding him like a dark cloud, before he turned swiftly, saying, "Your pardon, but I've got to be certain that my riders rest their dragons immediately."

"Of course," M'tal called after him. After a moment he added, "If you'd like, I'll fly with you."

H'nez paused mid-stride and turned back, eyeing M'tal carefully before replying, "If you wish."

"What about F'jian's Ladirth?" Fiona asked, glancing among the three Benden weyrfolk. "If the healthy dragons will be tired from the cure, will Ladirth be well enough to fly tomorrow? He's been coughing."

Kindan frowned and glanced at Lorana, who shrugged. "I don't know," she said.

"Perhaps M'tal could lead F'jian's wing," Fiona suggested to H'nez.

H'nez frowned and turned away. "I'll be back."

"Don't hurry," Fiona called after him. "You need rest, too."

H'nez waved a hand over his shoulder in acknowledgment, but Fiona got the distinct impression that the prickly bronze rider was surprised at her concern.

As he moved out of sight, Terin and Xhinna arrived, each bearing a well-laden tray.

"She'll be okay?" Xhinna demanded, gesturing toward Talenth. "You've found a cure?"

"Yes," M'tal told her, casting a sidelong look toward Fiona. Fiona felt that the old rider was amused by the possessiveness in Xhinna's reaction.

"Oh, thank you!" Xhinna cried. She placed her tray on the table and turned away for a moment. Fiona rose from her seat and went to hug her.

"We've all been so worried about Talenth," Terin explained apologetically as she served the Benden weyrfolk. She glanced toward Jeila lying in Fiona's bed and frowned. "Is she all right?" she said to Fiona. "Should I send for Bekka?"

"She's just tired," Fiona assured her, still comforting Xhinna and trying to absorb her own feelings. Now that she could set aside her worry for Talenth, she realized how discomfited she was by Kindan's presence. She'd felt both glad and angry that he had mistaken her for Koriana, and she was surprised that at a time like this, she even thought of it.

Shyly, Xhinna pulled away and began bustling about the room, searching out blankets for Jeila, arranging the pillows for the young weyrwoman's comfort, and generally busying herself.

Fiona returned to her seat, even as Terin chided her, "You've not eaten yet yourself, Weyrwoman."

Fiona smiled at Terin and beckoned to her. When Terin gave her a look of alarm, Fiona overrode her concerns, explaining to the others, "Terin was my headwoman at Igen."

"I recall," M'tal said.

Kindan frowned in Fiona's direction, fingering the brooch on his chest before turning toward Lorana and forcing a roll into her hand. "You've got to eat, love."

Fiona gave the older woman a careful look, then declared, "You need to rest. You haven't slept in at least a sevenday, have you?"

Lorana gave her a startled look, and a moment later, Kindan did the same.

"Terin, get with Shaneese and have the other weyrs prepared," Fiona said. "Jeila and her Tolarth can have one, Lorana and Kindan the other." She glanced toward M'tal, who was eyeing her with interest, then added to Terin, "And ask H'nez where M'tal and Gaminth should settle."

Terin gave her an amused look and, with a grin at the others, nodded and sprinted off.

Xhinna looked ready to follow her but Fiona forestalled her with a raised hand. "Can you get Bekka? I want her to look at the weyrwoman, just to be safe."

Xhinna nodded. "I'll be right back."

M'tal chuckled as Xhinna raced out of the room into Talenth's weyr, paused to give the sleeping queen a quick pat, and sped off on her mission.

"I congratulate you, Weyrwoman," M'tal said with a nod toward her. Fiona looked at him in surprise. "You not only did amazing things when you were at Igen, but you've produced a miracle here as well." He gestured toward the weyr where Terin and Xhinna had been. "It is not everyone who can command such loyalty."

Fiona caught Kindan giving her an appraising look, but he turned away the moment he realized she saw him.

They ate in silence until Bekka arrived, breathless and eager-eyed.

"The dragons are cured?" she piped excitedly, her gaze going over everyone in the room. Her eyes locked on Lorana and she rushed over, embracing the larger woman's shoulders and resting her head on her back. "Oh, thank you, thank you, thank you!"

Lorana was nonplussed.

"I know it was too late for your dragon or my father's, but at least no more dragons have to die!" Bekka explained.

"Your father's . . . ?" M'tal repeated in surprise but his words were lost as Lorana gave a heartfelt sob and began to cry. Everyone's attention went to her, and Fiona was already out of her chair and moving to her side.

"You heard her, Lorana," Fiona said, feeling her own tears overflow as she grabbed for Lorana's limp hand. She could tell that the dark-haired woman hadn't, until this moment, fully allowed herself to grasp that fact: Lorana, so overwhelmed with dragons dying, could only now consider that dragons might live. Because of her. "No more dragons have to die. You did it—*you* saved the dragons of Pern!"

TEN

With my life and my dragon's
I pledge ever to learn,
I pledge Thread to burn,
I pledge to guard all Pern.

Telgar Weyr, later, AL 508.2.10

Bekka prescribed fellis juice and a long rest as it became clear that fatigue and sorrow had overwhelmed Lorana—she did not stop crying for ten minutes, after which, wracked with exhaustion and coaxed to lie next to the resting Jeila, she curled up into a ball and fell asleep. Kindan held her close while M'tal and Fiona looked on helplessly.

"I'll stay with them," Bekka declared, pushing at Fiona and gesturing to M'tal. "You two should go to the Dining Cavern and see Shaneese."

"Terin—"

"I'll handle her," Bekka declared firmly, pulling a chair close to Fiona's bed and settling herself in as guard. M'tal glanced at her and then at Fiona in surprise. Fiona smiled at him and shook her head, gesturing for him to follow her toward the Dining Cavern.

"She doesn't sleep," Fiona explained as they walked across the Bowl. "They'll be in good hands."

"But what if she needs help?"

"I'll ask Talenth to check in with her periodically," Fiona told him.

"Does your queen talk to everyone?" M'tal asked.

"That's not normal?" Fiona shook her head, frowning as she admitted, "I know so little about being a proper Weyrwoman—"

M'tal grabbed her hand and laid it on his arm, bowing toward her with a flourish. "No, Weyrwoman, you are an example to us all!"

Fiona felt her face flush and looked away hurriedly. She maintained her silence until she and M'tal sat themselves at the high table and Shaneese bustled over to them.

"So?" she demanded of Fiona, "have you got everything the way you like it once more? All jumbled, rattled, and running just your way?"

Fiona grinned and she nodded in agreement. "Next, I'll send you back in time to Igen: It needs a good cleaning."

M'tal, who seemed torn between rising to Fiona's defense and jumping in on Shaneese's side, choked on his *klah*. Fiona gestured to him. "This is M'tal. He's been to Igen, so he knows how dirty it is."

"My lord," Shaneese said, inclining her head, her manner sobering abruptly, her next words directed equally to M'tal and Fiona, "I hope you'll forgive my banter. You brought news we never expected to hear."

"And wouldn't have, if it were not for D'gan," M'tal said, raising his mug in a half-salute to the late Weyrleader.

"How is that?" Fiona and Shaneese asked, nearly in unison. Fiona cocked her head firmly toward a vacant chair, ordering the headwoman to be seated. Shaneese glanced around the Dining Cavern and, deciding that nothing needed her immediate attention, complied with her Weyrwoman's demand.

"It's a sad story," M'tal said with a shake of his head, "and I don't know if we'll ever hear the full of it."

"Perhaps I should get Norik?" Shaneese suggested to Fiona. The Weyrwoman frowned, then relayed the request to Talenth.

He comes, her queen replied drowsily, in a tone that made Fiona resolve not to disturb her again.

"I've asked for him," Fiona said.

"And your dragon scolded you for waking her," M'tal said. "My Gaminth did the same with me, the day he got the injection."

Oddly, Fiona found his words a relief. Gaminth seemed completely healthy.

"Anyway," M'tal said, "as I understand it from Kindan, Lorana needed a word to open the door to the Teaching Rooms."

"The Ancient Rooms at Benden?" Fiona asked.

The bronze rider nodded, but Shaneese looked perplexed. "We've heard nothing of this here," she said.

"When the illness first started affecting dragons, we started examining the Records," M'tal said.

"I think Lina did that," Shaneese said in the late Weyrwoman's defense.

"We found nothing and so Lorana decided that we should check the Records at Fort Weyr."

Shaneese nodded. "It's the oldest—most likely to have ancient Records."

"The only reference found was to Ancient Rooms at Benden Weyr," M'tal continued. Shaneese raised her eyebrows in surprise and M'tal nodded in agreement. "We all thought it odd but discovered a section of corridor off the Hatching Grounds—an Ancient corridor—that was blocked by a rockslide.

"We got help from miners to dig the fall out and found a room, but it was the wrong room."

"Wrong room?"

"We didn't know it at first," M'tal said, his eyes going bleak with sadness, "and by then Lorana's Arith had caught the illness." He took a deep breath before he continued. "We found four glass vials, each filled with different colored powders.

"Lorana was desperate, her Arith was near to death, she thought to mix some of each of the vials and inject it into her."

"She killed her dragon?" Shaneese asked anxiously.

M'tal nodded.

"The mix was wrong—we only discovered that much later," he said. "Arith went *between*. It wasn't until Lorana recovered that we realized there were other rooms and she thought that perhaps the answer lay in them."

"She lost her dragon and she didn't give up," Shaneese said in awe. She sniffed once, dabbed at her eyes, then motioned politely for M'tal to continue.

"The miners returned and excavated another section above the rooms that led to a different entrance," M'tal said. "This was the entrance we should have found first, because when we entered, we were greeted by a voice."

"A voice?" Fiona asked, thinking of the voice that she'd been hearing in her head. "Did you recognize it?"

"More than that: It introduced itself to us," M'tal said. "It said it was a recording—almost like playing music on an instrument from a written score—and the voice was Wind Blossom's."

"Wind Blossom?" Shaneese repeated. "Two people? Or one person with two names?"

"Two names," Fiona told her. She glanced at M'tal as she continued, "I learned about her from Kindan. He'd been trying to find the words to a song that he'd read just before—"

"Just before the fire at the Harper Hall," M'tal interrupted her quietly. "He found the title; he remembered the song."

"It was important," Fiona said, recalling how often Kindan had striven to remember the song when she was growing up, how much it had driven him.

"The song saved Pern," M'tal said. He saw a man in harper's blue approach and waved him to a seat. "You must be Norik."

Norik nodded but said nothing.

"I was just saying that a song saved Pern," M'tal explained. "It is called 'Wind Blossom's Song' and it contained a question that Lorana had to answer to open the door to the final Teaching Room, the one where we learned how to defeat the illness."

He paused, silent for a moment, turning his head toward the queens' quarters. "But it wasn't enough to cure just one dragon. So Minith and Tullea went back in time to High Reaches Weyr, where she clutched and her dragonets grew to full size. With them—including Jeila's Tolarth—we had enough serum to cure all the dragons. And now, with Telgar here, we have done so."

"So that's why High Reaches was being so aloof!" Fiona exclaimed. "I remember Cisca talking about it, saying that they'd not had any contact for three Turns."

"They couldn't let anyone know," M'tal said with a grimace, "because no one did know."

"By the First Egg, I don't think I'll ever understand all the twitchiness in timing it!"

"And yet, timing it saved Pern," M'tal replied. A moment later he added, "And High Reaches' isolation, and Tullea's pluck."

He shook his head, with a sad look, before saying to Norik, "You'll have to ask Kindan for the full words, but as I was saying, the song recalled the loss of Telgar—"

"Recalled?" Norik interrupted. When M'tal nodded in confirmation, the harper persisted, "Was not the song written before the event?"

"Hundred of Turns before and yet after," M'tal replied. "It seems that the loss of Telgar opened a bridge back in time, a bridge across which Lorana could send one word—"

"A word?" Norik asked in disbelief.

"Why don't you let Lord M'tal finish, then you can ask questions," Fiona said firmly to the harper. Norik spared her a glance, then lowered his eyes as Fiona out-glared him. She turned back to M'tal. "My lord?"

"The words were clearly written by a harper—"

"A Masterharper, I think," Kindan spoke up from the entrance.

"Kindan, are you all right?" Fiona asked, rising from her chair.

Kindan gave her a smile and a nod. "I'm so well, in fact, that your Bekka sent me here."

Fiona laughed at the image his words invoked. She gestured for him to join them.

"You found the words to the song!" she exclaimed in delight.

"I did," Kindan replied gravely as he sat down. He turned to Norik and began to sing softly in a minor chord:

> *A thousand voices keen at night,*
> *A thousand voices wail,*
> *A thousand voices cry in fright,*
> *A thousand voices fail.*
> *You followed them, young healer lass,*
> *Till they could not be seen;*
> *A thousand dragons made their loss*
> *A bridge 'tween you and me.*
>
> *And in the cold and darkest night,*
> *A single voice is heard,*
> *A single voice both clear and bright,*
> *It says a single word.*
>
> *That word is what you now must say*
> *To open up the door*
> *In Benden Weyr, to find the way*
> *To all my healing lore.*
>
> *It's all that I can give to you,*
> *To save both Weyr and Hold.*
> *It's little I can offer you*
> *Who paid with dragon gold.*

Kindan spared nothing of his craft in his singing and when he was done, Norik had dropped his head in his hands, tears falling freely. Shaneese, Fiona, and M'tal were no better.

It was a long time before the Telgar harper recovered and when he did, he lifted his head to be met by Shaneese's bright eyes as she assured him, "Their loss was not in vain."

"Please sing this song again, Kindan," Norik said. "I must teach it to the Weyr."

"If you like, we could sing it tonight, together," Kindan offered.

"It would be an honor."

Softly, with all the strength he could still muster, tears rolling down his cheeks, Kindan began once more to sing "Wind Blossom's Song."

He was surprised and relieved to feel warm hands on his back, massaging him, comforting him as he relived the grief of the moments still fresh and bitter in his memory. It was only when he'd repeated the last, heartfelt phrase—"Who paid with dragon gold"—that he realized the hands were Fiona's.

"I knew you'd remember it when you needed," she whispered to him as she wrapped her arms around him and buried her head against his shoulder. "I just knew it."

She felt his gratitude at her praise, and was filled with a special warmth. She knew that she was the only person who truly understood what it meant to him.

"Vaxoram would be proud of you," she told him, hugging him tightly. "You didn't give up . . . again!"

"As you see, Kindan," M'tal spoke up approvingly, "I'm not the only one to acknowledge your virtues."

Fiona glanced up at the older dragonrider and smiled. The look in his eyes left her feeling a bit awkward and she released Kindan and, resuming her seat, sought out a new topic. "With the illness cured, how long do you think it will be before things return to normal?"

M'tal pursed his lips in a frown. "I'm not sure that normal has much meaning, Weyrwoman, during a Pass."

"I want to meet with Master Archivist Verilan soon and check the Records," Kindan said, glancing toward M'tal first, then Fiona. "We have less than three Flights of dragons at Benden—"

"Not even two wings here," Fiona added, her brows meeting in a frown as she followed the thrust of his words. "None at Igen, only five wings at Fort . . ." Her words trailed off and she bit her lip before looking up at Kindan once more. "We don't have enough dragons, do we?"

"Enough dragons for what?" asked Lorana, standing at the entrance to the Dining Cavern, a desperate Bekka following her in train.

"My lady, you need rest!" Bekka said.

Lorana turned back to her and smiled gently, reaching a hand down toward the younger girl who took it shyly, as Lorana told her, "As do you."

Bekka glanced apologetically in Fiona's direction, saying, "I fell asleep, Weyrwoman."

"Well, that's a first!" Fiona said, waving off Bekka's anxiety and asking solicitously, "Are you still tired? I'd like someone with weyrwoman Jeila when she wakes."

"Terin's with her," Bekka said, trying her best to stifle a yawn.

"Terin asked me if you'd mentioned anything about the box," Lorana said. She smiled shyly as she added, with her glance sliding toward Kindan before returning to Fiona, "She showed me her note and offered me her dragon."

"She would," Fiona said, as moved by Terin's offer as by Lorana's obvious refusal. "If you're not tired, we were eating, and Kindan was filling us in on events at Benden Weyr—"

"And you'd just discovered that we don't have enough dragons," Lorana said, stepping toward them. Bekka glanced at Lorana, then at Fiona for direction and when Fiona nodded for her to join them, she followed beside Lorana, her grip on the older woman's hand tightening just a bit.

"You'll think of something," Bekka told her confidently. "You saved the dragons of Pern; there's nothing you can't do."

Lorana kept her gaze on Fiona and only she shared the great pain in her eyes as they both recognized the error in Bekka's statement.

"I'll get some *klah*," Shaneese said hastily, putting actions to words with the air of one grateful for an excuse to avoid an awkward exchange.

"It needs warming," Fiona agreed.

At Kindan's beckoning, Lorana sat next to him and he drew her head to his shoulder and rested his against hers for a moment.

"Terin told me that you met Mother Karina when you were back in time at Igen Weyr," Lorana said, even as Kindan pushed a roll toward her suggestively.

"We did," Fiona said. "I learned a lot from her."

Lorana glanced at Kindan. "One of the traders had the gift of the Sight, they said." His eyebrows went up in surprise but he said nothing. "He left notes for Fiona and Terin here."

"Did he?" Kindan asked, impressed.

Lorana nodded and continued, but Fiona was sure she felt anxiety growing in the other Weyrwoman. "Yes, he left Terin a harness fitting made of gold in the shape of a soaring dragon."

Fiona suddenly stared at the twin of her own brooch gleaming on Kindan's breast. Tenniz had said, *"It will all turn out right."* What had he meant by that? Why had he arranged for her to get a brooch identical to Kindan's?

"Tenniz's note to Terin said: *'This is yours and no other's,'*" Fiona quoted. She glanced toward Kindan. "The queens will be rising soon."

"You think perhaps your friend Terin will Impress?" M'tal asked.

"She's got the makings," Lorana said. "Her heart is in the right place."

Kindan turned toward Lorana, glanced quickly toward Fiona, then back at Lorana with a question forming on his lips.

Fiona beat him to it. "Will you stand on the Hatching Grounds again, Lorana?"

Lorana held her breath for a long moment before letting it out again to say, "Perhaps I should see what Tenniz wanted to say to me."

Fiona turned to Kindan. She knew that he'd been left on the Hatching Grounds for over ten Turns and that he was far too old for tradition, but all the same she felt a sense of rightness in his riding a dragon and she could feel M'tal steeling himself to say the same.

Lorana beat them to it. "No matter whether I do or not, Kindan of Pern, *you* will be a Candidate."

Fiona met her eyes and they exchanged a look of firm agreement.

"No queen of my Weyr—" Fiona began only to be interrupted by Lorana who declared, "No queen of Pern will keep you from the Hatching Grounds."

"And for what you've done, they would be glad to see you ride bronze," M'tal added solemnly.

Kindan sighed heavily, signaling his defeat.

Fiona, however, ignored him; her attention was focused on Lorana. Her voice when making that declaration had sounded so startlingly familiar.

"Did *you* bring us back in time?" Fiona asked her suddenly.

"Me?" Lorana repeated in surprise. "Lorana?" M'tal said at the same time, giving Fiona an odd look. "She was at Benden the whole time."

"The whole *time*," Fiona repeated. Lorana looked no less confused and Fiona dropped the notion with a frown, explaining by way of apology, "Someone brought Talenth and me back in time to Igen—a gold rider."

"You mean a weyrwoman," Kindan corrected absently, his attention directed toward Lorana.

I don't know, Fiona said to herself with some surprise. Why is it that I always say "queen rider" or "gold rider" but never "weyrwoman"?

"We wouldn't have gone if she hadn't urged us," she said. "If she hadn't made it sound like we'd already done it." She glanced toward Lorana. "Her voice sounded something like yours."

"Arith was too young to go *between*," Lorana told her sadly.

"I'm not so sure," Fiona replied. "Talenth was not much older than Arith and *she* went."

Kindan shot her an angry look that Fiona understood all too well: The loss of Lorana's queen weighed heavily on the both of them.

"Would you," Fiona said softly to Lorana, "at least consider standing on the Hatching Grounds again?"

"I might," Lorana said with a small smile. "It would be good to hear the hatchlings; I've never tried that."

"She hears all dragons," M'tal explained.

"She feels them," Kindan corrected him, his hand unconsciously rising to pat Lorana's shoulder in comfort.

"Before you have a Hatching, you've got to have a mating flight," M'tal said, his gaze leveled at Fiona.

Fiona felt herself reddening and she ducked her head in embarrassment before answering, "Talenth is old enough to rise any day now."

"Who will be the lucky dragon to catch her?"

Fiona shook her head.

"The first queen to rise here will be senior, won't she?" Kindan asked with a quick, apologetic glance toward Lorana.

"Jeila's Tolarth is just as ready," M'tal said.

"But she'll be going back to Benden, won't she?" Fiona asked.

"Not if she's any sense," M'tal said with a chuckle. Fiona looked at him, confused, and he explained. "Tullea can be . . . a little difficult."

"I imagine she'll be better now," Lorana opined diplomatically. She told Fiona, "She'd been timing it back at High Reaches Weyr so her temper was difficult."

"But you weren't like that, were you, Weyrwoman?" Bekka asked Fiona, bristling with loyalty.

"No, I felt different," Fiona said. She glanced toward M'tal and Lorana. "I wasn't the only one. T'mar and several of the weyrlings felt much the same way. We were tired even before we went to Igen—all except Terin."

"Hmm," M'tal murmured thoughtfully. He glanced inquiringly toward Kindan.

The harper shook his head, lips pursed in a frown. "I recall nothing like that in the Records."

"But there wasn't much mention of timing," Lorana said. She glanced toward Fiona as she added, "I think the Weyrs were trying to keep it a secret."

"With good reason, if Tullea is anything to go by!" M'tal agreed.

"Speaking of secrets," Lorana said, glancing toward Kindan and M'tal, "when were you going to tell me that we don't have enough dragons?"

"Lorana, that's not fair," Fiona rebuked her gently. "You've only just discovered the cure! Before that there was no point in worrying about our numbers."

Lorana ducked her head in acknowledgment.

"So how many do we have?" Kindan asked.

"We've forty plus two here," Fiona said, looking around for a slate and, not finding one, gesturing for Bekka to get one. The young girl grinned at her, glad to be involved in the discussion, and raced off and back with the first slate she found. Fiona handed it back, saying, "This one has a recipe on it; I don't think Shaneese will thank you if it's erased."

Bekka's next sojourn was longer but more productive: She returned followed by a small procession of weyrkids towing a large teaching slate.

"*Much* better!" Fiona agreed as she erased the board with the duster and wrote down the names of the weyrs with columns for fighting strength and queens. She filled in Telgar first with 40 and 2.

She had arranged the chart from northeast to southwest, so Telgar was in the middle. With Lorana's aid they soon had it filled out:

High Reaches	328	2
Fort	156	1
Telgar	40	2
Igen	0	0
Ista	307	2
Benden	197	1
Total	1028	8

"We should have three thousand fighting dragons for a Pass," Kindan said sourly. "And as many as thirty queens."

He turned to M'tal. "As soon as possible, I'd like to visit Master Zist and Verilan."

"This distribution is very uneven," M'tal agreed. "We should have more dragons at Telgar; it's central to Pern and has the extra burden of the Falls it inherited when Igen was abandoned."

"Fort's weak, as well," Fiona added in fairness to her old Weyr.

"Perhaps we can get the Weyrleaders to meet soon and discuss this," M'tal said thoughtfully.

"I think that would be an excellent idea," H'nez said. They turned to see him approaching from the Weyr Bowl, pulling off his wher-hide gloves and scarf. Behind him, in the Bowl, other riders returned from drill were dismounting and sending their dragons to their weyrs. He gave the group a tight smile as he continued, "I was thinking much the same thing myself."

He found a seat opposite M'tal and examined the chart silently for a long while.

"Harper Kindan, Norik, am I right in recalling that the queens can be expected to rise twice a Turn and produce an average of twenty-eight eggs?" H'nez said, steepling his hands thoughtfully.

"That sounds right from Records I've read," Fiona told him, glancing at Norik and Kindan for any disagreement.

"So this Turn we can expect—" H'nez paused as he did the sum in his head. "—the queens to produce at most four hundred and thirty-two weyrlings."

"I think—" Bekka piped up hesitantly, then spoke with greater speed as H'nez nodded for her to continue. "I think it's four hundred and forty-eight, my lord."

"Yes, you're right," H'nez said after a moment's thought. "Well summed."

"I did a lot of sums for my mother," Bekka explained.

"Four hundred and forty-eight," H'nez repeated, absently waving Bekka back to silence.

"And at least two Turns before they're large enough to fight," Fiona added warningly.

"We could send them back to the past," H'nez countered.

"Where?" Fiona asked. "We've already used all the time at Igen."

H'nez frowned. "Well, couldn't we just send them again?"

"It doesn't work that way," M'tal told him. "If we *would* do it, then it would already have happened at Igen back in time and we'd know that we'd done it already."

H'nez's eyes widened in confusion.

"It could only happen in a place where we wouldn't have seen it already, H'nez," Fiona told him. "It didn't happen at Igen, or I would have met those riders from the future." She added, "There's only one past to go to."

"So we didn't do it at Igen," H'nez conceded with a mild irritation. "Where else could we do it?"

"It's not just location, it's supplies," Fiona said. H'nez gave her an inquiring look. "Three Turns, four hundred and forty-eight dragonets, riders, and there'd have to be others to care for them—that adds up to a lot of supplies. Where would they come from?"

"You managed."

"That's my point," Fiona said. "We did manage and we were noticeable. Another group, nearly three times as large, would be even more noticeable. The only decent place to hide them would be a Weyr."

"Tullea hid at High Reaches," H'nez pointed out.

"Which means they couldn't be there," Fiona said. "Nor could they be at Benden, nor Fort, nor Igen, nor Telgar."

"That leaves Ista?"

"I think that we can safely discount Ista, too," M'tal said. "The island can only support so much, and Ista Weyr's never been all that shorthanded. The difference would be observed, particularly by the traders."

"Traders can keep secrets," H'nez pointed out, with a nod toward Shaneese and another for Fiona.

"We could just ask them," Lorana said. "If they'd done so, now's the right time to tell us."

"Good point," M'tal agreed, his face taking on the abstracted look of a rider communing with his dragon. "C'rion's Nidanth tells me no."

He shrugged and said to H'nez, "Well, never mind, it was a good thought."

H'nez frowned. "Even with those extra four hundred fighting dragons, we'd still have only about half the dragons we'd need."

"And that's ignoring casualties," Norik added glumly. He looked at Kindan. "I don't suppose you've determined the sort of casualties we can expect?"

"I've an idea," Kindan replied, "but most of our experience has been with the added danger of the illness." He turned to M'tal. "I'd like to get with Verilan and see what the Records say."

"We have Records here," Fiona reminded him. "And, in fact, I suspect our Records are more complete with regards to Weyr details—"

"You'd be surprised, Fiona," Kindan interrupted her with a grin. It was a moment before he noticed the reproachful looks of both M'tal and H'nez, and even then, it took him longer to realize their cause.

"I mean, Weyrwoman," he corrected himself, flushing in surprise. To Fiona, he apologized, "I'm sorry, but I still remember you as someone whose diapers I changed."

Fiona's eyes flashed angrily even as the warmth seemed to vanish from the room.

"Thank you, harper," she told him coldly. "I still remember you as the one who couldn't save my sister's life."

But she was instantly contrite, even before M'tal's exclamation: "By the First Egg, Kindan, it still surprises me that you can be such a dull-glow at times!"

Fiona made a face and placed a hand on Kindan's arm. "I'm sorry, that was uncalled for," she said even as she flinched at the anguish in his eyes. "I will never forget that I owe you my life."

"You've grown up," Kindan said after a long, thoughtful silence. "I guess I haven't adjusted to it, Weyrwoman."

"I've lived three Turns that you don't know," Fiona said, hoping to put the incident behind them. "I've not just thirteen Turns, I've nearer seventeen."

"I'll try to remember," Kindan said. He pursed his lips tightly in consideration before adding, "And I'll try to remember that you're not your sister."

"Again, I'm sorry," Fiona said. "I can only guess how much you loved her."

"Perhaps," H'nez suggested diplomatically, "we should examine the Records?"

Fiona could almost kiss the man for his tact.

▾ ▾ ▾

They were surprised to hear voices as they climbed up the queens' ledge and past the sleeping Talenth.

"So you were the only girl?" Jeila's voice could be heard clearly.

"Fiona was there, too," Terin said. "After a while, we had the traders staying with us—"

"Really? In the Weyr?" Jeila sounded surprised and impressed. "You know, I've trader blood."

"Hush! Someone's coming!"

"It's just us," Fiona called as they entered her quarters. "We didn't mean to interrupt. We're going to the Records Room."

Terin groaned and explained to Jeila. "Anytime she goes into the Records Room it means trouble."

"Can I come?" Jeila asked, throwing off her blankets and sitting up.

"Bekka?" Fiona said, cocking her head to the young weyrgirl. Bekka examined the older woman's forehead for heat, took her pulse, and checked her eyes.

"How do you feel?" she asked the young weyrwoman.

"I feel tired but otherwise fine and a bit fidgety," Jeila confessed. Fiona glanced at her sharply: She felt fidgety herself.

"Well, you're definitely not pregnant," Bekka declared. Everyone turned to her in surprise. "It's really all I know, now."

"Whether someone's pregnant?"

"My mother's a midwife," Bekka explained nonchalantly. "After a while, you just know."

Fiona saw the way Bekka's eyes lingered on Lorana and how the older woman's lips tightened in surprise. Fiona glanced toward M'tal and the bronze rider met her eyes with a slight, confirming nod of his own. The air went out of Fiona's lungs with a finality that surprised her. He'd told her that Kindan and Lorana had formed a bond; why did it bother her so much now to see the truth?

"Are the Rooms over there?" M'tal asked Fiona politely, rescuing her from another awkward moment.

"Yes," she said. "I haven't had a chance to—"

"Shaneese had them cleaned the other day, my lady," Terin told her.

"Perhaps I should stay here with Terin," Lorana said. She glanced at Fiona. "I could see this box that your Tenniz left."

"Why don't you go on," Fiona called to the others. "I'd like to see this as well."

Kindan and Lorana exchanged a quick glance, after which Kindan nodded and followed the two bronze riders to the Records Room.

"The box is over here," Terin called out cheerfully, pulling it down from the shelves. She continued breathlessly, even as she placed it on Fiona's worktable, "I wonder what you'll get and what your message will be. I hope yours makes more sense than ours."

With an inquiring look at Fiona, Lorana opened the box and reached inside to pull out the final envelope, the one with her name on it.

"It's heavy," Lorana said nervously, and then she opened it and poured out its contents. Something golden and long, rod-like, dropped into her hands. She held it up and turned it until she made sense of the shape.

"That's odd," she said, as she held it up for the others to examine. It looked something like the twined serpents and staff symbol of a healer, but the top was shaped more like a dragon's head. The workmanship was brilliant but seemed somewhat incomplete. Fiona wondered at the small holes at either side, one third of the way up and one third of the way down.

"It looks like something else should hook there," Terin said, her eyes narrowing.

"What's the note say?" Fiona asked.

Lorana smoothed the note out on the table, and as she read it, her face drained of all color. Anxiously, Fiona moved behind her to read over her shoulder: *The way forward is dark and long. A dragon gold is only the first price you'll pay for Pern.*

▼ ▼ ▼

"Mine said that it would turn out all right," Fiona said, trying to reassure Lorana. "I'm certain it will."

Lorana gave her a small smile.

"Perhaps he was wrong," Terin said. "After all, he seems to think I'm going to be needing this." She fingered her gold dragon fitting longingly.

"He must have felt he was right," Lorana said, gesturing at the box, "to go through all this trouble." Her lips pulled into a frown as she added, "And he *did* know that I was going to be here."

"We can't be certain of that," Fiona said. "He could just have expected me to deliver this."

"Fiona," Lorana turned to her bleakly, "he knew that I'd paid with dragon gold. How many others knew that?"

Fiona couldn't argue her logic. "Whatever is needed, I'll do," she swore. She waved angrily at the note. "This will not be! You've paid enough already."

"Have I?" Lorana asked her softly. She met Fiona's blue eyes squarely with her almond-brown ones. "What price would you pay to save Pern?" She turned to Terin. "What price would you pay?"

"But it's not fair!" Terin said. "You've paid more than anyone!"

"Have I?" Lorana asked, gesturing toward the Records Room and Kindan. "Hasn't Kindan paid as much? Or Salina, or Seban? Or all those who have paid, even with dragon gold?"

"All the same, I agree with Terin," Fiona said. "It's not fair."

"No," Lorana said. "And as you've promised to help me, I'll ask that you—both of you—say nothing of this to Kindan." She met Fiona's eyes. "He's paid enough already."

"Very well," Fiona said. She chewed her lip thoughtfully before finding the courage to ask, "Does he know? About the child?"

Lorana shook her head. "It's far too early for anyone to know."

"Except Bekka," Terin corrected with a giggle.

"You *do* seem to surround yourself with the most amazing people," Lorana told Fiona.

"Just lucky," Fiona said with a shrug.

"Luck?" Lorana said. "Or something more?"

Fiona shrugged again. "Whatever it is, I'm grateful for my friends." She looked toward the Records Room. "We'd best join them unless you want Kindan to ask why we've been here so long."

"What should I do about this?" Lorana asked, gesturing to the brooch.

Fiona thought quickly and pulled out her brooch, passing it to Lorana. "Here, wear this."

"It looks just like Kindan's!" Lorana exclaimed as she examined it.

"Which is why I think there must have been a mistake," Fiona said. She felt Lorana's reluctance and told her firmly, "Look, if you don't wear it, Kindan will wonder."

With a sigh Lorana took the harp brooch and attached it. "I don't like lying to him."

"You're not lying," Fiona assured her. "You're wearing a brooch."

"And if he asks about yours?"

"I'll tell him it's none of his business," Fiona said waspishly. She shook her head and gave Lorana an apologetic look. "I'm sorry, but I'll handle it."

"You probably will," Lorana said. She grinned, then, and gestured for Fiona to lead the way. "Just as you'll figure out what to tell him about the note."

"Oh, that's easy!" Terin piped up. "Just tell him that it said that you'd pay a dragon gold to save Pern."

Lorana and Fiona turned back to face her, eyebrows raised.

"Well, it's not a lie, is it?" Terin said.

Fortunately, when they entered the Records Room they found all the others deep in concentration as they combed the older Records.

"They're mostly either too new or too faded to be useful," Kindan said as he irritably replaced a stack of musty Records, shaking his head. "The weather here is harder on paper than it is at Benden."

"Igen had clean Records," Fiona said.

"Perhaps we should go there?" H'nez said.

"That might be a good idea," Kindan said, his eyes slipping toward Fiona before returning quickly to the Records.

"But I've got some numbers to go by . . ." His words trailed off as he grimaced over a slate filled with numbers and terse lettering. He found another slate, glanced at its contents, and absently wiped it clean before transferring a cluster of numbers to it.

"Can someone check my numbers?" Kindan asked after a moment. Something in his tone alarmed Fiona. She reached for the slate, even as she said, "I'm not all that good with numbers."

The numbers were dragons lost in a series of Threadfalls compared with Weyr strength. She did a quick tally of each, divided the total losses by the total strength and then glanced at Kindan. "My numbers say nearly three dragons in every hundred."

"Three in one hundred?" H'nez asked, surprised.

"Per Fall," Fiona added grimly.

"So a full-strength Weyr lost nearly fifteen dragons every Fall?" M'tal said, gesturing for Kindan's slate and reading through it quickly. He put it down and glanced around. "Is there a clean slate about?"

Fiona passed him one and a stick of chalk. M'tal's eyes narrowed in thought as he drew numbers on his slate. Finally, he glanced up at the others. "That's better than Benden's average; we've been losing five for every one hundred."

"But we can't be sure how much of that was due to the illness," Kindan said.

"All the same, it lends credence to your number," H'nez said.

Lorana had been working on a separate slate of her own. "It tallies with the queens' clutches, too."

The others looked at her in surprise, so she explained, "Well, it makes sense that the queens would have to replace the losses. So a quick tally of clutches should roughly match the losses . . . and it does."

"With—what? Five queens in six Weyrs?" Kindan asked.

"Thirty queens," Lorana agreed.

"We've only eight."

"We can make more," Fiona reminded them, her lips quirked upward. "But will we have the time?"

On H'nez's suggestion, they agreed to say nothing of their findings to the rest of the Weyr.

"We've Threadfall tomorrow," H'nez reminded them as they made their way back into Fiona's quarters. He glanced at Lorana. "Will the dragons be fit to fly by then?"

"They could fly now," M'tal said. "Tullea's Minith had less time before she went back in time to High Reaches."

"But it would be better if they rested as much as they could," Lorana said.

"The Fall's not until after noon," H'nez said. "We wouldn't have to start getting ready more than two hours before then."

"That will be plenty of time for them to recover," M'tal assured him.

H'nez regarded M'tal for a long moment before saying, "Thank you, bronze rider. I think we have relied on your kindness more than enough."

M'tal looked at the rangy bronze rider with amusement in his eyes. "Are you dismissing me, H'nez?"

H'nez looked slightly flustered. "It's just that I'm sure you have duties to your Weyr and I wouldn't want to delay your return by imposing on your kindness."

Lorana gave Fiona a sympathetic look.

"Lord M'tal," Fiona said, "you are welcome to stay in Telgar as long as you'd like." She gave H'nez her brightest smile as she added, smugly, "You might have heard that my Talenth will be rising soon and I'm sure she would be very pleased to have your great Gaminth as a suitor."

"Fiona!" Terin murmured warningly under her breath.

M'tal inclined his head toward the Weyrwoman, his eyes twinkling as he glanced toward H'nez. "I shall certainly consider the offer, Weyrwoman."

"I'd like to stay here," Jeila added from where she sat in Fiona's bed. "Tolarth will be rising soon"—she glanced toward H'nez— "and I think that Telgar would benefit from two queens."

"But doesn't Weyrwoman Tullea expect you back in Benden?" Fiona asked quickly, suddenly feeling less smug.

"I suspect that Weyrwoman Tullea would be glad to see Tolarth established here," M'tal observed, inclining his head toward H'nez. "For the benefit of all Pern."

"With two queens so close to rising—" Fiona began, feeling suddenly very outmaneuvered.

"Not to worry, Weyrwoman," H'nez assured her. "As you know, it is easy for the other queen to take herself away temporarily."

"You want the best for the Weyr, don't you?" Jeila added.

"Of course," Fiona said.

"Sonia's Lyrinth has told me that High Reaches will fly this Fall with you," Lorana said. She glanced toward Fiona. "If you want, you could form a queens' wing."

"With both queens ready to rise, that might not be wise," M'tal said, his lips pursed tightly.

Dinner that evening was a subdued affair with undertones of tension that Fiona could not fail to notice. She was certain that some of the tension was from the spreading awareness that, although the dragon sickness had been cured, the Weyrs were still gravely understrength. Another part of the tension, Fiona guessed, was from the presence of so many new and different faces at the high table. Shaneese noticed it, too, and spent much of her time hovering near the Weyrleader's table, eyeing Fiona anxiously.

At Fiona's request, Mekiar was seated with them and she'd had him show some of his work to M'tal and Kindan, both of whom were impressed.

Still, Fiona found herself ceding most of the conversation to Jeila. The Benden weyrwoman was a thin-boned, animated person who charmed everyone around her, including Shaneese, who was thrilled to have another of the trader's blood in the Weyr.

F'jian and Terin were seated nearby and locked in their own intimate conversation, only occasionally exchanging words with the others at their table. Before dinner, F'jian had made a special point to thank Lorana for her sacrifice and Kindan for his persistence—remarks that both pleased and nettled Fiona.

T'mar was seated at yet another table, a cluster of his riders mingled with the Telgar weyrfolk. Fiona glanced his way several times, but he never seemed to look at her during the whole meal. She couldn't say why that irritated her so much. She shrugged. It seemed she was just a little touchy tonight.

"She's going to rise soon," Mekiar spoke up softly from his place beside her.

"Pardon?" Fiona asked, leaning politely toward the older man, remembering that he'd once ridden a brown dragon, Turns before she was born.

"Your queen," he said, "she's going to rise soon." He nodded firmly. "I can see it in the way you're acting."

"Me?"

"Yes," Mekiar replied. "You don't quite know how to feel, you can't concentrate, you're irritated, happy, sad—"

"How did you know?" Fiona interrupted sharply.

"I've seen many a mating flight," Mekiar told her. He gave her a grim smile. "Judging by you, I'd say you're going to have your hands full when the time comes."

ELEVEN

Heart pound,
Blood flow.
Soar high,
Mate nigh.

Telgar Weyr, late evening, AL 508.2.10

Shaneese had already arranged to have a weyr cleared for Jeila and her Tolarth and had also cleared another queen's weyr for Lorana—"If anyone deserves it, it's her"—so all Fiona had to do was politely see the others settled in and arrange for her own rest.

Terin wanted to stay with F'jian. Fiona wasn't sure how that would work out as the bronze rider would be flying a Fall the next day, so she found herself tossing and turning in her large, empty bed. She *hated* empty beds!

Finally, with a growl of defeat, she got up, dragging her blankets with her, and settled herself against Talenth's belly. That didn't seem to help—even though Talenth was warm and comforting, Fiona wanted something more. She dozed fitfully.

A chorus of noises and whispers woke her and she opened her eyes enough to see Xhinna and Taria herding their charges into place.

"We thought you could use some company," Taria confessed to her quietly as she passed by. Fiona gave the youngster a bright-eyed smile in thanks, grabbed a couple of the smaller children and nestled them softly against her before drifting back to sleep again.

She wasn't quite asleep when a deeper voice spoke up, "Are you all right?"

Fiona opened her eyes and saw Lorana crouching nearby her, a quizzical look on her face.

"I'm sorry," Fiona replied softly, "I hope they didn't disturb you."

"I wasn't sleepy," Lorana said, deftly avoiding an answer.

Fiona gestured invitingly with one free hand. "There's plenty of room."

Lorana's look was hard to fathom, especially in the dim light of distant glows.

"You could bring Kindan," Fiona said. "Xhinna and Taria are somewhere around here." She rested her head against Talenth's chest, near one of the younger boys; his hair smelled pleasantly of lemon, freshly washed. She sensed Lorana's reluctance and added, "I used to sneak out of bed when Kindan was visiting and curl up with him when I was younger." She smiled fondly at the memory, then gestured to the children nearby. "It made me feel like I had family, sleeping all together, so I'm passing it along."

Lorana's expression changed and Fiona felt the other woman's sorrow.

"What?" Fiona asked, her eyes open again, staring intently at the other woman.

"I was the last of my family," Lorana said. "My mother, brother, and sister all died when I was feverish." Fiona could tell that the memory was hard on her and Lorana recalled it with difficulty. Lorana took a ragged breath before continuing, "My father was a breeder, ranging between the holds and the locals thought we'd brought the Plague. They were going to kill him and us." She squeezed her eyes tight against the memory. "I remember feeling cold, oh so cold! And then realized that my mother, brother, and sister were cold and stiff. I cried out and Sannel, my father, rushed from the doorway. It was then that he realized what had happened and he turned back to the holders, shouting, 'They're dead! Now leave me with my daughter while we've still a chance!'

"So my last memory of family is with the cold and the dead." Lorana was silent for a long moment, her head hung low. "And then I had Garth and Grenn and I lost them and Arith to the illness." She raised her head to meet Fiona's eyes grimly. "So you see, everything I love dies." She glanced nervously back toward the weyr she'd left, the one with Kindan sleeping in it.

Fiona reached out a hand toward Lorana. Lorana examined it for a moment before shyly reaching out to touch it.

"I won't die," Fiona swore to her softly. She nodded toward the children. "They'll live and their children will live because *we* say so."

Beside her, little Aryar stirred and looked up at Lorana, her eyes wide with wonder. "Are you Lorana?"

Lorana nodded.

"My father says you saved his dragon," Aryar said, pushing herself up from the ground and wrapping her arms around Lorana's waist. "He said you gave your dragon to save all the other dragons."

"That's—" Lorana began, shaking her head, her eyes wet with tears.

"She did," Fiona told Aryar firmly, her look daring Lorana to argue.

"Does she have half a heart, Weyrwoman?" Aryar craned her head around to ask Fiona in all seriousness.

"Maybe she does," Fiona said with a lump in her chest. She looked up at Lorana and tightened her grip on the other woman's hand. "But if she does, we'll help her grow it back, won't we?"

"Yes!" Aryar said emphatically. She glanced up toward Lorana and added, "And if that's not enough, you can have my heart, too!"

A sob escaped Lorana and Fiona pulled her down close to her, settled her in against her in the spot Aryar had vacated. Aryar needed no prompting to snuggle on Lorana's other side.

"Talenth is big and soft," Aryar assured her. "Her cough is all gone, you'll have good dreams."

"Good dreams?"

"Yes," Aryar said. "You can sleep and grow your heart again." Shyly she added, "If you get scared, I'll be here for you."

Fiona felt Lorana tighten her hand on hers in a brief spasm before the other woman said to Aryar, "Thank you. And if you get scared, I'll be here for you."

"You will?" Aryar asked, suddenly all awake and wide-eyed. Lorana reassured her with a smile and softly pulled the youngster back down beside her.

"I will," Lorana promised as she leaned forward and kissed the crown of Aryar's head. "But first you must sleep."

Aryar let out a great, contented sigh, nestled her head into Lorana's shoulder, and fell asleep.

Fiona kept Lorana's hand loosely in hers even as she fell back to sleep, feeling warmer and more comfortable than she had since . . . since the last time Kindan had visited Fort Hold back when she was still little.

The sound of feet moving quietly and the rustle of fabric roused Fiona enough that she squinted one eye open. She smiled as she made out Kindan's form in the darkness and heard him quietly settle next to Lorana with Aryar sleeping, snug, between them.

When Fiona woke again, it was morning. Sunlight filtered wanly into the Weyr and lit Talenth's lair with a cold, drowsy light.

She woke because she was cold. Lorana was standing up beside her, saying softly to Taria as the other tried to quietly corral the children, "How can I help?"

"We'll manage," Taria assured her tersely. Fiona could sense that the youngster did not want her competence questioned.

"She's not trying to correct you," Fiona told her muzzily. "She's trying to help you."

"We'd be glad of it," Xhinna spoke up as she herded a small group of children toward Fiona's quarters. She gave Fiona an inquiring look to which Fiona replied, "Of course they can use the bath!" She smiled impishly at the youngsters arrayed before her. "We wouldn't want *stinky* children wandering around today, would we?"

The youngsters giggled and agreed loudly before trundling off, their faces full of glee.

Lorana looked back toward Fiona and then at Xhinna, who gestured for her to precede her. "I'll be right behind you, weyrwoman."

"It's just Lorana, now," Lorana corrected.

"I'm sorry," Xhinna said, flustered, "I didn't mean—"

Lorana raised a hand and shook her head. "No harm done."

She smiled as she strolled briskly after the youngsters, following them into Fiona's bathroom.

Xhinna paused long enough to give Fiona an anxious look. Fiona responded with an encouraging smile and a deliberate nod toward the bathroom and the now-loud children inside.

"Aryar has the right of it," Fiona said to herself as Xhinna disappeared, still not entirely relieved.

"That with our love, she'll grow her heart back?" Kindan spoke up, startling her. Fiona realized that the harper had been awake in the other room for the whole exchange, merely feigning sleep, and now, the way his eyes explored her left her feeling uncomfortable; his maleness, the spicy smell of him, unnerved her.

"Yes," she said, rising from her position all too near to him and moving toward her quarters. Her eyes flashed as she looked back at him and snapped, "You, of all people, should know that!"

Kindan's look of hurt and confusion almost made her relent and return to him. Almost.

"He's supposed to be a harper," Fiona murmured to herself as she followed the sounds of splashing into her bathroom and saw that it was full of children, mostly bathing, all wet.

How are you today, Talenth? Fiona asked as she turned back to her bedroom and pulled out fresh riding gear.

I'm feeling much better, Talenth replied. *Are we going to fly today?*

Oh, dear heart, I doubt it, Fiona told her, a small smile flashing across her lips. *I think that Jeila and I should stay here. When we have three queens, then we'll have a proper queens' wing.*

That will be nice, Talenth agreed. A moment later, she added, *Tolarth asks what can Jeila do to help?*

Have her meet us for breakfast and we'll plan from there.

I did, Talenth responded. After a slight pause she added, *He is quite confused.*

He? Fiona wondered to herself.

Kindan.

She remembered another time, Turns back. A time before she'd gone to Igen, when hatchling Talenth had woken, creeling.

What is it? Fiona had asked, rushing to the young queen's weyr.

He hurts, Talenth had said with a whimper.

I'm sorry, Fiona had said, not knowing how else to respond.

He hurts and you feel it, Talenth had said. *How is it that you feel it?*

"He"—Kindan? Did he still hurt now? And did Fiona still feel it? He shouldn't be hurting now: He had Lorana. And she, Fiona, shouldn't be feeling his hurt for the same reason. Still . . .

It wouldn't be fair. It wouldn't be fair to Lorana, it wouldn't be fair to Kindan. And, she thought, it wouldn't be fair to T'mar, either.

But does that mean it has to be unfair for me?

Fiona shook her head, dislodging the thoughts from her mind.

He'll feel better when he eats, she assured Talenth absently, cocking her head toward the sounds in the bathroom and deciding that it was time for her bath.

"It's a good morning for it," Shaneese said as she met Fiona at the entrance to the Dining Cavern and gestured her toward the high table. "I've hot *klah* waiting."

"Thanks!" Fiona called as she passed through.

T'mar, H'nez, F'jian, and M'tal were talking low among themselves when she sat at the table. T'mar smiled at her, as did F'jian and M'tal, while H'nez gave her a quick nod before returning to the conversation.

Sonia asks if they can meet us here, Talenth relayed to her just as Fiona had taken a gulp of *klah.*

Let me check, Fiona said, swallowing quickly.

"I think that would be a good idea," M'tal said when she relayed the request, glancing toward H'nez.

The wiry bronze rider looked nonplussed by M'tal's deference. "You're the senior rider here."

"Only temporarily."

"We'd be foolish not to take every advantage of your experience," H'nez said, shrugging his shoulders. "And I expect that you know Weyrleader D'vin better than I."

M'tal turned to Fiona. "Please tell the Weyrwoman that we'd be delighted."

"What about the firestone?" F'jian asked. "We don't have enough firestone for them."

Their own firestone problems had been temporarily solved by a loan from Fort Weyr.

"I'll remind them," Fiona said, sending the message to Talenth. Fiona was just thinking how difficult it was to relay messages from one dragon to the other before getting it to the rider when she spotted Lorana entering along with Taria, Xhinna, and all their charges. For the first time since she'd seen her, the ex-dragonrider seemed at ease, almost happy.

Her reflections were interrupted when she saw Norik bearing down on her with Bekka following in tow. The man looked intent, on a mission.

"Weyrwoman," Norik began as soon as he was within earshot. Fiona glanced at Bekka, but the young girl's expression was unreadable, her gaze intent on the old harper.

"Harper," Fiona said, giving him a smile. "Have you a song for us today?"

"No," Norik said brusquely. He looked at Lorana, then spotted Kindan entering the Dining Cavern. His expression changed.

"I was wondering—" he began, then broke off and closed his eyes in pain. When he opened them again, he met her eyes unflinchingly. "I was wondering if perhaps Harper Kindan and I could change places." He paused, choosing his words carefully. "I loved this Weyr. But after—" He broke off, a harper groping for words. "There's too much pain for me here."

"The illness is past," Fiona began soothingly even as her heart leaped at the notion. "Surely—"

"The memories, Weyrwoman," Norik cut in, gesturing to those around him, "the memories are here every day for me."

"And it would be different in another Weyr?"

Norik pursed his lips thoughtfully before answering, "Yes, I think so." He grimaced. "I hope so." The pain in his eyes was evident. "I won't know unless I try."

"Kindan was assigned to Benden at my request," M'tal spoke up softly from beside them. Norik glanced at him in surprise. M'tal glanced toward Fiona, his eyes gentle. "It may be well for me to consider changing Weyrs. And if I did, it is possible that Kindan might choose to follow me."

"Lady Salina—" Fiona began but M'tal cut her off with a kindly shake of his head.

"I believe that Salina would, just as Harper Norik, appreciate a change of Weyrs," M'tal told her, adding, "In fact, that consideration weighs on my offer."

What would H'nez say? Fiona wondered, her eyes going wide with a wicked sense of delight. Then she sobered as she thought, what would T'mar think? And if Talenth rose, would it be possible for her to refuse Gaminth, a superb bronze with proven ability?

M'tal must have sensed her worry for he told her gently, "This is not something to be decided this day." He added, "In fact, after the Fall, I'd like to invite Salina here to see if Telgar suits her."

"I think that would be an excellent idea," Fiona said. She turned back to Norik. "I suppose, if Kindan agrees, you could possibly go to Benden then for the same purpose."

Norik nodded, looking relieved.

M'tal glanced over at Fiona thoughtfully before saying, "Perhaps it were best if I talked to Kindan on this matter."

"Of course," Fiona said. She glanced at Bekka, who seemed agitated over something. "What is it?"

"Well," Bekka said nervously, darting a look at Lorana, "if she's staying, we'd better find a midwife." She added, "I've watched many times, but I don't feel ready just yet."

"We've three midwives, lass," Norik assured her, rustling her hair fondly. He turned back toward Fiona as he added, "I'll miss her most of all." Then he turned back to Bekka. "Though how you can say that Lady Lorana is with child and hope not to get beaten for it is beyond me."

"She is," Bekka said emphatically. "My mother and I used to play a game, I had to guess whether and when." She pursed her lips as she added, "She's about three sevendays along."

"That's too early for any to tell!" Norik chided her. Bekka gave him a haughty look. The harper laughed. "You're a caution, you are."

Fiona only half-listened to their banter, her eyes turning to Lorana. She remembered the hand gesture. She'd seen it before with other expectant mothers.

"Caranth flew Minith," M'tal murmured close to her ear. Fiona turned to him, realizing that the bronze rider had been watching her carefully.

"I'm glad for her, then," Fiona said, trying to sound as if she meant it. She'd caught the older rider's meaning easily enough and was perversely irritated that he should make the comparison between herself and Tullea.

"Being a weyrwoman sometimes means putting your hopes behind those of others," M'tal told her sympathetically. He patted her shoulder. "But it doesn't mean that you should be miserable."

"Being a weyrwoman means doing my duty," Fiona replied, her eyes grim. She rose from her seat and said in parting, "And, if you'll excuse me, I must be attending to it."

"What's got you so upset?" Xhinna asked as Fiona approached her.

"Nothing," Fiona snapped, keeping her eyes from straying toward

Lorana. "Shaneese suggested that your young ones might be good help setting up the aid tables."

Taria moved over to them with an inquiring look on her face.

"The weyrwoman wants our help with the aid tables," Xhinna told her. She leaned closer to Fiona. "I suppose Shaneese figures that if the little ones help, it'll shame the older ones into helping?"

"Something like that," Fiona agreed. Raising her voice, she said, "We'll have riders from High Reaches Weyr and they may need our help, too."

Fiona watched with amusement as the word spread from one excited child to another along the table and, finally, to the cooks and helpers in the hall. She sensed a mixture of apprehension and pride growing in the hall—pride that High Reaches was coming here, apprehension that they might not find the sort of welcome they deserved. Suddenly, every adult in the cavern was bustling, some rushing off to others. Fiona glanced meaningfully to Xhinna, who merely shook her head, unsurprised.

"Thread won't fall until afternoon," Fiona said. "But it's best for us to be ready now." She glanced at Terin, who caught her eye and rushed over to her. "We'll need someone to see to the firestone."

"I can spare you some of mine," Xhinna offered, gesturing to the youngsters.

"No," Fiona said. "Better to have them help with the tables. We need stronger backs."

Terin sought out Shaneese and found that Mekiar was ready to help with the firestone, having organized a group of sturdy weyrfolk already.

Fiona was busy laying out medicinal supplies and bandages when a shadow alerted her to another presence. It was Lorana.

"Can I help?"

"It'll be messy," Fiona warned.

"I'm used to it from Benden," Lorana said. "Although with forty dragons I think we can hope for few injuries."

"We might even get away with none," Fiona agreed. She glanced around at the tables set up nearby. "In which case all this effort will be for nothing."

"I would be happy with that."

"So would I," Fiona said with a grin. Her expression slipped as she added, "I just hope it's not too bad."

"You never really get numb to all the pain and screaming," Lorana said absently.

Fiona gave her an intense look. "They say that you can feel dragons."

Lorana nodded.

"What's it like?"

"It's like breathing," Lorana told her. "Sometimes it hurts, sometimes it's marvelous, but always it's just something I do."

"But you didn't always."

"Actually, I think I did," Lorana told her. "I only knew what I was doing after I Impressed Garth and Grenn."

"Your fire-lizards?"

A ghost of a smile crossed Lorana's face as she nodded. "When I thought I was dying, I sent them away to save them." Lorana explained how she'd been lost overboard in a storm, how the fire-lizards were sick even then, and how she'd sent them away from her.

"I would have done the same," Fiona said, even as, privately, she wondered if she would have had the courage.

"Somehow Grenn survived."

"He survived?"

"He went back in time, the First Pass or the end of it," Lorana said. "I think he was sick then and his sickness alerted them to our problem."

"So you saved Pern three times," Fiona said. Lorana looked at her quizzically. "Kindan told me all about it. First, when you sent your fire-lizard back as a warning, and then when you lost your queen—you said your locket had a piece of your riding harness in it—and finally when you called"—Fiona paused, looking at Lorana in growing surprise—"you called across time, didn't you?"

"I must have," Lorana agreed. "I wasn't trying to do that. I was trying to save D'gan and the others, to save Caranth and, instead . . ."

"And that's how Wind Blossom and Emorra—five hundred Turns back in time—knew what to put in the Ancient Rooms found at Benden.

And how you found the cure to the illness," Fiona finished when it was clear that Lorana was unable to speak. She reached out to the older woman and touched her gently on the shoulder.

Lorana looked up and met Fiona's eyes.

"Thank you," Fiona said, her eyes sparkling with emotion. "I'm sorry you lost your queen, but you saved mine and if there's anything I can do . . ."

Her words were cut short by Ginirth's bugle, immediately echoed by the other dragons as they swarmed down into the Bowl.

"It's time," Fiona said. Silently she asked Talenth to take station as watch dragon and was surprised to see H'nez's grateful look as he climbed aboard his great bronze.

"Is that a habit of yours?" Lorana asked, gesturing to Talenth.

"Well, someone's supposed to keep watch," Fiona said, wondering at Lorana's tone of surprise. She thought about it for a moment and decided that she'd probably developed the idea from all her time with her father's guards at Fort Hold—a Hold, or Weyr, should always have someone responsible looking out for its safety. Not to mention those times when she and Talenth had stood guard back in time at Igen Weyr—in penance to T'mar for one of her more foolish stunts.

The cold winter sun had done its job of burning through the early morning fog and was now, triumphant, nearly mid-sky, highlighting Talenth's gold hide and burnishing it to a brilliance that even the harsh glare of Igen's desert sun couldn't rival.

Suddenly the air above the Weyr was full of dragons—bronzes, browns, blues, greens—all arrayed in formation, wing after wing. High Reaches Weyr had arrived.

A gold sparkle separated itself from the amazing display of color and dropped quickly into the Weyr Bowl.

Talenth bugled a greeting that was answered by the gold as she passed by.

Lyrinth, Talenth told Fiona unnecessarily.

High Reaches' senior queen settled quickly nearby and her rider

jumped off. Fiona had a momentary glimpse of long dark hair punctuated by a shocking white forelock streaming behind a running figure before she found herself confronted by a pair of intense green eyes that
scanned her quickly, dismissed her, and turned themselves upon Lorana.

Weyrwoman Sonia was several centimeters shorter than Fiona. Her
body was tight, muscled, wiry, an intense reflection of an intense personality.

"You must be Lorana," Sonia said. She stopped her forward motion,
suddenly as still as a stone.

"Weyrwoman," Lorana said with a nod by way of greeting.

Fiona was surprised at the ex–queen rider's wariness. Sonia surprised
her further when she barked a quick laugh and declared, "Tullea's a
bitch."

Sonia ignored Fiona's startled gasp, keeping her attention on Lorana,
eyeing her reaction critically. Somehow satisfied by Lorana's surprise,
she continued, "It's not a requirement for Weyrwomen, even seniors."

"Cisca's nice," Fiona said. Sonia turned her eyes to her briefly and dismissed her with a flick of her head before returning her attention to
Lorana. Fiona's eyes narrowed at the insult.

"I wanted to thank you for what you've done," Sonia told Lorana.
"I'm sure you haven't heard it enough yet."

Fiona's temper flared and her eyes flashed angrily as she thought that
perhaps Lorana's worries about the manners of senior Weyrwomen were
not so misplaced after all.

"We appreciate your help, Weyrwoman," Fiona spoke up, calling
upon her memories of her father in his moments of diplomatic fury. "Is
there anything we can provide you with or will you be returning to your
Weyr for lunch?"

Sonia glanced at Fiona with a look of amusement before turning back
to Lorana, and asking, "Is there anything we can get you?"

"Weyrwoman Fiona has already seen to my needs, thank you," Lorana
said, shifting her position to stand closer to Fiona, resting a hand on her
shoulder.

"Sonia!" a voice shouted and a blur of a figure flung itself onto the dark-haired Weyrwoman. It was Jeila. She stepped back from the embrace quickly, saying, "It's good to see you here!"

"Jeila," Sonia said. "What brings you here?" Before Jeila could answer, the Weyrwoman guessed, "Tullea?"

"I asked for her to be here so that we could use Tolarth's blood for the cure if necessary," Lorana said. "Jeila did not feel well, so we had her stay the night here."

"And where will you spend this night?" Sonia asked, cocking her head questioningly toward Jeila. The other weyrwoman's eyes slid over to the Telgar riders, picking out H'nez.

Fiona was surprised by her own feelings when she noticed the other girl's look—how *dare* she? Lorana's hand tightened on her shoulder comfortingly while Fiona fought to control her jealousy—even as she sought to analyze the strength of the emotion. It wasn't like her; she had no real feelings for H'nez—did she?

Sonia took in the tableau with one quick look and smiled. "Oh."

Jeila flushed and met Sonia's eyes with a suffused look on her face.

"Tolarth is close to rising," Sonia said to Lorana by way of explanation.

"As is Fiona's Talenth," Lorana said.

Sonia held up a hand to Jeila. "Are you hoping to be Telgar's senior?"

Jeila snorted and shook her head, her free hand moving behind her toward Fiona. "I would be happy to be Fiona's second."

"Really?" Sonia said, her tone prickly with surprise.

Fiona felt somewhat vindicated by Jeila's declaration and Sonia's sudden reappraisal, but before she could fully appreciate it, Sonia angled her head toward her and asked, "And do you feel ready to assume such a burden?" She examined Fiona critically from head to toe. "You seem rather young for it."

"She was Weyrwoman at Igen," Terin spoke up, having moved, unnoticed, toward the knot of weyrwomen.

"And you are . . . ?" Sonia asked, her eyebrows raised demandingly.

"Terin was my headwoman," Fiona said. She smiled at the younger girl before explaining to Sonia, "She's a bit impetuous but she means well."

"So you *were* her headwoman," Sonia said. "And now?"

"I am," Shaneese said, stepping forward, attracted by the same play of emotions that had attracted Terin. She bowed to Sonia. "We've met before, Weyrwoman."

Sonia's eyes narrowed as she strained for recognition, then she brightened. "Shaneese! Weren't you Lina's headwoman?"

"I was," Shaneese said, a look of sadness crossing her face before she continued, "and now I'm Fiona's."

"I see," Sonia said in a doubting tone. She made a tossing-away gesture with one hand, dismissing the issue, asking Shaneese, "Do we have some time for *klah*?"

"I could bring it here," Shaneese offered, "or you could join us in the Dining Cavern."

"Come to the Cavern, Weyrwoman," Fiona said decisively, slipping her shoulder out from under Lorana's hand and grabbing it with her own to urge the ex–queen rider to accompany her. "We still have plenty of time before the Threadfall and I'd like to show you something that you might find interesting."

"Really?" Sonia repeated, clearly intrigued by Fiona's excitement.

"I'll stay here," Jeila said, glancing at H'nez, who was making final arrangements with his wings. "Until they're off."

Fiona felt that Jeila was making her some sort of offer, but she couldn't quite fathom it. She hesitated, feeling that perhaps she should wait, but Jeila waved her on. "I'll keep watch for you, Weyrwoman."

The dark-eyed woman's declaration was so firm, so warm, that Fiona smiled once more in response, nodded in agreement, and led the others off toward the Dining Cavern.

Talenth, could you ask Mekiar to attend us? Fiona asked. Beside her, Lorana jerked and Fiona realized that the other woman had heard the exchange. She clenched Lorana's hand in hers, her eyes darting up to Lorana's, dancing with joy at the notion that the other woman could share her moments with her queen.

"Talenth enjoys company," Fiona told her quietly.

"I know," Lorana responded. Her tone sounded hesitant, shy.

"What?"

"I—" Lorana began, then cut herself short, shaking her head. "Nothing."

Fiona felt Lorana's desire to drop the matter and, out of her gratitude for the other woman's sacrifices, decided not to press it even as her curiosity welled. Lorana, she was certain, was going to say something important, something that would answer a lot of Fiona's questions. She felt Lorana's hand twitch in hers and forced her thoughts into a different direction.

"This is amazing," Sonia declared as Mekiar guided her through her first finished vase, her eyes wide with the delight her fingers were reporting as they shaped the clay. She glanced longingly at Fiona, then Mekiar. "How hard would it be to set up one of these?"

"I imagine you'd have to inquire of the Mastersmith," Fiona guessed. "But Zellany may be amenable."

"You mean, he owes you for those new flamethrowers," Sonia observed.

"Actually, my lady," Mekiar told Fiona demurely, "these pottery wheels are something we make here in Telgar."

Fiona picked up on the other man's undertones and her brows rose as she inquired, "And this is a Telgar craft secret?"

"Well," Mekiar huffed, "not so much a *secret* as—"

"I understand," Sonia said, sounding deflated. She turned her head up to Mekiar, who was standing above her seat. "Perhaps you'll let me visit?"

"Weyrwoman," Mekiar said, at a loss for further words.

"Nonsense!" Fiona declared firmly. "Mekiar, too many arts were lost in the Plague. This one clearly gives such pleasure that we would be churlish not to share it."

Mekiar started to protest but Fiona forestalled him. "Weyrwoman Sonia clearly has a gift for this and will doubtless make many remarkable works that will command high trade, but there will always be a need for vases, for plates, for mugs, and I don't doubt that the glazes and colorings that will be favored by High Reaches will be quite different from those favored by us here."

Mekiar's protests died in a sigh.

"I'm sure we can convince Pellar to search out clays," Sonia suggested. "And we'd be willing to trade our clays and pigments for your wheels and expertise."

"Weyrwoman," Mekiar said, with a quizzical look toward Fiona, "it will be our pleasure."

Beside them, Lorana murmured a grunt of agreement, lost in her own forming.

From behind Mekiar, Jeila coughed delicately. "Sonia? If you're done, could I try?"

Sonia looked back down to her hands and the figure she was forming. "I'm not done yet."

Jeila sighed in resignation.

"Weyrwoman," Mekiar said, taking pity on her, "I believe we can set up another wheel before the day's end." He paused, adding, "Although if you'd like to try free-forming, you could work on the table over there."

Mekiar strode over to the clay barrel and dug up a nice lump of clay that he placed invitingly on a nearby table, arranging a pitcher of clean water close to hand.

Fiona giggled and, in explanation to all the heads turned to her in surprise, said, "Who would have thought that getting dirty could be so much fun?"

Sonia did not take her eyes off her work as she replied, "Me, for one."

"Sonia!" Jeila exclaimed in a reproving tone. The High Reaches Weyrwoman snorted in delight at the younger woman's outrage.

They've met the Benden riders, Talenth called suddenly, even as Tolarth and Lyrinth bugled loudly.

How are they doing? Fiona heard a voice ask Talenth. She glanced behind her to Lorana, who met her eyes with a wide-eyed look of amazement.

"You heard me!" Lorana said, her voice soft with shock. Fiona grabbed her hands and nodded her head.

Yes.

TWELVE

Chew stone,
Breathe fire.
Wheel, turn,
Fly higher.

Telgar Weyr, Threadfall, AL 508.2.11

With M'tal's approval and encouragement, H'nez arranged his forty dragons into two light wings, with F'jian flying with him and T'mar leading the other. D'vin of High Reaches had asked the Telgar riders to fly above the High Reaches flights until they had taken over the Fall from Benden. However, H'nez had seen how poorly the tired Benden riders were faring against the Fall and committed his two wings early.

This Thread falls strangely, Ginirth remarked minutes into the Fall. H'nez agreed but was too strained, swiveling his head in all directions to respond. The Thread did indeed fall strangely, roiled by currents of warm air rising from the tops of the mountains.

A Telgar dragon, threadscored, cried in pain before going *between.*

Zirenth, Ginirth told him. *T'mar was scored badly on the leg.*

Have F'jian take over the other wing, H'nez said, turning around in his seat to spot F'jian and make a broad arm gesture to the same effect. The young rider pumped an arm in acknowledgment and his bronze Ladirth wheeled sharply out of formation to race toward the other, now leaderless wing.

Thread was falling strangely.

Lorana's sharp intake of breath alerted Fiona just an instant before a cold prickle of dread coursed down her own spine.

"Come on!" she said, racing out of the Dining Cavern and into the Weyr Bowl.

On the far side of the Bowl, at her station near the Hatching Grounds, Terin looked up at Fiona's form, shouting, "What is it? It's too early!"

As if in answer, Talenth bugled loudly in warning and a bronze shape winked into existence.

"It's T'mar!" Fiona cried, racing toward the injured pair even as she heard Lorana and Kindan following fast behind her.

"It doesn't look too bad on this side," Lorana called after Fiona.

"It's his leg!" Terin called from her vantage point on his right side.

As though in response, T'mar raised his left hand to wave Fiona off— and that's when his riding straps broke. He plunged off Zirenth's right side.

With a cry of pure terror, Fiona put on an extra burst of speed. Terin, who was closer, was slower into motion, startled by the sudden turn of events.

Zirenth did what he could and sideslipped toward the Weyr walls in hopes of scooping up his fallen rider with his foreclaws.

The effort was well-intentioned but ill-timed. Instead of catching him, his foreclaw threw T'mar hard against the rock wall. The bronze rider went limp, bouncing off the stone to tumble toward the ground. Zirenth gave a heart-stopping cry.

Time seemed to stop for Fiona as she cried, *Don't let him go* between!

She reached with all her energy toward the panic-stricken bronze dragon even as she stretched her legs and arms in frantic motion, making a desperate attempt to get under T'mar. Somewhere in her mind she knew there was no way she could possibly catch him—she was too far away, he was too large for her, she could never take his weight—but nothing seemed to matter but getting under him and cushioning his fall.

Zirenth sideslipped away from the wall, his wings clawing for air as he tried to gain enough altitude to go *between*, unable to sense life in T'mar's body.

No! a voice cried. *I won't lose you!*

Later, Fiona couldn't say whose voice it was. She fervently added her strength to the cry even as she ran.

And then, as she saw T'mar's legs pass her outstretched arms, she felt a hand touch her shoulder and she *knew* that she would catch him, alive or not. Energy coursed through the hand and into her; it redoubled again even as a voice shouted, *Hold him! Don't let him get away!*

Fiona glanced upward and gripped Zirenth in her thoughts. The bronze dragon roared in agony and writhed in the air as though fighting off an entanglement, then gave another defiant bellow and angled his flight back down to the ground.

Time returned to normal as the weight of T'mar's body fell full onto Fiona's outstretched arms and, with a grunt of pain, she collapsed on the ground under him, his head and arms cradled on her lap.

"Don't move," Lorana ordered hoarsely.

"Are you all right?" Terin asked, her voice near hysterical.

Kindan! Fiona was surprised that she heard Lorana's call, and then the harper arrived beside her and knelt over T'mar's head. He examined it carefully, his eyes taking in everything before he moved his hands.

"We've got to get his headgear off," Kindan said. Blood was on his hands and Fiona realized with a start that T'mar's scalp was bleeding. She made to wipe it away but was halted by Kindan's harsh, "Don't move!"

Kindan turned to Terin. "Get scissors!"

Terin paused mid-stride, then turned and ran back to her station.

How is he?

"He's breathing," Kindan said, pointing to T'mar's chest. "So he's still alive."

"Look at his leg!" It was Bekka. Fiona followed the youngster's finger and was horrified to see that T'mar's right leg was not only broken from the fall but also chewed up by Thread. She could see bone near the knee.

"Bekka, get your gear," Fiona said. The girl nodded once and tore off to her station.

"I'm worried about his head and his neck," Kindan said aloud. He glanced toward Fiona. "If his neck is broken, one wrong move will kill him."

Fiona nodded, then checked the movement, afraid of jostling T'mar.

"Zirenth thought he was dead," Lorana said, her words coming with great effort.

"Not yet," Fiona said. She glanced toward Lorana. "How did you hold on to him?"

"I didn't," Lorana said in surprise. "I thought it was you."

"I thought it was you," Kindan said to Lorana. "You did much the same when you pulled Caranth back."

"I felt like I was pulled this time," Lorana said, glancing at Fiona.

"I didn't think it was me," Fiona repeated. "I thought it was you."

Terin arrived with the scissors, and a moment later, Bekka returned with her aid bag.

"Terin, Lorana, hold his head steady while I do this," Kindan said.

"What about his leg?" Bekka asked.

"Wait until I get his helmet off," Kindan said. Gently, he cut along the top seam of the wher-hide helmet, peeling it slowly away from T'mar's head. Fiona gasped when she saw what lay beneath it. "His skull's been smashed."

"Will he live?" Fiona could see the white of his skull amid the freely-flowing blood, could see thin lines where the bone had cracked, but otherwise, the wound did not look as bad as others she had seen. She had never dealt with a head wound like this. If it had been his leg, she'd have given him a month before trying him on crutches.

Kindan pursed his lips. "It will depend upon him. He's been concussed; he might be in a coma."

"That would explain Zirenth's behavior," Lorana said. "He couldn't hear T'mar, so he assumed the worst."

"If Zirenth had gone *between*, T'mar wouldn't have survived," Kindan said.

"So what do we do?" Fiona asked.

"All we can do is wrap the wound and keep an eye on him."

"We should get him to the Healer Hall," Fiona said.

"I don't think he'd survive the trip *between*."

"Then we should get a healer here," Fiona said. She gave Bekka an apologetic look as she added, "Someone who could help Bekka in her learning."

"Perhaps Ketan would come?" Lorana suggested to Kindan. The harper pursed his lips thoughtfully.

"Perhaps."

"Get a stretcher and let's get him to the infirmary," Lorana said.

"No, put him in the empty queen's weyr," Fiona said. The other two looked at her. "Zirenth will want to be near him and the stretcher-bearers can negotiate the queens' ledge easily enough."

"I'll get a stretcher," Lorana said, standing up, pausing only long enough to say to Fiona, "when I come back, I want you to take a cold bath—you strained all the muscles in your arms and back."

"I'll show you where the stretchers are," Bekka said, trotting along after her.

It was only when Lorana mentioned it that Fiona thought to take stock of her own injuries and she realized that the other woman was absolutely right. Ruefully, she asked herself, "Does she boss weyrwomen around all the time?"

"Usually," Kindan said with a grin. Fiona's eyes widened in surprise.

Lorana was back moments later with Bekka, two sturdy weyrfolk, and a stretcher. Between her, them, Kindan, and Fiona, they managed to gently place T'mar in the stretcher, his neck braced, leg straight.

Zirenth, we're putting T'mar in the other queen's weyr, Fiona called. Ahead of her, Lorana snorted, turned her head and said, "I told him already."

"You heard me talking to him, too?" Fiona asked in surprise.

"Of course."

"I thought you just heard dragons."

"Usually I do," Lorana said with a bemused look.

They reached the start of the ledge and conversation stopped as they carefully negotiated it and their way through the empty lair to the quarters beyond. T'mar was delicately moved from the stretcher onto the empty bed.

"Thank you," Fiona said to the weyrfolk, who nodded and, with a worried look toward the comatose bronze rider, left with their stretcher, heading back to the aid area.

Bekka leaned over T'mar and gently rested the back of her hand on his head for a moment, testing his temperature. When she was done, she moved her hand lower so that it hovered over his nostrils and she could feel his breath. Satisfied, she straightened up and moved back to tell Fiona, "He's not too hot, and resting gently."

"We should get back," Fiona said, turning toward the entrance even as she looked back at the stricken rider.

"I could stay with him," Lorana said. A rustle of wings and the sound of Zirenth's claws alerted them to the arrival of the bronze dragon, who quickly entered the weyr, circled once around, and poked his head through the gap between the weyr and the quarters to eye T'mar worriedly.

"I'll stay with you," Kindan told Lorana, pulling two chairs closer to the bed and gesturing for her to take one.

Fiona turned her head back to the entrance, then back once more toward T'mar, Lorana, and Kindan, giving them a quick nod before gesturing for Bekka to come with her.

As she stepped back down into the Weyr Bowl, Fiona saw Sonia with Lyrinth nearby.

"I must get back," Sonia said as she started to climb up on the gold's foreleg. She nodded toward the recently occupied queen's weyr. "There'll be injured at High Reaches soon, too."

"Do you need help?" Fiona asked, glancing around for Jeila. She spotted the swarthy weyrwoman striding toward them from the aid tables, dressed in riding gear, and waved to her. As Jeila got closer, she said, "We think alike, if you're thinking of helping at High Reaches."

Jeila smiled and nodded. "With Kindan and Lorana, I think you've got enough helping hands."

"They're with T'mar," Fiona said. She gestured toward Bekka. "But I'm sure Bekka and I can manage."

Jeila smiled at the younger girl, who smiled shyly in return, awed to be under the approving gaze of no less than three Weyrwomen.

"I'll come back as soon as I can," Jeila said, as her Tolarth landed close by.

"Stay there and rest, if you need it."

"Don't worry," Sonia said, "I won't let her fly if she's too tired."

The two queens were soon airborne, their departure cheerfully acknowledged by Talenth from her place back on the watch heights.

"Come on," Fiona said to Bekka as the two queens winked out *between*, "we should rest while we can."

She led the young girl back to the aid tables. They spotted Seban and in no time Bekka had squirmed into his lap, closed her eyes, and curled up tight against his chest.

"She's not sleeping, is she?" Fiona whispered to the ex-dragonrider in surprise.

"This is about all the sleep she ever gets," Seban said with an answering grin and an affectionate glance for his youngest. "She takes little naps, worse than a baby fire-lizard, and then she's up again, and just as much trouble."

Bekka got to nap for little more than twenty minutes before the next injured dragon arrived. Fiona had no more than finished dowsing the injured rider with numbweed before another dragon arrived and another.

Somewhere during the tumult, Talenth and the other dragons sounded the keen that indicated that a dragon had been lost, and then another, and another.

At the end of it all, H'nez, F'jian, and M'tal returned leading only twenty-six dragons and riders.

Eight others, beside T'mar, had returned beforehand. Two were severely injured and would take many months to heal, six were more lightly injured, but not so lightly that they would be able to fly for many Falls to come.

"High Reaches had it worse," M'tal said as he and the others regrouped in the Dining Cavern. He glanced around the room. "Where are Kindan and Lorana?"

H'nez heard the question and looked around, adding, "Where's T'mar?"

"He's in a coma," Fiona said. "Lorana and Kindan are keeping watch on him." She explained how he'd fallen, victim of a threadscored riding strap, how she'd caught him, but not before he'd banged his head on the rock of the weyr wall so badly that his skull had been fractured.

"It's a wonder you didn't lose Zirenth," M'tal said. "With an injury like that, the dragon wouldn't hear the rider and might think the worst."

"We nearly did," Fiona said. "I think Lorana convinced him to stay."

"Like she did with Caranth?" M'tal mused. No one who had a dragon could forget that day when Lorana had pulled all their power for her desperate failed grab for the dragons of Telgar Weyr and her subsequent successful grab of Caranth from *between*.

"Something like that."

"I should go check on him," H'nez said, forcing himself wearily to his feet.

"That's my job, wingleader," Fiona said, waving him back into his seat. "You should rest."

"You should all rest," Shaneese said, approaching the table and glancing around the nearly empty cavern. She glanced toward M'tal. "If you'd like, we can put you and your brilliant Gaminth in a weyr for the evening."

"I put T'mar in the empty queen's weyr," Fiona said apologetically, "or I'd let you have it."

M'tal rose and gave her a gracious half-bow. "I think that Gaminth will have no trouble giving me a lift to our weyr."

Fiona rose as well, pausing as H'nez rose more slowly from his chair. "Do you need a hand?"

"I'll be fine."

"Don't be such a baby," Fiona said, grabbing his arm at the elbow. "You can barely stand, much less walk."

H'nez tried to move away from her, but M'tal blocked the wing-leader's movement with a deftly timed lurch of his own.

"If anyone's watching, they'll just think that the Weyrwoman is conferring with the Weyr's senior rider," Fiona assured him.

"I need to check on the riders," H'nez protested.

"They've been seen to, my lord," Shaneese said, coming up behind them and deftly propping H'nez's other elbow. "Telgar takes care of its own."

Realizing himself overborne by both Weyrwoman and headwoman, H'nez permitted them to escort him back to his quarters.

"I'll walk you back to your quarters, too," Shaneese said as Fiona started across the Weyr Bowl.

"Thanks, but I don't—"

"You won't be as stubborn as he is, will you?" Shaneese asked, jerking her head back toward H'nez's weyr.

"No, of course not," Fiona said with a long relenting sigh.

"Wise."

Fiona waited only long enough to be certain that Shaneese wouldn't see her before she left her weyr to check on T'mar.

Zirenth roused at the sound of her feet outside his lair and regarded her quietly for a moment, his multifaceted eyes whirling a slowly green, before returning to his slumber.

Zirenth's actions alerted Kindan and Lorana. They looked up expectantly from their seats placed beside T'mar's bed.

"How is he?"

Kindan frowned. "His breathing is steady."

That description didn't sound very reassuring to her. She moved closer to the bed, standing behind Kindan's chair, to peer down on the sleeping bronze rider.

"He looks peaceful," Fiona said. She turned to Kindan. "Does he have a fever?"

Kindan shook his head; halfway through, the motion dissolved into a wide yawn. Fiona frowned toward Lorana who, as expected, followed the harper a moment later with her own yawn. With a look of exasperation, Fiona joined them a moment later.

"Where are you going to sleep?" Fiona asked, trying to imagine where to set a bed. She saw the way Kindan set his jaw and gathered that the harper and Lorana had discussed this earlier and had decided to sleep in their chairs. "Oh, no you're not."

Talenth, Fiona called, *would you be a love and ask Seban if he and Bekka can watch T'mar tonight?*

I was sleeping, Talenth responded petulantly.

Just be a dear and ask.

There was a pause before Talenth responded: *They come.*

Fiona shivered in the cooling night air. "It's too cold."

She went into the bathroom and came back out with a bundle of blankets. Kindan reached for one but Fiona pulled it away from him. "These are for Seban and Bekka."

The sound of approaching footsteps alerted them to the ex-dragonrider's approach. He was carrying his daughter cradled in his arms.

"Oh!" Fiona cried in surprise. "I didn't mean to wake you!"

Seban smiled and shook his head. "I was still awake when Talenth called." He glanced down tenderly at Bekka and added, "And she'll want to check on T'mar."

"I can kit you out with blankets," Fiona said, gesturing with a firm nod of her head for Kindan to relinquish his chair. "I'm going to take

Kindan and Lorana to my weyr, that way they'll be close by and rested if there's any need."

"That sounds wise," Seban said. He waited until Fiona was satisfied with her arrangement of blankets before taking his seat and was immediately wrapped with another set of blankets over him.

"Warm enough?" Fiona asked, wondering if they might need more blankets.

"We're fine, Weyrwoman," Seban told her with a smile.

"Then we'll take our leave of you and wish you a good rest," Fiona said, gesturing for Lorana and Kindan to precede her.

"We could sleep somewhere else," Kindan said, glancing toward Lorana for confirmation.

"What? And have *me* freeze?" Fiona retorted, stepping forward and linking her arms with the other two. "I'll sleep at the outside, so that I can be closest to Talenth," she added winningly. "The bed's so large, you two probably won't even notice me at all."

"I doubt that!" Kindan said. He glanced toward Lorana. "When she was still a child, her favorite trick was to figure out a way to get me to stay the night at Fort Hold, then crawl into bed with me." With a snort, he added, "By morning, she'd have me either on the floor or stuck in a corner."

"I've gotten older," Fiona said with a sniff. "I'm much better at sharing." She shivered again, pulling the other two closer to her and asking with wide-eyed woefulness, "Besides, you don't want me to freeze?"

"No, not after all your kindness," Lorana said. She glanced at Kindan. He frowned but said nothing.

Talenth did not stir at all as they passed her, stepping quietly into Fiona's quarters. Lorana glanced back at the golden queen, her expression unreadable. Fiona followed her gaze and was surprised to see Talenth twitching in her sleep, as though flying away in a dream.

"She'll quiet down, I'm sure," Fiona assured them as they passed into her quarters. Fiona urged the other two into bed before her and climbed in quickly after them. Settled, she turned the glows at the head of the bed and the room got dark. It wasn't long before all three were warm, and not much longer before they were asleep.

Fiona woke abruptly, alarmed. She sat up quickly, tilting her head to identify the source of the sound. A girl's voice, high, nervous, followed by a man's voice, soothing but feigning confidence.

"Zirenth, it's all right!" the man called. Seban. The girl was Bekka.

There was a roar from Zirenth followed by the sound of him launching himself skyward.

"No!" Fiona yelled, reaching across Kindan for Lorana. The other woman was instantly awake.

More bugles were heard in the Bowl outside, deep, loud, threatening. Bronzes.

"See to Talenth!" Lorana ordered, pushing Fiona out of bed in front of her. As she rolled over Kindan, she snapped to the drowsy harper, "Get up! Talenth is rising!"

Rising? Fiona thought in horrified surprise.

"Stay with her, don't let her gorge," Kindan said as he suddenly erupted into motion, joining Lorana in pushing her out of the bed.

"We have to see to Zirenth," Lorana said to him as the two stood on the cold stone floor, grimaced, and quickly found their slippers.

Kindan sprinted ahead, shouting, "We're coming!" And Fiona found herself left behind, still in shock. Lorana turned back to her at the entrance to Talenth's weyr. She mustered a soothing smile. "You'll do fine."

Fine?

Another dragon bellowed in the morning air. Talenth twitched in her sleep, turned her head toward the Bowl in puzzlement.

Fiona reached her thoughts to her queen lovingly. She jerked when her mind met a roil of emotions, of intense desires.

Echoing back from the far end of the Bowl, Fiona could dimly make out the sounds of herdbeasts crying out in surprise and fear before being silenced by the rapacious bronzes.

Talenth's eyes snapped open, whirling a brilliant, dangerous red.

Talenth!

The gold dragon turned her head toward Fiona for a moment, her whirling eyes slowing and then, with a bellow, she leaped out of her weyr, into the sky, and down toward the waiting herd.

"You mustn't let her gorge!" a voice called to her urgently. Fiona looked up in surprise. It was Kindan. He grabbed her arm and dragged her out onto the ledge. "Reach out to her, control her!"

Fiona reached—and found her jaws locked on the neck of a felled herdbeast, the hot blood enraging her. She hissed at Kindan and twitched away from him. *She* would eat this beast whole!

No, a voice called to her. The voice was strangely familiar. Lorana? *Don't let the dragon control you. Control her!*

The blood tasted so good, so hot. She could smell the fear of the dead beast, hear the rising panic of the others and she wanted more. She wanted to rend, to tear, to rip—

"No!" Fiona cried out loud. With a grunt, she lashed back at Talenth, who recoiled in surprise, then resisted as Fiona exerted herself. *Only the blood!*

No! Talenth roared, her thoughts emphasized with a bellow that filled the whole Weyr and echoed on.

Yes, Fiona thought back, tightening her grip on her bond with her dragon. *Drop it now. There's another nearby. Drink the blood. Hot blood! You want it!*

With a cry mixed equally with anger and anticipation, Talenth launched herself up high and dove on her next victim. Fiona reveled with her in her flight, in her pounce, and felt the hot, warm blood course into her veins.

Fire, she was fire. She was wind, she was heat. She was queen!

More! A voice cried and Talenth leaped again before Fiona could even wonder if the voice was hers or her dragon's. Was there any difference?

Again Talenth pounced, again she resisted, again she relented to Fiona's will.

A rush of feet punctuated the morning air and Fiona had a brief flash of anxious faces gathering around her, their excitement both arousing and threatening.

More! Talenth cried, pouncing on her fourth buck, the largest by far. She tore its throat out with a quick deft movement and drained the dying beast's blood into her waiting jaws.

Sated, she lifted her head up and cried in delight and challenge, then turned back to her kill only to startle all the waiting bronzes by launching herself in the air.

Fiona gasped as Talenth bounded into the air, her wings clawing, pulling her higher and even higher with each muscle-straining beat, up through the thick cold air of morning and into the thinner warmer air above.

With a cry of pure delight, Talenth dove and rose again, higher, and higher until even the Telgar mountains seemed only tiny dots below.

Yes! Fiona cried in exultation. *Higher, higher!*

Below them, Talenth could make out the bronzes, dots striving piteously to match her prowess.

With a bellow of anger, Talenth noted that there were only four—just four!—dragons following her. It was an insult. She was half-tempted to fly to Fort Weyr or High Reaches in search of greater honors but something held her back.

She craned her neck down again, examining her escort. There was Gaminth—a noble and wise dragon, able to lead a Weyr. And Ladirth: young, virile, able. There, leading the pack was—it was Ginirth!

Talenth let out a bellow and dove, down, down, down, scattering the group of bronzes before soaring back into the air, the strain on her wings pulling at her muscles and causing her chest to heave with the extra exertion of her climb and the thin air.

Another bellow below her. Zirenth.

There was an interesting choice.

Talenth remembered something odd about Zirenth and glanced back at the bronze once more. The dragon seemed colored differently, lighter—tired?

No, that wasn't it. Talenth flipped a quick circle on her wingtip, reversing her course and allowed herself a squawk in pleasure when the bronzes only noticed moments later.

She dove again, this time directing herself toward Zirenth, curious.

Ginirth bellowed a challenge, climbed up toward her, and reached for her with his claws, but she folded her wings and slipped by him easily.

Nearby Gaminth roared in delight and turned sharply to give chase.

Ladirth was last, flagging.

Zirenth was ahead of her and, to her surprise and consternation, the bronze beat away from her, pulling farther away.

With a roar of outrage, Talenth put on a burst of speed and clawed her way up beside him.

Just as she looked toward him again, to issue a challenge and a triumph, the bronze flipped himself on his side, his claws reaching out for her and grasping her tightly.

Talenth screamed in surprise at the maneuver and then—

They were falling, rolling over and over, Zirenth on top, then on bottom, Talenth on top in his stead. As they plummeted, Zirenth would beat his wings when he was on top, his bugle challenging her to emulate him.

Intrigued, Talenth tried and discovered that their plummet became a dance in the air. She bellowed in delight and then—

Zirenth's neck twined around hers, his tail about hers and—

They were one.

And more.

Fiona felt the explosion of pleasure, the primal lust sated, and found herself clinging tightly, passionately, lost in the moment that reflected the joining of the dragons thousands of lengths above. Just as Talenth was locked with Zirenth, she was locked with—

Who?

"It is time to bring them home," a voice spoke low in her ear, respectful, soothing, loving. Lorana.

The man whose body was wrapped around hers was too short to be T'mar. Fiona recovered her senses enough to realize that T'mar was still in bed, eyes slitted open but otherwise motionless.

Who?

An arm touched her shoulder, soft, warm, not the man holding her. Fiona felt the love of that touch. Even as she started to recover from the frenetic events that had so completely controlled her, Fiona recognized the depth of that love. And as she did, with a mental gasp, she knew without doubt whose body was twined around hers.

Kindan.

Don't, a voice touched her softly, stilling her incipient alarm. The voice sounded something like the strange voice Fiona had heard so many times before, but she realized, just then, that it was only Lorana's voice; it had none of the echo she had come to associate with that other voice.

Kindan must have felt her stiffen, for he suddenly surged backward, away from her.

"No," Lorana spoke aloud. Fiona felt the arm that had touched her shoulder slide around her side and felt the tension as Lorana moved her body closer to them, holding them together in her arms. "This is my moment, too."

We must bring them home now, Lorana continued in thought. Fiona reached out to Talenth and felt, to her surprise, not just Zirenth but the presence of Lorana and Kindan, and the fainter presence of T'mar all bonded with the bronze and, through him, with her.

We must come back now, Fiona said to Talenth. She felt her gold's languorous response, Zirenth's delicate, loving agreement, and then the two broke their grasp, spun upright, and started a glide back toward the Weyr.

Fiona opened her eyes quickly to see Kindan's blue eyes focused intently on her. She settled her clothes. Kindan blew a rueful snort but followed her actions. When she glanced up again, he was looking at her once more, his eyes dancing.

"You arranged this, didn't you?"

"Kindan!" Lorana said. "When dragons rise, passion flies."

"You felt it," Fiona said to Lorana. "You felt it all."

"I did," Lorana agreed. She looked to Kindan. "And you felt Zirenth's passion. You responded as a dragonrider."

"But T'mar—"

They all turned guiltily toward the still form of the bronze rider.

"I saw his eyes open earlier," Fiona said.

Kindan frowned.

"I felt him," Lorana said. She turned to Kindan. "I think the mating flight roused him."

"One would hope," Kindan replied feelingly.

Outside, the air darkened and Zirenth landed on the ledge. They drew aside to allow the bronze dragon entrance to his weyr. He blew a quick breath of thanks in their direction, peered into T'mar's quarters, and made a soft, wistful sound at his still form, then curled up swiftly into a deep sleep.

A bugle from nearby alerted them that Talenth had also returned, and at a motion from Fiona, they moved outside to watch the gold land and scamper into her weyr.

"You were marvelous!" Fiona called as they entered after her. Talenth turned to greet them, her eyes whirling with the green of contentment, her body radiating a newfound strength and maturity.

I'm tired.

"Get some rest, love, you earned it."

"We should get someone to check on T'mar—" Kindan began, only to be interrupted by the sound of feet approaching from Fiona's quarters.

"The flight went well?" Seban asked, his arm draped over his daughter's shoulders. Close behind were M'tal and H'nez, who had left the room when their dragons had lost their chase of Talenth.

"Zirenth flew her," Kindan said in answer to the ex-dragonrider's unspoken question.

Seban's eyes widened. "Zirenth? And T'mar?"

"Please check on him," Fiona said. Seban nodded quickly, his expression full of curiosity. Fiona took pity on him, blushing lightly as she said, "Zirenth flew Talenth with aid from Kindan and Lorana."

"A good mating flight," M'tal's voice boomed out. He nodded toward Fiona respectfully.

"But it solves nothing," H'nez said, brooding. "Zirenth flew Talenth: Does that make T'mar Weyrleader?"

"So it would seem," M'tal agreed.

"But he is not capable," H'nez protested. He gestured irritably toward Fiona, Kindan, and Lorana. "So incapable that we don't see him where he should be."

"He was there," Fiona said softly. "And what he could not do himself, he ceded to Kindan for him."

"He's not even a dragonrider—how can we call *him* Weyrleader?"

"This discussion needs to come later," M'tal declared, pointing H'nez toward the door. "Now it is time for the dragons to return to the weyrs, and for their riders to rest."

"Hmmph!" H'nez snorted, but he preceded the other bronze riders to the exit.

"Kindan?" Seban repeated, glancing toward the harper in surprise.

"Lorana can talk with any dragon," Kindan said, his own face flushing with embarrassment, "and formed a link with Zirenth into which I was drawn."

Seban glanced at Fiona, then back to the harper. A smile blossomed on his face. "Then congratulations are due to all!"

"T'mar stirred, I think, during the flight," Fiona said. "Would you please check on him and keep him company?"

"Of course."

What now? Fiona asked herself as she eased into the warm tub. What do I do now? I didn't mean for this to happen.

Lorana and Kindan had a bond; she had no right imposing herself on it. And yet . . . if it hadn't been for Lorana, T'mar's Zirenth would have gone *between* forever, and just as surely as the dragon died, the rider would have been lost with him.

She couldn't lose T'mar. She cared for him too much. And the Weyr needed him, needed him as Weyrleader. H'nez was too rigid, too much like the old leadership.

But . . . Lorana. What about her? Surely she deserved better than—

Don't.

Talenth? Fiona thought, reaching out to her queen only to find the slow, steady sleepy feeling in return. The gold was asleep. Lorana?

Lorana had given her a gift beyond measure when she'd arrived with the cure to the dragon sickness: She'd saved her beloved Talenth. And now, she'd given another priceless gift again. Was that what Tenniz meant with:

A dragon gold is only the first price . . . ?

Was this part of the price Lorana must pay? Fiona's brows furrowed in anger at the thought. No, she would not let it be. She was no thief of hearts, and she would do everything to avoid hurting this woman, who had paid so much already.

With determination, she scrubbed herself down, rinsed, and rose from the bath, dressing quickly. She needed to be seen by the rest of Weyr and to check with Shaneese in the Dining Cavern. Besides, she was sure that Kindan and Lorana would be grateful for some time to themselves.

She went through Talenth's weyr to check on the sleeping queen, who looked well-pleased with herself even as she snored, deep in slumber.

"Good flight, Weyrwoman!" J'gerd called as he spied her entering the Dining Cavern.

"Thank you!"

It was the first of many such accolades Fiona accepted, maintaining a graceful air even while entertaining the notion sardonically that she had had very little to do with the outcome.

As if in answer, the ex-dragonrider, Mekiar, sat gruffly next to her, nodded brusquely in her direction, saying, "Seen many mating flights. You did well, didn't let her gorge, let her fly high, made it look easy."

Fiona found her cheeks heating at the potter's compliment.

"You did well," M'tal chimed in agreement as he pulled up the chair opposite Mekiar and sat.

"I'd be surprised at any less than thirty eggs, and a queen among 'em," Shaneese added from behind Fiona's shoulder, startling Fiona with her quiet approach. The headwoman reached around Fiona and set a plate of fresh scrambled eggs in front of her and another plate of fresh, hot rolls to the side. As a garnish, she plopped down a small bowl of sliced red peppers.

"Try them if you need more waking," Shaneese challenged.

"Fresh *klah* should be enough," Fiona said, eyeing the red hot peppers warily.

"How many mating flights have *you* seen?" Shaneese snorted disrepectfully.

Fiona shook her head in acknowledgment but reached instead for the black pepper and sprinkled some on her eggs.

"If this isn't enough, I'll try the other," Fiona promised. She took a mouthful and savored it, closing her eyes in relish. When she opened them again to reach for another bite, she noticed M'tal eyeing her thoughtfully.

"How long have you been tired?" he asked, his voice soft but not concealing some intense urgency.

"Ever since I Impressed Talenth," Fiona said with a shrug. "I thought it was from timing it back to Igen."

"Do you get edgy, irritable?"

"Sleepy, muzzy-headed," Fiona said. "Some days worse than others." She couldn't suppress a grin. "Today, I feel more awake than not."

M'tal shared her grin with one of his own.

"T'mar felt the same, and many of the weyrlings," Fiona said, wondering what had caused the bronze rider to consider this particular issue interesting.

"Headaches?"

"Yes," Fiona said, her eyes narrowing. "Do you know something?"

"Tullea had similar symptoms," M'tal said, stirring in his chair, a frown on his face. "She had been acting odd pretty much since she'd Impressed her Minith—three Turns back."

"And?" Fiona asked, raising a hand and motioning peremptorily for the ex-weyrleader to continue.

M'tal's eyes flashed briefly with amusement before he continued, "Sometimes, Weyrwoman, you have flashes of her behavior."

"I take it you don't approve."

"Only when it's uncalled for," M'tal said. He waited for her response, but she merely smiled at the gibe and pleaded with her eyes for him to continue. M'tal relented, pursing his lips for a moment as he recovered his thoughts, before saying, "Now I wonder if some of your behaviors aren't related in another way."

"Timing?"

"Tullea went back three Turns in our time to High Reaches Weyr," M'tal said. "It seems that being in the same time caused her bad temper in both times."

"But we went *back* in time—" Fiona began in protest.

"So far," M'tal agreed.

"You think that perhaps some time soon we will go back in time again? Now?" A moment later, Fiona expanded, "I mean to *this* now? Why?"

"I have no idea."

Fiona distracted herself with another bite of food. She chewed carefully and took a drink of her *klah* before continuing, "What effect would timing have on Talenth?"

"I don't know," he said with a frown. "I assume that you're referring to her eggs."

Fiona nodded and then sighed, shaking her head. "I can't see myself leaving Talenth with a clutch on the Hatching Grounds."

"Perhaps you will take her someplace else," Mekiar said, looking from Weyrwoman to bronze rider and back.

"But where?" Fiona asked. "It can't be Igen—there are riders recovering all through the last ten Turns."

"Perhaps it is something else," M'tal said, his expression troubled.

"Else?" Fiona said. "Worse?"

"It's never wise to borrow trouble," Mekiar reminded them.

Fiona snorted acidly. "No, certainly when we've enough of our own already!"

A noise from the entrance attracted her attention and she turned in time to see Kindan and Lorana saunter through the entrance. Something in Lorana's walk made Fiona curious and she sent a thought toward

Talenth, only to find her queen still deep in slumber. Thwarted, Fiona tried an experiment and focused her attention on Lorana.

The dark-haired woman glanced up toward her, her eyes dancing, cheeks flushed.

Caranth flew Minith!

Fiona whipped her head back around to catch M'tal's eyes, but the bronze rider showed no signs of having heard the news.

"Caranth flew Minith," Fiona told him. "Did you know?"

M'tal looked abstracted for a moment, then shook his head. "No, Gaminth is still sleeping." He quirked his eyebrows up at her. "How did you know?"

Fiona turned her head toward the approaching pair and M'tal followed her gaze.

"You guessed?" he said. "Just because they're late?"

"Lorana can talk to any dragon," Fiona said by way of broaching her new notion.

"Yes."

"That's rare, very rare," Mekiar said, glancing toward the approaching couple. "The last one who could was Torene of Benden, wasn't she?"

"I believe so," M'tal said with a note of home pride in his voice. "But, as far as I know from the Records, Torene could only hear and talk to the dragons." He paused, forcing a quick grimace from his face. "It appears that Lorana can also *feel* the dragons."

"It's not *all* bad," Lorana said as she and Kindan drew within earshot. Kindan gestured for her to take the seat near M'tal while he strode quickly to sit opposite her beside Mekiar.

"Did you say that Caranth flew Minith?" Fiona asked, even as Shaneese efficiently bustled about with two more place settings and fresh mugs.

Lorana grinned, her eyes dancing. "You heard! I thought maybe you did, but I wasn't sure!"

I heard, Fiona thought, glancing at Lorana and smiling when she noticed the woman's reaction. She turned to M'tal. "If a person can talk to all dragons, is there any reason that they might not also be able to talk to people the same way?"

M'tal turned to Lorana, then back to Fiona. "*She* told you?"

Before Fiona could respond, Lorana gave a large gasp and turned to M'tal. "Quickly, Jeila comes! The bronzes—"

M'tal jerked in unison to a loud, raucous bellow, which was instantly reinforced by several others.

"The bronzes are blooding their kills!" J'gerd shouted from near the doorway.

"T'mar!" Fiona cried, rushing out of her chair.

"No, stay here!" Lorana called to her, jumping to her feet. "Kindan, come with me." She assured Fiona, "We'll go to him."

Fiona nodded once quickly in agreement and waited until they had turned the corner out of the Cavern's entrance and out of her sight before sitting back down with a heavy sigh.

"I've never heard of so many mating flights in one day," Mekiar said, his eyes rheumy with pain. He rose from his seat slowly and raised a hand invitingly to Fiona. "Perhaps you'd care to join me in some clay?"

It took Fiona a moment to recognize that the ex-dragonrider was offering her a chance to throw some pots on a potter's wheel. The thought of sensuously occupying her hands and mind was deeply appealing to her. She smiled and reached for his hand.

They were seated and deeply engrossed in their work when Jeila's Tolarth bellowed near the Star Stones, her tone lustful.

Tell them to meet in Zirenth's weyr, Fiona thought hastily to Lorana, anxious about the one time when she, as Weyrwoman, couldn't perform her duties as Weyrwoman.

Fiona was relieved to hear Tolarth glide toward the queen's wing before tearing off to bellow challengingly in the pasture at the far end of the Weyr. She caught a fleeting snatch of thought from Lorana, partly accepting, mostly amused, and snorted as she realized that the older woman would probably have selected that course of action without Fiona's prodding, and had gathered the bronze riders in Zirenth's weyr.

Her concentration faltered and she twitched in her seat, feeling the urge to rise, to be there, to help Jeila who was not much older than herself, to know that T'mar and Zirenth were all right—

"Stay here, Weyrwoman," Mekiar's voice came to her, calmly, firmly. She glanced at the ex-rider.

"Your dragon is only sleeping now," Mekiar reminded her. "This is Tolarth's time. You don't need me telling you the dangers of fighting queens."

Fiona forced herself to sit back down, nodding slowly. She sent a quiet, fleeting tendril of thought toward Talenth and was glad to note that the gold was still slumbering, although her dreams were clearly becoming influenced by the sounds and emotions rising around her. Fiona realized that she, too, was feeling those emotions and found her breath quickening when she heard Tolarth's challenging bugle warble as the queen soared into the sky above.

"If you put your mind to it, the clay can be your lover," Mekiar told her softly. "Done right, you can make the most beautiful works."

"How?" Fiona asked, aware of the rising emotions all around her, filling the Weyr as the bronze dragons—including one from High Reaches and another from Benden—bellowed and leaped into the air after the challenging queen.

"Close your eyes, still your breathing, put your mind in your fingers, shape the clay with your thoughts," Mekiar told her calmly. She drew a breath to ask for more guidance but he forestalled her. "Hush now! Quiet, close your eyes. This is a time of silence."

Fiona closed her eyes and—found herself soaring through the air. Startled, she opened them again. Zirenth, she had been with Zirenth. She reached out to Lorana, felt a welcoming echo tinged with concern and forced herself, regretfully, to withdraw once more.

"Lorana and Kindan are flying with Zirenth," Fiona said quietly.

"It would have to be, if T'mar is still unconscious," Mekiar replied, his tone not wholly devoid of emotion but also not overwhelmed by it. "Ride with them if you wish."

Fiona caught some hint of disapproval—no, it was less than that—in the older man's tone. Caution.

Fiona thought she understood even as she felt the passions grow. She forced her feelings back to her fingers, felt the clay, reached for some cool, wet water with which to slick up the shape she was working and felt her fingers flow once more over the shape as her leg pumped the wheel round and round.

Even as her fingers reported their sensations, Fiona felt a counter pull from high above her as wings beat, hearts pounded, lungs pumped, all joyfully, purposely. Tension grew, threatened to pull her apart until— finally—

Fiona felt the maleness of Kindan come to her through her connection with Lorana. She felt T'mar's steady, calm breathing, felt the passion of his breath on her cheek, felt the roar of the wind high in the sky above, felt Lorana's heat as she stood next to Kindan, felt Zirenth's growing elation—mixed with approval—felt herself at the potter's wheel, felt—

Suddenly she gasped and opened her eyes. The clay was a misshapen mess, all mashed together.

"Sometimes that happens, too," Mekiar said softly from beside her, his words sounding somewhat forced. She looked up at him and he smiled calmly, then she saw his work.

He must have stopped spinning his wheel early on. For on his wheel stood a mix of wings and limbs, as though dragons and riders were each clutched in the same mating embrace.

He frowned at it. "I'm not sure if that'll fire well."

"It's beautiful all the same," Fiona said, even as her breathing returned to normal.

"I'm afraid we can't keep it," Mekair said sadly, folding the wings inward and slowly lumping the shape back into a ball. "Some beauty is only for an instant, to be admired just in the moment."

Fiona nodded in understanding. "Thank you for sharing it with me."

"My pleasure as well, in your company," the ex-dragonrider said.

From on high, a loud contented bellow filled the sky.

"Ginirth," Fiona said.

"About as I would have expected," Mekiar said. Fiona raised an eyebrow at him questioningly. "There was a way the lass looked at the lad, and she came back here on purpose."

Fiona nodded once more in understanding. Then a thought struck her. "And me? Could you tell?"

Mekiar smiled. "You, Weyrwoman, love everyone."

Fiona looked at him in confusion.

"It's your way," he told her gently. "And it would be foolish to deny it." He saw the pained look in her eyes and added, "If your heart is big enough, there is nothing better than to love as many as you can."

"And is my heart big enough?"

"Only you know the answer to that."

THIRTEEN

Bronze and gold,
Fleet and bold.
Entwined as one,
Passion's done.

Telgar Weyr, morning, AL 508.2.13

"So, Jeila plans to stay here," M'tal said as he saw her and H'nez arrive for breakfast the next morning.

Fiona glanced over at the two, nodding and smiling encouragingly in their direction. Jeila responded with a big grin while H'nez merely gave her a dignified nod. Jeila leaned in close to the taller bronze rider and said something that Fiona didn't catch. H'nez jerked upright, then glanced down in surprise at the diminutive woman by his side. Jeila looked back toward Fiona, shaking her head ruefully, but her eyes were dancing.

"She seems to have him well in hand," M'tal said quietly even as Jeila changed their direction toward the head table.

"Weyrwoman," H'nez said stiffly as they approached. Fiona schooled her expression, gesturing to empty seats, saying, "Wingleader, please join us."

H'nez sat woodenly, seeming surprised at the offer.

"A good flight, from all accounts," M'tal said, nodding to Jeila and H'nez. He grinned at the tall, thin bronze rider and added, with a gleam in his eyes, "Although you'd best be careful next time. Gaminth swears that he's got the way of it with two mating flights in the same day."

H'nez regarded the ex-weyrleader seriously for a moment until Jeila's snort alerted him that M'tal was joking.

"Ginirth is ready any time, sir," H'nez said, joining into the spirit of things.

"Two queens on the Hatching Grounds at the same time," M'tal said. "I don't think I remember a time when such ever happened at Benden."

"Kindan and Lorana insisted on spending time in the Records Room to see if they found any Records of that occurring here," Fiona said. She smiled at Jeila, as she added, "But I'm not worried: Neither Talenth nor Tolarth seem at all concerned."

"I'm hoping for a queen egg and thirty others," Jeila said, as she snagged a roll and put it on H'nez's plate. She gestured for the butter, which M'tal pushed in her direction, and lathered the roll with it copiously before pushing it toward H'nez's mouth. The bronze rider looked askance at the treatment until he caught the look in his mate's eyes, and resignedly took the roll and ate it whole. She nodded appreciatively as he did, saying, "You need some more padding if you're going to continue to share a weyr with me." To Fiona, she said, "I thought *I* was bony!"

"Petite," H'nez corrected her, his near hand reaching unconsciously for hers. "Thin-boned."

"Perhaps for not much longer," Jeila said, glancing up doe-eyed at the bronze rider. "Will you still want me when I get all bloated with child?"

"You're with child?" H'nez asked, his eyes going round with alarm. "I mean, we just—I didn't think—"

Jeila's chuckles silenced him and, as he strove to recover his composure, H'nez looked around the table daring anyone to comment on his reaction. Taking pity on her mate, Jeila turned to Fiona, saying, "And how about you, Weyrwoman?"

H'nez cleared his throat hastily in alarm. Jeila leaned over to him and he bent down for another whispered conversation. When he straightened up again, Jeila was looking in Fiona's direction with great interest.

"That must have been quite a mating flight," the smaller weyrwoman told her.

"It was," Fiona agreed.

"And how is T'mar?"

"When I checked on him this morning, he seemed better," Fiona said, working to keep her worry out of her voice.

"Seemed?"

"You were there in his quarters during your mating flight," Fiona reminded her. Jeila glanced up at H'nez, as if to check his response, before nodding in agreement.

"I didn't pay much attention to T'mar or anyone in the room," Jeila said. She pursed her lips as she added thoughtfully, "Except that I was surprised, at first, to see Lorana there and not you—and then I was suddenly grateful to have someone there talking me through Tolarth's gorging."

Fiona nodded sympathetically. Her eyes caught Jeila's and the two shared a moment of understanding, tabling parts of the discussion for a time when they could be alone together. Again, Fiona found herself warming to this kind, perceptive person.

"Anyway, Seban said that afterward, he thought he heard T'mar murmur something," Fiona said, returning to their original topic.

"He spoke?" M'tal asked, surprised. "What did he say?"

"'Three times,'" Fiona answered, trying and failing to hide her blush.

"Three times?" H'nez repeated in confusion. "What does that signify?"

"I, when we were back at Igen, I decided that I needed some . . . instruction." Fiona found herself blushing even redder.

"With T'mar?" Jeila asked, her eyebrows arching high. She pursed her lips tightly, even though there was a definite upward curve to them, before adding judiciously, "From all I've heard, he would have been an excellent instructor."

"Anyway, as with all his lessons, I insisted that we perform the exercise three times," Fiona finished lamely.

"I see," H'nez said, his voice more diplomatically neutral than Fiona had thought possible. He glanced at her, asking, "So you feel that he was recalling the same reference?"

"A third mating flight will revive him?" M'tal wondered. He furrowed his brow. "Here or could it be any queen's mating?"

"Because Minith and Caranth—" Fiona began thoughtfully only to find herself interrupted by a sudden call from Talenth. *Come quickly!*

"I must go," Fiona said, rising from her chair. "Talenth wants me in T'mar's quarters."

Fiona raced across the Weyr Bowl toward the queens' ledge. Her intent expression was such that weyrfolk and dragonriders alike veered out of her way, rather than delivering polite greetings and congratulations on the multiple mating flights. She acknowledged their kindness with a quick smile and a wave, keeping her pace quick and her course firm.

She was so quick that she was breathless by the time she made it up the ledge, past her quarters, Jeila's quarters, and finally to the queen's quarters that had been allocated to the injured bronze rider and his dragon.

Zirenth regarded her warily as she approached, his head flinching away from her, his eyes whirling a slow, steady red.

In T'mar's quarters, Fiona found Seban, Bekka, Lorana, and Kindan all huddled around the dragonrider's bed.

"What is it?" Fiona asked, edging her way in to look down at T'mar.

He was sweating and tossing from side to side.

"I don't know," Kindan said, shaking his head. "Seban called me when he first noticed and T'mar's been getting steadily worse." His blue eyes met Fiona's, his expression somber. "With a head injury, there's a great deal of pain, headaches, nausea, and sometimes memory loss."

"Memory loss?" Fiona said, wondering how much T'mar might forget.

"Lorana and I were looking for similar cases in the Records," Kindan said. By his tone, Fiona gathered that he hadn't found any matches and that what he had found was disturbing. "Sometimes a serious knock on the head can cause the loss of months of memories. Most often the memories return slowly over time."

"Most often?"

"Sometimes they don't," Kindan said, confirming her worst fear. "The Records suggest that a person who is in familiar surroundings recovers quicker than those who are in a strange location." He waved at the quarters here. He grimaced as he added, "Also, the presence of a long-term relationship, a partner of long standing, has been shown to aid recovery."

"Is this why he's thrashing about so?"

"No," Kindan said, shaking his head. "There was no mention of this in the Records."

"Among those who survived," Lorana added darkly. She glanced to Kindan, saying, "Tell her the rest."

Kindan sighed heavily, and beckoned for Fiona to bend her ear close to his mouth, as he whispered, "A person who doesn't regain consciousness in the first day rarely survives at all."

"But why is he moving so? He seems upset," Fiona protested. "And didn't Seban hear him speak earlier? Isn't that a good sign?"

Her eyes narrowed as she examined T'mar closely. Pushing the others aside so that she could kneel, she grabbed his hand and leaned over his face, trying to follow the movements of his lips.

"Three times, is that it, T'mar?" Fiona asked. She was certain that his hand had spasmed briefly around hers.

"If we have to wait for another mating flight, half a Turn or more, he won't make it," Kindan said.

"No, not here," Fiona said, rising and turning to examine Zirenth. "Fort."

"Fort?" Kindan said. "I've heard nothing of Melirth rising."

Lorana's eyes grew distant for a moment and then she grabbed Kindan's arm and pulled him away forcibly, crying, "Come on!"

"Where are we going?" Kindan asked, holding his ground with a worried look toward T'mar.

"We're going to Fort!" Lorana said, dragging him after her. "The bronzes are blooding their kills. We have to get there in time."

"But you don't know the coordinates!" Seban cried in warning.

"I do," Fiona said, turning to start after them.

Stay here, Lorana told her. *Just give us the image.* Aloud, she said, "Zirenth! Rouse yourself, we're going to Fort Weyr!"

To Fiona's surprise, the bronze dragon stood up quickly and raced out of his weyr, jumping over the queens' ledge and sidling up close to it, ready to receive Kindan and Lorana.

"You've no straps!" Fiona cried.

"Then we'd better not fall off!" Lorana said, increasing her pace into a full sprint. Kindan followed her lead, his reluctance lost.

"What are they doing?" Bekka asked in confusion. She gestured toward T'mar. "All the noise seems to have made him worse."

"No," Seban said, "not the noise, the dragons at Fort." He glanced up at Fiona in confirmation. "He knows that the bronzes are blooding their kills."

"Yes," Fiona said. Outside she heard Zirenth's bellow and the sound of the bronze beating his way into the air, then silence. The bronze, with Lorana and Kindan as his riders, went *between* to Fort Weyr.

"But if they're blooding their kills now, how will Zirenth arrive in time for the mating flight?" Bekka asked. "Won't he need to blood kills, too?"

"Yes he will," Seban said. He shot a glance toward Fiona before adding, "Which is why Weyrwoman Fiona sent them *back* in time."

Fiona took a deep breath and nodded, hoping that Lorana had realized her intent.

A noise from T'mar caused all eyes to turn to him.

"I'll watch him now," Fiona said.

Seban caught her eyes and nodded, placing his hands on Bekka's shoulders and guiding his daughter toward Zirenth's weyr and the queens' ledge.

"He shouldn't exert himself too much, Weyrwoman," the ex-dragonrider cautioned her.

"I understand."

"If you have Talenth call us when it's over, we'll see about changing his bandages," Bekka said, a hopeful look flashing across her face when she mentioned Talenth. Fiona smiled and nodded, guessing how exciting it was for the youngster to have Telgar's senior queen talk to *her*.

Fiona was pleased to realize that there was a little girl still lurking inside Bekka's earnest, adult demeanor.

Her eyes dancing at this revelation, Fiona nodded in agreement, keeping her eyes on T'mar while their footsteps faded away. She turned then, to look at his bandaged leg. Yes, Bekka was not mistaken, the leg would need re-bandaging soon. Fiona frowned as she compared T'mar's still body with the lively, energetic dragonrider she knew.

Kindan's words came back to her: "A person who doesn't regain consciousness in the first day rarely survives at all."

But if T'mar didn't survive, what would happen to Zirenth? Would the bronze remain, bonded to Lorana and Kindan? And what of the Weyr? How would the riders react to having someone like Kindan, a respected harper indeed but no dragonrider, in the position of Weyrleader?

Would Kindan stay? Would Lorana want to stay, under those circumstances? Why did they want to stay now, anyway?

For a moment Fiona regretted Talenth's choice of mate and the strange outcome that had produced.

But was it Talenth, really? Fiona asked herself, recalling her thoughts from the day before. How much of the outcome had been her own desire?

You love Kindan, she told herself. You always have.

Ah, but how much of it was because he was safe? she taunted herself. How much because he was always there, out of reach, a constant reminder of things lost, of hopes never achieved?

He had Lorana now.

And you would poach his love away from her? she chided herself.

It's only poaching if you refuse to share, the thought came to her with the force of the spoken word. This was not herself, Fiona realized, this was Lorana.

I would never hurt you!

I know, Lorana responded. Fiona got the impression that Lorana was straining, exerting herself, and needed to focus solely on the events immediately before her. With a soft touch, Fiona released the attachment, with the gentle wish that Lorana be happy.

"What am I?" Fiona asked herself aloud. Did other queen riders behave this way? Had there ever been such a connection? What would happen? How could she handle this?

Below her, she heard a change in T'mar's breathing and looked down. The bronze rider's face was contorted in a mixture of pain and pleasure. Touched by his pain and wishing to help, Fiona used her free hand to stroke his cheek.

"Fiona." The word was the barest whisper.

"I'm here," she assured him even as her heart leaped and her mind struggled with yet another worry: Do I love him?

"Three times," T'mar breathed.

"Yes, three times," Fiona agreed quietly. "Melirth rises. Zirenth is there."

"Cisca?" T'mar's brow furrowed, his expression troubled. "I love her."

"Of course," Fiona said. T'mar's expression eased, his lips curling up slightly. Why shouldn't he love her?

Just then, a wave of emotion engulfed Fiona. A murmur from T'mar proved that he had felt it, too.

T'mar's hand spasmed around hers.

Gently, tenderly, with a passion no less intense for her controlling focus, Fiona traced his face with the fingers of her other hand. She traced his brows, which boldly framed thoughtful, passionate eyes, his gentle cheeks, the firm line of his nose, the sweet curve of his lips.

She could see the child still in the man and railed that she'd never had a chance to meet T'mar when he was younger. She could see, mirrored in the crow's feet around his eyes, the easy smile, the long days spent squinting against the brilliant sun, the pain of friends lost, wounds not healed.

"I love you." The words were hers. And, in saying them, she realized it to be true. He was a hard taskmaster, a person steadfast in his convictions, sometimes angry, always thoughtful, often kind. But, as his heart beat, so did hers.

"Kindan?" T'mar's question was barely above a whisper but the name was spoken clearly.

"I love him, too," Fiona said. She gave him a sad smile. "You'll have to make do with someone who loves more than one man."

"'Course, you're a Weyrwoman," T'mar said, struggling to open his eyes. "'S your job."

"Shh!" Fiona whispered, gently rubbing his brow. "Close your eyes, you've got to rest, regain your strength."

"As you say, Weyrwoman."

She moved back then, thinking to call Bekka and Seban, but his hand tightened around hers once more, begging.

"Rest, and I'll stay with you a bit longer," she told him softly. "You've had a nasty fall, near smashed your skull. You might have headaches or worse, so rest easy."

Again, his hand tightened on hers in an unspoken plea.

With a sigh, Fiona relented, not too reluctantly, and resumed her examination of his tanned face, looking more lively now with just the slight animation that his consciousness provided it.

They remained that way until she heard the noise of Zirenth's return and, not without misgivings, had Talenth send for Bekka and Seban.

Footsteps, a pair of them, approached from Zirenth's weyr and when a hand reached gently for her shoulder, she reached up behind her and clasped it gratefully.

"He woke," she said quietly, even as Kindan came into view at her side. "He spoke."

"That's good," Kindan said, sounding weary.

"I've sent for Seban and Bekka," she told them. She smiled at the fatigue in Kindan's voice. "You two should get some rest, timing it is very exhausting."

Lorana snorted humorously. "To say nothing of mating flights!"

The sound of another two sets of feet, one quicker and softer than the other, heralded the arrival of Seban and Bekka.

"He woke?" Seban asked as he joined them. Fiona nodded. Seban gestured to her politely and, reluctantly, she released T'mar's hand and stood back, allowing Bekka and Kindan to examine him.

Kindan's face was lined with more than exhaustion when he was finished.

Fiona met his eyes demandingly and the older man gave her an astonished look in response. "What is it?"

"I don't know," Kindan said. "I'd like to send for Tintoval."

Talenth? Are you up for a flight? Fiona asked her dragon. *We should pay our respects to Melirth and Cisca.*

Talenth's response was an enthusiastic, *Of course!*

"I'll see if she'll come," Fiona told him. She nodded to him and Lorana. "You two should get some rest—"

"A bath first," Lorana said wistfully.

"Just be careful not to fall asleep in it," Fiona warned. "Timing it can make you *that* tired."

Lorana raised an eyebrow in surprise, then nodded compliantly when she saw that Fiona was deadly serious.

Fiona was still so concerned with their weariness that she put off her departure until they were both safely in bed.

"Are you going to tuck us in?" Kindan teased sleepily.

Fiona shook her head silently, her face going red. She quietly put on her riding gear, went to Talenth's weyr, put on and double-checked the riding straps, and then urged her queen out to the queens' ledge.

Talenth was glad of the exercise, even though Fiona could feel that the gold had some muscles that were still sore from the previous day's exertions. To warm her up, Fiona had Talenth do a slow, lazy circuit above the Weyr before fixing the image of Fort Weyr firmly in her mind and giving Talenth the order to go *between*.

The cold of *between* was a tonic to Fiona, seeming to banish all the nagging thoughts that had been quietly demanding her attention. She counted slowly to herself, one, two, three—

And burst out above Fort Weyr without any bother. The watch dragon challenged her and Talenth bugled a response, the watch rider waving at her. Fiona waved back, surprised to see V'lex again, even though it hadn't yet been a fortnight since their return from their journey back in time to Igen Weyr.

Fiona smiled to herself as she remembered the mating flight of V'lex's green Sarinth; the first mating flight she'd ever experienced after her Impression of Talenth. Beneath her, Talenth rumbled in amusement.

Soon, you'll be a mother, Fiona thought to her queen with a mixture of pride and teasing.

I'll clutch, Talenth corrected her, adding wistfully, *maybe there will be a queen egg.*

Or two!

Two would be more, Talenth observed abstractedly. All the same, Fiona understood her dragon's meaning: While two would be good, it would be more than Talenth could imagine.

It was another question for the Records, Fiona thought as she guided Talenth in a spiral down to the Weyr Bowl below. Did queens ever produce two gold eggs in the same Hatching?

The thought of two queen eggs hardening on the Hatching Sands brought another thought—would Lorana stand again? Briefly Fiona entertained the notion of Lorana dragon-borne, smiling and waving as she soared on a beautiful gold. Or would it hurt too much?

Fiona pushed the question from her mind, uncertain of how much of her thoughts were shared with Lorana.

"Lady Fiona!" a woman's voice came to her from across the Bowl, toward the Dining Cavern. Fiona turned in time to see an older woman bearing down on her. She was familiar, Fiona realized, her mind straining to match the features and then—

"Merika!" Fiona called in response. "How are you? I'm sorry that I've been monopolizing Bekka but she's—"

"Ah, you've been doing me a favor," Merika said with a dismissive wave of her hand. Her expression changed as she added feelingly, "Not to mention the good it's done her father."

"But I'm sure that you miss her."

"I do," Merika said with a savage nod. "I miss her every day and I send a special thought her way." She straightened. "But she's doing good, as you say, and good for her father." Her eyes danced as she added, "And for all that I love her, and she's the youngest of my four, she's worse than a nest of tunnel snakes some days."

"Which is probably why she's so dear to my heart," Fiona said. "I made a fair number of marks hunting tunnel snakes."

"I thought you two were well-matched," Merika said in a tone which indicated that that had been a part of her willingness to let her youngest go to Telgar. "And I'd be doing both of you a disservice if I didn't admit that I was much the same at the same age." She smiled as she added, "After all, it takes a fair bit of flirting to catch the eyes of a blue rider, duty or no!"

"Well, I know for certain that Seban loves his daughter," Fiona said, not certain how to deal with the question of blue riders and their duty.

Merika nodded wisely. "'Love knows love,'" she recited. "Or perhaps it should be: love loves love."

The phrase echoed thrillingly down Fiona's spine. "Yes, that about sums it up between them."

Merika brought a finger to her nose as though sharing a secret. "And not just them, for all the word's been."

Fiona was startled to think that her exploits were the talk of the Weyr and then, on reflection, somewhat pleased. "It seems that I'm in good company," she teased the older woman.

Merika chuckled. "It's not for nothing that they made up that saying about love knowing love."

"I suppose not."

"You'll be looking for the Weyrleader or the Weyrwoman?" Merika said, glancing toward the senior queen's weyr.

"Actually, I'm hoping to get Tintoval for a consultation," Fiona said.

She smiled toward the queen's weyr. "I imagine that Lady Cisca probably won't want to be disturbed."

"Probably," Merika agreed, her eyes dancing once more. "It was quite a mating flight." She leaned in closer as she confided, "I wasn't sure if Melirth was ever going to come close enough to any dragon to mate. After all, she'd just risen not a sevenday before!"

"The Igen Records said that it happens sometimes, especially when there are other mating flights that day. A second flight gives plenty of eggs," Fiona said.

"Indeed," Merika said. "But it seemed for the longest time that Melirth was torn between Rineth and Zirenth."

"If so, I'm glad to hear it," Fiona said. "T'mar regained consciousness." Briefly, she told the older woman of T'mar's injuries and their worries.

"Perhaps that was it, perhaps Melirth was encouraging him to recover," Merika said, although she didn't sound convinced. "And by the First Egg, we've never heard of one bronze rider being Weyrleader to two Weyrs!" She shook her head and chuckled, "Awkward, that'd be."

"Awkward indeed," Fiona said, wondering if such a thing had ever occurred in all the Records. Once again, she regretted the necessity that kept the Records of the Weyrs separate. She wondered how much more could be gleaned from reading the Records of all the Weyrs combined? She pushed the thought from her mind, returning to her present issue.

"Is Ellor about?"

"You'd find her in the Dining Cavern if she is," Merika said. She gestured toward the far end of the Weyr. "I've got to check on Perilla, the mating flight's probably brought on her contractions."

"Do you need help?"

"Shards, no, Weyrwoman!" Merika said with a laugh. "I've been doing this for Turns now, since before you were born. I'll manage."

And with that, the older woman continued on her way, leaving Fiona behind, shaking her head at the similarities between mother Merika and daughter Bekka.

▼ ▼ ▼

As predicted, Fiona found Ellor in the Dining Cavern, bending over a pot gently simmering and ordering the attendant to add more spices.

"There'll be a lot of hungry mouths here later on!" Ellor said. To herself she muttered, "And no one can say when they'll wander in."

She looked up at the sound of Fiona's footsteps, her expression cloudy, her lips pursed for an angry outburst only to burst into a huge grin when she recognized the Weyrwoman.

"Fiona!" Ellor said, rushing forward to crush the younger woman in a tight hug. She pushed herself away, gripping Fiona's shoulders as she examined her. "I swear by the First Egg, you've grown a full hand since I last saw you and that not even a sevenday ago." She shook her head. "They must be feeding you well at Telgar, and well they should, after all they've been through and you've done for them."

"Ellor!" Fiona said, more to find the time to regain her breath and her thoughts than for any chiding. She laughed, saying, "They've been most kind to me at Telgar. Shaneese is the headwoman and she's quite something."

Ellor's lips pursed disapprovingly. "I've heard of her," she said shortly. "She's got trader's blood, hasn't she?"

"There's nothing wrong with trader's blood," Fiona rebuked her softly. "And, in case you've forgotten, I'm beholden to traders for my time in Igen."

Ellor allowed her frown to fade. "Of course you are," she said. "Not that they didn't profit from the encounter, by all rights."

"Profit was had by all," Fiona agreed. "And is there harm in that? The Weyrs work to the profit of Pern by providing protection; our wares cannot be bartered, should we frown upon those whose can?"

Ellor shook her head, her expression mulish as she admitted, "No, I suppose we can't."

She looked up and met Fiona's eyes squarely. "Why, you certainly have your father's way about you to shame me in my own hearth."

"I don't mean to shame you," Fiona said soothingly. "I merely wish to be fair."

"Fair!"

"And it's not that you aren't, Ellor," Fiona hastened to add. "If it weren't for you—"

"What?"

"If it weren't for you, I wouldn't know half of what I know about running a Weyr," Fiona told her. "Not to mention how to cook."

"Ah, hungry, are you?" Ellor asked, relieved to find the conversation turning to matters closer to her mind.

"I am," Fiona said, surprised at the admission. "It's been a strenuous"—she ignored Ellor's accusing chuckle—"several days and I've not eaten as well as I should." She raised a finger and waggled it at the headwoman. "But don't tell Shaneese, she'd be desolate after all she's done to feed me."

"Are you eating for two now?" Ellor asked.

Fiona made a face. "I don't know."

"It'd be early days yet," Ellor agreed. She glanced up to Fiona's eyes. "And perhaps you've enough on your plate with all that's going on."

"I promise to tell you all, if you feed me," Fiona said, glancing wistfully toward the nearest table.

Ellor snorted once more and waved her to a chair. "For all that I've heard of Shaneese, even with your pining, I'd be addled not to know that she sets a good table, good enough that you wouldn't be here just to be fed." As she spoke, she bustled up a plate, soup bowl, and mug, and filled each, setting them and utensils in front of Fiona and gesturing for her to start eating. "What is it, then, that brings you here?"

Predictably, the question was asked when Fiona had just swallowed. Fiona gave Ellor an apologetic look as she cleared her throat. "T'mar's conscious. I want Tintoval to check on him."

Ellor pursed her lips thoughtfully before responding. "You'll bring her back?"

Fiona gave her a look of surprised hurt in reply.

"It's just that so many people seem to stay in your wake once attracted," Ellor said, working hard to keep her expression neutral. "Lorana, Kindan, even that weyrwoman from High Reaches, Jeila."

"I think Jeila chose Telgar more for H'nez than me."

Ellor shook her head. "And why do you think H'nez is at Telgar?"

The question caught Fiona off balance. "He'd been fighting with K'lior, he wanted to be posted to another Weyr."

"All true," Ellor said, clearly believing none of those reasons to be the principal one.

"I've no love for H'nez!"

"No," Ellor said. "And I'm sure he knows that, too."

"So why would he want to be at Telgar?"

Ellor sighed, clearly debating something with herself before deciding to say, "Because you are good for him."

Fiona raised her eyebrows in response.

Ellor gave her a quick grin. "Sometimes, even when we don't want to admit it, we know that someone has something we can learn from them."

"H'nez can learn from me?"

Ellor nodded. "And you can learn from him."

"He's not without his strengths," Fiona admitted reluctantly. "And Jeila seems a good judge of character."

"And while I've never known him not to be a bit bullheaded, H'nez is perceptive enough to know his weaknesses," Ellor said. "And driven enough to strive to remove them."

"I certainly see 'driven,'" Fiona said, taking a sip of her *klah*.

Ellor smiled in agreement. Deftly changing the subject, she asked, "And how long do you think you'll need our Tintoval's services?"

"How about if I promise to have her back in time for dinner—unless there's an emergency?"

And so it was agreed. Fiona found Tintoval in her quarters and the healer was more than willing to accompany her, on one condition: "I want us to stop at the Healer Hall and see if Masterhealer Betrony has any journeymen or apprentices he'd like to have consult on this."

Fiona grinned. "Thinking of educating the next generation?"

"That," Tintoval conceded, adding with a grin, "and perhaps to tantalize some with the allure of Weyr life."

"Well, anything that gets me more healers is all to the good!" Fiona said, adding, "But, as I recall, there were three apprentices sent there from Fort Weyr."

"There were, and I've made sure that Cisca and K'lior know how grateful we are for it," Tintoval replied. "They're able, too, but they've a ways to go before they'll walk the tables."

They stopped briefly at the Healer Hall. Fiona had just enough time to look wistfully toward her father's Hold before Masterhealer Betrony packed Talenth with three journeymen—two men and one woman, all older than Fiona—and sent them on their way.

"They've never been *between* before," he warned Fiona just before she mounted. He smiled at her; he'd been one of the healers who'd tended her many scrapes as a youngster, so they were well acquainted.

"I'll be careful with them," Fiona said. She paused, thinking of Bekka. "And Master—" Betrony gave her an expectant look "—would you be willing to take on another apprentice?"

"How old is she?" Betrony asked, wryly guessing that Fiona's candidate was a girl.

"She has twelve Turns," Fiona said. She saw Betrony's look but forestalled him, "Her mother is one of Fort Weyr's midwives, and her father was a dragonrider."

"Was?"

"He lost his blue to the sickness," she replied sadly. "I think it's only her love of life that's kept him going."

"So I'd be getting a package, eh? Father and daughter?"

Fiona nodded; she hadn't thought of it that way.

"Is she as bad as you were?"

"Worse; she doesn't sleep," Fiona said. The Masterhealer's eyes widened in surprise. "She takes little naps from time to time."

"Oh, like our Tintoval," Betrony said with a sideways look at the Weyr Healer. "Does she follow orders?"

"She's dutiful," Fiona allowed. "But willful."

"And I've never dealt with that," Betrony muttered sardonically, nodding toward Tintoval, who stuck her tongue out at him in response. Betrony snorted and shook his head. Then he turned to Fiona. "Where is she now?"

"She's at Telgar with me," Fiona said. "And I'd need a replacement for her."

He nodded toward the healers. "Those are my best," he told her. "I'd not let them go, only you say that she comes with her father."

"Seban," Fiona agreed. "Between them, they know enough about healing to handle a Threadfall."

Betrony's eyes widened in admiration. "Very well, if you wish, you may send her whenever you can spare her."

"Thank you!" Fiona said, turning back to Talenth.

He took two long strides toward her and spoke quietly into her ear, "You can use this time to see which of these healers might work with you. I was about to send them off to the holds, so they're all packed and ready to leave."

"If they don't work out, I've got Kindan and Lorana," Fiona said.

"And," he wagged his head at her with a grin, "from what I've heard, you've learned a fair bit yourself."

Fiona nodded. "All those lessons you gave me."

"I thought you were asleep!"

Fiona smiled, shaking her head. "Not all the time."

She turned to hug the Masterhealer, who took the opportunity to say, "When you see Kindan, you might remind him that there are several people here—at both the Healer Hall and the Harper Hall—who are eager for a word with him."

"I will!"

As she climbed up behind Tintoval, she said loudly, "Healer, be sure the others are properly hooked on with the riding straps. The weyrfolk are under strict orders to let plummeting healers fall."

Tintoval turned back long enough to give Fiona a droll look, recalling their first meeting and how Fiona had been rebuked for risking the life of a queen and her rider for a mere healer, before turning back to be certain that the others were secure. Fiona craned around her side to make her own inspection and, satisfied, sat upright before ordering Talenth to leap once more for the sky.

"Remember, *between* only lasts as long as it takes to cough three times!" Fiona shouted loudly before giving Talenth the image of Telgar and the order to take them *between*.

They arrived as predicted on the third cough—Fiona was certain that she heard one hastily stifled—and Talenth began a gentle descent into the Weyr Bowl. Fiona was pleased by the exclamations and pointing hands of the journeymen gawking at the sights of the Weyr below them.

"I'm taking us to the queens' ledge," Fiona told Tintoval, as Talenth altered her course slightly, did a half-circle, and gently landed within a wingtip of the queens' ledge.

Fiona was the first off, then Tintoval. Between them, they got the other three down. The girl—she looked to have perhaps seventeen Turns—was the last down and lightest. The middle man looked to have two more Turns than she, and the last was the eldest, seeming closer to T'mar's age—old to be a journeyman.

The man sensed her curiosity and smiled at her as he introduced himself, "Birentir, formerly harper of Red Sands hold." He gestured to the other two. "These are Cerra"—the woman—"and Lindorm."

"I'm glad to meet you," Fiona said, giving them all a brisk nod. She clambered up the side of the queens' ledge and was surprised when two arms fastened on her legs and gave her a boost. She turned back and held out a hand for Tintoval, who took it and accepted a second boost from Birentir and Lindorm. Cerra had balked at the ascent and had trotted to the end of the ledge, climbing the rise as quickly as she could. Birentir turned to follow her progress and with a polite nod to the two women on the ledge, elected to follow her less strenuous route. Lindorm looked torn between clambering up and trotting around. Tintoval decided the issue by waving him toward the others. "Master Betrony would have my hide if you were hurt climbing the ledge!"

Fiona, feeling slightly guilty, waited for the others to join them, then led them into T'mar's quarters.

"This is Seban and Bekka," Fiona said as the other two rose at the sound of their arrival. A slight sound caused Fiona to glance over her shoulder and she was surprised to see Tintoval step back to the wall, where she leaned with arms folded, nodding pointedly to Fiona to indicate that she was going to monitor the proceedings, rather than lead them.

Fiona accepted her decision with a nod of her own and turned back, and, noting that Lorana and Kindan had joined them, she stretched her hand toward them, adding, "And this is—"

"Kindan!" Cerra cried, rushing toward him. "It's good to see you!"

"You must be Lorana," Birentir said with an engaging smile, raising a hand in greeting. "There are not enough thanks on all of Pern to repay you for what you've done."

Lorana shook her head wordlessly. Fiona moved to her side and touched her hand briefly, just enough to let the older woman know that she understood her ambivalence, as she whispered, "You *paid*."

Lorana twitched at her words but said nothing. Changing the subject, Fiona turned to look down at T'mar. "How is he?"

"Awake and wishing you'd all be quiet," T'mar spoke up tetchily. "If you're hoping to speed my recovery by shouting, it's not working."

Birentir's features twisted into a frown as he bent down to the bronze rider, looking over his shoulder to ask Lorana, "How long since his concussion?"

"This is the second day," Kindan said.

"When did he regain consciousness?" Birentir asked, turning back to gaze at T'mar.

"Today, after the third mating flight," Fiona said. Birentir glanced her way with a dismissive look. Fiona felt her temper rising and was surprised to feel Lorana's hand on her shoulder, soothingly.

"Mating flights are a strong emotional stimulant," Birentir said. "And you said it took three?"

"Mine, Jeila's, and Melirth's at Fort," Fiona said.

"What of his dragon?" Cerra asked, looking over her shoulder toward the sleeping bronze. Birentir glared at the interruption. "If he was unconscious, who controlled Zirenth?"

Fiona nodded at Kindan.

"You?" Cerra asked in surprise.

"Lorana and I, actually," Kindan replied, reaching to grab Lorana's free hand.

"If they hadn't, Zirenth would have gone *between* forever," Fiona told her.

"Who flew Talenth?" Lindorm asked, glancing from Fiona to T'mar.

"Zirenth flew her," Seban said. "And, would you all, as our patient has asked, talk more softly?"

"Sorry," Lindorm replied, glancing down at T'mar. "Does it hurt very much?"

T'mar nodded, unwilling to trust himself to words.

Birentir was still absorbing Seban's revelation. "If Zirenth flew your queen, then who . . . ?" His voice trailed off as his eyes settled on Kindan.

"We're here for T'mar," Fiona reminded the older healer testily, glancing pointedly in his direction.

"Masterharper Zist will be eager for your report," Birentir told Kindan. "I'm surprised you—"

"Oh, please!" Cerra cut him off. "Would you get out of the way, so we can see to the patient?"

"*I* am examining him," Birentir said haughtily.

"No, you're not," Fiona declared, gesturing for him to move away from T'mar. "In fact, you're just leaving. I think you'll find some food in the Dining Cavern."

"You can't—" Birentir spluttered in amazement "—I'm the senior here and you're—you're just a girl!"

Shh, Talenth! Fiona called as she felt her queen readying to bellow in angry support of her rider.

"You idiot," Bekka snapped, with an impertinence that surprised everyone, "she's the Weyrwoman, she can do anything she farding well pleases!"

"Shh," Fiona said to Bekka. "You're hurting T'mar's ears." She turned to the older healer, saying coldly, with all the dignity learned from Turns watching her father deal with such arrogance, "Journeyman Birentir, I believe that we no longer have need of your services."

"I—" Birentir's eyes shifted around the room nervously and he licked his lips. "I'm sorry if I offended, Weyrwoman."

"I'm sure," Fiona agreed, gesturing for him to move away. "My head-woman's name is Shaneese, you might meet her in the Kitchen Cavern."

Reluctantly, Birentir rose and backed away from the group, his lips moving as he searched for some words that might heal his breech.

Fiona turned her back on him, gesturing toward Cerra and Lindorm to take the older healer's place. After he'd left, Fiona leaned over to Bekka and shook a finger at her warningly.

"Sorry," Bekka said contritely, "but he wasn't *listening* to the patient." She glanced up at her father. "And if you don't listen to the patient, how can you know what's wrong?"

"We'll talk about this later," Fiona said, turning her attention back to T'mar.

Cerra ceded her position to Lindorm, saying, "I've not had much work with head injuries."

"I'm no better," Lindorm said, kneeling beside T'mar. "Really, Weyr-woman, for all that he's an ass, Birentir probably knows the most of the three of us."

"No he doesn't," T'mar corrected him softly, his eyes closed against the pain.

Cerra raised her eyebrows in surprise.

"If he did," Kindan explained, "he'd know better than to irritate a Weyrwoman in her own Weyr."

"We haven't moved him much," Bekka said, deciding that everyone was spending far too much time on unimportant matters—like manners—

and not enough on her patient. "His leg was threadscored, we've dressed it and changed the bandages.

"We haven't given him fellis for the pain nor numbweed for the wound for fear of affecting his coma," she continued briskly, "but I'm getting worried about keeping him in the same position for too long—he'll get bedsores if nothing else."

Lindorm glanced at her in surprise, then asked calmly, "So what do you recommend?"

Bekka frowned in irritation. "If I didn't know any better, and I could be certain that he had no spinal injuries, I'd say that we should try to move him in his bedsheets into his pool to let him soak a bit." She frowned. "It'd be difficult with the bandages—maybe we'd be best off removing them while he's bathing—but I think the warm water would aid in circulation."

"Who did you study under?" Cerra asked her, amazed.

Bekka shrugged. "My mother mostly." She threw a hand toward Fiona, adding, "And Weyrwoman Fiona knows a lot about Thread injuries, human and dragon."

"Your mother?" Lindorm asked, his eyes going to Seban.

"Merika, midwife at Fort," Seban said.

"Have you considered apprenticing at the Healer Hall?" Cerra asked. She glanced up to Seban, adding, "She has the gift."

"Actually," Fiona chimed in, "she's a place at the Healer Hall as soon as we can let her go."

Bekka's eyes lit up and she leaped into the air in excitement but, with an apologetic look toward T'mar, did not shout in glee.

The import of Fiona's words were not lost on the two healers and they exchanged wary looks.

"I know something of spines," Cerra said. She glanced up to Bekka approvingly. "I think if we follow apprentice Bekka's suggestion, we could use the chance to examine T'mar's spine in the water."

"The only danger is in moving him," Lindorm pointed out.

"I've got to move sometime," T'mar said.

"If only to use the necessary," Fiona said, surprised at herself for not considering that need sooner.

"He flew a Threadfall when he was injured, so he was dehydrated," Seban said.

"And his metabolism was slowed by the coma," Lindorm added.

"If he's to get better, he'll need to get mobile, won't he?" Fiona asked, glancing down to give the bronze rider an encouraging smile.

"Let me check his neck," Cerra said, glancing up to Lindorm for agreement. When he nodded, she turned to Bekka and beckoned to her.

"Kneel beside me," she said. Bekka knelt and was surprised when Cerra turned to her, placing her hands on either side of her neck.

"Your fingers are smaller, more gentle, so you'll go first," she told the young girl.

"Feel how I'm moving my fingers? I'm probing for anything out of place, anything that doesn't feel right." Bekka's eyes widened in brief panic, then she closed them, her expression intent as she absorbed Cerra's movements, ready to replicate them.

"Now, you do it to me," Cerra said. "That way I'll know that you've got it right."

"'Cos if I don't, he could die?" Bekka asked, wide-eyed.

"It's possible but not likely," Lindorm spoke up.

"Perhaps—" Seban began, only to stop himself with a deep sigh.

"Most likely, with your small fingers, you'll do no harm," Cerra assured the young girl. "That's why we'll start with your hands."

Bekka took a deep breath, glanced up to Seban for an instant, then placed her hands gently behind Cerra's neck. "Okay."

Cerra closed her eyes and said nothing as Bekka ran her fingers up her neck, fingering each veterbra in succession.

"There's a spot here, just before the last bone," Bekka said, opening her eyes.

Cerra raised an eyebrow in surprise, put her hands to her neck, and felt the spot before nodding. "Yes, there is," she said, smiling at the youngster. "Good for you! It's nothing, just a misalignment—" She twisted her head quickly and Bekka jumped as the apprentice's neck gave a loud *pop*!

"There, back in place again." She smiled at Bekka and gestured for Lindorm to join them. "Lindorm, let her practice on you, too."

The other healer was only too willing and, after Bekka repeated her examination, pronounced himself completely satisfied with her abilities.

"You'll make a great healer," he told her with a smile. Shyly, she smiled back. Then he nodded toward T'mar. "Are you ready for the examination now?"

"Are you ready, Weyrleader?" Bekka asked, standing up and bending down over the Weyrleader, poising her hands on either side of his neck.

"I'm in your hands," T'mar said.

Bekka ignored the remark, instead closing her eyes and reaching her hands down to delicately touch his neck. She went over it twice, before standing up and turning to Cerra. "I can't feel anything wrong."

"Okay, let me," Cerra said. Bekka was happy to move away, particularly after Kindan assured her, "Whenever possible, healers like to get a second opinion."

And a third. After Cerra had finished her examination, she moved aside to let Lindorm repeat the examination.

"I don't feel anything broken," Lindorm said as he straightened up after his examination. He smiled at T'mar as he added, "I think it's safe to move you, Weyrleader."

"Good," T'mar said a bit distractedly. "In which case, the soonest the best."

Bekka and Fiona scurried aside, willing to let the larger and stronger adults take on the burden of moving the fully-grown Weyrleader in his bedsheets.

Fiona watched the proceeding carefully, noting how Lindorm had no hesitation when it came time for him to step—fully clothed—into the warm bath so that he and Kindan could be on the far end of T'mar's makeshift stretcher.

"We're going to just lower the whole thing into the water," Lindorm said to T'mar. "You'll float off."

"That sounds quite relaxing," T'mar said.

Bekka quickly lifted her skirts and, with a quick twist, knotted them higher up as she stepped into the pool, declaring, "I'll keep your head above water."

"Hold his shoulders," Cerra said.

Soon the whole maneuver was completed, the bedsheets removed and T'mar, still in his clothes, was floating in the water. His features relaxed into a look of pleasure.

"I'm afraid we're going to have to remove your clothes to complete our examination," Lindorm said.

"I'll be glad to get them off," T'mar said.

"Perhaps Bekka should be excused," Lindorm said.

"Not if I'm going to be a healer," Bekka said. Her expression changed and she glanced down to T'mar, "Unless you don't want me, Weyrleader?"

T'mar smiled. "Were you the one who changed the bandages on my leg?"

"Yes," Bekka replied offhandedly, not seeing any connection.

"She's been watching mothers give birth since she could crawl," Seban said by way of assurance.

"But if you're going to be embarrassed, Weyrleader, I promise I won't look," Bekka said in assurance.

T'mar's lip twitched. "Do what you must, healer."

Bekka's face flamed into a brilliant smile at the compliment.

Safely in the water, Cerra had Bekka repeat her performance, this time checking T'mar's spine. First she and then Cerra and Lindorm pronounced themselves satisfied.

"But this is no guarantee, Weyrleader," Lindorm warned. "Your head injury could have caused injury to your spine as well. It could be that if you move the wrong way, you'll sever your spinal cord."

"And if I do?"

"You'll be paralyzed," Bekka told him. "The spinal cord is the nerve that runs the length of your body."

"Which would make it difficult to fly Thread," T'mar said drolly.

"But not impossible," Fiona said. T'mar glanced at her in surprise and exasperation before saying, "With you, I believe it could be done."

"Be certain of it," Fiona told him.

"Very well," T'mar said, "with such assurances, I think we should give it a try."

Cerra glanced at Lindorm, who turned to Bekka. "What would you suggest?"

"To see if he's paralyzed?" Bekka asked. When the others nodded, she continued, "Well, he's not."

"How do you know?"

"Because he couldn't help twitching when I bandaged him," she said. "If he was paralyzed, he wouldn't have been able, would he?"

Lindorm exchanged a surprised look with Cerra, before shaking his head, "No, I suppose not."

"And having said that," Cerra continued, "the chances of his having a spinal injury are slight."

"Because if he had, he would already have severed the cord?" Bekka guessed.

"Yes."

"Well, that's a relief," Kindan said, glancing at T'mar's face.

"So he's all right?" Fiona said.

"He still had a major brain injury," Lindorm reminded her. "That can cause long-term problems."

"Memory loss, mood changes, and other such-like," Fiona said, glancing toward Kindan. "That's what Kindan said."

"Harper Kindan has the right of it."

"We should get him out of the water, before he turns into a giant wrinkle," Bekka said.

It was not quite as difficult an operation as the job of getting him into the water, particularly once Cerra and Lindorm had satisfied themselves that T'mar could move all his limbs freely.

"Does this mean I can get some fellis for my head?" T'mar asked testily as he reclined in his bathrobe, with Fiona gently drying his hair by rolling it in a towel and squeezing it.

"I'd recommend against it," Lindorm said. "I know you're in a lot of pain, but with a head injury such as yours, until we know you've fully recovered, we don't want to do anything that might dull your wits."

"That way we'll know if your wits are dulling from the blow," Fiona said.

Cerra gave her a surprised look; Lindorm merely nodded in agreement.

"When can I get back to my duties?"

"Duties?" Bekka snorted, as she worked to bandage T'mar's leg. "Your leg has to heal yet!" She shook her head. "A month at least, just for that."

"Probably six weeks," Fiona said, glancing at the rebandaged wound.

"You can try sitting up later this week," Lindorm said. "You shouldn't walk, though, without someone to help you." Seeing T'mar's frown, the healer explained, "You were in a coma; it's doubtless that you have a concussion. That can leave you disoriented, even feeling like you're walking on air—which is not recommended with stone floors."

"When you do sit up, have a care for any signs of dizziness or muzziness," Cerra warned.

"Muzziness?" Fiona repeated, glancing at T'mar. "Muzziness can be caused by head injury?"

"Often," Lindorm said, his eyes narrowed. "Why do you ask, Weyrwoman?"

"Because Fiona and I—and many others—have been suffering from some sort of muzziness for the past several Turns," T'mar said in answer.

"Like Tullea," Kindan spoke up suddenly.

"That's what M'tal said," Fiona said. T'mar looked at her questioningly, so she said, "Tullea timed it back to High Reaches Weyr and was there for the last three Turns. That's where Minith clutched and the sickness-immune hatchlings grew. Jeila's Tolarth is one of them."

"During which time at Benden Weyr," Kindan picked up the tale, "Tullea was the most difficult, irascible, and vindictive"—he shot a glance at Lorana—"person I'd ever seen."

"M'tal thinks we could be timing it, too?" T'mar asked. "Or is this a result of our timing it back to Igen?"

"If it is," Fiona said, "then wouldn't all the injured riders from the other Weyrs feel the same effects?"

"The Benden riders were tired but they recovered quickly," Kindan said, glancing at Lorana for agreement. His brows furrowed as he turned back to Fiona. "Are you saying that you still feel this way?"

Fiona nodded.

"And it's slowed you down?" Kindan asked. When she nodded once more, his lips twitched and he said, "I was hoping that you'd just calmed down."

Fiona's eyes flashed and she deliberately turned away from him. Catching sight of Tintoval, who had observed the entire proceedings without saying anything once—a feat Fiona recognized was beyond her own capabilities—she asked, nodding toward Bekka, "So, do you think she'll do?"

"Cerra, Lindorm?" Tintoval said, deferring the question to them.

Lindorm smiled and Cerra ruffled Bekka's hair affectionately.

"She'll do," the young woman said. She frowned thoughtfully before adding, "In fact, I'm worried that she'll outshine some of the older apprentices."

"And it may be a detriment having her father with her," Lindorm added thoughtfully.

"Seban goes with her," Fiona said, even as Bekka started to make her own protest. "Seban, how would you feel about apprenticing yourself to the Healer Hall?"

Seban took a step back in surprise.

"What were your plans?" Lorana asked the ex-dragonrider.

Seban furrowed his brow. "I suppose I hadn't thought about it," he said, glancing toward Bekka. "My only thought was to help my daughter, here." He pursed his lips as he added with a sad look toward Bekka, "But that includes, one day, leaving you to your own devices."

"Here's my request," Kindan said, glancing to Fiona briefly, then smiling at Lorana and grabbing her hand. "I ask that you go present yourself to the Halls—Harper and Healer—as an apprentice." He smiled at an old memory, adding, "There has been a long tradition of weyrfolk finding a calling at the Halls."

"You're not thinking of Mikal?" Seban asked, surprised at the comparison. M'kal—ex-dragonrider—had become a legend among healers in his lifetime before the Plague.

"Yes," Kindan said catching Seban's eyes with his own. "I most certainly was."

"You're a natural teacher," Lorana said. Seban gave her an incredulous look.

"She's right," Tintoval said. "Half of teaching is knowing when to be silent and"—she gestured to her position at the outside of their group—"observing."

"If nothing else, your memories of Weyr life would be invaluable," Kindan said.

It was Bekka who brought up Kindan's unspoken meaning, as she stepped forward and slipped her hand into his, "And, Father, you know what it means to lose a dragon."

Seban's face twisted with pain and Bekka tightened her grip, continuing, "I promised to become a healer so that this would never happen again."

"Dragons are lost to Threadfall," Seban murmured in response. "You can't save them all."

"No," Fiona said, remembering F'dan and his blue Ridorth, and glancing sympathetically at Lorana, "we can't."

"You are a healer in your own right," Seban said, also looking at Lorana.

"And if she wants to go, she'll go with all my support," Fiona said, nodding at Kindan and Lorana before adding, "But with her ability to hear any dragon, I would hope that she would stay at the Weyr."

Seban nodded. Kindan gave Lorana an inquiring look that the older woman answered with a quick jerk of her head toward Fiona, saying, "Someone has to keep her from bullying all the other Weyrwomen!"

Fiona surprised everyone—including herself—with an indignant squeak. Kindan, Lorana, Bekka, and Seban allowed themselves a quick chuckle at her reaction while the healers all looked on, too anxious to make any noise, although Fiona was pretty certain that Tintoval's eyes danced with glee.

"Well, Seban?" Fiona asked with all the dignity she could muster.

"Master Zist and Master Betrony would be overjoyed," Kindan said.

"It's a lot of hard work, little sleep, and you'd have everyone muttering about your age," Tintoval cautioned. Fiona bit off a retort, realizing that the healer was taunting the ex-dragonrider with exactly the right tone.

"And you think that I'd let my daughter take up a challenge her father couldn't handle?" Seban snorted. "Can we think about it?"

"No," Fiona said. "I've promised to get Tintoval and two of the healers back before dinner and you're to go with them."

Seban turned his eyes toward T'mar who had watched the whole exchange silently. "Weyrleader?"

"I will stand by your decision," T'mar told him softly.

"If you go as an apprentice in your own right, no one can say that you are there to guard Bekka," Fiona said. Seban gave her a look that made it quite clear that he'd arrived at the same conclusion and Fiona felt her cheeks blushing at the unspoken rebuke his eyes conveyed.

"Very well," Seban said, reaching down fluidly and pulling Bekka up into his arms, "we'll go!"

Bekka buried her face in his shoulder but even so, her squeal of delight filled the room.

"You said two healers?" Tintoval asked, facing Fiona. She turned quickly toward Zirenth's weyr and the Weyr Bowl beyond, saying, "I'd best get Birentir."

"Leave him," Fiona said. The others all looked at her. Apologetically she told Cerra and Lindorm, "I don't question your abilities, nor your desires. But, as I have been recently reminded, sometimes my duties require me to learn new abilities."

Lorana smiled at her in agreement.

"Birentir came to the Healer Hall not long after the Plague," Tintoval said, her expression grave.

"As a patient," Fiona guessed. Tintoval nodded even as her brows rose in surprise. "When he recovered, he—like our Bekka here—made a vow."

"Yes," Tintoval said.

"How did you know?" Cerra asked in surprise.

"I'd even guess that he had a daughter near my age," Fiona continued, "and lost her in the Plague."

"Yes," Lorana said, following Fiona's line of thinking.

"'Arrogance is usually born of fear,'" Fiona said, nodding toward Kindan, who had told her that many Turns ago. Kindan jerked in surprise, delighted that she'd remembered. With a wry grin, she added, "I seem to have made it a habit to collect arrogant people."

"It's because you conquer your fear," T'mar spoke up from his bed. All eyes turned toward him. "You still feel it, but you don't let it rule you."

"I don't know about that," Fiona said. The thought flustered her and she sought a means to divert herself from it. "Regardless, I think that we should get everyone back soonest, including Bekka and Seban."

"I don't think Talenth is up to eight," Kindan said, a quick gesture including himself and Lorana in the count.

"Zirenth needs exercise," T'mar said. Kindan and Lorana turned to him in surprise. T'mar met the ex–queen rider's eyes, saying, "If you wish, I'm certain he'll be happy to carry you."

"And we'd like to work on this experiment," Fiona added with a nod toward T'mar for his planning. "We've been trying to see if we can mix riders and dragons."

"Uninjured riders paired with uninjured dragons?" Kindan asked, glancing from T'mar to Fiona and back. He pursed his lips thoughtfully. "That's an interesting proposition."

"So go test it," T'mar said.

"Some more?" Lorana asked. "Remember that we already brought Zirenth to Fort Weyr."

T'mar's eyes narrowed. "Really?" he looked distracted as he probed his memories. "I hadn't realized."

"You've been through a lot," Fiona told him. "You're lucky to be alive

and, if you don't get some rest"—she gestured for the others to leave—
"I'll kill you."

T'mar's lips twitched but he closed his eyes, resolutely following her
orders.

Fiona left it to Lorana and Kindan to organize the loading of Zirenth
and Talenth while she went to the Dining Cavern. She was not surprised
to find Birentir at one of the pottery wheels, working the clay under the
tutelage of Mekiar.

"How is he doing?" Fiona asked, startling the older healer and causing him to ruin the bowl he was forming on the spinning wheel.

"He is learning," Mekiar replied drolly, glancing up to Fiona. "I would
say that at this moment he is learning patience."

"Good," she replied, "see that he does."

Birentir looked askance at her words.

"You're staying," she told him. Birentir's eyes widened further in surprise. "Bekka and her father are going back to the Healer Hall and I don't
need you there causing her grief on a daily basis."

"You would prefer me causing 'daily grief' here?" Birentir asked with
a flash of humor.

"You won't be causing *me* daily grief, healer," Fiona assured him. She
softened her tone as she confided, "I'm more worried about fighting
Thread without enough dragons."

"I'd heard," Birentir said, rising from his chair, his expression grave.
"How bad is it?"

"No one really knows," Fiona said. She shook her head, adding, "We
all know that it's bad but we haven't exact numbers until we can figure
our losses per Fall."

"Master Archivist Verilan could help with that."

Fiona cocked her head at him measuringly. "So, when you get over the
fact that I'm nearly the same age as your late daughter, and deal with me
for myself, you are willing to think, aren't you?"

Birentir flushed hotly and Fiona held up a hand in apology.

"I don't recall seeing you whenever I visited the Harper Hall," Fiona
said. "Were you hiding?"

"I was studying."

"You're older than most."

Birentir nodded in acknowledgment.

"Tell me about it," Fiona said.

"It was the Plague," Birentir said. "I lost my whole family, wife, two boys, three girls." He glanced into her eyes as he added, "My youngest would be about your age now."

"I've nearly seventeen Turns," Fiona told him.

"Yes," Birentir said, "she had five Turns when the Plague struck."

"I had only two," Fiona told him. Birentir gave her an inquiring look. "I spent three Turns back in time at Igen Weyr."

Birentir's eyes widened. "I hadn't heard."

"We haven't been back for very long, and we were sent here after . . ." Her voice trailed off, but Birentir nodded. The news of the death of Telgar Weyr had traveled quickly to the Harper Hall. Fiona shook herself. "So, you'll be staying here," she told him. "I'll ask Master Betrony to give me your stuff and we'll put you in the healer's quarters."

"Are you certain, even with my daily grief?"

Fiona smiled at the taunt and nodded.

"I'll be sure to bring your gear back from the Healer Hall," she told him.

"Thank you," Birentir said, and Fiona knew he wasn't referring to her promise about his belongings. She smiled again and, with a wave, hurried out of the Dining Cavern in time to climb up behind Bekka and Seban, who were already perched on her eager queen. The older man had stored their gear and secured them ably onto Talenth.

To Bekka, she asked, "Are you ready?"

"I hope so," Bekka said.

"You'll do fine," Fiona assured her. Silently, she gave Talenth the instruction to rise and, after they circled the watch heights once, went *between*.

▼ ▼ ▼

When they came out again, Bekka took one look down and gasped in surprise. She turned back to face Fiona, an accusing look on her face.

"I promised Ellor I'd get Tintoval back first!" Fiona said, stifling a laugh. Her expression softened as she added, "And I thought you might want to see your mother, too."

"Thank you," Bekka said, peering down intently into the Weyr Bowl below.

Zirenth appeared just behind them and followed Talenth as she spiraled down for a landing.

They were met by Ellor and Merika first. In the distance, Cisca could be seen on the queens' ledge, walking quickly toward them.

"Should we wait?" Fiona asked Seban, glancing in Cisca's direction. But Bekka rendered the question pointless, quickly untying herself and jumping down, running toward her mother while screaming at the top of her lungs, "Mother! I'm going to be a healer!" Seban gave Fiona an apologetic look, but Fiona waved it aside. Grinning, she jumped down from Talenth, patting the golden queen softly on her leg while Seban clambered down.

"Queens are a lot bigger than blues," Seban said, glancing back up at their perch on the queen's neck.

"Tolarth is even bigger," Fiona reminded him.

"Is that a complaint?" Seban teased.

"Oh, no!" Fiona said, patting Talenth once more. "My queen and I are exactly the right size for each other." She turned to face him, asking softly, "Wasn't it that way with you and Serth?"

"It was," Seban said in a choked voice.

"I'm sorry," Fiona said, reaching out a hand consolingly. Seban glanced at it and took it, wrapping both his hands around it.

"Here's the Weyrwoman," Seban said, glancing in Cisca's direction.

"Let's go see her, then," Fiona said, turning and using his grip on her hand to tug him along beside her.

Cisca met them halfway across the Bowl. "Fiona, is that Zirenth in the distance?"

"It is," Fiona said. "We're bringing back some healers to the Hall and needed another dragon." She gestured toward Lorana and Kindan, adding, "T'mar's still recovering, but he was willing to oblige us with his bronze."

"And not for the first time," Cisca said, giving the blond Weyrwoman a knowing look.

Fiona met her eyes squarely. "If it weren't for Lorana and Kindan, we would have lost both Zirenth *and* T'mar."

"Come with me," Cisca said, waving toward the Kitchen. "It's far too cold to converse out here; you'll have to forgive my manners."

Inside, seated with warm *klah* and fresh rolls, Cisca was much more relaxed.

"Congratulations on your flight," Fiona said, raising her mug in toast.

"And on yours," Cisca said, raising her own mug in response. She glanced around at a sudden eruption of noise and spotted Bekka with a group of friends, helping themselves to a snack. Glancing at the youngster, she asked, "Did she wear you out, too?"

"Hardly!" Fiona said, smiling. "Especially not with Seban to mind her." She waved at Bekka and the youngster waved back before flying out of the Kitchen toward the living quarters. "But an opportunity arose to get her healer training, and so we're taking it."

"Wise."

"I learned from the best," Fiona said, nodding back at Cisca.

"And you're here because of her?"

"No," Fiona said. "I'm here returning Tintoval." She explained how she'd purloined the Weyr's healer, had gone to the Healer Hall, and had acquired the three journeyman healers.

"So you kept the older grouchy one?" Cisca said when Fiona had finished. "And why is that?"

Fiona shrugged, not quite certain of her reasoning. Cisca gave her a thoughtful look, then cocked her head toward Lorana and Kindan. "Are you keeping them, too?"

"I don't know if 'keep' is the right word," Fiona said defensively.

"We really haven't made any plans," Kindan said, looking over toward Lorana.

"We're staying with Fiona," Lorana declared. She glanced to the younger woman. "If you'll have us."

"I don't see what's in it for you," Cisca said, pursing her lips thoughtfully as she gazed at Lorana.

"Well, for the time being, they get to ride Zirenth," Fiona spoke up quickly. "And, of course, Lorana can ride Talenth any time." She thought furiously for more inducements, but just then K'lior entered the Cavern and the conversation ebbed as they all waited for him to seat himself beside Cisca.

"You're not twitting her, are you?" K'lior asked Cisca after he'd had his first revitalizing sip of *klah.*

Cisca pretended not to know what he was talking about and K'lior snorted in response, telling Fiona, "She's jealous, you know."

"I am not!" Cisca said, her eyes flashing with anger.

"Just the other day she said that she wanted a group of men, too," K'lior said, smiling wickedly at Fiona.

Fiona was out of her chair in an instant, her cheeks burning.

"Fiona!" Cisca called even as she batted at K'lior and Kindan and Lorana rose from their chairs to follow the Telgar Weyrwoman. "I did not say that. I merely said that it must be hard—"

But Fiona merely turned back to her, saying carefully, "Weyrwoman, we've taken too much of your time," before heading out to the Weyr Bowl and her queen.

Talenth! Tell Seban and Bekka we're leaving!

"Fiona!" Lorana called from behind her. Fiona turned toward her, furious, her lips trembling. When Lorana caught up to her, she grabbed Fiona's shoulders and looked into her eyes. "I don't think she was trying to be mean. I think K'lior's right: She's just jealous."

"Of what?" Fiona cried. "Of a mating flight?"

"No," Lorana told her softly, "of us: what we are."

"What are we?" Fiona asked quietly.

"Friends, I should hope," Lorana said. "And more."

"How can we be friends? We love the same person," Fiona cried. She shook her head, tears flowing down her cheeks as she continued, "I can't take him away from you, I swore I wouldn't." She looked up at Lorana. "Maybe it's best if you and he were in another Weyr."

"And what about T'mar?"

"I love him," Fiona said, even as she realized, with the words, that he could be her anchor, he could save her from her misery.

"If we leave, what about T'mar?" Lorana said. "And Zirenth?"

Fiona absorbed her words slowly, her tears stilling and her eyes going wide. "Are you bound to them like you are to me?"

"I don't think so," Lorana said. She smiled at Fiona as she added, "But I'm glad to see that you realize we're bound to each other."

"I don't want to hurt you."

"Well, that's something that you're going to have to get over," Lorana told her firmly. Fiona took a step back, straining at Lorana's hold, her eyes wide. "If you love someone, you have to accept that sometimes you'll hurt them, too."

"But I don't want to hurt you," Fiona repeated. Her tears started again as she added, "And I love Kindan; I'm sorry, but it's true."

"Shh," Lorana said softly, pulling Fiona closer to her. "Why shouldn't you love him? You've got a big heart and you give it to everyone."

The sound of footsteps broke the moment and Fiona looked up to see K'lior and Cisca standing by them.

"I'm sorry," K'lior said, "I spoke without thinking."

"He does that sometimes," Cisca agreed, punching him lightly on the arm. "But, you know, he always *means* well."

"Will you forgive me?" K'lior begged Fiona.

"Of course she will," Lorana spoke up firmly. "She knows that sometimes we hurt those we love the most."

"At least I do now," Fiona said, dabbing away her tears.

"Come on back with us and we'll give you a proper Fort lunch," Cisca said, gesturing toward the Kitchen Cavern. "Besides," she added, "Ellor would never forgive me if she didn't get to feed up Lorana, here."

"Oh," Fiona said, trying for a lighter tone, "so this is *all* about Lorana, is it?"

"Of course it is," Cisca said, holding out a hand toward Fiona. "It's only because she can talk to all the dragons, you know." When Fiona accepted her hand, Cisca maneuvered the smaller Weyrwoman until she had her arm wrapped around her shoulder. As they walked back to the Kitchen Cavern, she leaned down and said quietly, "You have a knack for making your life difficult."

"My father preferred the word 'interesting,'" Fiona said, glancing up into Cisca's warm brown eyes.

"Well, just so you know, I'm not jealous," Cisca told her. "I've seen a few of these relationships with the blue riders and green riders and—"

"They don't last," Fiona finished for her. Cisca's eyes widened. "I know, I've seen them, too."

"Just so you know what you're getting into," Cisca said. She looked measuringly at Fiona and then added more kindly, "Although, sometimes they do work out."

"I know that, too," Fiona said. "It takes a lot of work."

"All relationships take work," Cisca said. She shrugged. "Really, when you think about it, anything you care to do well takes work."

"**N**ow, you be good and *listen* to your father," Merika called up from the ground below as Bekka settled into her perch behind Seban and in front of Fiona on Talenth's golden neck.

"I will," Bekka promised.

"And *you*," Merika said, wagging a finger at Seban, "be good and listen to your daughter."

"I will," Seban called back with a chuckle.

"And both of you," Merika went on, waving a hand in disgust at Seban's amusement, "remember that there are those who love you and they're only *between* away."

"We will!" Bekka called back loudly.

"You too, Weyrwoman," Cisca called, jumping up and down to gain Fiona's attention.

"We will!" Fiona called back just as loudly, causing Cisca to gape in surprise and then laugh.

Come on, Talenth, let's go! Fiona said to her queen as she waved good-bye to the Fort Weyr riders and weyrfolk gathered to see them off. *Fort Hold.*

The gold and bronze climbed up quickly in the afternoon air, circled the Star Stones once, and were gone, *between* to Fort Hold.

Fiona insisted upon circling Fort Hold's Great Hall before they glided down for a landing in the field outside the Healer Hall.

"So, you're back?" Betrony said as he approached from the Healer Hall. "And you've brought trouble?"

"We'll need Birentir's gear, sir," Fiona said.

"Birentir, eh?" Betrony said, his eyebrows arching. "Good choice, good choice." He glanced inquiringly toward Seban and Bekka.

Fiona got the hint and gestured toward them. "Masterhealer, may I present, with my compliments, Seban, formerly rider of blue Serth, and his daughter, Bekka." To Bekka and Seban she said, "This is Masterhealer Betrony."

"Kindan!" A loud voice boomed from the distance. "Report!"

"He's supposed to use a drum," Kindan growled affectionately. He turned to Lorana. "I'm sure he'd like to meet you, too."

"And Kindan wants the protection," Fiona added with a giggle. She waved Lorana off with Kindan. "I'll catch up when we're done here."

Kindan waved a hand behind his back in acknowledgment.

"Don't be too long and we'll drill on recognition points!" Fiona shouted after them. She turned back to Betrony just as Lindorm and Cerra strode by with Seban and Bekka in tow.

"We'll get them settled in, Master," Cerra said in passing.

Betrony waved them on, adding, "I'll have a longer meeting with you later."

"Don't worry," Lindorm told Bekka as she turned wide, worried eyes toward the Masterhealer, "he's not half as fearsome as the Masterharper."

"You'll be meeting him, too, tonight at dinner," Betrony added with a smile.

"Don't worry, Bekka," Fiona told the young girl, "*I* survived."

"You spent most of your time hiding up at the Hold, as I recall," Betrony said reminiscently.

"Not true," Fiona said. "Half the time I was down here, hiding from Father."

"Or hunting tunnel snakes."

"That, too," Fiona agreed. She glanced toward the retreating forms of Seban and Bekka as they entered the hall. "They're really very good."

"We'll see," Betrony said judiciously. "Of course," he cocked his head at her, "if they are, you know I'll be wanting *more*."

Fiona chuckled. She turned toward the Hold and said to the Master, "If you'll forgive me, I think I might have time to pay my respects."

"Your father's up with the Masterharper," Betrony said, gesturing in the other direction.

"Then I'm *certain* to have enough time to pay my respects!" Fiona said, marching off toward the distant Fort Hold.

The guards were overjoyed to greet her and waved her in through the great doors; once inside, Fiona turned to her left, heading toward the kitchen.

"There's no use coming here—there'll be no food until this evening, as you should well know!" a voice called out peremptorily as Fiona approached.

"Perhaps a cup of *klah*?" Fiona asked in her most waifish, pleading voice.

"Fiona?" the voice called.

"Neesa?" Fiona asked as she rounded the bend. She was met and hugged immediately by a round woman with gray hair and bright eyes.

Immediately, Neesa thrust her away again with her hands on her shoulders, crying, "My, how you've grown!"

"I've nearly seventeen Turns now," Fiona said. "I was back in time at Igen."

"Back in time?" Neesa said. "Sallit, did you hear, Fiona went back in time."

"She did, did she?" Sallit said as she bustled forward. "You're so tall!"

"I grew," Fiona said with a small smile.

"And you've got your own Weyr from what I hear," Neesa said as she gestured toward the worktable. "Sit down, I want to hear all about it."

"That's good," Fiona said, moving toward the table. Something in her manner alarmed Neesa who gave her a worried look and said, "What?"

Fiona's face crumpled and she was in tears even before she found the bench. "I think I've done something terribly wrong!"

"Probably no worse than the tunnel snakes," Sallit said, setting some mugs on the table and dragging a hot kettle from the nearby stove. "Let me brew us some fresh *klah* and see how the rolls are doing."

"While you tell me all about it," Neesa said, sitting beside Fiona and wrapping an arm around her comfortingly.

"You'll hate me," Fiona said.

"I doubt that," Neesa said. "But it's obvious you need to get this out of your heart."

Slowly, Fiona told the two older women everything. Neesa had been her confidante, anchor, and disciplinarian all through her childhood at Fort Hold. The old cook doted on her and spoiled her, but only up to a certain point.

"You're a Lady Holder and must act like it," Neesa had told her many times.

Now, she haltingly told them about her time in Igen Weyr, about going to Telgar, about Talenth getting the sickness, how Lorana and Kindan came with the cure—

"He's always been a good lad!" Neesa interjected.

—about T'mar's injury—

"And *he* was the one . . . ?" Sallit asked when Fiona got to that part of the story and Fiona nodded. "Ohhh!"

"Keep going," Neesa prompted. Fiona told them about the mating flight and its consequences and how she was trying—

"You've taken a load on your plate and that's no mistake," Sallit said, glancing to Neesa.

"But you're not the first," Neesa told Fiona soothingly.

"What should I do?"

"You do what's right for you," Neesa told her. "You do what your heart tells you."

"But my heart—"

"If you go this way, understand that it's hard," Neesa said. "For some it works, but for most it doesn't."

"Lorana said that there'd be pain."

"She's a smart one," Sallit said. "There's no love without pain, don't let anyone fool you."

"So I'm not terrible?" Fiona asked them. "I can do this?"

"I didn't say that you could," Neesa replied quickly. "Nor did I say that you couldn't, either." Fiona gave her a miserable look. "It's your path, child. You're the only one who can know for certain. And you're *not* terrible."

Neesa rose and Fiona rose with her. "You'd best get back to them, either way," Neesa said. "You said you were going to drill them on going *between*?"

Fiona nodded.

"So it's best you be about it, then," Neesa said, motioning Fiona toward the door. "Come on, I'll walk you back."

When they reached the Healer Hall, Neesa stopped and hugged Fiona.

"You know, you had his heart a long time ago," Neesa said. "Maybe you did him a kindness, taking those Turns in the past."

Fiona shook her head. "I can't be Koriana."

Neesa smiled at her. "You never were: You were always your own person." She reached out a finger and touched Fiona's nose lightly. "You remember that. Remember that you're special."

"I'll try."

"Good," Neesa said. "Now leave." Fiona's eyes widened and the old cook grinned at her. "The sooner you're gone, the sooner you can come back."

FOURTEEN

▼▼▼▼▼▼▼▼▼▼▼▼▼▼▼▼▼▼▼▼▼▼▼▼▼▼▼▼▼▼▼

Sands heat,
Dragons prove.
Times meet,
Eggs move.

Telgar Weyr, morning, AL 508.2.15

Birentir's ministrations to T'mar the following morning proved Mekiar's point: The healer was courteous, attentive, and efficient. T'mar, however, was querulous, difficult, and restless.

"You be careful, bronze rider, Talenth is certain that she'll rise before the Turn's out, and she might choose a different dragon next time," Fiona chided him.

"Was it the dragon or the rider?" T'mar asked, giving her a knowing look. "Or will you arrange it that there's another comatose bronze rider to suit your whim?"

"I might at that," Fiona answered calmly, her anger tempered by a warning glance from the healer. "Although, seeing as I've gotten rather good at catching you when you fall, I might just stick with Zirenth."

With a sour look, T'mar subsided. Birentir finished his inspection and rebandaged the bronze rider's leg in silence.

"I'm sorry, I'm not much of a patient," T'mar told the healer grumpily as he left.

"A head wound is debilitating and can leave a person feeling out of sorts, my lord," Birentir said. He glanced at Fiona, adding, "The Weyr-woman assures me that your normal behavior is much more agreeable."

T'mar smiled at that.

"And how soon can we expect normal behavior?" Fiona asked quietly as she and Birentir slipped by Zirenth onto the queens' ledge and into the Weyr Bowl proper.

"If he doesn't improve in a sevenday, I'll ask you to bring the Master-healer here," Birentir said. Fiona bit her lip anxiously until he added, "I haven't seen too many cases but, if my memory serves, he's progressing pretty much on schedule." He paused. "But stress always delays recovery and he's not sleeping as much as I'd like."

"We've Threadfall here in four days and not even a full flight to fly against it," Fiona said. She turned her head back to T'mar's weyr. "It's a wonder he sleeps at all." She frowned as she added, "And the meeting today won't help, either."

"He's not to be moved or move himself beyond trips to the necessary and back," Birentir warned.

"Which is why we're bringing the Weyrleaders here."

The healer nodded unhappily. He had reluctantly consented to Fiona's suggestion only when she'd included the Masterhealer among the attendees. She was glad that he'd agreed: The man had visibly mellowed in the past two days, but he still had trouble thinking of her as anything else than a tall lass of thirteen Turns with her father's lordly airs.

"Telgar was the logical choice anyway," Fiona continued, more to herself than Birentir. "We're in the middle time zone, which makes it convenient to everyone."

"Including the Istan Weyrleader," Birentir remarked drolly.

"Including the Istan Weyrleader," Fiona agreed, her eyes dancing.

▼ ▼ ▼

Lorana had surprised everyone two days before when, just after their return from the Healer Hall, she announced that High Reaches' queen, Lyrinth, was rising. No sooner had she made her announcement, than she'd added that Ista's Bidenth was also rising.

"I'd better go, they'll need help at Ista; they've too few bronzes," M'tal had said immediately on hearing the news, calling silently to Gaminth, who darted in to land beside him in the Weyr Bowl.

"Come back when you can, we've more to discuss," Fiona had told him. M'tal had waved an acknowledgment before clambering up his bronze and departing *between*.

What Fiona hadn't realized with her blithe dismissal was that the ex-Weyrleader would not be able to return until this day and then only as Weyrleader of Ista.

"I thought he loved Salina!" Kindan had exclaimed angrily when Lorana told them that M'tal's Gaminth had flown Istan Dalia's Bidenth, making him the Weyrleader of the southernmost Weyr. Salina had been M'tal's mate for Turns; her queen was the first to die of the sickness.

"He does," Lorana assured him with a puzzled look at his outburst.

"'How big is your heart,'" Fiona breathed to herself. She realized that M'tal, in giving her advice, may also have been advising himself.

Lorana had insisted on going to Benden on Zirenth to ferry Salina to Ista. Kindan had gone with her.

When they returned, they had several carefully wrapped parcels and Kindan wore the expression of someone keeping an important secret.

Knowing Kindan, Fiona had asked Lorana about the contents of the parcels.

"They're ancient artefacts," Lorana had told her simply. "We used them to make the cure for the sickness."

"And you want to use them here?" Fiona asked, her eyes going wide. "Is there more work to do?"

Lorana shook her head. "Not with these, at least," she'd replied.

"Emorra's last request was that we honor her mother's promise and return them to the sea at Tillek." She hefted a smaller parcel, adding, "The instructions are here."

"Shouldn't we keep them? Just in case we need them again?"

Lorana shook her head. "I don't think we'd know what to do with them. Our training was very specific, directed toward this one problem."

"Can I come with you? Do you need any help?"

Lorana shook her head again, smiling sadly. "I don't think we'll need any help, but you're welcome to come with us."

She glanced quickly at Kindan, who was hunched inward on himself. "We could use the company."

And so it was arranged.

They left midday the next day, after Fiona had assured herself that T'mar had settled in for the day and that Shaneese and Terin, between them, had all the Weyr matters well in hand.

Because High Reaches was to the west, the sun rose four hours later than it did at Telgar, allowing them to make a leisurely noon departure and arrive at first light. With Talenth leading and Fiona carrying all the precious artefacts, and with Lorana and Kindan on Zirenth, they rose to the watch heights, circled once, and went *between.*

When they emerged from *between,* Fiona could easily see the outline of Tillek Hold in the growing light of the sun. They had no trouble finding their landing—Zirenth landed so lightly that it was only when Lorana started to move that Kindan realized they were once again earthbound.

A hoarse bugle greeted them, to be echoed more loudly by the dragons.

Tillesk, Talenth said to both Fiona and Lorana.

"They've got a watch-wher!" Kindan exclaimed, a look of delight blossoming on his face.

"Disaller at your service," a richly clad man said as they passed through the large gates of Tillek Hold.

"Lord Disaller," Fiona said, nodding slightly.

Disaller nodded politely back, but his attention was fixed on Lorana. He strode up to her quickly, grasped her free hand, and bowed. He was a great bear of a man, one fully built for the needs of the premier sea hold.

"News of your deeds, and your sacrifice, were heard throughout Pern," he told her, his eyes full of sympathy. "It is an honor to have you here."

He glanced at Kindan and pumped his hand firmly. "You, too, harper," he said. His wagged his great bushy eyebrows at Kindan and his bearded mouth twitched up in a smile. "Perhaps we'll get a proper song of the events from you, soon?"

"There is no better song than Wind Blossom's," Kindan told the holder honestly.

"But he is composing another," Fiona said, her lips curved and her eyes twinkling. "Aren't you?"

"I've only just started," Kindan said, giving her an exasperated look.

"Pern is grateful to the both of you," Disaller said, turning and waving toward his Hold. "And we'd be happy to let you take your ease with us for as long as you desire."

"Not too long, my Lord," Kindan said with a shake of his head.

"We've a promise to keep and then we must return," Lorana added, gesturing at her carisak.

Disaller directed them away from the gates. "My watch-wher relayed your message," he said. "Although I'm not sure I completely understand it."

"A rope, a bell, a raft, and a beach with low surf is all we need," Kindan said.

"Ah." Disaller sounded relieved. "That is what we have. Although I took the liberty of laying in wet-weather clothing as well."

"Thank you," Lorana said.

"And some soup for the fog and chill of *between*," Disaller added as he guided them through a narrow cut in the hills surrounding the hold.

They walked less than a kilometer before they heard the roar of the surf and caught the smell of the sea.

"In good weather, the children come here to swim," Disaller told them as he indicated a stone outbuilding set well back from the shore.

It was no more than three walls and a roof, with an opening facing on to the sea. Inside there were the supplies Lorana had requested and, on a trestle table, a large container of soup covered with a warming mitt.

Disaller handed them all bowls and poured the warm soup into each, handing them large spoons after he finished.

They ate standing and the soup was quickly gone.

Disaller eyed the sea critically. "Not the best day for the beach."

"Not the worst, either," Lorana said, shuddering in memory of her last moments on the *Wind Rider*.

"True," Disaller said. "I forgot you were aboard the *Wind Rider*." He glanced at her thoughtfully, then added, "Was she a good ship?"

"Yes, she was," Lorana said. "And fast."

Disaller grinned at that, satisfied. "I've got Tanner building me another at that Half-Circle Sea Hold, in their deep docking caverns. He's almost a better builder than a ship's captain."

"How will you get it up here?" Lorana asked.

"I might not," Disaller said with a shrug. "But as long as she's hauling goods, she'll turn a profit."

"She will," Lorana said. She glanced at him curiously. "What will you name her?"

"I was thinking, if I might—" Disaller broke off. Then, somewhat abashedly, he asked, "Would you mind if I called her *Lorana*?" Quickly he added, "It's not much of a tribute, I know."

"I'd be honored," Lorana said, smiling.

Disaller beamed at her. "Thank you," he told her. "We'll take good care of her, you can be certain."

"You needn't fear, she'll take a lot of punishment and she'll be a good ship, with Tanner building her," Lorana told him.

"I wouldn't mind if you treated her gently," Fiona told the Lord Holder. "Then we'd have at least *one* Lorana who wasn't overworked."

Beside him, Kindan muttered a hearty approval.

"We should get to work," Lorana said, ignoring them. She moved outside of the hut, eyeing the gear Disaller had brought.

"I presume you're hoping to set the bell up on the raft," Disaller said as he approached. "Who are you hoping to attract?"

Fiona and Kindan exchanged glances, wondering how Lorana would answer.

"Dolphins," she told the Lord Holder directly.

Disaller nodded to himself. "Good," he said. "If you were hoping to attract one of the Deep Ones, I'd say you wouldn't have a chance."

"'Deep Ones'?" Fiona repeated questioningly.

"Surely you've heard the stories of the huge dwellers of the deep?" Disaller said, raising an eyebrow in surprise. "They go to depths well beyond the range of our trawlers."

"Have you ever caught one?"

"Caught one?" Disaller repeated, sounding outraged. He shook his head fiercely. "We'd no more catch one than we'd harm a dolphin.

"They help us; sometimes I think they herd the fish like the dolphins." He nodded toward Kindan. "Harpers tell us they came on the Great Crossing."

"Really?" Fiona asked in surprise. She turned to Kindan. "I'd never heard anything about them."

"Nor had I," Kindan said. He had a faraway look in his eyes, which Fiona recognized as a desire to dive into Records; a look rare for Kindan.

"My instructions say the dolphins," Lorana said, gesturing to the raft. "We're to get their attention and then return their gifts."

"Gifts?" Disaller asked, eyeing Lorana's carisak carefully. "Gifts from the sea?"

Lorana nodded.

Disaller's beard twitched again in a smile. "I checked our Records," he said with a nod toward Kindan. "I don't suppose it would surprise anyone to learn that Wind Blossom had visited here."

"I'm surprised your Records survived," Kindan said, eyeing the corrosive sea mist critically.

"These did," Disaller said. "They were carefully preserved, written by Lord Holder Malon himself." His eyes twinkled. "He seemed to think it important." He cocked his head to the distant hills. "Something to do with the dragons?"

"Lord Malon was very perceptive," Kindan said.

"Wind Blossom said we had to return them," Lorana said, her tone verging on anxious.

"The tools used to save the dragons?" Disaller guessed. "What would the dolphins do with them?"

"I don't know," Lorana said. "But Wind Blossom's daughter made it clear that it was important that they were returned."

"Very well," Disaller said, gesturing to Kindan to help him as he took one end of the raft. The two men hauled it to the surf and Disaller, wearing oiled waders, pushed it behind the surf with a stiff pole while Lorana and Fiona held firmly on to the mooring rope.

Satisfied, Disaller returned to them and tugged on another rope that lay nearby. "This'll raise a sail," Disaller said, tugging on the rope. "The wind's in the right quarter."

A small sail appeared above the raft several dragonlengths in the distance. They could hear the faint sound of the bell ringing out on the water.

"There," Disaller said, satisfied by the raft's position. He jerked his small rope again and the sail disappeared. "Now what?"

"We wait for the dolphins," Lorana said.

"And when they come?"

Lorana hefted her carisak. "We give them these."

Kindan rolled closer to Lorana to shelter her from the wind and keep her warm. In the next hour, the others also huddled around her, keeping themselves nearly as warm as she was.

The sun rose higher and the mist cleared. Lorana was dozing, half-awake when a noise startled her.

The bell. It was ringing loudly. Disaller jumped up, peering into the distance.

"I see fins," he called back. "Dolphins."

"Pull the raft back," Lorana said. "We'll load it up."

They pulled the raft back and loaded the contents of the carisak on it. Disaller eyed the strange enclosures carefully.

"I've never seen the like," he said. "How do you open them? Are they watertight?"

"Yes," Kindan said. "We tested them."

Disaller pulled off a glove and ran his finger over the surface of the matte material. "It feels slick; do you know what it's made of?"

Kindan shook his head. "There are some Records written on something similar, but we don't know what it is or how to make it."

"Pity," Disaller said, putting his glove back on. He glanced at the handiwork of the others as they placed the enclosures on the raft. "They'll not stay, you'll want to tie them on."

"No," Lorana told him. "This is the right way."

"Very well," Disaller grumbled, shaking his head. He pushed the raft back out past the surf and raised the sail once more, sending the raft skidding out farther before lowering the sail yet again.

The bell rang once more, then started pealing rapidly.

"Something's jostling the raft!" Disaller said. Before he could react, the raft had overturned. Fins raced around it for a moment and then were gone. Disaller turned to Lorana, worry and surprise on his face. "We could run back to the Hold and maybe launch a ship!"

"Why?"

"To recover your artefacts," Disaller said, glancing from Lorana, to Kindan, and finally to Fiona in surprise.

"No, they're fine," Lorana said, her eyes closed. She had a slightly quizzical look on her face.

Kindan stepped closer to her, his arms held out protectively. "Lorana?"

Lorana shook her head. "I'm fine," she told him, glancing up and nodding encouragingly. "It's just that—"

"Look!" Fiona said, pointing off to the distance. The others followed her finger and saw a spout of water burst into the air, followed by another, and another.

"The Deep Ones," Disaller said, his eyes wide with awe. As they watched, something huge and stately broached the surface of the water where the last spout had appeared and then dove below the water once more. Disaller could spot dolphin fins racing toward it.

Lorana smiled. "They're beautiful!"

"They don't often come this close to land," Disaller said, glancing at Lorana incredulously. "How did you know . . . ?"

Lorana shook her head. "I didn't," she told him. "*They* did."

"Lorana?" Fiona asked.

"I can almost hear them," Lorana said. She turned to Kindan. "They're like the dragons, only different."

"Telepathic?" Kindan asked in surprise.

"Almost," Lorana said. "Or just different." She shrugged. "They thanked us. I got the impression that there was more but I couldn't understand it."

"Sea dragons?" Disaller asked wonderingly.

"No," Lorana said. "Not dragons." She stared back out to sea, hoping for one final glimpse of the Deep Ones. "More like dolphins, only bigger, much bigger. And different."

"How different?" Fiona asked.

"Like I doubt I could ever understand them," Lorana said. She turned to Disaller. "You'll want to recover that raft, for the bell."

"The bell?" Disaller asked, giving her an inscrutable look.

"Yes," Lorana said. "They like the bell."

Disaller's brows narrowed in surprise. "How did you know—"

Lorana turned back to the sea and that was answer enough for the Lord Holder.

"*They* told you," he breathed in awe, pulling gently on the mooring line. To the others he said, "That bell was the same one used by Wind Blossom."

They stopped at High Reaches Weyr on the way back. Weyrwoman Sonia was happy to see them, as evidenced by Lyrinth's proud bugling when she spotted Fiona's queen.

"Congratulations on your flight!" Fiona said to Sonia and D'vin when they met.

"And you on yours," D'vin returned.

"On your *two* flights," Sonia added. "I take it that I've lost my queen to Telgar." She raised an eyebrow questioningly as she added, "Unless you're here to request a transfer?"

Fiona smiled and shook her head. "No, Kindan and Lorana were at Tillek returning borrowed gear and insisted on stopping here."

"They did, did they?" Sonia said, eyeing the pair speculatively.

"If we could, we'd like to check in your Records Room," Lorana said, hefting a carisak onto her shoulder.

"Let me send for some *klah* and we'll join you," D'vin said.

"Actually, my lord, we'd prefer to do this ourselves," Kindan responded smoothly, gesturing to Lorana and himself. Fiona hid her surprise and hurt at the exclusion, giving Sonia a look of resignation as if to indicate that one had to make allowances for harpers.

"Well, then, we'll meet you in the kitchen," Sonia said, waving them away and motioning for Fiona to precede her.

When Kindan and Lorana rejoined them half an hour later, Fiona saw the way that Sonia's eyes darted to Lorana's now empty carisak and the Weyrwoman's thoughtful expression.

D'vin waved them toward chairs and continued saying, "I understand that we'll see you tomorrow."

Sonia gave Kindan a triumphant look as if to say "Take that!" but the harper merely nodded, saying, "So you'll be at Telgar tomorrow noon?"

"A bit later than noon," Sonia said in response. "I'll need *some* sleep."

Recalling the conversation now, with the arrival of all the Weyrleaders and Weyrwomen of Pern imminent, Fiona wondered if perhaps Sonia wasn't also obliquely giving Telgar more time to prepare.

Certainly Shaneese had worked wonders, although, to judge from the fatigue-smudged eyes of the Cavern staff, she'd kept most of the weyrfolk up through the night.

"I'll not have it said that Telgar doesn't know how to entertain!" Shaneese had said as soon as she'd recovered from the shock of Fiona's news.

And, indeed, the Weyr looked cleaner than Fiona had ever seen a Weyr look before. Even the dirt on the Weyr Bowl floor looked freshly washed and raked.

H'nez, for his part as senior wingleader, had ensured that all riders and their dragons were turned out smartly in their finest. The watch dragon was a bronze—Fiona had offered Talenth's services, but had quickly demurred under the weight of H'nez's affronted look and Shaneese's gasp of indignity.

"If you've no further need for me, Weyrwoman," Birentir said as they neared the entrance to the Dining Cavern, "I should make my rounds."

Fiona waved him away with a smile, entering the Cavern alone. She was not surprised to see Xhinna and Taria hustling their young charges through their breakfast.

"Will we be able to see the Weyrleaders?" Aryar asked hopefully as she pranced alongside her older carers.

"I think they're going to be busy," Taria said.

"But will they hear our singing? With harper Norik?" little Rhemy asked, eyes wide with hope.

"I'm sure, if there's time, we will be delighted," Fiona told her.

The group halted and whirled around, breaking away from their minders to rush over and crush Fiona in a hug and a chorus of giggles.

"The Weyrwoman's busy! You need to let her go!" Shaneese called crossly from across the kitchen.

Fiona gently shooed the youngsters from her side, telling them, "And you'll need to practice very hard if you're going to sing for us!"

"We will!" Aryar said, shoving the others back to Taria and grabbing the older girl's hand in hers, tugging her toward the exit into the back corridors. "Come on, Taria! We've got to practice!"

Fiona waved farewell and turned her attention back to the area prepared for the Weyrleaders' council. When they'd first planned for it,

Fiona had naturally assumed that they'd just use the Council Room of the Senior Queen's quarters. But once she'd checked out the size of that room and tallied up the number of attendees, she decided that the room would be far too small to accommodate everyone—not only were there to be Weyrleaders and Weyrwomen, but also many of their healers, wingseconds, and junior queen riders, as well as harpers from the Harper Hall, smiths from the Smithcrafthall, and a smattering of interested Lord Holders.

Fiona had despaired of housing them all, but Shaneese had strung thick canvas curtains in the Cavern to separate the designated section from the rest of the room. Fiona looked inside and was pleased to see that the chairs were also festooned with canvas covers, grouped in pairs on opposite sides of the long table, the backs and tops marked with Weyr symbols for Fort, High Reaches, Telgar, Ista, and Benden.

In addition there were chairs for the Masterharper, the Masterhealer, the Mastersmith, Lord Bemin of Fort Hold, Lady Nerra of Crom Hold, and Lord Gadran of Bitra Hold.

"That old wherry!" Kindan had snorted when they'd learned that he'd been invited by B'nik of Benden Weyr. "I suspect B'nik's hoping for pointers on how to deal with the old goat."

"My father is a Lord Holder," Fiona reminded him. "I'd expect more deference from a journeyman harper."

"Ah, so you've not met him!" Kindan said.

Fiona nodded in agreement, adding reluctantly, "And Father made it a point to introduce me to all his favorite Lord Holders."

Kindan smiled. "That's when he was planning to install you as the next Lord Holder of Fort, so he was currying favor," he told her. Shaking his head, he added, "Gadran has too many sons to ever consider such an outrageous idea."

"So how ever did he approve of Lady Nerra?" Lorana asked.

"It doesn't take a majority to seat a Lord Holder," Fiona told her.

"Lord Gadran was the leader and sole member of the vocal minority," Kindan noted.

"So this meeting will be interesting on many levels," Fiona said.

A rustle of wings and the bugling challenge of the watch dragon alerted them to the arrival of the first of their guests.

"M'tal and Daria from Ista," Lorana told them as they left the enclosure. She cocked an eye at Kindan. "Are you ready?"

"Yes." With a flourish and a bow toward Fiona, he said, "By your leave, Weyrwoman, my lady and I will start conveying the Lord Holders to this meeting."

"Who first?" Fiona wondered, feeling oddly stung at Kindan's reference to Lorana as his lady. "Please, not Gadran!"

Kindan snorted. "You haven't been so ill-behaved recently as to deserve *that* fate."

"Thank the First Egg!"

"I think, with your permission, it will be your father—"

"And his lady," Lorana added.

"I'd hardly think that Kelsa would accept being anyone's lady!" Kindan said with a laugh.

"Yet you claim me," Lorana retorted in a low voice.

Kindan looked surprised and groped for words, saying, "I—I only thought—"

"You didn't think, I'd say," Fiona cut him off. She waved a hand toward Zirenth. "You'd best go."

Sort it out later. Fiona wasn't sure if that was Talenth, Lorana agreeing with her, or her own voice talking to Lorana. From the surprised look on Lorana's face, it was clear that the older woman was just as unsure.

"Later," Kindan agreed, turning with alacrity toward the bronze dragon's lair.

Lorana spared a smile for Fiona before joining him.

"Now," Fiona said to herself, "what other trouble can I get into today?"

"Trouble comes without asking for it," a sour voice spoke up beside her. Fiona spun and saw Norik. The older man grinned a strained smile. Fiona fought down the sudden tension in her gut.

"It's true," Fiona agreed. "But I've often found that diving right into it puts it off guard."

"Indeed?"

"It at least has the virtue of being novel," Fiona told him. "And what trouble were you bringing me today?" She glanced around. "I thought you were instructing the youngsters in their singing."

"I was," Norik said. "I took a break when I learned you were here."

Fiona gave him an attentive look.

"I don't know, with all that has transpired, if you remember my request for a new assignment."

"No," Fiona assured him with a relieved smile, "I haven't forgotten. In fact, I thought that you would be able to appeal directly to Master Zist when he arrives."

Norik pursed his lips and nodded. "So I'd hoped."

Fiona nodded, waiting attentively to see if their conversation was over. It was not.

"I think, if I might, I'd like to be posted to Benden Weyr."

"Yes, you'd mentioned that. But I have to ask, why another Weyr?" Fiona said, surprised. And why, from what she'd heard, would anyone choose to be posted into the care of the prickly Weyrwoman Tullea? Of course, given Norik's taciturn nature, perhaps the two would be a good match, Fiona thought impishly to herself.

"I've not heard of any open holds," Norik said. He met her eyes squarely as he added, "And, truth be told, I like the freedom of the Weyrs."

"As a former holder lass, I can't argue with you!"

"I appreciate that, my lady," Norik said. His normally flat eyes seemed to have found some sparkle as he continued, "And now, if you'll forgive me, I must get back to the lessons."

"Of course," Fiona said, turning to the two dragons gliding down to the ground before her. She heard the sound of footsteps racing up beside her and was not surprised to hear H'nez say, "They're early, aren't they?"

"I suspect M'tal wants a word with us beforehand," Fiona said.

Bronze and gold settled on the ground, greeted warmly by Talenth and Jeila's Tolarth, who bugled in greeting.

Bidenth is a great queen, Talenth declared.

Another sound distracted Fiona and she turned to see Zirenth exit his weyr and Lorana and Kindan climb quickly aboard.

"It's traditional for the Weyrleader to greet guests," H'nez said from the corner of his mouth as they approached the new Istan Weyrleader, putting up a cautioning hand and moving ahead of Fiona.

"Bronze rider," Fiona said tartly, her hand grabbing his and pulling him back, "in case you haven't yet noticed, I make my *own* traditions."

"As you will," H'nez said with a resigned sigh.

"M'tal!" Fiona cried, rushing toward the older man uninhibitedly and throwing herself into his arms. "It's good to see you!"

M'tal crushed her against him in a quick hug, then pushed her back again. "I've not been gone that long, Weyrwoman!" he said. Then, with a worried look, he added, "Has something *else* happened?"

"No," she assured him with a grin, "I haven't destroyed anything yet today."

"The day is young," M'tal said, entering into the spirit of things.

"You, on the other hand," Fiona said, "have been quite busy." She glanced over toward Bidenth and was surprised to see not one but two women dismounting. Her expression cleared instantly and she turned to him with a look of contrition and pride. "Have you found how big your heart is?"

"Let us say that I've discovered that it is bigger than I thought," M'tal replied, his voice soft and sounding troubled in the admission.

"And," he added, "for all my Turns, I've discovered that you and I have much in common." His eyes twinkled as he declared, "I should have told you that in my youth, I was considered something of a rebel."

Fiona snorted with amusement. The two women approached and M'tal introduced them. "This is Dalia, Weyrwoman of Ista."

Dalia's face was lined, the corners of her eyes marked with crow's feet and her cheeks with laugh lines. Her eyes were brown and her hair a fading red. Freckles speckled all over her face.

Fiona nodded and extended her hand, feeling her lack of years in the presence of the older woman.

"Congratulations, Weyrwoman," Fiona said as she released her hand. "I hope you had an excellent mating flight."

"Well, it was *interesting*, to say the least," Dalia said drolly. "But perhaps not quite as interesting as the tale of *yours*." Dalia glanced around. "Where are Kindan and Lorana?"

"They just left on Zirenth," Fiona said. "They are going to ferry the Holders and Crafters." She gave the older woman a grin as she added, "I'm not sure if it was Kindan's idea—to get more time a-dragonback—or Lorana's—to permit me to greet you first."

"Probably a little of both," said the other woman in the party. Salina seemed near the same age as Dalia but was much taller and had an elegant, thin-boned form. Her hair had lost almost all its color but her eyes were still bright blue.

"You must be Salina," Fiona said, extending her hand again, adding solemnly, "I grieve for your loss."

"Mine is nothing compared to Lorana's," Salina said dismissively, "and from what M'tal's said, you've done more than most to make good her loss."

"Thank you," Fiona said. She wasn't sure that she agreed with Salina; she cast a glance toward Dalia and wondered if the Weyrwoman had the same misgivings about her queen's mating flight with M'tal's Gaminth as she had with her Talenth's mating flight with Zirenth. For all that Lorana denied it, Fiona was still not certain that the ex–queen rider was unhurt by Fiona's mating-flight relationship with Kindan. And, deeper inside herself, Fiona was still not sure if her own heart was big enough to share a love.

Fiona realized that Salina was eyeing her intently and raised her head to meet the older woman's gaze. Salina nodded silently as if to herself and raised a hand to break the moment.

"M'tal's also told me about your work back at Igen," Salina told her quietly. "*That* accomplishment is yours alone."

"You've acquired a following in Ista," Dalia added, her lips curving upward. "My daughter was quite impressed with M'tal's reports, as was I."

"Thank you," Fiona said, her cheeks going hot. She sought to change the subject. "As you know, T'mar is still recovering from his fall. H'nez is our senior wingleader and will take his place in the Council." She glanced around and waved a hand toward H'nez, who strode forward and made his introductions.

"I understand you're to be congratulated as well!" Dalia said with a grin, adding, "And I've heard that Sonia was none too pleased to lose her only other queen to such a handsome man."

"My Ginirth was lucky to catch her."

"In my experience, which bronze catches a queen is one thing," Salina corrected him, "what the riders choose later is another."

"Jeila has asked me to grace her quarters," H'nez replied, his stiff mask of control slipping for a moment to reveal a nearly boyish glee. Fiona found the expression as charming as it was unexpected. H'nez seemed to notice her reaction and, with a twitch of his eyebrows in acknowledgment, resumed his normally stiff look.

"I think I see why she'd make such an offer," Dalia said approvingly.

M'tal glanced toward the three weyrwomen's quarters near the entrance to the Hatching Grounds and said, "How is T'mar? May I see him?"

"He's querulous, tetchy, irritable, and snappish," Fiona replied. "But our healer, Birentir—"

"Birentir?" Dalia interrupted. "From Ista?"

Fiona agreed, explaining how she'd borrowed Tintoval from Fort Weyr to examine T'mar and had arranged with Masterhealer Betrony to bring his three journeymen along for observation—and trial.

"Birentir was a very sad and bitter man," Dalia said when Fiona had finished. "I'm glad that he's found peace."

"I've been told that I surround myself with difficult people," Fiona said, careful to keep her gaze from straying in H'nez's direction.

"The traders call you the desert flower," M'tal told her with a smile. He nodded toward T'mar's quarters. "Would it be possible to pay respects to the Weyrleader?"

Fiona frowned, not wanting to overwhelm T'mar with a crowd of visitors. Before she said anything, Dalia spoke up, saying, "I'd like to visit with Birentir, for myself."

"I'd be happy to escort you," H'nez said, offering up a hand while glancing at Fiona for agreement.

"We'll have to keep the visit brief," Fiona said warningly, nodding permission to H'nez, who directed Dalia on a new course toward the healer's quarters.

T'mar was awake, lying stretched out on his bed when they came in.

"I'm checking Lorana's coordinates," T'mar told them with a strange expression on his face. "She's on the way here with Verilan, Master Zist, and Betrony." He made a wry face as he added, "Apparently there was a . . . discussion with the blue rider sent from Fort Weyr over who would have the honor of bearing the Masters."

"I'll bet that was short," M'tal said.

"The blue bears Bemin and Kelsa," T'mar said in agreement. He glanced toward M'tal. "Congratulations on your flight, Weyrleader."

M'tal nodded, saying, "It wasn't quite what I'd intended."

"Often things don't turn out the way we intended," T'mar said, glancing toward Fiona.

"See," Fiona said, throwing up a hand in mock disgust, "just as I said, he's tetchy and irritable."

The others chuckled.

"Seriously," T'mar continued, glancing toward Fiona who forced herself not to stick out her tongue in pique, "the Weyrwoman and I have talked, and I've talked with Kindan and Lorana about today's meeting."

"And now you'll rest and leave it in our hands," Fiona told him pointedly.

"I will," T'mar said. "But as I've a chance to stretch the ear of the Istan Weyrleader, I thought I'd mention our worries about the number of fighting dragons once more."

"There's been no change since our last conversation, T'mar," M'tal said. "During that, I agreed that we need to have a meeting of all the Weyrleaders to plan a combined course of action." He patted the younger man's shoulder and stood back. "Rest easy, bronze rider, we'll do our best."

They left him immediately afterward, Fiona leading the way to the Dining Cavern.

"We would have set up a pavilion in the Weyr Bowl but," she gestured to the damp ground and shivered at the freezing air, "we decided it would be more difficult than setting aside a meeting place in the Cavern itself."

"**A**ssuming that the losses I've read about in the Records are a reliable standard, at our current rate, the strength of the Weyrs will fall below one Flight each—ninety dragons—in less than half a Turn," Verilan concluded grimly, glancing at each of the Weyrleaders in turn.

"So, even though we've found a cure, we have no hope," Tullea said, turning to the Master Archivist for confirmation.

"If the casualties follow the historical numbers," Verilan cautioned.

"So the solution is to fight wiser than our ancestors," H'nez said. He asked Verilan, "What casualty rate is required for us to survive?"

"At the risk of sounding overly pedantic, wingleader, I must ask you what do you mean by survive?" Verilan asked.

"Have enough dragons to fight Thread," the bronze rider said, glowering at the Master.

"Again, meaning no disrespect, what is enough?" Verilan asked, glancing around the room to include the other Weyrleaders and Weyrwomen present. "The Records tell me that ninety dragons is the bare minimum deemed suitable to fight a Fall, yet even the Records imply that more—two Flights or even the full strength of a Weyr—is preferred.

"Would a mere ninety dragons be enough for all the Falls on Pern? And for how long could they be expected to hold out?" Verilan mused. "Those are questions that the Records do not answer."

"Because they were never asked," D'vin said gloomily.

"All the queens—save Darial's Somarth—have mated recently and will mate again in half a Turn according to the Records," H'nez said, glaring again at Verilan who met his gaze steadily. "So it would seem to me that all we have to do is wait for these weyrlings to hatch."

"And how long before they are strong enough to fly Thread?" Tullea asked. She gestured to B'nik, Benden's Weyrleader, for an answer.

"At Benden," B'nik told the group, "we prefer to wait three Turns if possible."

"Eighteen months was the minimum time I found in the Records," Verilan said. "Although, from what I can read, those riders and dragons fared worse fighting Thread than those who'd trained longer."

"You're telling us nothing new in that," H'nez snorted. "The more time to train and grow, the better the fighting dragon."

"But we don't have time," K'lior, Fort's Weyrleader, reminded them. He glanced at Verilan. "So, eighteen months and we'll have how many more dragons?"

"Queens clutch as few as a dozen and as many as three dozen eggs," Verilan said, thinking aloud. "The first mating flight usually produces fewer eggs than later flights. If we were to take an average number for the eight queens, we could hope for an additional two hundred and forty dragons—somewhat less than three Flights of dragons." He nodded at K'lior and Cisca, adding, "But the eggs have yet to clutch—let alone hatch—and that adds another four to five months to the number."

"Nearly two full Turns, then," M'tal said.

Fiona exchanged a bleak look with Lorana.

"I did not take my calculations out two Turns," Verilan told the council miserably.

"Why not?" H'nez asked. Fiona kicked him under the table but the bronze rider ignored it. "Given what we know, can't you tell us how many dragons we'll have when these hatchlings are ready to fight Thread?"

"Given what I know, bronze rider," Verilan said quietly, "there will be no dragons left when those hatchlings are ready to fight Thread."

"None?" Salina gasped.

"My lady, we stopped when we reached fifty-nine fighting dragons," Verilan said, glancing at his group of apprentices and helpers, who were waiting outside the pavilion.

"And when was that?" D'vin asked.

"Forty-seven weeks from now," Verilan replied, glancing down at his slate with a sour look.

"And when do your calculations say the total strength will be down to just one Flight of ninety dragons?" H'nez asked.

"Thirty-eight weeks from now," a voice outside the canvas called in response. Fiona recognized Bekka. She'd seen the girl when she'd arrived with the Master Archivist and assumed that she'd been sent to help Birentir.

"Who dares listen in on this council?" H'nez demanded angrily, rising from his seat.

Bekka poked her head in through the entrance. "I do," she told him simply, adding, with a shrug, "And pretty much everyone else. After all, this concerns us, too."

"As indeed it does," Fiona agreed, raising a hand to pull H'nez back to his seat, "but we already have enough voices in this discussion." She gestured for Bekka to leave. "Listen if you must, but speak only if absolutely necessary."

"Something," Verilan added menacingly, "that I'd already mentioned to you."

Bekka paled at the Archivist's words and slunk out of the enclosure.

Fiona turned to him with frank surprise at Bekka's immediate and fearful obedience of the Master Archivist. "How did you do that?"

Verilan shrugged. "I've been dealing with apprentices since not long after you were born, my lady."

"Which still does nothing for the issue at hand," Weyrwoman Sonia said.

"No," Masterharper Zist agreed sadly, "it does not."

"Have you figured how much better we'd have to fight to survive long enough for the hatchlings to mature to fighting age?" K'lior asked Verilan.

"We're working on it!" Bekka's voice called from outside the pavilion. Fiona glanced sharply toward the entrance before giving Verilan a droll expression.

"She is, perhaps, one of the more challenging apprentices," Verilan allowed.

"Nothing we wouldn't have expected," Zist added, "given the source."

Fiona ducked her head in appreciation of the gibe, then turned her head toward H'nez. "I presume we've got Terin helping with the calculations?"

"Bekka suggested her," Verilan said. He gave Fiona a hopeful look, as he added, "She's quite good with numbers. If she were to come to the Harper Hall . . ."

"I'll put it to her," Fiona replied.

"I'm not sure that F'jian would approve," H'nez said.

"As long as dragons have wings, F'jian won't be far from her," Fiona said. "He's no fool, nor she—I can't believe either would want her talents to go to waste." Her expression made it clear that she thought H'nez wouldn't want Terin's talents to go to waste, either.

"At another time," Zist said, "we really should discuss how to identify and encourage such talents."

Fiona nodded in agreement.

"What I don't understand is why are we in so much danger," D'vin said. "Did they not survive the same sort of problems in the last Pass?"

"From all that I've seen, we have no Weyr Records from the time two hundred and fifty Turns back," Kindan said. He glanced toward Fiona. "Unless some survived at Igen?"

"They did. But I don't recall any problem like ours."

"They must have survived worse problems in the First Pass," K'lior said. "Back then they started with *no* dragons and still survived!"

"Ah, but they had the aid of their amazing machines," Mastersmith Zellany responded. "I'm afraid we can offer not much more than the agenothree throwers inspired by Weyrwoman Fiona."

"That's not much help from the past," Weyrwoman Tullea said. Beside her, Benden's Weyrleader gave her a pained look, but Tullea persisted. "We had help from the First Pass before, why not ask for more now?"

"Are you willing to sacrifice your dragon to send the message?" Sonia asked. Tullea gave her an irritated look.

"I doubt that they can help any more," Lorana said. As the others glanced her way, she continued, "Wind Blossom is dead, and, from what Emorra said in her audios, her special knowledge died with her."

"What about all those ancient artefacts you were so desperate to sink at Tillek?" Tullea asked.

"Their usefulness to us was over when the last of the materials were used in the cure," Kindan said.

"I," H'nez began, "for one, am of the opinion that we here can solve this problem." He glanced at Tullea. "I think we don't need more hand-holding from the past."

"You say that with less than a wing of fighting dragons?" Tullea asked scornfully.

"Speaking now for Ista, some of us have seen worse days," M'tal said. "And yet we recovered." He looked around the table as he added, "Ista has three hundred and seven fighting dragons." He paused, glancing at Dalia and Salina before continuing, "I'm willing to redistribute that strength to bring the other Weyrs up to decent fighting numbers."

"Really?" Tullea asked acerbically. "What, you'll give away a wing?"

"To Benden, yes," M'tal replied. With a wink for Fiona, he added, "I think we can send another ninety-seven here, to Telgar." Over the gasps of the others he added, "Telgar is central to Pern and could well be expected to be taxed more than most."

"We were thinking along the same lines," D'vin said, turning toward K'lior. "Sonia and I would like to bring your strength up to two Flights, if you're willing."

"We'd appreciate it," K'lior replied, grinning.

"And we'll send two wings here, to Telgar," Sonia added, smiling at Fiona. "A queen's due, as it were."

"For our part, we promise to share any queens with Weyrs that need them," Fiona said in response, glancing at Cisca, who nodded in thanks.

"This still won't solve our problem," D'vin said.

"No, but it will make it easier to bear," B'nik said.

"And we'll fly to your aid, when needed," H'nez declared solemnly.

"Only if you're not fighting Thread yourselves," M'tal said.

"For the Crafts," Zellany said, "we and the Holders might be able to provide better ground cover."

"As soon as we get enough of those new flamethrowers," Lord Holder Gadran of Bitra Hold growled.

"And training," Lady Nerra of Crom Hold added.

"To be honest," Lord Holder Bemin spoke up reluctantly, "we really don't know how much better these new flamethrowers will perform until we've used them more."

"I'm certain, my Lord, that they'll do better than the old ones," the Mastersmith said. "If only because your crews won't have to worry about them exploding."

"*That* would be a relief," Gadran said.

"What else can we do?" H'nez asked. "It seems that we need to provide the time—"

"That's it!" Tullea exclaimed. "Go back in time, raise the new weyrlings back in time."

"Where?" Fiona asked after the first rush of excitement had flowed over her. Tullea looked at her dumbfounded, so she continued, "I mean, Weyrwoman Tullea, we've already used all the time we had at Igen Weyr."

"Used all the time?" Tullea repeated, brows furrowed thunderously. "How can you use time?"

"Every Turn back all the way through ten Turns has been used already," Kindan said. "If we'd sent more weyrlings back in time, we'd already know about it."

"You can't break time," B'nik told his mate quietly.

"And we don't know quite when the sickness started," Lorana said, "so we can't go back further in time."

"Not only that, but before then I don't think the holds had recovered sufficiently from the Plague to provide supplies," Fiona said.

"We can bring supplies," H'nez said.

"From where?" Sonia asked.

"From wherever we'll get them to feed our new weyrlings, I suspect," K'lior said.

"It still won't work," Fiona said. The others looked at her. "If it had happened in the past, there would have been signs at Igen."

"But you said yourself that someone had worked the firestone mine nearby," Kindan reminded her. "And it was the new firestone, not the flamestone we'd been using."

"Perhaps we could use timing itself," M'tal said while Fiona absorbed Kindan's comment with a thoughtful frown.

"How?" D'vin asked.

"Dragons could go back to a Fall to aid in the fight," M'tal said.

"How would they know to go back?" K'lior asked.

"Because they would have seen themselves come back," M'tal said.

"So . . . when we do it, we'll do it?" Sonia said.

"That seems to be the common case with timing," M'tal replied dryly.

"Who has the most experience with timing?" D'vin asked, looking around the room, his eyes settling on M'tal.

The older rider chuckled. "Guilty."

"Well, then, it makes sense to go with the advice of the most experienced in this matter," D'vin said. "I've only done it once, myself."

"I've done it once as well," Tullea griped, "for *three* bloody Turns!"

"Yes, dear," Sonia said in a tone that was both calming and dampening, "we remember."

"My experience isn't all that much different from Tullea's, except that I never stayed back in time as long as she has," M'tal said, nodding diplomatically toward Tullea, who gave him a mollified look in return. "But I think that journeying *between* time is more fatiguing than going *between* places."

"I'd agree," Fiona said.

"So what that will mean for the riders is that they should be well-rested before going *between* times and have time to recover before another Threadfall," D'vin surmised. He turned to M'tal. "Is that right?"

"I'd say so."

"According to what I've learned from Kindan and the other Weyr harpers," Verilan said, careful to note his sources, "the pattern of Thread-falls repeats every fifty days."

M'tal pursed his lips thoughtfully and nodded, turning to D'vin and B'nik, who each made gestures of agreement.

"According to my sources, then," Verilan said, "it seems that as things stand, Benden flies in seven Falls, Telgar in six, Ista in five, while the High Reaches and Fort Weyrs fly four Falls."

"Then Benden should have more dragons," Tullea said.

"I'd prefer to see how things work out, first," B'nik said, glancing reprovingly at his Weyrwoman. "There was a reason our ancestors established six Weyrs."

"*Six* Weyrs," Tullea said, "and Benden's had to take a higher proportion of the Falls that used to be flown by Igen."

"I don't think we can hope to reestablish Igen until we've solved the current problem," Sonia said with a nod toward Tullea. "But if you run into troubles, we'll provide you with aid."

"Benden will fly its own Falls, thank you."

"That's really for me to decide," B'nik told her. He glanced around the room. "Still, I think for coordination, it's always best to assume that the assigned Weyr will handle a Fall unless prior arrangements are made."

The dragonriders all nodded in agreement.

"We've got an answer for you," Bekka called from outside the pavilion.

"By all means, please tell us," Verilan said, his voice a mix of somber gravity and resignation.

"From what I can figure," Terin's voice piped up from outside the canvas, "and Bekka has checked me, the Weyrs must lose less than two dragons every Fall if they're to maintain their strength for two Turns."

"There hasn't been a Fall yet where a Weyr hasn't lost at least three," Verilan said. He cocked his head toward the outside group, demanding, "Is that losses or casualties?"

"Casualties," Terin responded after several tense moments of whispered conversation between her and the others.

"The injured come back," Bekka said.

"That doesn't help if every dragon and rider is injured," Fiona pointed out.

"Oh!" Bekka said in surprise. "I hadn't thought of that."

"Can you work out how long the Weyrs have until they have less than a Flight of fighting dragons?" Sonia asked.

"We'll work on it, Weyrwoman," Verilan said, rising from his chair and adding, "I think it best if I go supervise."

The Weyrwoman waved a hand in agreement.

"I don't see how we have any other choice but to do better," D'vin said in the silence that followed.

"Perhaps timing will help," M'tal said hopefully. He pursed his lips tightly for a long thoughtful moment, then rose from his chair, bowing toward Fiona and nodding at H'nez.

"Weyrwoman," he said, "I think it best if we take our leave of you. I have many preparations to make and"—he nodded toward H'nez again—"I'm certain that you will want as much training time as possible between now and your next Fall."

The others rose, too, and the meeting adjourned.

As M'tal peered down from his perch on Gaminth, he sketched a quick salute to Kindan, calling out, "As you seem to be something of the acting Weyrleader, I thought you might like to know that I'll be sending J'lantir and his wing to you." He smiled drolly as he added, "Try not to lose them, will you?"

From the ground, Kindan smiled and waved an acknowledging salute, calling back, "We'll do all we can!"

Gaminth leaped into the air, beat his wings twice, and was gone *between* even before he'd cleared the watch heights.

"Show off!" Sonia swore affectionately as she sat astride her Lyrinth alongside D'vin on his bronze Hurth.

"I'd prefer it if he were less flashy," D'vin said with a frown. M'tal was now the oldest Weyrleader left and the High Reaches Weyrleader could not help feeling a sense of foreboding.

Across the distance of dragonlengths, Sonia shot him a probing look and nodded in silent agreement, her expression shifting to match his.

"Fly well!" Fiona called up to them.

"Don't be strangers!" Jeila added in agreement, her arm wrapped possessively around H'nez's lanky waist.

The High Reaches Weyrleaders waved back and then they, too, were gone, *between*.

"They should have flown to the watch heights first," H'nez commented sourly.

"They know what they're doing," Jeila said in their defense.

"They're tired, and tired people should never deviate from tradition," H'nez groused. "Not only that, but we'll be certain to have those here foolish enough to think they can do the same—and I'll have to show them otherwise."

Tullea and B'nik were more careful, particularly as Norik had achieved his ambition of attaching himself as Benden's harper, and rode clinging to Tullea's back, talking ingratiatingly to the Weyrwoman. The dour Gadran eyed him critically from his position behind B'nik on Caranth.

"It's not as though we'll see Kindan, at least until T'mar has healed fully," B'nik had allowed when the notion had been proposed to them.

"And he seems a lot more competent than Kindan," Tullea had agreed, her eyes flashing sharply toward the younger harper. She added venomously to Fiona, "Not that I'm sure you didn't get the better of the bargain, my dear."

"Two for one, and both the most famous on Pern?" Fiona purred in response. "I cannot thank you enough."

"Of that I'm certain," Tullea rejoined, not willing to let the exchange go in Fiona's favor.

Fiona merely nodded, lips pursed tightly, in response.

Cisca and K'lior were the last to leave and they left reluctantly, clearly tempted by the offer of a warm meal.

"We've much to do ourselves," K'lior said by way of apology, as he and Cisca headed out the archway of the Kitchen Cavern and into the Weyr Bowl.

"Thread falls over Fort in six days," Cisca reminded them.

"They're both night Falls, too," Fiona remarked with a grimace.

"Why don't we fly them together?" Cisca asked. Beside her K'lior choked in surprise. "Just we two queens?"

"Queens together?" K'lior gasped in surprise, his brown eyes nearly popping out of his head.

Fiona shook her head apologetically even as Cisca laughed and slapped her mate on the back, saying, "I did it just to see you squirm!"

"Besides," Fiona said, "as both queens have just recently risen, it probably would be unwise to risk them, at least until they've safely clutched."

"I'm afraid you're right," Cisca agreed with a sigh. She glanced at K'lior as she added slyly, "But perhaps we could cadge a ride with Kindan and Lorana?"

"I suspect they'll be busy enough looking out for themselves," K'lior said.

"I hadn't thought of them flying this Fall," Fiona admitted anxiously, adding a moment later, "But we need all our dragons and I doubt we could keep Zirenth on the ground."

"I didn't mean to alarm you," Cisca said. "I'm sure they'll do fine."

"It's a night Fall," K'lior said by way of agreement, "and the air here is cold, so much of the Thread will be dead."

Less than a month had passed in the present time since the two night flights that Fort Weyr had fought with the aid of Nuella and the watchwhers, and even though Fiona's memories of the events were faded by the three Turns she'd spent back in time at Igen Weyr, still her recollection of the anguished cries of riders, dragons, and watch-whers was a searing memory. She fought to suppress a shudder of fear.

Cisca sensed her feelings and wrapped her in a hug. "You'll do fine, Weyrwoman."

It was only after they'd left that Fiona realized that the Fort Weyrwoman hadn't suggested that Kindan and Lorana would be safe.

FIFTEEN

Weyrfolk, keep your riders true,
Help them to their battle hew.
Aid them, keep their troubles few
And thus grow their strength anew.

Telgar Weyr, next morning, AL 508.2.16

J'lantir and the three Istan wings arrived early the next morning. Shaneese and the Telgar weyrfolk had worked through the night to prepare the additional one hundred and forty-five weyrs required for the welcome influx of fighting strength.

"We've found enough of our weyrfolk who'd like to swap for warmer climes that we've no worries providing space for their weyrfolk," Shaneese had assured Jeila as she grew anxious at the scope of the whole affair.

"It's like we're getting a whole new Weyr!" Jeila said, eyes wide.

"Well, we've been poaching from Fort, High Reaches, and Benden," Fiona said. "I think it's about time we stole from Ista as well."

The junior weyrwoman had snorted in response and recovered her humor, only repeating darkly, "But I still don't know why you left the arrangements to *me*."

"I have it on highest authority that it's a Weyrwoman's duty to be sure that her replacement is well-trained," Fiona told her, grinning. "After all, you never know when you'll need a new one."

Jeila grabbed her right arm tightly with both of hers and implored, "Promise me you'll give me some warning before you do anything!"

"I'll try," Fiona temporized, her grin slipping. "But there are times . . ."

Like the night before. She hadn't expected to find Kindan awake; she'd been avoiding him, not certain if she ever would find the courage to discover if his prior passion was only dragon-flamed, but Lorana practically threw them at each other, insisting that she had to help in the Kitchen Cavern.

In the morning, Fiona was surprised to find that Lorana had crept in with them sometime during the night.

"Are you all right?" Fiona asked as she felt Lorana shift against her.

"I'm fine," Lorana said.

"You are?" Fiona asked. Confused, she added, "Then why did you . . . you don't mind?"

"No," Lorana said. Fiona pressed herself against the older woman in thanks.

"Besides," Lorana added, "if anything were to happen to me, I'd need to know that there was someone there for Kindan. And the child."

"Always," Fiona said firmly, realizing how much trust Lorana placed in her: That Lorana would choose her as a surrogate. "And in response, I'll ask—"

"I'll love any child of yours, no matter who the father," Lorana said. "You're a special one; Kindan's right to love you."

"Love me?" Fiona could only mouth the words.

"Of course," Lorana said. "Hasn't he always?"

"I thought he loved me for my sister, for Koriana," Fiona said.

"Maybe once," Lorana said. "But after the mating flight, no."

"But he doesn't seem to even notice me!"

"Notice you?" Lorana asked, smiling.

"I mean, until last night."

"He did," Lorana said. "But I don't think he understands yet."

"That he loves me?"

Lorana shook her head. "That he doesn't have to choose."

"I always thought that I would be married to a Lord Holder, one man, and maybe one love," Fiona said.

"So did I," Lorana said. "And I think I've found him." She made a face as Fiona started to protest. "He wouldn't be the man I love, if he weren't in love with you, too." Her eyes twinkled as she added, "What was it that little one said? 'I'll help you grow your heart.'"

"Aryar," Fiona recalled fondly.

"You help me grow my heart," Lorana told her. "Besides, I've never heard of two people *speaking* to each other the way we have."

"I found no mention of it in the Records."

"Perhaps we should ask Kindan."

"I think Masterharper Zist," Fiona said. "I think we shouldn't tell Kindan just yet."

"Perhaps not," Lorana said. "We wouldn't want to shock him *too* much just now."

"Did you tell him about the baby?"

"No," Lorana said, amusement spilling out of her voice. "I was hoping we could present him with a double event, as it were."

Fiona giggled. "That *would* be nice."

And now Fiona, Lorana, and Kindan were arrayed side by side to greet J'lantir as he jumped nimbly from his perch atop bronze Lolanth. The air was still cold and the clouds above threatened rain or, more likely, snow later in the day. Dragons' breath was clearly visible as streams of fog wisping through the air. Fiona noticed some of the Istan riders shiver and was glad she and Shaneese had preparations made to keep them warm—used, as they were, to the much warmer climate of Ista.

"Kindan!" J'lantir exclaimed, racing over to hug the shorter man quickly. "M'tal told me I'd have a surprise, but I didn't expect it to be you!"

In the background, Fiona noted, weyrfolk spread out with mugs of warm *klah* and extra sweaters for the colder Istan riders. Fiona took a careful breath, not wanting to freeze her nose, just enough to get a good sniff of the amazing pine scent that wafted down from the trees in the mountains surrounding the Weyr. She could never get enough of that special, fresh smell.

"I suspect I'm only a part of it," Kindan said with a smile, gesturing to Lorana. "This is Lorana."

J'lantir's eyes widened in recognition and he drew himself back, bowing low in front of her. "My lady, I grieve for your loss and applaud your extreme fortitude in saving all the dragons of Pern."

Fiona could feel Lorana tense beside her. Not all, she thought, remembering that her beloved friend felt every dragon's loss.

"Fiona, Weyrwoman," Fiona said in introduction, distracting the bronze rider from his gaffe.

"Weyrwoman," J'lantir returned with a brisk nod, his frank eyes clearly registering his surprise. "Aren't you awfully young for the duty?"

"I've nearly seventeen Turns, bronze rider," Fiona corrected him.

"Nearly," J'lantir said, his brows rising with his words. "That many; I hadn't realized."

"I spent three Turns back in Igen," Fiona said. She gestured to one of the weyrfolk, who handed J'lantir a steaming mug, and she added, "I remember all those warm days very fondly."

J'lantir chuckled appreciatively, muttering thanks to his server and draining his mug with evident relish.

"We'll try to keep you warm," Fiona said.

J'lantir raised his bushy eyebrows in surprise and turned his head enough to see how his other riders fared. He gave Fiona a grateful nod as he saw that they were being bundled up and hastened out of the cold morning to their quarters.

"So I see!" he said.

Fiona gestured to H'nez, who stepped forward. "Weyrleader T'mar is recovering from injuries, and in the meantime H'nez is senior flightleader."

"Flightleader," H'nez said with a nod toward J'lantir. "I believe you outrank me."

"I might at that," J'lantir said.

"We've a Fall tomorrow; how would you like to array the wings?" H'nez asked.

"I think I'd like to get settled in first," J'lantir said. "If you've any training you've planned for your Flight today, please proceed."

"Gladly," H'nez said. He turned to Fiona and nodded to her. "Weyrwoman."

"Fly safe," Fiona said with a wave. Once he was out of earshot, she muttered to herself, "Old stick in the mud."

"I've been called that, yes," J'lantir said, turning to her.

"Not you," Fiona corrected, pointing to H'nez's retreating back. "Him."

J'lantir's brows rose once more as he registered the comment, but before he could make any remarks, Fiona continued, "We've weyrs set to your disposal and fresh food if your riders feel the need, Flightleader."

"As soon as we get settled and pay our respects to the Weyrleader, we'll probably want to join H'nez and get a feel for the air," J'lantir said.

"Excellent," Fiona said joyfully. At J'lantir's surprised look, she added, "I had a bet with our headwoman and you've made me a winner."

"Glad to oblige," J'lantir said, smiling. "Are there any other wagers I should aid?"

"I wouldn't know," Fiona replied innocently, glancing significantly toward Kindan. "A Weyrwoman has to maintain decorum."

J'lantir startled at that, asking, "Aren't you the same Fiona who was so fond of tunnel snakes as a youngster?"

"I was more fond of the marks I earned catching them," Fiona corrected him with a grin. "However, I now have reason to believe that I was never in any danger, having been protected by my continued existence."

J'lantir gave her a blank look, so she said, "My snake-hunting companion was someone who knew that I would live long enough to go back in time to Igen and so had no worries inciting me to greater and greater levels of danger."

"Oh!" J'lantir said, enlightened. "Not the sort of thing one encounters often."

Fiona nodded in agreement. "If you need anything, bespeak Talenth."

"Or have your dragon ask me," Lorana said.

"Yes," Fiona said. "Lorana can hear any dragon."

"Oh," J'lantir said, thinking quickly. He turned back to the taller woman. "Then you have my heartfelt commiserations; the past few months must have been quite a trial."

Fiona linked hands with Lorana at the same time as Kindan encircled the dark-haired woman's waist protectively.

"I am lucky in my friends," Lorana told him.

J'lantir nodded and, somewhat bemusedly, turned back to the remaining Istan riders.

"Oh, Flightleader!" Fiona called as he departed. J'lantir turned back to her expectantly. "As time permits, see the headwoman, she's proper Telgar garb for the riders."

J'lantir nodded absently, then brightened. "I shall arrange it at the earliest moment!"

Fiona nodded and waved him back to his duties.

The riders from High Reaches were the next to appear. They arrived just after the former Istan riders departed to join H'nez in drill. The sun was well in the sky and the chill of the morning had vanished.

"I wonder who they'll send to lead the wing," Kindan said, craning his neck and sheltering his eyes to spot the lead rider.

Fiona picked out the rider and discovered that her eyes were better than Kindan's as she said, "He's threadscored on the cheek. He's missing an ear, too!"

"C'tov!" Kindan shouted, racing across the Bowl to greet the rider as his dragon landed. Fiona and Lorana followed after him, exchanging looks of surprise.

"Sonia sent her best," Fiona said to herself as she examined the tall rider clambering down from his perch.

"She honors you," Lorana agreed.

"Us," Fiona corrected her firmly, reaching once more to grab Lorana's hand and give it a quick squeeze. "I've got a lot to live up to."

"You'll do fine," Lorana said. Fiona's lips twitched but she made no response.

Kindan led C'tov over to them and the bronze rider bowed to Fiona. "Weyrwoman, I present you with thirty-seven of High Reaches' best."

"We're honored, wingleader," Fiona said. "You are welcome here."

"May I pay my respects to the Weyrleader?" C'tov asked, looking beyond her to the queen's weyr where Zirenth peered out.

"I think it would be best to wait until evening," Fiona told him. "J'lantir and his Flight from Ista have just gone off to join flightleader H'nez in drill."

C'tov nodded in understanding. "Then, with your leave, Weyrwoman, as soon as we've stowed our belongings, we'll join them."

"Headwoman Shaneese was expecting you," Fiona told him, waving toward a group approaching from the lower caverns. "They'll take your gear and stow it in your quarters."

"Thank you," C'tov replied, his eyes twinkling as he smiled at her. Fiona realized that disregarding the scorched side of his face was easy given the animation the bronze rider brought to his expressions, particularly his piercing blue eyes.

"My pleasure."

"I should have been there!" T'mar said when Fiona recounted the events to him later. He shifted nervously in his bed.

"You're not leaving that bed until Birentir says," Fiona told him, pressing a hand against his chest forcefully. "Even if I have to sit on you."

"Or Birentir does," Lorana added in agreement. "I can't imagine he'd want to have a Weyrleader be the first patient he lost."

T'mar lay back, fuming. "Well, at least tell me what's going on."

"Nothing more than you would have guessed," Kindan told him with an easy wave of his hand. "H'nez led off the drill this morning, J'lantir has joined with a Flight from Ista, and, just recently, C'tov from High Reaches brought another thirty-six fighting dragons with him."

"By the First Egg, we've got a fighting Weyr and a lamed Weyrleader," T'mar growled, his eyes going accusingly to Fiona.

"And do you suppose, Weyrleader," Fiona returned hotly, "that in all these Turns that situation has never before arisen?"

T'mar pursed his lips mulishly.

"The Records are pretty clear on the issue," Kindan said. "Even here at Telgar, the Weyrleader has been injured for months at a time."

"And?" T'mar demanded.

"And he's appointed seconds, had reports made to him, and proceeded as best he could with due regards to his injury *and* his eventual recovery," Fiona told him. Her voice softened as she added, "I know it's hard, particulary with H'nez in charge, but it is part of a Weyrleader's duty to train his replacement."

"And you, Weyrwoman?"

"I'm doing very well in that department, thank you," Fiona replied primly.

T'mar held her eyes for a moment more, then blew out a breath in resignation, forcing some cheer into his response as he said, "You are at that."

"Thank you," Fiona said. After a moment she added, "I can only imagine how difficult this must be for you."

"Well, what cannot be changed must be endured," T'mar said with a sigh. From his weyr, Zirenth craned his neck and blew a sympathetic sigh toward his rider. T'mar smiled at him and then turned back decisively to Kindan and Lorana. "But my incapacity is no reason that Zirenth should get out of shape."

Kindan cocked his head at the bronze rider inquiringly.

"If Tajen could do it when I was lamed before, why not you and Lorana now?" T'mar asked.

"No!" Fiona snapped without thinking. The others turned to her and she shook her head in confusion.

"I could do with the exercise," Lorana said, casting a glance toward Fiona. "I think Kindan's up to catching firestone."

"It takes Turns of training to make a proper fighting pair," T'mar said. "I was thinking more of reserve than fighting."

"Or we could observe, and report back," Kindan said.

"Dragons aren't good with subtleties," T'mar said.

Fiona gestured toward Lorana. "She can talk directly with me—"

"She can?" T'mar asked, surprised. His expression broadened when he noticed the same look of surprise on Kindan's face.

"You can?" the harper asked, looking from Fiona to Lorana and back. "And you didn't tell me?"

"We're not sure how well it works," Fiona said, temporizing. She glanced at Lorana and took in the other's stance and the look of excitement on her face, and added hastily, "But this would be a good time to learn."

"Zirenth is willing," T'mar said. Fiona thought she heard some sudden reluctance on his part, but the bronze rider shrugged, adding, "And who am I to argue?"

"You're the Weyrleader," Fiona said in answer.

"And this is a way to adapt, isn't it?"

"It is," Fiona agreed, still reluctant. She turned to Lorana and Kindan. "But if you fly the Fall tomorrow—or any day—stay behind and report in."

"She's right," T'mar said. He glanced at Kindan, smiling. "Much though I trust you both, I'd hate for either you or Zirenth to get injured."

"Dragonmen must fly when Thread is in the sky," Lorana quoted, her expression stolid, firm.

"And of us all, I suppose you have the best right to call yourself dragonman," Kindan found himself saying. Fiona and T'mar nodded in agreement.

"No one knows what would happen to the dragons if anything

happens to you," Fiona warned Lorana. The older woman nodded in understanding.

"Enough of this!" T'mar said, raising both arms to wave them off. "Get your harness on Zirenth and have Fiona inspect it, then we'll see."

Fiona brightened at the thought, then slumped as T'mar cautioned her, "And don't think to keep them dirt bound on a pretext."

Glumly, Fiona nodded, following the other two out. She turned at the entrance to Zirenth's lair, and called back to T'mar, "As soon as they're safely airborne, I'll come back."

T'mar's eyes flashed in gratitude.

As it was, Kindan and Lorana had no trouble at all in getting Zirenth's fighting straps properly arrayed. Fiona, with some foresight, had them load up with eight sacks of firestone, allowing them to refuel the fighting dragons.

Jeila came running up as they completed their preparations.

"I could help," she said, looking imploringly to Fiona. "I could fly with firestone, too."

"Not until after Tolarth's clutched," Fiona told her. "Right now our two golds are more valuable as breeders."

Jeila, pouting, agreed. To lift the dusky weyrwoman's spirits—and her own—Fiona added, "But if we get some gold eggs in our clutches, we'll be able to consider other options!"

"We'll have to wait Turns yet," Jeila said.

"Perhaps," Fiona said. "Although some of us have found the Turns come easier than others!"

At the reminder of Fiona's time in the past, Jeila brightened.

At Fiona's request, Jeila joined her in T'mar's quarters. T'mar gave the petite weyrwoman a cheerful greeting and the three of them alternated between discussing Weyr matters and dissecting the messages from the drilling dragons.

"I think we should offer J'lantir the lead," T'mar said just after Fiona relayed how the Ista flight had outperformed its Telgar and High

Reaches counterparts. He caught Jeila's frown and nodded his head toward her. "You disagree?"

"No," Jeila said, sighing. "He's led a Weyr as well as a Flight, he's had more experience than any bronze rider here."

"H'nez will be disappointed," Fiona predicted.

Jeila glanced sharply toward her, a calculating look on her face. "It would be wrong to hope he behave any other way."

"It would," T'mar agreed. "I would feel the same in his position."

"In fact, you do," Fiona pointed out. T'mar gave her a pained look even as he nodded in acknowledgment of her words.

"His first concern is Pern," Jeila said, almost to herself. "Then his Weyr, his Flight, his wing, his dragon." With a rueful smile, she added, "After that he considers himself and the feelings of others."

"He is a hard man," Fiona said.

"Tough times call for such," Jeila replied. Her eyes flashed as she said to Fiona, "I know that you and he have quarreled in the past—"

"Our ways are different," Fiona said.

"But your interests are the same."

Fiona smiled at the dark-haired woman. "What I do know is that anyone who attracts your affection has my friendship."

"But, even so, we should let J'lantir lead," Jeila said in agreement. She lifted her head to meet Fiona's eyes, then turned to T'mar, saying, "Weyrleader, I agree with your decision."

"While I'm still recovering, I'll let H'nez lead the Fort riders," T'mar said.

"No, you will not!" Fiona found herself shouting in unison with Jeila. They turned to each other in shock, and Fiona gestured for the other woman to speak first. Jeila cleared her throat, then said with as much control as she could muster, "Weyrleader, if you give J'lantir the authority to lead the fighting dragons, you must leave how to lead and arrange the wings and Flights up to him as well."

"Besides, we should mix up our riders as quickly as we can," Fiona said, after nodding in agreement with Jeila's declaration. "We are *Telgar* now."

"Exactly," Jeila said.

T'mar's lips rose in a small grin. "I believe you have made excellent points, Weyrwomen."

Fiona made sure to accompany Birentir as he checked on T'mar shortly before the fighting drill was to end. She and Terin brought him a lunch tray and waited until Birentir had inspected him before setting it in front of him and helping him sit up enough to eat.

"Another two days at least, Weyrleader," Birentir said. "After that, we'll see how you are at standing."

"I feel fine," T'mar protested.

"Lying down, yes," Fiona snapped back. "Wait until you try standing."

"With a concussion, people often feel as if their feet are floating above the ground," Birentir said. "Given the condition of your leg, the last thing you need to do is strain your sutures, particularly with a fall."

T'mar grumbled in reply.

"You rush your recovery and you won't recover," Fiona warned him. T'mar made a face and waved at her in a feeble display of irritation. She was about to voice an angry reply when she felt Lorana and brightened. "They're coming back."

A moment later, they heard the sound of a dragon bursting out of *between* and Zirenth bugled happily at his low arrival. They reeked of firestone, the sort of smell that only comes from a flaming dragon.

"Zirenth, you know better!" Fiona called chidingly to the bronze dragon even as Lorana and Kindan jumped from the dragon's haunches to the queens' ledge nearby. Fiona ran out to the ledge, wagging a finger at the pair. "And you two! You should know better!"

The broad grin on Lorana's faced slipped for a moment, then redoubled. "We knew where we were, Fiona!"

Seeing the ex-dragonrider looking so happy robbed Fiona of any response, leaving her to shake her head wordlessly.

"You look just like your father after you were caught hunting tunnel snakes," Kindan declared, laughing.

Fiona felt her cheeks burning. Embarrassed, she turned away, stamping her foot loudly on the ground of the ledge.

She was surprised a moment later when Kindan wrapped his arms around her from the back in a strong hug. She twisted in his arms to face him and realized that she was very nearly at eye level with him.

Kindan said nothing, merely looking deeply into her eyes until she buried her head against his neck.

"We were careful," he told her soothingly.

"Be more careful next time," Fiona huffed, still grumpy with worry.

"You knew what we were doing," Lorana said, coming up to them, looking not the least upset at their embrace. She smiled as she added insightfully, "You're jealous!"

Fiona lifted her head and stuck her tongue out at the older woman, who chuckled in response.

"Of course I am," Fiona said. She broke free from Kindan, maintaining her grasp on one of his hands, reached and grabbed Lorana's right hand with her other hand and tugged them both gently into T'mar's quarters. "Tell us everything."

Their report was not quite complete when it was interrupted by the sound of the return of the remaining dragons in one great rush of cold air from *between*.

T'mar and Fiona glanced at each other for a moment, then turned their heads to strain for the sounds of the descending dragons. The four of them—T'mar, Fiona, Kindan, and Lorana—nodded approvingly as they heard the various wings descend and disperse, one after the other.

"Lorana, could you ask J'lantir to report?" T'mar asked when they heard the last of the dragons rising on their way back to their weyrs.

"I've asked Lolanth," Lorana said. She glanced at the blond-haired Weyrwoman, adding, "I think Fiona's the only one I can talk with directly."

"Probably just as well," Kindan quipped and instantly found himself the center of two piercing glares: one of blue eyes, the other of brown. He raised his hands defensively, saying, "Well, could you imagine how awful it would be if you could hear *every* dragonrider as well as every dragon?"

Lorana nodded, conceding the point, but Fiona held the harper's eyes for a moment longer before looking at T'mar to ask, "And why do you suppose that is?"

T'mar paused before answering and was rewarded with the sound of J'lantir rushing up the ledge to them. He gestured pointedly toward the entrance and held his breath.

"Weyrleader," J'lantir called as he entered, then seeing Fiona and the others added with a polite nod to each, "Weyrwoman, harper, Lorana."

"I wanted to talk with you about the drill," T'mar said.

"Should I invite H'nez?" Lorana asked. T'mar nodded in agreement.

"Should we wait?" J'lantir asked, with a quick smile for Lorana.

"No, I don't want to take up too much of your time," T'mar said. "I know you've still got to settle in to your quarters."

"And you'll be hungry, too," Fiona said.

"We were watching from behind you," Kindan said, gesturing to himself and Lorana.

"And?" J'lantir asked invitingly.

"I learned a lot," Kindan said.

"I think you'd be best integrating the wings and riders as quickly as possible," Fiona told him.

"My thoughts as well," J'lantir agreed. He glanced at Lorana and raised an eyebrow in invitation.

"I'm afraid I have nothing to add," the dark-haired woman said with a rueful look. She glanced slyly at Kindan, adding, "We were learning how to flame."

"Well, your additional unused firestone was much welcome," J'lantir said in response. "And I did see your flaming; I think you have nothing more to learn."

"But you will *not* fight Thread," Fiona warned them.

"Weyrwoman," J'lantir began diplomatically, "let us hope that they never *need* to fight Thread."

"But we need every fighting dragon," Kindan and T'mar declared in chorus. The harper glanced in surprise at the Weyrleader, who shook his head, saying, "Kindan has the right of it, we need to learn if we can cross-mount dragons and riders."

"*Trained* dragons and riders," Fiona said, glancing anxiously toward Kindan.

"Our need is great," J'lantir told her. He looked at Kindan, adding, "But there is no reason you can't be trained."

"It will be a bit of a change to get training before getting a dragon," Kindan said.

"Your dragon will come, lad," J'lantir assured him and was surprised to see Fiona and Lorana nod in agreement. "There's no reason you shouldn't know all you can beforehand."

"But we won't have time to drill him on recognition points before tomorrow," Fiona said. She felt Lorana's hand tighten on hers and leaned against the taller woman, murmuring, "I can't lose you."

"You can do whatever it takes," Lorana assured her, wrapping her other arm around Fiona and pulling the shorter woman tight against her, adding fondly, "You are strong, you will survive."

A shiver ran down Fiona's back and she buried her head against Lorana's chest. After a moment, she pulled away again and gave Lorana a wan smile.

"A Weyrwoman sets the example," Fiona said.

"She does indeed," J'lantir said in an approving tone. The sound of H'nez's approaching feet stalled further conversation.

"Weyrleader," H'nez said to T'mar as he drew up. He nodded to J'lantir and threw a general look at Fiona, Kindan, and Lorana. "What can I do for you?"

"I'm pretty sure you know," T'mar said, partly turning to J'lantir.

"I think I do," H'nez said, facing the older bronze rider. "Flightleader J'lantir, you are the most qualified to lead the Weyr, I'll be happy to fly wherever you see fit for me."

"Well said, lad, well said," J'lantir rumbled in response, his gray hair and grizzled features emphasizing his age and ability. "Your riders flew well today."

"They could have flown better," H'nez said with a frown. "I'll be talk-ing to them later."

J'lantir barked a laugh. "Of course! They can *always* fly better," he agreed. He wagged a finger at the wiry rider, adding, "But it would be a mistake to make every flight a lesson. Sometimes it is enough to let the riders find their own shortcomings. Sometimes," he added in a more somber tone, "it is our duty to lift their spirits no matter what their fail-ings."

H'nez nodded. "I shall try to remember."

"You do that!" J'lantir agreed heartily. "Do that and you'll be a great Weyrleader."

H'nez raised his hands, palms open in protest but the Istan rider shook his head, saying, "Every bronze dreams of a queen."

"I have a queen," H'nez replied quickly, then flushed and amended, "My Ginirth was lucky enough to fly Jeila's Tolarth."

"One of the youngest and strongest queens on Pern, I believe," J'lantir said. "Weyrleader, indeed."

T'mar coughed from his bed and J'lantir barked another laugh. "No offense meant, T'mar! There are Weyrs aplenty. One even now goes beg-ging."

"I'm Telgar now," H'nez said.

"As are we all," J'lantir agreed. "As are we all."

For a long moment, no one spoke, savoring the force of the older rider's declaration.

"I'd appreciate it, J'lantir, if you and the wingleaders could meet with me here after dinner," T'mar said.

"This is going to be a night Fall," Fiona spoke up, glancing at J'lantir and T'mar. "Have we coordinated with Nuella?"

"Worse," Kindan added, "it spills over to High Reaches. They'll be fly-ing the darkest part."

"Thread should arrive the seventh hour after noon," H'nez said, cast-ing an inquiring look toward Kindan, who nodded in agreement, "so we'll have sun for the majority of our part of the Fall."

"I haven't had the honor yet of flying with Nuella," J'lantir said. He caught the surprised look on H'nez's face and correctly guessed that the other was not yet convinced of the utility of the watch-whers. "You should know that it was I, along with M'tal, who first discovered their true worth."

"You flew Thread at night over Southern Boll, H'nez; do you still doubt their ability?" T'mar asked.

"It's not that," H'nez replied with a shake of his head. "We took a lot of casualties that night."

"And we haven't trained with them since," T'mar said by way of agreement. He asked J'lantir, "Is there a chance to arrange training tonight?"

The bronze rider pursed his lips thoughtfully, then shook his head. "I think our riders are too tired. It was a strain to drill at all today; usually I prefer a day of rest prior to a Fall."

"It was necessary with all the influx," H'nez said.

"Oh, absolutely," J'lantir agreed. "But we're now all too tired to consider more drilling."

"We're not," Lorana said, gesturing to Kindan. "We could coordinate with Nuella."

"And you could talk to the watch-whers, too!" T'mar exclaimed enthusiastically. He glanced at Fiona, who flushed when she noticed his gaze and shook her head resignedly.

"It could work," she said. "In fact, Lorana, why don't you tell Sonia's Lyrinth of your plan and offer to fly the full Fall?"

"At night?" H'nez exclaimed. "With no training?"

"Needs must," Fiona told him. With a sly look toward Lorana and Kindan, she added, "Besides, your ability to coordinate will make you too valuable to risk fighting Thread directly."

Kindan groaned in response but Lorana merely nodded serenely.

"We should leave after dark," Kindan said. "Nuella and Nuellask won't be awake before then."

"I'm coming with you," Fiona declared, her expression daring anyone to defy her.

"If," T'mar responded slowly, his expression neutral, "Weyrwoman, you feel it in the best interests of Pern to disturb your queen's rest before she has clutched, I will say nothing against it."

"Good!" Fiona said. "Because Talenth says that she's bored lying around all day and wants to get out while she still can!"

They left with the last of the evening sun hovering on the horizon in the west. A light rain was falling and threatened to turn into a cold winter downpour.

The evening meal had been a spirited affair with riders from three Weyrs discovering their differences and similarities while the Telgar weyrfolk, grateful for the further infusion of strength, outdid themselves in making the new riders feel welcome and at home.

Fiona announced J'lantir's position as fighting leader, which was greeted enthusiastically by all—except for a few grumbles from the older Fort riders, which died down as they considered the sensibleness of the decision.

Worries soon surfaced about fighting at night and were soothed by Fiona's revelation of the mission to Nuella. It seemed that every one of the one hundred and eighty-five fit riders found a chance to pay respect to Lorana, each profoundly grateful for her sacrifice and deeply moved that she had chosen Telgar as her new Weyr. Fiona was surprised to hear murmurs of approval about herself, too, mostly in praise of her ability to attract the likes of Lorana and J'lantir to the Weyr.

"That's as silly as a wherry bathing!" Fiona declared the first time she heard it from one of the older riders who should have known better.

"It isn't," Jeila chided her. "Think of how jealous Sonia must be."

"Or Cisca," Terin added from her place near F'jian. Strictly speaking, the displaced headwoman should not have been seated with the dragonriders, but the Telgar weyrfolk had learned to respect the youngster and had discovered that their new Weyrwoman tended to ignore such traditions in favor of the comfort and enjoyment of all.

"Or Tullea," Fiona said in rueful agreement. "Of course, she probably saw Lorana as a threat."

"Almost certainly," Jeila said.

"Maybe Tullea will get better now that she's not time-fuddled," Fiona said, taking a long sip of *klah* herself and remembering M'tal's comment. If she *was* time-fuddled like Tullea, then when would she be going back in time . . . and where?

"What?" Kindan asked, leaning across the table toward her, with a look of concern on his face.

Fiona shook her head, smoothing her expression. "Nothing."

The harper's lips tightened into a frown.

"It's not important now," Fiona assured him. Kindan gave her a look that reminded her that he knew her all too well and made it clear to her that he would pursue the topic later, she could be certain. "Finish your *klah* and let's go."

Grudgingly, Kindan did as she ordered and, with a glance at Lorana, rose from the table as soon as he'd finished his drink.

They were all still dressed in their riding gear, so it was only a matter of moments before they were airborne, circling the Star Stones before winking out *between* to the wherhold.

They arrived with the last of the light, circling down quickly to the landing just outside the stone hold. A bugle from the ground announced their arrival, followed quickly by Talenth's warbled greeting in response.

Nuellask is awake, Talenth relayed eagerly, diving so steeply that Fiona had to lean back and clutch her flying straps tightly.

Sorry! Talenth said as she caught her rider's flash of fear just before she pulled up into a perfect landing.

No, you're not, Fiona replied testily, *you're showing off.*

Talenth answered with a chagrined silence.

Fiona relented and patted the golden neck hard before loosening her grip on her straps and sliding down Talenth's foreleg to the ground below. *Off you go, have fun!*

Talenth sauntered off, taking a quick leap to cup the evening air beneath her wings and glide slowly in the darkness. She was joined shortly after by Zirenth, who flew protectively at her side.

"Well, she's enjoying herself!" Zenor's deep voice exclaimed in the night air.

With a yelp of joy, Fiona raced to the sound of his voice and threw herself into his arms. "Zenor!"

"Hey, easy there!" the red-haired holder declared as he wrapped his arms around her. "You're not as small as you once were and I've ten more Turns to my name."

"Indeed you do," Kindan said. "You're practically gray with age."

"Kindan!" Zenor exclaimed, unceremoniously dropping Fiona to race over to his lifelong friend. He paused long enough to pull Fiona back to her feet and along with him, adding, "So have you discovered the identity of your secret admirer?"

"I have," Kindan said. He gestured toward Lorana on his other side. "And this is Lorana."

"Ah?" Zenor said in surprise. "And . . ."

"It's complicated," Kindan said.

"Only to confused harpers," Lorana said, reaching a hand forward to Zenor who shook it absently.

"Zirenth flew Talenth," Fiona said by way of exclamation.

"But we'd heard that T'mar was injured." A new voice, Nuella's, joined in the conversation.

"He was," Lorana said, turning toward the approaching woman who was led by a young girl who was easily recognizable as her daughter.

"Zirenth would have gone *between* except that Lorana and Kindan restrained him," Fiona said.

"And you," Lorana said. "It took the three of us."

"The three of you?" Zenor said.

"And so when Zirenth flew Talenth . . . oh!" Nuella said, her expression brightening. "Then congratulations are due all around, aren't they?"

"I think so," Lorana said. She glanced at Kindan. "Some of us are still adjusting to the reality."

"Shards, Kindan!" Zenor said, his eyes going wide. "Only you would have partnered with the two most amazing women on Pern!"

"Present company excluded, of course," Kindan added with a half-bow toward Nuella.

"He bowed at you, Momma," the girl said.

"I know, Nalla," Nuella assured her daughter easily. "He learned manners at the Harper Hall."

"He's the one who gave you your first watch-wher, isn't he?" Nalla asked.

"Yes, he did," Nuella told her patiently. Only the adults heard the pain in her voice.

"It's good to see you again," Fiona said, rushing forward to hug Nuella and discovering, in surprise, that she was taller than the wher-handler.

"I was hoping you'd come tonight," Nuella said in agreement.

"She had Sula lay out some dainties," Nalla declared eagerly.

"Sula's dainties?" Kindan asked. He turned to Lorana and Fiona, saying, "You really have to try Sula's dainties."

"I have," Fiona reminded him. She added to Lorana, "Remind me to see if we can pry the recipe from her."

"That good?" Lorana asked.

"*That* good," Kindan agreed, gesturing them forward.

"We're here to talk about the Threadfall tomorrow," Fiona said as they made their way into the hold.

Nuella nodded. "So I'd guessed."

Quickly, Fiona brought them up to date with the news.

"J'lantir?" Nuella exclaimed in delight when Fiona mentioned his arrival. She gave Fiona an approving look, then turned to Kindan, saying, "She certainly has a way of attracting the best, doesn't she?"

"She does," Kindan said when he recalled that Nuella could not see his nod.

"See?" Lorana said triumphantly to Fiona. "Everyone notices."

Fiona blushed in embarrassment.

Seated in the comfort of Nuella's quarters, even as Sula distracted Nalla and the younger Zelar, Lorana explained her plan to Nuella.

"You can speak to any dragon?" Zenor said, his eyes going wide with surprise as he absorbed the notion.

"She can feel them, too," Kindan told his old friend, with a dour look.

"Oh," Zenor said, his face falling. "That could be . . . must have been . . . painful."

Lorana nodded in response.

"What's important now," Fiona said, with a sympathetic look toward her friend, "is that Lorana has offered to coordinate between dragons and watch-whers."

"Can you speak with the watch-whers, too?" Nuella asked.

In response, Lorana grew still with the inward look of one communing mentally. A moment later she looked up and smiled even as a surprised squawk echoed in from the night air. "Yes, I think I can!"

"Yes, you can," Nuella agreed, adding wistfully, "Nuellask says she's never heard a voice like yours before."

"You don't suppose you could teach Nuella . . . ?" Fiona asked hopefully.

Lorana shook her head. "I wouldn't know where to begin," she replied, frowning as she glanced thoughtfully at Fiona, "but maybe you could."

"Me?"

"Why not?" Zenor said. "You're full of surprises."

Fiona grumbled irritatedly.

"You can hear my thoughts," Lorana reminded her.

"And you could plant images in my mind," Nuella added hopefully.

Fiona shook her head. "Anyone could do that," she told Nuella, turning to Lorana and adding, "And you taught me how to hear your thoughts. I'm nothing special."

"I'm not so sure," Nuella and Lorana said in unison.

"And I agree," Zenor said. "But Thread will not wait. Perhaps we should consider the issue at hand."

"I suppose," Nuella said, still wistful with the thought of communicating more closely with her watch-wher. She shook herself, dismissing the thought from her mind. "So you are here to coordinate on tomorrow's Fall."

"Indeed," Kindan said. "Given that Lorana can talk with any dragon—"

"Or watch-wher," Fiona added.

"Or watch-wher," Kindan accepted the correction with a nod, continuing, "we think it'd be best if we coordinated through her."

"Aren't the next four Falls all night Falls?" Zenor asked, nodding toward Nuella. "That's what we've heard here."

Lorana and Fiona glanced expectantly toward Kindan, who frowned in thought, his lips moving silently. After a moment he nodded, saying, "Telgar, Fort, and High Reaches twice."

"High Reaches flies tomorrow," Fiona said.

"It does, but the sun sets later there so the Fall will last from mid-afternoon to late evening there," Kindan told her.

"Up to the twenty-first hour," Nuella agreed. "And then their next one actually starts the day before—on the twenty-third, falling through into the twenty-fourth."

"For some reason," Zenor said with a droll grin toward Kindan, "the Threadfall charts are all based on Benden time."

Kindan shrugged and grinned in response.

"It's only natural," Nuella said. "That's where you were posted."

"You know," Zenor said, stroking his chin, "if you and Lorana are going to fly this first night Fall, it might make sense for you to fly all of them."

Fiona gasped in surprise.

"It makes sense," Zenor told her. "Lorana can speak to any dragon. Her coordination will help save lives—dragon and watch-wher alike."

"If you're going to do that," Fiona said, turning to Lorana and then Nuella, "then Nuella should ride with you."

"What?" Nuella barked.

"Lorana can't talk to you directly by mind but your ears work well enough," Fiona said.

"Besides, with Kindan's eyes, you'll not need worry about more threadscore," Zenor added hastily, giving Fiona a grateful wink.

"Can Zirenth manage three?" Kindan asked.

"Of course," Lorana said with staunch loyalty for her surrogate mount.

It would be an honor to carry the WherMaster, Zirenth declared with an accompanying rumble from outside.

Nuella's face lit with a smile, making it clear to Fiona that the bronze's announcement had been made to all present.

"Well!" Fiona said. "When Zirenth speaks, it's foolish to argue."

So it was arranged. Fiona tried her hardest to convert her worry and disappointment into a method of acquiring Sula's recipe for dainties, but she was thwarted and made the return trip to Telgar in frustrated silence.

"That's excellent news!" J'lantir said. He glanced at Kindan and Lorana, confiding, "I'd been most concerned about our coordination with the watch-whers." He paused before adding wistfully, "We at Ista have never had a chance to work with them."

"Well, you'll get it tonight," Fiona said, her tone grumpy. Her worry for Kindan and Lorana increased with each passing moment.

J'lantir frowned and looked over at H'nez. "This is going to be a difficult Fall, even with the aid."

"How so, sir?" H'nez asked. Fiona was surprised to hear the amount of respect in the usually self-possessed bronze rider and leaned forward to better hear J'lantir's answer.

"We'll be flying into the setting sun," J'lantir said. "It may make it much harder to spot Thread."

"It could also light it up," H'nez countered.

"Or both," Fiona said. She turned to J'lantir. "I see your point. With such conditions a rider could get too self-assured, especially with the falling chill of night to dull the senses."

"Indeed," J'lantir said. "And I'm concerned that it may not be dark enough for the watch-whers to use their abilities."

"Or even to fly," H'nez said, his face set in a grim frown.

"What can we do, then?" Fiona asked, feeling more desperate than before.

"Fly Thread," H'nez answered simply.

"Hope for the best," J'lantir said in agreement. He took a long sip of his *klah* and toyed with the eggs on his plate before saying to H'nez, "If anything happens to me, you lead."

"Yes sir," H'nez said and for once Fiona could tell that the bronze rider held no joy in the thought of leading the Weyr.

"You've done a good job," Fiona said as she inspected the set of the riding straps on Zirenth's neck and shoulder. "You've room enough for four sacks of firestone and yet you'll all be secure in your mount."

Kindan nodded. "I should, for all the times I've been made to inspect weyrlings."

"Just part of your training, love," Lorana assured him with a smile that she extended with a nod toward Fiona. Fiona answered it with the same look, causing Kindan to mutter, "You'd think you've got my egg all picked out."

"I haven't," Fiona said, her eyes dancing as she jerked a hand toward her weyr and the sleeping Talenth, "*she* has."

Kindan snorted in amusement, a sound that died quickly as he began his climb up to his place on the great bronze dragon's neck. He reached a hand down to Lorana, who climbed quickly to her place behind him, leaving the rearmost position for Nuella.

"Don't hurt my dragon!" T'mar bellowed from his bed, forcing good cheer into his voice.

"We'll do our best," Kindan called back in promise.

"Fly safe," Fiona said, looking up at the pair of them. "I need you back."

Kindan said nothing, Lorana nodded gravely in response, and then Zirenth moved away from the ledge, into the Bowl proper, took a leap, cupped air, rose swiftly above the gathering dragons, up to the Star Stones, and was gone, *between*.

"I've got to get better," T'mar grumbled from his bed. Fiona cast one last glance at the after-image of the bronze dragon and his riders, then turned to march briskly back into T'mar's quarters.

"You will," she assured him, "if you are willing to rest."

"By the First Egg," T'mar swore, "I've never known anything harder!"

"Fly well!" Fiona called to J'lantir less than half an hour later as the last of the assembled wings made ready to take to the air. Above them the other five wings of Telgar Weyr circled, ready and eager for the night's fight.

"We'll see you in three hours' time," J'lantir said. "We hand off the Fall to High Reaches over Nabol."

Fiona knew this and she was certain that J'lantir knew she knew this, so she gathered that the flightleader was making the announcement for the benefit of the knots of weyrfolk gathered around the outskirts of the Bowl to see off the fighting dragons.

This was only the second Fall since the disastrous time when D'gan and all the dragonriders of the Weyr were lost. Fiona could understand that they were naturally anxious, particularly as in the first Fall since then, their new Weyrleader, T'mar, had been seriously injured.

She could sense the feelings of anticipation and worry and fought to keep them from settling on her, too.

"Good flying!" Fiona called loudly, waving J'lantir and the last wing into flight.

The dragons rose gracefully, assumed their position at the head of the upper Flight, and, together, one hundred and eighty-five dragons disappeared *between*. To Thread. To battle.

"It will get darker soon," Lorana assured Nuella as they followed slowly behind the fighting dragons, gouts of flame marking their progress in the battle against Thread. The dragonriders had been fighting for more than an hour, with only two more hours left before they would meet with the High Reaches riders above Nabol Hold.

Even so, the fight had been difficult. For Lorana, who felt as well as saw the carnage, the first loss was the most shocking, as she saw the small blue and his rider engulfed from behind by a clump of Thread that had been hidden in the gloam of the dusky night air—invisible one moment, mortal the next. She had cried out in unison with the tormented blue, had known that the small dragon had received its deathblow and then—he was gone, forever, *between*.

Nuella had wrapped her arms around her and buried her head against her spine in comfort while Kindan had tried his best to turn in his perch to console her.

"Keep flying!" Lorana had told him. "I'll recover."

"Yes, you will!" Nuella had agreed fervently, sitting back enough to rub Lorana's shoulders in a soothing motion.

Moments later a brown cried out and disappeared, but winked back into the fight, having frozen off an assaulting strand of Thread *between*.

"I think it's getting darker," Kindan said now, straining to pick out the dragons in the night air.

"This is the most dangerous time," Nuella said. "When it is still too light for the watch-whers, and too early for the Thread to have frozen."

As if in answer, ahead of them, a pair of dragons bellowed in pain, their cries stifled as they went *between*. Only one returned.

"Karalth made it back to the Weyr," Lorana reported, referring to the missing green. Her lips curved upward in relief as she added, "Fiona's with him."

"That's good to know," Kindan called back over his shoulder. "I'm going to close up or we'll lose sight of J'lantir."

In response, Zirenth swooped forward with easy wingbeats, closing up to the nearest dragons.

Lorana strained forward over his shoulder for a sight of J'lantir.

"There's J'lantir!" Kindan shouted, raising an arm and pointing.

Lorana strained over his shoulder to follow his aim and had just spotted the flightleader when she shrieked, "J'lantir! Behind you!"

Too late, the bronze rider reacted to the clump of Thread that had twisted on the rising turbulence of the night air to fall directly onto the backs of rider and dragon alike. For one brief moment it flared, gorging upon the leathers of the bronze rider and the skin of the unprotected dragon, and then they were gone *between*—but not before Lorana could make out the pulsing red of blood as Thread ate through the last of J'lantir's wher-hide jacket and feasted on his flesh, even as it grew in its feeding on Lolanth's spine.

"He was too late," Lorana cried, balling her fists and pounding them feebly against Kindan's back. "Too late!"

J'lantir is no more! The voice rang out clearly, devoid of hope, bereft of all happiness, dry only with despair.

H'nez, lead the flight.

Ahead a dragon rumbled in acknowledgment and the dragons of Telgar Weyr hastened to re-form their confused assault against the falling Thread.

When Fiona finally staggered into her quarters after ensuring that the last of the four injured were comfortably settled into their weyrs and certain to recover, she was too tired to notice much of her surroundings. She shucked her clothes into the bathroom, threw on her nightgown as quickly as tired fingers, spurred by the evening chill, could manage, and slipped herself into the warm bed with a sigh of contentment.

She was surprised to realize that she was looking into Kindan's eyes.

"Lorana's keeping an eye on T'mar," he said.

Fiona murmured noncommittally and closed her eyes. A moment later she opened them again. Kindan was still looking at her.

"Who ordered H'nez to lead the flight?" he asked. "Was that you or Lorana?"

"I think it was me," Fiona said.

"It sounded mostly like you," Kindan agreed, his brows furrowed. "But it sounded like Lorana, too."

"A bit of both," Fiona agreed.

They looked at each other for a moment longer then, reached out and hugged tightly, comfort against the pain.

Fiona felt her tears come and let them flow freely. When they were gone and Kindan was still in her arms, she felt a different feeling wake in her. Awkwardly she moved her head to peer into his eyes and darted her lips against his for a kiss.

Throwing despair away for passion, Fiona let her hands flow over his warm body, and had the reassuring pleasure of his hands moving in response. Slowly they maneuvered, touching, moving, silently, passionately.

Long afterward, Fiona reached a hand up to his cheek and stroked it gently. Kindan cupped her hand with his and smiled down at her.

"Three times," he told her with a smile.

Fiona chuckled and raised an eyebrow in challenge.

"**W**hat do you mean, I can't go out?" T'mar demanded testily when Birentir told him. "I waited an extra two days because you said so!"

He turned to Fiona, who was eyeing him with one eyebrow raised archly. "And you—dowsing my wine with fellis juice so I slept an extra day! Give me those crutches!"

Fiona pulled them away from him, saying, "Not until you get some sense in your thick skull. You're acting like an addle-pated wherry!"

"I'm acting like a Weyrleader," T'mar declared, but his words lacked conviction.

"A Weyrleader sets an example, or so I'm told," Birentir said dryly. "And a Weyrleader recovering from a severe *pair* of injuries would best set an example by listening to the Weyr Healer, wouldn't he?"

T'mar scowled stubbornly before leaning back in his bed, asking in a grudging tone, "So, healer, what can I do?"

"If you wish to recover fully," Birentir responded, emphasizing the last word, "you'll restrict your movements to your weyr for the next sevenday or so."

"And then?"

"Then we'll see," Fiona told him, shaking her head in exasperation as she added, "You're just as bad as the worst were back in Igen, you know."

T'mar's face twisted as the barb struck home. He had vivid memories of the younger Fiona arguing with grizzled old-timers—and winning.

"Ah, you're remembering," Fiona said, taking in the look on his face. "Perhaps you'll also remember that all of my charges recovered and are now fighting Thread?"

"I do," T'mar growled with a resigned look on his face. He brightened as he turned back to the healer, saying, "So, just around here?"

"If you don't tire yourself."

"How will I know?"

"You'll know when you fall over back into a coma," Fiona said with a shake of her head. "Or, if you're sensible, you'll *listen* to your body and limit yourself accordingly."

T'mar jerked his head to Zirenth's lair. "You could *make* him stop me."

"I could," Fiona agreed, turning with a half-smile toward the slumbering bronze in the weyr beyond. She turned back to T'mar. "But they're desperate for him and the night crew for the Fall at Fort this evening, so I'm going to rely on your common sense instead."

And with that, she thrust the crutches toward him, turned, and walked briskly out of the room, passing through Zirenth's weyr and murmuring a fond greeting to the dozing bronze before moving on to the rest of her day's business.

Birentir and T'mar were left behind to exchange surprised looks.

"She has a way about her," Birentir said.

"Makes you forget her Turns, doesn't she?" T'mar asked with a grin.

"If there's one thing this Weyr doesn't lack, it's a strong Weyrwoman," Birentir said.

"For which," T'mar said, his voice straining as he raised himself on his crutches, "I am extremely grateful."

"And does she know that?"

T'mar greeted the healer's question with a glowering silence marred by a wince as he took his first step.

▼ ▼ ▼

"**Y**ou two will be careful," Fiona said as she glanced up at Lorana and Kindan perched atop bronze Zirenth later that evening. "And you'll make sure that Nuella doesn't get hurt, won't you?"

"Of course," Lorana assured her. Kindan added a nod in agreement.

"Zirenth, I hope you're well rested," Fiona said, patting the great bronze on his foreleg. The bronze rumbled in amused agreement. "Talenth and I are expecting you to be here for the Hatching, you know."

"Yes, you'd better take good care of him," T'mar called from the entrance to Zirenth's weyr. "He and I expect many more mating flights!"

Fiona smiled at that and, with one last wave to Lorana and Kindan, stepped back from the bronze.

"In which case," she said to T'mar, "you'll need to get some rest."

"Come up here and I'll show you how much rest I need, Weyrwoman," T'mar responded teasingly. To his surprise, Fiona jumped up onto the queens' ledge and trotted over to him, even before Zirenth had leaped up to go *between*.

"I wish she wouldn't do that," T'mar muttered for her ears alone. "She should take him up to the Star Stones first."

"She said she always knows where and when she is," Fiona assured him.

"It's not that," T'mar told her, shaking his head, "it's that it sets a bad example for the rest of the Weyr."

"Good point," Fiona said. "We should tell her when they get back."

"We should," T'mar said, jerking his head invitingly toward his weyr. "In the meantime, perhaps you'd care for a demonstration of my newly regained strength."

Fiona gave him an arch look. "Are you so desperate to put yourself in a coma?"

T'mar snorted. "Really, Weyrwoman, I think you overestimate yourself."

"Probably," Fiona agreed. "But there are some experiments I'm not willing to try."

T'mar's expression softened at the tone in her voice. "So, exactly *what* experiments are you willing to try?"

Fiona snorted and waved for him to precede her into his quarters.

They were lying together, asleep, much later when the sound of Zirenth's wings awoke them. Fiona untangled herself from him and, with a restraining look, gestured for him to remain while she went and helped Kindan and Lorana.

They reeked of firestone, as did Zirenth.

"You've been flaming?" Fiona said, her lips set disapprovingly.

"Had to," Kindan said. "When one of the wingleaders was injured, K'lior assigned us to take over."

Fiona's eyes widened in surprise.

"It was for the best," Lorana said. "It got us closer to the fighting, so we could coordinate better." She smiled as she looked at Kindan. "He did all the fighting while Nuella and I did the controlling."

"It worked out well enough," Kindan said diffidently as they walked into T'mar's rooms.

"You had my dragon flaming?" T'mar asked, sitting up in his bed.

"As you knew," Lorana said without any sign of apology. "You were in touch with Zirenth so much you nearly distracted him."

"You were?" Fiona said, glaring at the Weyrleader. "Even while we . . . ?"

"No, not then," T'mar assured her hastily.

"I'm sorry," Fiona said to Lorana, "if I had realized he was interfering, I would have distracted him more fully."

"Don't," Lorana said with a smile for T'mar, "you'll only encourage him."

Kindan's features sharpened grimly as he absorbed their banter, eyeing Fiona appraisingly. Fiona sensed that he was disappointed somehow and her elated mood evaporated.

"It's late," Kindan said, "we shouldn't detain you too long, Weyrleader."

"How bad was it?" T'mar asked.

"They lost four dragons, had two seriously injured, and two who will take a good month to recover," Lorana reported.

"High Reaches flies at night in three days' time," T'mar said with a sigh. He glanced up at Kindan. "They'll want you again, won't they?"

Kindan didn't reply, looking distracted, so it was Lorana who answered, "I expect so, Weyrleader, if that's all right with you."

"It's for the good of Pern," T'mar said. He cocked his head toward Kindan, adding, "Though I'll be happy when you get your own dragon."

Kindan glanced sharply at T'mar and shook his head. "I'm not sure that'll happen, Weyrleader."

"Only because the right dragon's not been hatched," T'mar declared stoutly. Fiona and Lorana nodded emphatically in agreement but Kindan kept his doubtful expression.

For the next three days, until the next night Fall at High Reaches Weyr, Fiona felt Kindan grow more distant from her. At first, she put it down to nerves, exhaustion, and drill, but when he returned from the second night Fall at High Reaches, his attitude toward her was unmistakable. Rather than speaking to her, he made his report to T'mar only, excluding her from his line of vision and holding tightly to Lorana while he spoke.

"A lot of their losses were because they were unused to flying with the watch-whers and wouldn't listen to Lorana," Kindan said, running a hand through his dark hair in exasperation.

"How bad was it?" Fiona asked. Kindan said nothing; it was Lorana who replied, looking up from the seat into which she'd half-fallen on their return. "Bad. They lost three dragons, had three seriously injured, and five minor injuries."

"Between their losses from the first night Fall and this one, they've only five wings now fit to fly," Kindan said.

"One hundred and fifty fighting dragons," Lorana murmured, her eyes wide with worry.

"We'll find a way through," Fiona assured her, curving her lips up into a smile. "We're here now because of you; we won't fail."

Lorana made no response. Kindan gave Fiona a sour look that both startled and hurt her.

"We need to rest," Kindan said to T'mar, gesturing politely toward Lorana and helping her up from her seat. T'mar nodded and waved them away. When they were gone, his eyes sought Fiona's.

"He hates me," Fiona said, her voice a hoarse whisper.

"Of course," T'mar agreed. "Who else could he hate?"

Fiona's brows furrowed at his question.

"He can't hate Lorana, and hating himself is much the same," T'mar told her. "You, on the other hand, are a living reminder of all his faults and failings." He shook his head wearily. "You are the obvious target."

"But I didn't do anything!"

"Which is all the more reason," T'mar told her with a wry grin. "He hates that he's so angry that he has to find someone to take it out on. He's chosen you because you're the Weyrwoman and he's hoping you're strong enough to weather his storm." T'mar pursed his lips and gave her an inquiring look. "Are you?"

Fiona was about ready to protest once more that it wasn't fair but the words died on her lips. Was it fair that Koriana died of the Plague? Was it fair that Lorana lost her queen in her attempts to save Pern?

"Is he afraid to love me?" Fiona asked at last, feeling her heart churn heavily in her chest, as though weary of beating.

"Yes," T'mar told her gently, "just as much as he's afraid that you don't love him."

"What?"

"In that, we're not all that different, he and I," T'mar said, glancing up at her from under his eyebrows, his expression guarded.

"I . . ."

"M'tal and I had several long conversations before he left for Ista," T'mar said to comfort her. He grinned as he added, "Apparently his obversations about you quickly became pertinent to his own situation."

"We've a saying at Fort Hold: 'When you're talking to someone, two pairs of ears are listening,'" Fiona said.

"Precisely," T'mar said. He laid his head back on his pillow, his eyes gazing unfocused toward the ceiling as he confessed, "It is impossible not to love you."

"I love you, T'mar," Fiona replied slowly. "I just don't know—"

"No, of course you don't," T'mar cut her off. "For all your maturity, you've still Turns of learning in ways of the heart." He roused himself and grinned at her wickedly. "I expect you'll prove as quick a study there as you have with all things related to the Weyr."

"If I could, without hurting too much," Fiona said, "I'd love everyone."

"Actually," T'mar said, lowering his head once again, "I think you already do—in your own way."

"And that's the problem."

"Weren't you the one who quoted: 'Problems are just challenges'?"

Fiona snorted at the taunt.

"And aren't you always up for a challenge?"

"Sleep well, Weyrleader," Fiona said, marching to Zirenth's lair. "You need your rest."

SIXTEEN

▼▼▼▼▼▼▼▼▼▼▼▼▼▼▼▼▼▼▼▼▼▼

Dragonrider:
Dance in clouds
Soar to stars
Touch mountains
Skim rivers.

Telgar Weyr, morning, AL 508.4.15

"Fit to fly?" Fiona asked as she raced up the queens' ledge toward T'mar. The Weyrleader grinned and nodded emphatically. The air was full of the fresh smell of spring and while clouds danced overhead, Fiona felt that they wouldn't make rain that day, at least. The morning air was chilly but without the harsh, biting cold of winter.

"Come on, Zirenth, let's see if you remember!" T'mar called to the bronze dragon, who followed him eagerly out of his weyr. He cocked a glance toward Fiona. "Care to join us?"

Fiona shook her head ruefully. "Talenth is too gravid to be interested."

"She's six weeks or so shy of clutching," T'mar said, his expression growing serious.

"Queens can clutch any time from twelve to fifteen weeks after mating," Fiona reminded him. "Although the norm seems to be about fourteen."

"Three and a half months, then," T'mar said. "So she's due near the end of next month."

"Or sooner," Fiona cautioned.

T'mar raised a hand. "Don't say that! An early clutch is small."

"We'll hope for a late clutch, then," Fiona said, nodding toward Zirenth.

"And a queen egg," T'mar said, as he moved to the side of Zirenth's weyr, allowing the great bronze easy egress.

"Queen eggs are rare on the first Hatching," Fiona warned him.

"We need queens," T'mar said, as Zirenth backed up against the ledge and crouched down to let his rider jump on his shoulders.

"Indeed we do," Fiona agreed. With an approving glance at T'mar's grasp of his riding straps, she added, "And we need Weyrleaders, too!"

"She won't rise again until after her clutch hatches," T'mar reminded her as Zirenth turned away from the ledge and moved out into the Weyr Bowl proper.

"So keep safe and fly well, Weyrleader!" Fiona called, waving merrily after him.

T'mar waved back over his shoulder and then, with two bounds, Zirenth was aloft, pumping mightily toward the Star Stones and being greeted cheerfully by T'mar's fighting wing. The remaining wings of Telgar Weyr joined them and together they winked *between* to drill in preparation for the next Threadfall.

After they were gone, Fiona's expression slipped. The clutching would change things, she was certain. But the steady erosion of the Weyrs' strength had only been recently reversed by the recovery of the first of the wounded.

Telgar Weyr now had—with T'mar and the other five recovered dragonriders—five full-strength fighting wings, a full wing less than they'd had when the Weyrs had redistributed their strength. And while Telgar was the worst off, none were all that much stronger—as both Fiona and T'mar had taken pains to point out to H'nez, who'd resumed command of the fighting wings after J'lantir's sudden death.

The wiry, dour bronze rider had grown so distraught over the losses that Jeila had begged Fiona to intervene.

"I've heard nothing but good about you," T'mar had told H'nez when Fiona brought the issue to his attention. "I'll be hard pressed to match your ability when I return to health."

"I wish you had recovered a month ago," H'nez confessed.

"But I didn't," T'mar said. "And you've not complained in all that time." He gave H'nez a grin. "Keep up the good work, I'll soon relieve you!"

T'mar's encouraging talk was still not enough for H'nez and the bronze rider grumbled that when T'mar recovered, he'd request to be allowed to return to Fort Weyr.

"No, you won't!" Jeila had told him heatedly. "You'll stay here, with me, where you belong."

And that, as Jeila told Fiona later, was that. Although, Fiona thought with a grin, perhaps Jeila had produced some extra inducements as she had confided all this as a prelude to announcing her pregnancy.

"It's still too early to tell," Jeila had cautioned when she'd shared the news. "And I'm worried."

Fiona raised her eyebrows inquiringly.

Jeila gestured to her petite frame and thin waist. "I'm worried that the way I'm built, I might not carry to term."

"Wasn't your mother much the same as you?" Fiona had asked. When Jeila had nodded in response, Fiona had continued, "And how many children did she have?"

"Four," Jeila admitted. "But she miscarried the first."

"Well," Fiona had replied, "we'll guarantee you the best midwife."

"I want Bekka," Jeila told her.

"She's not a midwife."

"Her and her mother, then," Jeila had replied.

"I'll see what we can do," Fiona said. "After all, I've reason to believe that Lorana may have need of one soon."

"And what about you?" Jeila had asked, casting a probing look her way.

"I think two will be enough to getting on with," Fiona had replied, turning the question aside. Jeila had given her a thoughtful look but had not pressed the matter.

It *was* just possible that she was with child, but Fiona had always been erratic in her cycle, so she wasn't entirely certain. Surely she hadn't noticed any change in her eating habits and, if she felt a bit more emotional, it was far too easy to ascribe to the current mood of the Weyr—even, of all Pern.

There was no escaping the steady, slow attrition of the fighting strength of the Weyrs. High Reaches had fared best of all, while the other Weyrs found themselves nearly a full wing short—and this after only two months of fighting. With losses up to a wing every two months, there would be no dragons flying at any Weyr—save perhaps High Reaches—when the still-unclutched hatchlings were barely old enough to fly.

The advent of the new agenothree throwers eased the requirement of the dragonriders to perform endless patrols looking for any stray burrow after a Fall—except that, alarmingly, more and more Thread had made it through in the latest Falls to cause burrows larger than the holders could contain.

Fiona heard that Lord Holder Gadran of Bitra was practically dyspeptic with fury when Weyrleader B'nik of Benden had to burn yet another of the Bitran's forests to check the spread of burrows. Telgar had been no luckier, having to fire two valleys—one in Telgar Hold and the other in Crom—much to the despair of all involved.

The discussion around the Weyrleaders' table of late had turned to the issue of when to start going *between* times to previous Threadfalls.

"Hold off as long as you can," Fiona had urged. "The dangers of timing it are so great that I fear you'll lose more than you'll save."

"It matters not," T'mar had said. Fiona looked at him sharply and he shrugged. "You can be certain we won't be timing it until after we've timed it."

"You mean that the first we'll know of timing it will occur when a flight from the future comes to our aid?" H'nez asked.

"Precisely," T'mar said, raising a hand to disguise a yawn, a move not unobserved by Fiona who snorted and handed him his mug of *klah*.

"Well, at least you know the dangers," she'd observed sourly. Thoughtfully, she added, "Although, given how tired you are, going *between* times might be doubly dangerous."

"Perhaps I'm tired because I've already done it," T'mar said. "Perhaps we're more accustomed to the effects."

H'nez gave the Weyrleader a doubtful look, then turned imploringly to Fiona, who snorted and told T'mar, "And perhaps you're eager to let H'nez have the Weyrleader's position permanently!"

"I'll be careful," T'mar said.

Fiona bit back a tart rejoinder and converted her breath into a long sigh.

"Our strength is returning," T'mar told her soothingly. "We've five fighting wings as of today—we've been as low as four." He turned to H'nez. "We've time enough before the next Fall, I think we should practice timing it."

"If you are, then I'm coming with you," Fiona warned.

"If you can get Talenth roused, we'll be happy to have you," T'mar said, knowing that the gravid queen was spending most of her time resting. Fiona glared at him in response, turned on her heel and stomped off.

"I'll be happy when her queen clutches," T'mar admitted to H'nez once she was out of earshot.

"It'll be awhile yet," H'nez said. T'mar nodded in agreement, then shook his head to clear it of distractions, before saying to H'nez, "Now, let's consider how best to practice timing it."

"I would never have believed it if I hadn't seen it with my own eyes," F'jian said as the dragonriders milled around the Dining Cavern later that evening. He pointed at T'mar. "There he was"—and then he pointed to a spot above him—"and *there* he was—two of him!"

"Two of you, as well?" Terin asked, her expression troubled.

"I didn't see me," F'jian said, "I was too busy looking at the Weyr-leaders." He shook his head in bemusement. "If I hadn't seen it myself, I never would have believed it."

The conversation was a sample of the murmuring throughout the Cavern as dragonriders joked and swapped tales of seeing themselves— "I never knew I was that fat!" "We did!"—and explaining to the wary weyrfolk the events of the day.

"We'll jump back tomorrow," T'mar said to H'nez as they gathered at the wingleaders' table. Timing it was difficult enough to *do* but some-times harder to explain—as they hadn't jumped back immediately in time after seeing their future selves, the jump from some future point still had yet to occur.

"So soon?" Fiona asked, eyeing him carefully.

"That will give us more time to recover before the next Threadfall," T'mar said. He frowned. "I'm sure I wouldn't have considered jumping back any later than that."

"You didn't look too tired," H'nez said.

"The worst of the exhaustion usually sets in *after* timing it," Fiona said.

"So it will only be a problem if we don't have enough time to recover."

Fiona looked at T'mar and they exchanged a frown, the Weyrleader saying, "I'm not sure it's quite that easy."

Fiona pulled the pitcher of *klah* toward her and refilled T'mar's mug. "I'm not sure that either of us are good examples," she said, shaking the pitcher emphatically before placing it back on the table.

"How did Kindan and Lorana do on Winurth?" Fiona asked, glancing toward the couple who sat at the opposite end of the table, engrossed in their own conversation.

"Well enough," T'mar told her. He pursed his lips, adding, "If we had more injured riders than dragons, this idea of pairing spare riders with dragons would work better."

"Dragons are larger than riders," Fiona said, "so they're more likely to get injured just because of their greater size."

T'mar flipped the fingers of one hand up in agreement. Dragons were injured nearly eight times more often than riders; Fiona was right, it was a simple question of size.

"We're doing pretty well all the same," Fiona said, catching T'mar's eyes and glancing significantly toward H'nez, who wore a glum look. "We've only twenty-three injured, and nine of them only slightly."

"And twenty-one are lost forever," H'nez reminded them grimly. Jeila, who was sitting beside him, reached for his near hand and cradled it comfortingly. "Of all the Weyrs, we've lost the most."

"No more than Ista," Fiona said.

"And High Reaches is close, with nineteen," T'mar added, shaking his head emphatically. "So, if you're to make comparisons, H'nez, remember that you're comparing yourself with M'tal and D'vin—both of whom have been Weyrleaders Turns longer than you've been leading Falls."

H'nez started to reply, thought better of it and, with a sigh, nodded glumly.

"Besides," Fiona said, "if you'll recall, J'lantir led the Weyr for the earliest Fall."

"He was a good man," H'nez said.

"Even good men can make mistakes," T'mar said. He shook himself and rose from the table. "And with that, I will say good evening, I think we can all use our rest."

He cast a questioning look toward Fiona, hand outstretched. She frowned thoughtfully before rising and grabbing his hand. Together they paid their compliments to Shaneese and departed into the darkened Bowl.

Much later, Fiona found herself taking a hurried bath in T'mar's quarters before quietly sneaking back to her own weyr. She paused in Talenth's lair for a long time, watching the flanks of her queen as they rose and fell with her breathing. Her stomach had turned lumpy with the growing eggs.

Talenth twitched in her sleep, as though reacting to Fiona's presence.

To soothe her, Fiona moved over to the queen's great head and gently scratched her eye ridges. Talenth exhaled noisily, twisted slightly on her side as though trying to get comfortable and slid back into a deeper slumber.

A smile played across Fiona's lips as she watched her queen, marveling that such an amazing person could love *her*.

A slight noise from the entrance of her quarters warned her that she was not alone. Without turning, she knew it was Kindan. She couldn't say how long he'd been watching her. Beyond him she felt the comforting presence of Lorana, asleep. For a moment Fiona allowed herself once again to be amazed at how she felt Lorana's presence, much like she felt Talenth—like fabric brushing against her skin or her hair when the wind tossed it—part of her and, yet, apart.

It was not like that with Kindan. Her heart pounded in her chest and her breath came faster to her, his very presence energized her.

She turned then, her eyes seeking out his in the gloom. For a long moment they stood there; Fiona waiting, expectant, and vaguely surprised at her own serenity. Then Kindan moved forward. She waited for him, only moving when his arms wrapped around her, folding herself into his embrace.

"**N**ever again!" T'mar groaned as he slipped down off Zirenth's neck. Fiona caught him, disregarding his scolding look. She looked beyond him to Lorana and Kindan as they dismounted Winurth in the distance. Lorana carefully helped Kindan down, his face was as ashen as T'mar's.

"I feel like I've been trampled by Talenth and buried under her eggs," T'mar said, as he allowed himself to collapse against the Weyrwoman. Fiona gestured desperately for Xhinna and Taria and between the three of them, they managed to guide the fatigued Weyrleader up to his quarters, where he collapsed into his bed.

The rest of the riders were no better. It took no urging from Fiona for the weyrfolk to rush out into the Bowl and, in groups, guide each returning rider to their weyrs.

"Let them rest," Fiona said as she returned to the Bowl and took in the scene.

"It was like riding a Fall twiceover," H'nez murmured weakly as Fiona came to Jeila's aid in propping up the much taller rider. "I've never felt so bad."

Fiona gave him a sympathetic look but secretly she wondered why the riders were so overwhelmed by it all—hadn't she been dealing with the same problem for Turns? Perhaps it was worse when they actually timed it. Even so, she decided, *she* would not behave as poorly as the rest of the Weyr.

Hours later, when T'mar had recovered, the Weyrleader told her, "If you think this is anything like what we've been feeling, I can assure you that you're wrong."

Fiona gave him a studious look but her disbelief leaked into her expression.

T'mar wagged a finger at her. "Just you wait, Weyrwoman, you'll see."

"Either way," Fiona said, dismissing the issue, "if the riders are this fatigued, surely timing it is too dangerous."

"As compared to letting Thread fall unchecked?" T'mar said, shaking his head. Adding the old Weyr saying, "'Needs must when the Red Star rises.'"

"All the same."

"I'm not eager to try it, Weyrwoman, but we had to prepare," T'mar said.

"Lorana's warned the other Weyrs," Fiona said.

"And well she should," T'mar said. "But the problem remains, the first we'll know of timing it is when we see ourselves back in time."

Fiona's expression darkened as she took in his words. How terrible would it be for riders, exhausted from a Fall, to know that they would soon be even *more* exhausted going back in time to save themselves?

"Casualties will be heavy," Fiona said. T'mar nodded in wordless agreement. "It should only be used as a last resort."

"We may be at last resorts soon," the Weyrleader said grimly.

"The queens will clutch soon."

"Those dragons will only be ready to fight three Turns from now," T'mar said. "It's *today* and tomorrow that concern me."

Fiona had no response to that.

Every three days and three hours, Thread came again. Telgar flew over Igen Weyr, then over north Keroon, then over the Weyr itself and Telgar Hold.

And each time Thread fell, Lorana would grit her teeth in response to the anguish, the pain, and the loss of dragons and riders fighting against it.

Fiona found herself carefully orchestrating a watchful group to tend to the ex-dragonrider's special needs: Jeila, Terin, Xhinna, Mekiar, Shaneese, even Birentir took part in the comforting, always solicitous, always available.

Kindan was at first resentful and then grew grateful as he realized how much of Lorana's pain he had taken upon himself.

It was during the last Fall that Fiona discovered that she herself also had a steady group of companions. It was Rhemy, the wide-eyed girl who seemed to have feelings beyond her years, who was most often at Fiona's side.

"You feel it too," Rhemy said. As Fiona drew breath to protest, the young girl blurted out, "Maybe not as much but you feel it."

Fiona let out her breath in surprise.

"You do, don't you?" Rhemy persisted.

"Not as much as Lorana," Fiona said. She was sure hers was only an echo of the dark-eyed woman's feeling.

Finally, the Thread fell elsewhere, outside of Telgar's borders and the Weyr rested, the dragonriders trained, and more recovered to gladly rejoin their Wings. Even so, the Weyr flew only five Wings—and one of those Wings light by four dragons.

While Telgar rested, the other Weyrs were busy. Ista Weyr flew Falls over Igen Hold, then Ista Hold, while High Reaches Weyr flew their Fall over High Reaches Hold and then Fort Weyr flew Fall over Ruatha Hold.

The dragonriders of Telgar Weyr—and the weyrfolk—kept up to date with the losses of every Fall.

"Fort's down to four full Wings," F'jian remarked glumly that evening.

"One hundred and forty fighting dragons," H'nez said. "That's nearly five full Wings."

"Ista's worse, they've got three and a half Wings," brown rider J'gerd pointed out.

"There'll be eggs on the Hatching Grounds soon enough," Terin said, trying to improve F'jian's mood.

"Not too soon," H'nez said. "Another fortnight yet."

"They might clutch early," J'gerd said.

H'nez shook his head. "An early clutch is a light clutch. We need all the dragons we can get."

"I think I'd prefer some sooner than too many later," Jeila said.

Fiona listened to the discussion silently. For herself, the sooner Talenth clutched, the happier she'd be. Oh, she didn't want a small clutch, but she'd be glad when Talenth wasn't so bogged down with the weight of the eggs, especially the way her gravid state seemed to give her such distressing dreams—dreams that Fiona sensed in a garbled way.

"You are not going to lose your eggs," Fiona had told her that very morning. "You're doing fine."

Talenth rumbled in disagreement.

"It's your first clutching, you can't expect everything to be perfect," Fiona assured her, raising her hand once more to scratch Talenth's eye ridges, her hands still slippery from her morning oiling of Talenth's stretched hide.

It just doesn't feel right, Talenth complained, gently angling her head so that Fiona could reach to a particularly itchy spot on her eye ridge.

Fiona continued scratching and made no response. She'd felt enough of her queen's dreams to understand Talenth's words—the dreams had been unnerving—always predicting that something would happen, something horrible.

Fiona dug deep into herself to find enough cheer to spread it to Talenth and counteract the dragon's despair, but she realized that even her reserves were stretched. She knew how much the rest of the Weyr looked to her, how they shook their heads in amusement when they thought she wouldn't notice over her ever-cheerful manner, how she managed to find something good in the hardest of times. Oh, the old ones would prattle on and warn her that she was taking things too easily, but Fiona knew with a certainty that the mood of the entire Weyr was influenced by her cheerfulness and that mothers would tell their daughters, "See? The Weyrwoman's not worrying, why should you?"

Dragonriders, too, took their cues from her, as did Jeila and even Lorana.

Fiona's lips turned down as she thought of Lorana. The ex–queen rider was finding it increasingly difficult to bear up under the weight of the loss of dragons and riders in Threadfalls, which she felt all too keenly. Fiona had a secondhand glimpse of Lorana's pain; she felt it more fully than Kindan, but she also knew by dint of the same strange bond that allowed Fiona to feel Lorana's pain that Lorana purposely shielded her from a lot of it.

Ironically, it was their strange connection that kept up Fiona's spirits. If two people could form such a tight bond, then anything was possible, wasn't it? At least, that's how Fiona reasoned the matter.

Theirs was a strange relationship, Fiona mused. In some ways, Lorana reminded her of Tannaz . . . Fiona's hand stopped moving on Talenth's eye ridge as that notion froze her into stillness. Lorana was like Tannaz; would Lorana choose Tannaz's course if the situation continued to get worse?

Fiona realized that she'd stopped breathing and forced herself to take a fresh breath. The difference was that Fiona was older, knew herself more—she could help Lorana where she couldn't help Tannaz. Still . . .

She started as a hand clasped her back at the base of her neck and turned quickly, her sea-blue eyes flashing, only to find herself looking up into Kindan's face, his blue eyes framed by stray locks of dark hair.

The harper's lips were quirked upward. "Woolgathering?"

Since that night three sevendays before, Kindan's manner with Fiona had thawed into a warm, easy companionship.

"Yes, I suppose so," Fiona said, glancing back affectionately to her dragon. "She says she feels heavy."

Kindan chuckled. "No doubt she does with all those eggs weighing her down."

"How's Lorana feeling?"

Kindan's eyebrows furrowed.

"No, I wasn't referring to that," Fiona said. Lorana was just starting her twelfth week and only just beginning to show—although, having been in close proximity with her for some time, Fiona had known that she was pregnant for a while. Her lips tightened into a frown, as she added thoughtfully, "Though that might have something to do with it."

Kindan nodded. "She's at the stage where going *between* should be avoided."

Fiona turned back toward him, eyes flashing. "That's not it at all, Kindan!"

The harper took a step back, arms raised defensively, alarmed at her fierce reaction.

"What is it, then?" Kindan asked, lowering his arms and stretching out his hands beseechingly.

"It's . . . everything," Fiona said, throwing her arms open wide. "It's that Talenth and Tolarth both will soon clutch, that we're losing dragons every three days and all the clutches on Pern will be too little too late and that, on top of it all, she has a child coming into the world and she doesn't know where she fits."

"With me," Kindan said with a decisive nod of his head.

"With us," Fiona corrected. Kindan gave her a questioning look. "Here, in this Weyr—Telgar—where she's central to everything, where she can speak to all dragons, coordinate with Nuella and the watch-whers, and be surrounded by those who love her."

"So where is the problem?"

"The problem is with her, Kindan," Fiona replied tetchily, surprised at his obtuseness. "The problem is that she sees all she is *not*—not a Weyr-woman, not a mother, not a mate—and it worries her."

"How do you know so much about her feelings?"

"I didn't," Fiona said. "Mostly I learned it from Shaneese and Mekiar."

"Do they have any suggestions?"

"Patience, sympathy, comfort," Fiona said with a heavy sigh. "All the things I'm not very good at."

Kindan grunted in disbelief.

"It's true!" she said, giving him a sour look. "I'm better at cheering, at encouraging than I am at comforting."

"I think you're wrong," Kindan said. He raised a hand to forestall her hot retort. "It may be that you feel inadequate to meet her needs but I can't see how"—and he gestured toward Talenth's egg-laden belly—"you can't be sympathetic about her pregnancy."

Fiona let out the breath she had gathered for her argument with a rueful grin. "I suppose I *do* understand something of that."

"And," he continued, his voice going soft, "I expect you've dealt with the same issues of being a mate—"

"True."

"—and I think you can imagine her concerns about not being a Weyr-woman," Kindan concluded.

"Ever since T'mar's recovery, I've watched her slip deeper and deeper into sorrow," Fiona said, her expression bleak. Kindan nodded in understanding.

"I've seen it, too," he said. "Although I question whether she wasn't just distracted from her sorrow when we were flying Zirenth."

"If I could," Fiona said, "I'd give her Talenth."

"No you wouldn't," Lorana's voice answered from outside the weyr. She stepped into Talenth's weyr and made her way to the queen's head, reaching up a loving hand to scratch Talenth's eye ridges. "Once you've Impressed, only *death* can separate you."

Kindan and Fiona exchanged alarmed glances at Lorana's words. Lorana caught the look and smiled wanly at them, shaking her head, her hand going to her belly.

"There are other loves than dragons'," she said, reaching her hand out toward them. Kindan grabbed it firmly and Fiona moved to the taller woman's side, wrapping an arm around her waist and laying her head on her shoulder.

"I love you," Kindan told Lorana feelingly.

"So do I," Fiona added, clutching Lorana tighter even as she wondered in the depths of her soul whether their love would be enough.

A moment later, Fiona felt Lorana stir and pulled away from her far enough to look up into her eyes. "What is it?"

Lorana sighed. "Thread falls at Igen today."

"M'tal's a good man, he'll handle it," Kindan said.

"They have four full Wings," Fiona added cheeringly, "more than enough for a Fall."

Lorana made no argument but Fiona could feel the other woman's deep sense of foreboding. To distract her, Fiona placed a hand on Lorana's belly. "Is he sleeping?"

Lorana frowned thoughtfully, then shook her head. She grabbed Fiona's hand and moved it over slightly. Fiona's eyes widened and her mouth broke into a huge grin. "He kicked me!" She turned to Kindan, eyes wide in awe, exclaiming, "Our baby kicked me!"

SEVENTEEN
▼▼▼▼▼▼▼▼▼▼▼▼▼▼▼▼▼▼▼▼▼▼▼▼▼▼▼▼▼▼▼

Fly high,
Scan sky.
Brave all,
Fly Fall.

Ista Weyr, afternoon, AL 508.5.5

"We'll keep one Wing in reserve," M'tal said, glancing thoughtfully at the three other wingleaders standing in the archway joining Ista's Kitchen Cavern with the Weyr Bowl. "S'maj, your Wing's been in the thick of things far too often, I want you to sit back this time."

The grizzled old dragonrider snorted and nodded. "It's time you others picked up the slack."

The two remaining wingleaders chuckled. Both were younger than either M'tal or S'maj, but both had been dragonriders for close to twenty Turns. J'lian, a veteran of J'lantir's famous "lost Wing," was the youngest, having "only" thirty-three Turns.

"We'll take care of the Fall for you, grandpa," J'lian said, his eyes twinkling.

"Just make sure you get older, young one," S'maj growled.

"As long as there are queens in the sky," J'lian said.

"If we need any more help, we'll call up the reserves," M'tal said, re-

ferring to the half-wing that he'd decided to leave behind in reserve at
the Weyr.

"Well, it's not like they'll be shirking," S'maj said, "seeing as they're
hauling our firestone."

"All the work and none of the glory," J'lian said, shaking his head and
glancing pointedly at the older wingleader.

"It's enough to fly, dragonrider," S'maj said, picking up on the bronze
rider's implied gibe.

M'tal smiled at the banter. He waved for the others to precede him
onto the warm sands of the Weyr Bowl where all the fighting dragons
clustered in a small portion of the vast expanse.

Thread would be falling over Igen, roiled and tossed by the turbulent
air rising from the hot desert sands below. M'tal was worried about that
turbulent air, but he kept his fear to himself, projecting a carefully
schooled air of professional nonchalance.

"Fly well," two voices called from behind him. He turned and spied
Salina with Dalia by her side. M'tal smiled and sketched a salute to the
two women. As he turned away from the two very different women in
his life, M'tal found time to send a stray hope in Fiona's direction that
she, Kindan, and Lorana had managed to cement their relationship as
well as he had with Dalia and Salina. It helped that both were mature
women and not given to fits of jealousy. He couldn't imagine Tullea in a
similar situation but, he reflected as he clambered up Gaminth's side,
perhaps the Benden Weyrwoman would come to surprise him as well.

What! M'tal thought as Gaminth bucked and dipped the moment they
came out of *between* over Igen. He was thrown first forward and then
backward violently as Gaminth searched for an altitude where the winds
were calmer. The hot air roiling up from the roasting sands below
churned and swirled unpredictably, making it impossible to keep formation. The turbulence was far worse than he'd feared.

Spread out! M'tal ordered. *Gaminth, have S'maj's Wing go high as lookout.*

The bronze dragon rumbled in agreement as he relayed the messages and the three fighting Wings spread out, seeking desperately to maintain what little formation they could in the fierce winds. Dimly, M'tal had the impression of S'maj's Wing clawing upward, searching for a less turbulent level from which to scan for Thread.

This is going to be rough, M'tal thought.

The air is troubled, hot, Gaminth thought. *Perhaps too hot for Thread?*

No, I don't think so, M'tal responded even as he heard a dragon bugle warningly, its voice distant and thin in the rough air.

S'maj has spotted it, Gaminth said. M'tal nodded, craning his neck upward and twisting from side to side to spy the thin wisps of deadly Thread.

There! he called, pointing at a clump and willing Gaminth to rise to meet it. With a bellow, the bronze surged upward in response to his unspoken command, jaws open, ready to flame. But as they approached, a buffet pushed them to one side while pushing the Thread away to another. Instinctively, Gaminth dove after the twisting Thread, twisting around to follow it as it slipped away again and again, saved by the fickle wind. Finally, to their surprise, the winds favored them, nearly blowing the Thread directly onto them but not before Gaminth's flame rendered it harmless ash.

Good! M'tal cried, slapping his dragon affectionately on the neck. *Let's get back to the others.*

But even as they resumed their climb, M'tal found himself astonished as he saw how scattered his Wings had become, each dragon following their individual clumps of Thread on the fickle winds.

Shards! M'tal swore to himself as he tried to imagine a way to reunite the dragons into a coherent fighting force. This is going to cost us.

As if in confirmation, two dragons, one after the other, bellowed in pain and vanished *between* as they tried to fight off Thread that had fallen upon them unseen or were suddenly blown by the churning winds aloft.

One returned quickly, the other, M'tal noted with a grimace, did not return at all.

Tell S'maj to join in, M'tal said. *We're going to need every dragon.*

Should we call up the reserves?

No, M'tal said, *it's going to be hard enough to get more firestone without exhausting them beforehand.*

They rejoined the forward line of dragons in their fight against Thread. Gaminth spotted and dove for a new clump, burned it, and rose again in search of more prey—all with the ease of previous Falls. Perhaps they were beyond the turbulent air, M'tal mused hopefully.

A sudden shout, a hiss of air and a dragon's bellow were all the warning M'tal had as another dragon dove over his head, its jaws agape with flame roaring into a clump of Thread directly above and just behind him.

M'tal had only a moment to recognize that the other rider's sudden appearance was all that had saved Gaminth from a terrible Threading— and probably death—before the dragon and rider veered upward sharply and disappeared once more *between.* They were not gone so quickly that M'tal didn't get a good look at the rider's back—and the large double black bars encased in a bright red diamond on the back of his leathers.

M'tal knew those colors well, for he'd worn them himself for many Turns. The man who saved him was wearing the colors of Benden's Weyrleader.

M'tal had barely time to send an unspoken thanks after the rider before another clump appeared and he and Gaminth dove upon it, flaming it quickly to char.

As they scanned for more Thread, M'tal glanced over the condition of his Wings and saw that all were spread out, ragged, many had holes left by missing dragons—injured or killed by the Thread blown erratically by the hot desert air.

Here and there, however, M'tal spotted another dragon winking into existence above them, burning through unseen clumps in the same manner as he'd been saved. Each time, it was the same dragon and, whenever he could see, the rider the Benden Weyrleader's badge. Light glinted off the dragon's hide, specks of gold mixed in with darker colors.

A rumble from Gaminth distracted him and M'tal leaned forward as his dragon burned through another clump of Thread and another. M'tal forgot about the Benden Weyrleader as he resumed his fight against the fickle Thread.

"Shards, M'tal, I don't know what you're talking about!" B'nik protested once again, pulling back from the older dragonrider's hearty embrace.

"You don't?" M'tal repeated, his hands on B'nik's shoulders, pushing the other man away from him so that he could see his eyes. B'nik had not much of a sense of humor, but it was foul enough that he might try to play a trick on his ex-Weyrleader, especially if Tullea had urged him on.

"No," B'nik repeated firmly, using his own hands to push M'tal's hands off him and stepping further away, "I don't."

M'tal's face fell. "Then if it wasn't you, who stole your jacket?"

"My jacket?" B'nik repeated blankly.

"Your Weyrleader's jacket," M'tal insisted. "I might have been mistaken in you—the distance was great—but the jacket and its emblem are unmistakable." Which hardly bore the mention, as the purpose of the Weyrleader's jacket was to be visible at all distances.

"No one stole my jacket," B'nik assured him. "It's in my quarters, just oiled."

"Someone rode Fall with us," M'tal said. "Someone rode Fall and saved us."

"But it wasn't me."

"No," M'tal said after a moment of thoughtful silence, "I think it was."

B'nik drew breath to make a heated retort but M'tal raised a hand placatingly. "Not today, but perhaps some time in the future."

"You mean I timed it?" B'nik asked in surprise.

"Yes," M'tal said. "I expect you did."

"But when?" B'nik asked. "And why only me? Why not a full Wing at least?"

"I don't know," M'tal said. "I suspect perhaps you wanted firsthand knowledge of the effects."

B'nik pursed his lips thoughtfully. "That would be prudent."

"Indeed it would," M'tal said. "Nothing less than I'd expect from you."

"Expect what?" Tullea demanded as she strode up to join them in the Weyr Bowl.

"M'tal thinks I timed it back to his Fall today," B'nik said.

"Saved my hide," M'tal said.

Tullea paled. "Timed it?" she said to B'nik. "When?"

"Not yet, apparently," B'nik said, "or I'd remember."

"You certainly would," Tullea agreed feelingly. She turned to M'tal. "How many others were there?"

"I only saw him," M'tal told her. He glanced over to B'nik's quarters and Caranth lounging in his weyr. His eyes narrowed as he added, "Caranth looked darker than he does now."

"It could have been a trick of the light," B'nik said.

"Possibly," M'tal said, shrugging off his doubts. "I only caught glimpses of you."

"So you're going to time it, eh?" Tullea asked, turning her head up appraisingly to her Weyrleader and mate.

"Apparently."

"In a way, I'm saddened," M'tal said. The others looked at him in surprise. "I was hoping that we wouldn't need to time it."

Tullea gave murmured heartfelt agreement.

"Why?" B'nik asked, turning from her to M'tal.

"Because it means that we soon won't have the strength to fly alone," the older dragonrider said.

B'nik pursed his lips and nodded in grim agreement.

"The baby's fine," Lorana told Fiona, barely keeping her irritation out of her voice. "Why don't you check on Talenth? She's ready to clutch."

"She's got nearly a fortnight before that," Fiona said, glancing from their quarters back to Talenth's weyr, where the gold was dozing; shifting once in a while to find a more comfortable position. Fiona turned back to Lorana and added quietly, "But if you want time to yourself, I'll let you be."

Lorana gave her a grateful smile. "I appreciate your efforts but—"

"You need some time to yourself," Fiona finished for her with a smile. "I understand." She rose and made her way to Talenth's weyr and the Weyr Bowl beyond, turning back to add, "Call if you need anything."

Lorana raised a hand in weary acknowledgment and then stretched herself out on the bed. Shaneese and Bekka both assured her that she would feel worse before the baby arrived, but for the moment Lorana did her best not to consider the notion. She was only in her sixteenth week with easily another twenty-four before the baby was born, but she was already heartily sick of "peeing for two" as Shaneese had so succinctly put it.

The baby certainly seemed to enjoy its confinement to the fullest extent possible, going so far as to kick his mother awake in the middle of the night. And, through their strange and special link, whenever Lorana woke, Fiona woke with her. Deep inside her, Lorana recognized how much of a gift that was. She was extremely grateful that the younger woman not only never complained but positively delighted in doing everything she could to help. A warm flood of love for Fiona's kind nature warred within Lorana against her need to vent, to release all the tension that was forever building in her, to get away from all the demands of her life.

And lately, she'd been having dark dreams. Her mind went to the strange brooch Tenniz had given her and his note: *The way forward is dark and long. A dragon gold is only the first price you'll pay for Pern.*

The first price? Lorana thrust the thought away as the baby kicked once more, as if in protest.

"You're worrying too much," Bekka said as soon as she caught sight of Fiona in the Kitchen Cavern. Bekka and Seban had been delighted with the request that they return—as healer apprentices—to Telgar and be-tween them had convinced Jeila, Lorana, and Fiona that they and Tel-gar's established midwives would be more than capable of handling any pregnancy. The two were welcomed back to the Weyr with such enthusi-asm that Fiona suspected it would be hard for them to consider return-ing to the Healer Hall. Not only that, but Seban exerted a steadying influence on Birentir while still maintaining a respectful deference for the journeyman's greater medical knowledge. Fiona got the distinct impres-sion that while Masterhealer Betrony would sorely miss Bekka and her father, that he'd been quite happy to force Birentir to take on the mentor-ing role. For her part, Fiona found herself looking at Birentir as someone who was being groomed as a future Master himself.

Fiona's eyes danced with delight at the young girl's complete lack of respect. She gestured toward an empty table, saying, "Why don't you tell me what's on your mind?"

Bekka followed her and sat opposite, immediately continuing, "You worry too much about Lorana."

"She practically threw me out of our quarters," Fiona confessed. She raised her eyes to meet Bekka's and her tone shifted. "I *do* worry about her," she said. "She's like a big sister to me, more even, and Kindan loves her so and it's *his* child, so . . ."

"It's going to be all right," Bekka told her firmly. The incongruity of the small, ever-active young girl assuring the senior Weyrwoman was not lost on her. She leaned forward to peer up into Fiona's face. "I've seen a lot of pregnancies, there's nothing wrong with this one."

Bekka's assurance had assumed greater merit after she'd been instru-mental in the last two of Telgar Weyr's deliveries. The two established midwives had both found themselves quite relieved to have her addi-tional knowledge—not to mention her irrepressible energy—available for their aid.

"But I'm still worried," Fiona said, her voice low and troubled.

"Your worry isn't helping either Lorana or the baby, Weyrwoman," Bekka told her as gently as she could. "It makes the both of them more nervous."

Fiona nodded and took a long steadying breath. "What should I do, then?"

"Stop fussing so much," Bekka said. "You're acting like you're afraid she'll lose the baby at any moment."

Fiona started to speak but Bekka stopped her with a raised hand.

"Honestly, Weyrwoman, it'll be all right," Bekka said. "The baby seems to be thriving, Lorana's doing well—"

"She's having nightmares," Fiona told her.

"That's normal," Bekka assured her. "Many mothers, particularly first-time mothers, worry and have nightmares."

"She's afraid she'll lose the baby."

"And you're afraid you'll lose the both of them, aren't you?" Bekka asked knowingly. When Fiona, frowning, gave her a reluctant nod, the young girl continued, "Isn't it possible that the *both* of them are picking up on your distress?"

Fiona bit her lips glumly and nodded once more. "What can I do?"

"Just be certain that they're both loved and cared for," Bekka said. "Lorana's tall, taller than you, and she's broad enough in the hips that she'll have no problem birthing this child."

Fiona frowned, still unable to rid herself of a deep foreboding.

"If you can't keep your moods in check, then it would be better if Lorana found quarters by herself," Bekka said.

A new voice joined in from Fiona's side. "Perhaps you're worrying about Lorana to avoid worrying about other things."

Fiona turned; it was Shaneese. The headwoman sat beside her, laying a basket full of warm rolls on the table. Bekka dove in and shamelessly grabbed one, gesturing for Shaneese to continue talking.

"Like what?" Fiona asked.

"Like Talenth and her clutch," Shaneese said. "Or you and Kindan."

"Or her and T'mar," Bekka added around a mouthful of roll and a mischievous look.

"So what do I do?" Fiona asked, turning toward the older woman.

"Spend more time with T'mar," Bekka said. "Let Lorana and Kindan have time together; let Lorana have time alone."

"She's got some good ideas," Shaneese told Fiona. She turned to the young healer, her eyes twinkling. "You know, she's just about as difficult as you, Weyrwoman!"

Fiona smiled even as Bekka growled in response.

"I'll be right next door," Fiona said to Talenth as she made her way to T'mar's quarters that night. Lorana and Kindan had both protested her plans, but she had heard the hidden relief in their voices. She kept Shaneese's and Bekka's words firmly in her mind and kept her expression neutral, her thoughts calm as she bade them good night and made her way to her queen's lair.

Talenth gave her a drowsy acknowledgment and went just as quickly back to sleep.

I'll bet you'll be happy to fly again, Fiona thought to her queen, only to be met with silence. With a sympathetic grin, Fiona walked out of the dragon's lair and over to T'mar's quarters. She greeted Zirenth warmly and crossed the distance to T'mar's room quickly.

T'mar met her at the entrance. "Weyrwoman—?"

Fiona wrapped her arms around him. "Just hold me," she said. "Hold me all night."

Wordlessly, T'mar scooped her up and brought her to his bed. He left her there as he finished readying for sleep, pausing only long enough to pass her one of the nightgowns she'd left in his closet. She slipped into it, carefully folding her day clothes and placing them on a nearby chair neatly, in readiness for any need.

With a nod, he gestured for her to get up as he pulled the blanket aside and motioned for her to get into the bed first, carefully removing the warming stones that had been set at the end of the bed. Fiona scampered in gratefully, her feet finding the warm spot and relishing it even as T'mar crawled in beside her and pulled the blankets over the both of them. Silently, she nuzzled her head up under his and was soon asleep.

She awoke in the middle of the night, her face wet with tears and she realized, in surprise, that they were hers.

"What is it?" T'mar whispered, hugging her more tightly.

"Something's going to happen," Fiona said, her chest tight with dread. "Something horrible."

"We'll survive," T'mar said.

"Not all of us."

The dark mood remained with Fiona over the next several days, even as three more riders returned to full fighting ability, giving Telgar a strength of one hundred and forty-six—nearly five full Wings.

Perhaps, she reasoned, it was because she spent so little time now with Kindan and Lorana, or perhaps it was because Talenth was so lethargic, burdened with the weight of her eggs.

Terin caught up with her as she was finishing her morning rounds of the injured.

"I haven't seen you in a while!" Fiona called in greeting. The younger girl blushed brightly.

"I'm sorry," Terin stammered, "it's just that F'jian . . ."

"I can understand," Fiona said. She raised an eyebrow conspiratorially. "Should I have Bekka see you?"

"Oh, no!" Terin said, raising her hands defensively. She blushed again. "It's not—well, we—I mean, I'm not ready for *that* just yet."

"Anyway, it's wise to wait a Turn and a half," Fiona said, referring to an old saying: "A Turn and a half proves the love."

"Not everyone waits that long," Terin said, her eyes flashing challengingly.

"Some wait longer," Fiona said with no bite in her tone. Terin drew breath for a quick retort and cut herself off, a thoughtful look on her face.

"But when dragons rise . . ."

"Dragons are a passion of their own," Fiona reminded the younger girl. Terin blushed again and ducked her head in a quick nod of agreement. The thought caused Fiona to reach out tenderly with her mind to her queen, even though she was certain that Talenth was sleeping—

"She's clutching!" Fiona yelled, turning on her heels and sprinting toward the Hatching Grounds.

Why didn't you tell me?

I knew what to do, Talenth said, sounding a bit strained as she passed another egg. *Come see.*

Lorana, Talenth is clutching! Fiona called excitedly.

I know, come quickly, Lorana responded, causing Fiona a moment's chagrin at the notion that her dragon had chosen Lorana to escort her to the Hatching Grounds—until she dismissed the notion as silly; doubtless Lorana had heard Talenth's departure from her weyr and had, naturally, followed.

Fiona was down the stairs and racing across the Weyr Bowl as she realized that Talenth's clutching was early.

"Fiona!" T'mar's voice called out from the Kitchen Cavern. "What is it?"

"Talenth's clutching!" Fiona shouted in response, not breaking her stride as she raced on by.

"Talenth?" she heard H'nez's voice echo. "What about Tolarth?"

"It's early!" another voice declared ominously.

Fiona disregarded the complaint, passing into the Hatching Grounds, her feet registering the warmth of the sands as she raced to the far end where Talenth lay exhausted after her labors, her eyes whirling in a swift green of pure contentment.

"I count twenty-one," Lorana said as Fiona approached. She reached out for the younger Weyrwoman, giving Fiona a cautioning look. "I've heard that's very good for a first clutch."

"Talenth, you're marvelous!" Fiona agreed even as she eyed the eggs and tried to hide her disappointment. No queen! Twenty-one eggs and no queen egg. And, were the eggs smaller than normal?

There's no queen egg, Talenth said, sounding disappointed in herself.

"That's normal for a first mating flight," Fiona assured her steadfastly. "But now that you've figured out how to do it, you'll be certain to have a queen next clutch."

"Having them early will mean that they're ready for flying against

Thread that much sooner," T'mar told the queen, his tone full of approval. Fiona shot him a questioning look, which the Weyrleader subdued with a quick jerk of his head.

And the clutch is small, Talenth said. *Are the eggs smaller, too?*

Don't worry, love, they'll be fine, Fiona told her. She continued to comfort her queen for several minutes, only leaving when Talenth was calm enough to lay her head down on the warm sands for a well-deserved rest.

Let me know if you need anything, Fiona said, as she made her way from the Hatching Ground once more into the Weyr Bowl. Talenth made no response; the sound of her slow, steady breathing carried clearly to the entrance: She was already asleep.

"She's asleep," Fiona said as T'mar joined her. She looked up worriedly. "Did we do wrong, to have that mating flight the way we did?"

T'mar pursed his lips thoughtfully. Finally, he shook his head. "A queen rises when she's ready," he said. He gave her a wry look as he added, "Do you think you really managed to align her passions to yours rather than the other way around?"

The notion startled Fiona and T'mar chuckled at her expression. "A queen often mates for the good of the Weyr, often against her rider's desires or interests," he said. "In the course of your life, there's no guarantee that you might not find yourself with several partners."

"Several *more* partners," Fiona corrected with a smile.

"Riders are often much like their dragons," T'mar allowed noncommittally, although his eyes gleamed humorously.

"You still haven't answered the question."

T'mar shook his head. "I've given you all the answer I have, Weyrwoman."

"But if—"

T'mar cleared his throat and grabbed her by the arm, forcing her closer to him. "What I'm more worried about," he told her in a voice pitched for her ears alone, "is whether the low numbers and early clutch are related to the cure to the dragon sickness."

Fiona paled as she absorbed his meaning.

"We won't know until the others clutch," T'mar said, gesturing for her to start moving once more. "As I said, and as you know, it's not uncommon for a queen's first clutch to be smaller than her norm."

"And she was ill not long before."

T'mar acknowledged that with a nod. "That would have an impact, certainly."

"So what do we do?"

"Wait," T'mar replied. "If the other clutches are normal, then we've probably no cause for alarm."

It was odd, Fiona thought as the days passed, that T'mar's worries about the possible effects of the dragon cure would cause Fiona to dismiss or at least downplay the various whispered conversations that abruptly ceased when she came near. She knew they were talking about Talenth's clutch and was certain that some of the conversations were condemning her for allowing Talenth to select Zirenth—as if she had a choice!—over a different dragon, one with a conscious rider and not the pairing of Lorana and Kindan.

Fiona was pretty certain that some of the more traditional weyrfolk were also chatting critically about her own choice of partners, but Turns of similar such chatter as she grew up at Fort Hold had inured her to the effects of such gossip—"Some people can't live without carping" had been Neesa's response Turns back when a very young Fiona had been taunted by some of the Hold youngsters.

Fiona's reaction was quite different if she overheard any criticism of Lorana or Kindan, as one group of weyrfolk discovered when she overheard them.

"Lorana and Kindan saved the dragons of Pern!" Fiona roared at them. "And anyone who cannot give them all due honor for their sacrifices need not remain in this Weyr."

The women blanched, one looking beseechingly in Shaneese's direction. That was a mistake, as Shaneese bustled over to the group and weighed in heavily on Fiona's side.

"I can see that you've all had too much idle time on your hands," Shaneese had said in conclusion, "and I'm glad that you've all volunteered to help the healers with their medical laundry." She glanced toward Fiona, who gave her a slight nod of encouragement. "The Weyrwoman and I are certain that you will give all your efforts to ensuring that all their fabrics and tools are thoroughly sterilized—steamed for a full ten minutes."

Stunned beyond words, the women could only nod in mute agreement.

Fiona's determination to talk with Lorana and Kindan about the issue was undermined the next morning just after breakfast when Lorana announced, wide-eyed, "Minith has clutched!"

Before Fiona or any of the others could react, Jeila dashed up, crying, "Tolarth is clutching!"

Everyone raced to the Hatching Grounds where Fiona quickly set herself as guard, turning back every gawker with a stern, "She needs no distractions!"

Indeed, Jeila was the only one the queen would allow into the Hatching Grounds. Talenth, a mother with only a sevenday's more experience, was tolerant of the other dragon's mood.

It's easier when no one's watching, Talenth told her rider calmly, adding tantalizingly, *Ooh, that's a large one!*

Lorana shared a smile with Fiona but said nothing, waiting patiently with H'nez and the other riders until Jeila finally called them in.

"That's a queen egg, for sure!" H'nez said as he noticed the larger gold-hued egg that Tolarth had pushed off to one side and was watching protectively.

"Aren't you wonderful?" Jeila cried, scratching her queen's eye ridges and beaming with pride. She turned to Fiona, saying, "Twenty-two and one's a queen!"

"I'm glad we've got a queen egg," J'lian said as he and the other riders approached.

"That's forty-three altogether," Kindan said.

"That makes a good dent on our losses," T'mar said, bestowing a huge grin on Jeila and H'nez both.

"And a queen!" H'nez said, as proud as if he'd done the clutching himself.

"Not bad at all for a first clutching," one of the blue riders allowed. Catching sight of Fiona, he added hastily, "Meaning no disrespect to you, Weyrwoman."

Fiona waved a hand dismissively. "None taken."

"Tullea's Minith clutched twenty-two," Lorana reported. "One queen egg."

T'mar and Kindan exchanged worried looks to which Fiona added a frown and then, with a jerk of her head toward Lorana, gestured for them to head back to the Weyr Bowl.

The two men followed her lead, catching up to where she waited out of earshot of the others.

"Could this have something to do with the cure to the illness?" Fiona asked the question that was troubling all of them.

"That's only three queens, Fiona," Kindan said. She gave him a look; his tone had made his own unease quite clear.

"If the cure means that the queens clutch early and light, how will that affect us?" T'mar asked, glancing first at Fiona, then at Kindan.

"Well," Kindan said, "it will mean that we have fighting dragons sooner—"

"Only a little—" T'mar interjected.

"—and that we'll take longer to replenish our numbers," Kindan finished, nodding in agreement with T'mar's remark.

"We don't have enough at the moment," Fiona said. "Getting only a few—"

"We can't say what the future holds," T'mar said. "It could easily mean that the queens will clutch more often."

"It could also be just a response to whatever was in the cure," Kindan said. Fiona arched an eyebrow inquiringly. "It would make sense for the queens to have clutches quickly right after they've been cured so that they can produce more queens to increase the dragon population."

"Then why didn't Talenth have a queen?" Fiona said. "For that matter, why didn't each clutch consist only of queens?"

Kindan shrugged. "Lorana and I only learned enough—and were taught enough—to know how to make the cure; we don't know nearly enough to understand all that was involved."

"From what I remember, Kitti Ping, who made the dragons, spent her entire life learning her trade and couldn't pass it all on to her daughter," T'mar said.

Kindan frowned. "I'm not sure how much of our knowledge of Wind Blossom is accurate; it seems that that watch-whers were created more by design than mistake." He held up a hand to contain T'mar's objections. "I think our Records from the times were purposely misleading."

Weyrleader and Weyrwoman gave him shocked looks.

"It wouldn't be the first time that Records were changed according to the feelings of the times," Kindan said.

Fiona made a face and nodded in agreement. "I saw plenty of that in the Records at Igen," she said. "It was obvious that those writing the Records had their own views of things."

"And, as they were writing the Records, those were the views that are remembered," T'mar said with an understanding nod of his own. He turned back to Kindan. "But that still doesn't answer our question now."

"No," Kindan said, "it doesn't."

"I'm more worried about how Lorana will take it," Fiona said. Kindan gave her a sharp look, so Fiona explained, "How could she, after all that she gave to find the cure, handle learning that that same cure has caused such harm?"

"We don't know that it has," T'mar said. "If the other queens clutch early and light, that would be another matter."

"And so, in the meantime we do nothing?" Fiona asked, looking askance at the Weyrleader.

"I think better that than assuming the worst."

Fiona's expression made it clear that she was not content with that answer, but she chose not to argue it.

"The next question is what to do with all the onlookers once the excitement has died down," T'mar said, partly to distract her from her concerns.

"Well, I've already spoken to Talenth and she's no problem with having some of the younger ones sleep in the Hatching Grounds with her," Fiona said. Her eyes flashed in challenge as she continued, "And I'm definitely going to have Xhinna touching all the likely eggs."

"There's only one queen egg," T'mar said.

"Who said anything about a queen egg?"

More news came at lunch—Melirth at Fort Weyr had clutched, again only twenty-two eggs—and then again before dinner, when Lorana relayed the news that Bidenth of Ista had laid twenty-two eggs as well.

"All the queens are laying light," Lorana remarked anxiously to Kindan.

Kindan shook his head, flexing open a hand in a dismissive manner. "There were queen eggs in the clutches at Fort and Ista."

"We talked about this earlier," Fiona said to the ex–queen rider, trying to assuage her concerns, "and we thought it might be possible that the cure caused the queens to clutch early." She heard Lorana's horrified gasp and added quickly, "To get them started again, and rebuild our numbers."

"But they're laying light!" Lorana said, her eyes wide and worried. "Kindan, what if they only lay light?"

"They might lay more often," Kindan suggested, shaking his head. "We don't know what Wind Blossom planned, perhaps this is normal."

"And, even if they don't, at least they're not going to die of the sickness," Fiona said. "I think we should consider this a good thing."

"What if it isn't?" Lorana asked. "What if this is a sign that something's wrong?"

Nothing Kindan nor Fiona could say to the ex–queen rider seemed to console her. And it was clear that Lorana hadn't been the only one to come to that conclusion.

Naturally, Tullea chose to appear in person to vent her ire.

"Saved the dragons!" Tullea snarled as she confronted a stricken Lorana in the middle of the Weyr Bowl the very next day. From the Hatching Grounds, Talenth shrieked angrily, echoed immediately by Tolarth and the bronzes of the Weyr.

Fiona saw the ruckus and raced over to it, coming in on the last of Tullea's words.

"I don't know about you, Weyrwoman, but I owe Lorana not only my queen's life, but my own sanity as well," Fiona cut in quickly, her blue-green eyes flashing ominously even as all the dragons in the Weyr backed her up with a tremendous roar of discontent. "If my queen had gone *between*—as hers had—I doubt I would have had the courage to continue seeking to cure others."

"Maybe she didn't," Tullea said with a bitter smile. "Maybe all she did was create a way where the rest of us would suffer her same agony."

Fiona's hand flew from her side but she contained herself before actually striking the Benden Weyrwoman. A bronze dragon burst into view overhead and warbled anxiously—B'nik with Caranth.

"I understand your worry, Weyrwoman," Fiona said, folding her fingers against her palm to leave only the index finger pointing. "Lorana shares your concern, too. And you may be certain that I—and she—will do all in our power to solve this problem if it is, truly, a problem."

B'nik leaped down from Caranth and raced to Tullea, wrapping an arm around her waist and tugging her away from the others.

"There's a queen egg at Benden, isn't there?" Fiona called to forestall any futher outburst.

"Yes," Tullea snapped. "Just the one."

"Talenth laid none," Fiona said. "Perhaps you should count yourself lucky."

"I'm sure they're all greens," Tullea said, "given the way they were mated."

Fiona firmly stood on her temper, letting her anger dispel with one long sigh and only acknowledging Tullea's words with a curt nod.

"Greens are good fighters," T'mar said breathlessly, having raced from his weyr up to Fiona's side. "We could use as many of them as we could get."

Tullea snorted in response but allowed herself, finally, to be led away by B'nik.

It was only after the gold and bronze dragons had disappeared *between* that T'mar allowed himself a sigh and gave Fiona an appreciative look. "B'nik has much on his hands."

"**W**e're well shut of her," Kindan assured Lorana later that evening over a quiet dinner in their quarters. Fiona was present although she'd already declared that she would be staying with T'mar that evening.

"She is a bit . . . difficult, isn't she?" Fiona said. She turned toward the older woman. "I don't know how you managed with her."

"Not very well," Lorana admitted. "Nor very long, when it comes to it." She glanced speculatively at Fiona and the younger woman easily guessed that the ex–queen rider was wondering how long their relationship would remain equitable.

Fiona reached for one of Lorana's hands, grabbed it, and pressed it to her cheek. *Always.*

Lorana gave her a surprised look and then shook her head, her lips parted in a smile.

"Whatever we have, the Records at Igen—and here at Telgar—never mentioned," Fiona told her feelingly.

"There have been plently of multiple partnerships," Kindan said.

"That's not what I'm talking about," Fiona said.

"I know," Kindan said. "I was going to say that the Records do not mention any mating flight like ours."

"Another thing for which to be grateful to Lorana," Fiona said, catching the dark-haired woman's deep brown eyes. "She was the only one who could keep Zirenth from going *between* when T'mar had his concussion." She paused for a moment, reflecting on her own frantic memories of that horrid day, and added, "Without Lorana we would have suffered a triple tragedy, perhaps worse."

"Which only goes to say that you," Lorana retorted, nodding first to Fiona and then to Kindan, "both of you, have very prejudiced views."

"For which I, for one, am extremely grateful!" Fiona said with a chuckle. She released Lorana's hand and gently gave it back to her. "And now, I think it best if I left the two of you—I mean, the *three* of you!—to your rest."

T'mar was already asleep when she entered his quarters. He'd resumed drilling the wings as soon as Tullea had left, in preparation for their next Fall over Upper Crom in four days' time and, perhaps in response to Tullea's tirade, he'd worked the entire Weyr into exhaustion.

Fiona spent a moment examining his features. He seemed more careworn than she'd ever recalled him, his face pinched in a combination of pain and anger. She turned away, shucking off her clothes and slipping into her nightgown before looking back toward him once more, her own expression anxious. Was this the right thing to do? Should she leave Kindan and Lorana to themselves, instead of being a constant reminder—goad, if one were honest—of the things neither had? She, a queen; he, a bronze—and both a love uncomplicated by third parties?

Some hint of displeasure seeped into her from the distance, words unspoken but their intent clear: *Stop that!*

In the same unspoken, unvoiced manner, Fiona apologized and then buried her thinking deeper, beyond the ken of either Lorana or Talenth. And what if something were to happen to either? How would Fiona survive without her queen? How would she survive without Lorana? The bond between her and the older woman wasn't quite as strong as that between rider and dragon, Fiona knew, but it was also *different*. Beyond love, beyond friendship, beyond—even—being. They weren't two halves of the same whole; they were two women bound not just by their love for the same man—which, in itself, ought to be an endless well of jealousy and betrayal—but also by mutual respect, caring, and love for each other and the two dragons in their lives. Fiona sighed as she realized that Lorana was even more than that; she was the only person on

Pern who felt all dragons, and their deaths, intimately. Fiona's eyes snapped open for a brief worried moment as she pondered: How could anyone suffer such pain and survive? Until she realized, as her eyes closed and her breathing slowed once more, that the pain was balanced by an equal measure of joy.

She turned toward T'mar, seeking to bury her head against his shoulder and wrap herself around his warmth, and opened her eyes for a moment. Still asleep, he moved with her, his arms going around her and, even as she watched, the care and worry etched in his face smoothing away, vanishing. Fiona stretched her neck up and kissed him on the cheek before burrowing once more into his warmth and drifting into a restful, dreamless sleep.

EIGHTEEN
▼▼▼▼▼▼▼▼▼▼▼▼▼▼▼▼▼▼▼▼▼▼▼▼▼

Chew stone,
Flame Thread.
Craft hone,
Else dead.

Keroon Threadfall, morning, AL 508.5.21

The sun had been up for several hours when the riders from Ista burst forth over the lush Keroon plains. They were light, three full wings and a reserve of scarcely twenty-four.

M'tal looked to his left and his right, to his wingseconds, wingmen, and the Wings on either flank. Their spirits were good, he knew, buoyed by the clutching two days before and the sight of a queen egg on the Hatching Grounds.

Even so, they were tired and wing light. The spare Wing was heavy with firestone sacks, ready to rearm the fighting dragons or drop them and join the fighting Wings as replacements, as needs be.

M'tal looked up, scanning the heavens above him for the silvery shimmer of Thread. Beneath him Gaminth rumbled ominously.

It feels wrong, the bronze declared. M'tal said nothing in response; he felt the same. He scanned to the left and right, extending his vision to the distant right and left horizon. Perhaps Thread had been blown off course, he considered nervously, his throat going dry in the hot morning air.

Have the others keep a lookout, M'tal said. *Remind them that we're early on purpose.*

Gaminth relayed his thoughts even as M'tal wondered if they could be that early. A gust of wind blew Gaminth to one side and M'tal heard shrieks behind him to indicate that the rest of the Wing had been similarly buffeted.

The wind. Always the fardling wind! It broiled off the ground below, rose and billowed in ways that were unpredictable. He craned his neck to look directly above him, wondering if perhaps the Thread had been blown back up by the heated wind and had only an instant to cry, *Shards!*

And then the clump of Thread engulfed him and it was too late.

Gaminth gave one horrified shriek and disappeared *between*, taking himself and his lifelong mate to a cold beyond forever.

S'maj had only a moment to wonder why Gaminth had cried before the Thread struck, lacing into his dragon's back and then they, too, were *between*.

The rest of the three Wings disintegrated as their Weyrleader and wingleaders were engulfed from behind by the fickle Thread.

Help! One forlorn cry went out, from whom or where, no one could later say.

Help! Lorana heard the cry. Fiona heard her gasp and turned toward her in surprise. They were in the Hatching Grounds performing their morning check—and praise—of the two queens and their charges.

Ista! Ista needs help! Lorana responded, her words sounding louder than Fiona had heard before.

"We're not ready!" Fiona cried in warning, as she heard the anxious bellows of dragons echoing around the Weyr Bowl. "T'mar's drilling, they've no firestone!"

Help comes, Lorana called. She turned to Fiona. "They need help now, at this instant."

Fiona felt the blood draining from her face as she realized what Lorana was saying.

T'mar, she called with no reluctance, *we need you to come back and then to time it.*

She felt a rustle of surprise and then nothing as the bronze dragon and rider were suddenly no longer where she'd found them. She turned to race toward the Weyr Bowl even as she heard more dragons bellowing outside.

"Get firestone! Get it now!" Fiona shouted as she burst out of the Hatching Grounds. She raced toward the firestone shed and skidded to a surprised halt as she spied a group of weyrfolk lined up outside, sacks of firestone ready in their hands, looking at her in surprise.

"My lady?" Shaneese asked her in surprise. Fiona glanced at her, eyes wide with questions. "You ordered me to prepare the firestone an hour ago, my lady."

Lorana caught up with her, gasping and holding her belly protectively. She and Fiona exchanged one glance and then Fiona called *Talenth! I need you!*

The dragon appeared from the Hatching Grounds to the surprise of all.

"Get them loaded up!" Fiona called as she ran to her dragon and clambered up to her perch, ignoring the lack of riding straps, and waving toward the landing Wings of dragons. *Talenth, we must go back in time one hour.*

I know, Talenth told her calmly. *I heard you the first time.*

The first time? Fiona asked, surprised.

When you told me not to say anything, Talenth told her calmly. She took two steps and leaped into the air and *between* in the same instant, ignoring the indignant squawks of the descending dragons.

Fiona had only a few moments *between* to consider this strange turn of events before they returned from *between* right above the Weyr Bowl. Talenth flipped one wing up and one down in a sharp turn to avoid flying into the wall of the Weyr itself and executed a neat landing almost in the exact spot from which she'd departed.

How—?

I knew where I would be, Talenth told her smugly. *I remembered.*

Fiona slapped Talenth's neck affectionately, her pride in her dragon stronger than words could convey.

Now, you need to tell Shaneese, Talenth said. *You weren't here long before we went back.*

Fiona raised an eyebrow in surprise at her queen's determination and then her lips quirked into a smile as she realized that the young queen was nearly as perplexed by the whole event as she was.

Fiona raced to the Kitchen Cavern and caught Shaneese's attention as soon as she entered, beckoning the headwoman toward her.

"Weyrwoman?" Shaneese asked, her brows furrowed.

"I'm not here, don't tell anyone," Fiona said. "You're to get the weyrfolk readying firestone for a Fall."

"For a Fall?" Shaneese said. "But Thread's not due until tomorrow, my Lady."

"We'll be flying Thread in an hour," Fiona assured her. "Get your people moving, I've got to get back!"

"Back?"

"To the future," Fiona told her. "I'll be just as surprised when I find you then as you are surprised to find me now."

Outside Talenth rumbled in agreement, echoed a moment later by Talenth from her spot in the Hatching Grounds.

"You timed it?"

Fiona nodded and, with a wave, raced back to her queen.

As she clambered into her place on Talenth's back, she told her, *When we return, we'll go to the Star Stones. I don't want to cause any accidents.*

As they returned *between* and Talenth answered the watch dragon's challenge, Fiona felt relief in the wisdom of her decision: The Weyr was a rainbow of colors as dragons hastily landed, loaded firestone, and leaped airborne once more, re-forming into their fighting Wings.

Fiona had Talenth land near the Hatching Grounds, understanding the queen's dilemma, torn between the need to guard her eggs and the excitement of the moment.

"Go on, you've done your part," Fiona said, as Talenth's eyes whirled with a reddish tinge of worry. "Although I'm sure that Tolarth wouldn't let anything happen to your eggs while we were gone."

From within the Hatching Grounds came Tolarth's strident assurance. Fiona laughed and patted her queen once more before urging, "Go on, you can count your eggs for yourself, just to be certain!"

Talenth scrambled inside, a small echo of surprise winding back to Fiona as the queen thought: How did she know that she was counting her eggs?

I'm your rider, I know everything! she called as she turned and raced back to the work parties hastily loading the fighting dragons.

"I'm Weyrleader, how come I didn't know about this?" T'mar asked in an inverted echo of Fiona's earlier words when she caught up to him.

"Because there wasn't time," Fiona said. He glared at her. "I had just enough time to realize that I would have to time it myself, not enough time to explain."

"Well," T'mar said, sounded slightly less mulish, "Lorana explained it to me while you were gone."

"So you asked merely to vent at me?" Fiona said, eyebrows arching menacingly.

"I don't see how we'll get there in time," T'mar continued, ignoring her. "We've taken the better part of an hour."

"Lorana will give you the coordinates," Fiona said.

"But they've been fighting unaided for an hour."

"No," Fiona told him, "they haven't."

"They haven't?" T'mar said. "Then who's been helping them? And why are we going?"

"You've been helping them and that's why you're going," Fiona said, smiling as she took in his confusion and dawning comprehension. "You're going to time it, too."

"It's the only way," Lorana assured him from where she stood beside the work parties. She flinched, as though struck by a burning brand—or as though struck by a searing strand of Thread—and hissed in pain before adding, with a look of concern, "Fly carefully."

T'mar gave her a long, hard look and then nodded slowly.

"I'll bear that in mind," he said, moving toward Zirenth. He turned back to Lorana. "How bad is it?"

"Best not to know," she told him. "Besides, the Fall's not over."

T'mar's eyes widened as he realized that she would already have felt the pain of the injured Telgar dragons—the same dragons who had yet to go back in time to Ista's aid.

"You'll take charge as soon as you get there," Fiona said, distracting him. "M'tal's dead."

T'mar nodded slowly, his lips pursed tightly. Fiona raced to his side, wrapped him in a quick hug and whispered, "Fly safe." He hugged her back and she looked up at him, her eyes firm as she told him, "Be certain you come back to me."

"I will," T'mar declared, then turned and vaulted up to his perch on Zirenth's back. He urged Zirenth into the air, found his place with his Wing, and made the hand signal for the dragonriders of Telgar to go *between*, back in time, to fight a Threadfall they'd not anticipated, a Threadfall they'd been fighting for over an hour already.

A silence descended upon the Weyr and Fiona turned to Lorana. "He will come back, won't he?"

Lorana looked at her a long time before turning away, saying sympathetically, "He hasn't been injured yet; I can no more see the future than you."

"We should set up the aid stations," Fiona said after a moment, turning to Shaneese and the weyrfolk.

▼ ▼ ▼

*S*he gave good coordinates, Zirenth said in approving tones as they burst out into the hot morning air over Keroon. T'mar nodded silently as he gazed out over the flight of Istan dragons arrayed before them.

Ginirth says they fly well, Zirenth relayed. T'mar snorted, guessing that behind that observation lay H'nez's question: What were they doing here? M'tal was in the lead, flying well and—

As suddenly as T'mar could think, a clump of Thread whirled around in a dangerous looping arc, at first unseen in the distance, and was entangled around M'tal. T'mar heard Gaminth's bellow of pain, saw the bronze rider slump even as the Thread burnt through his wher-hide and into his flesh—and then dragon and rider were gone.

T'mar barely had time to realize that the same thing had happened to three other Istan riders at the same moment—two of them wingleaders—before he cried out, "'Ware, Thread!"

Zirenth lurched suddenly, arching his neck, his muscles straining mightily as his wings fought to gain even more height and his mouth opened in a long arc of flame burning a clump of Thread out of the sky that just a moment before had threatened to engulf them the same way M'tal had been surprised.

Later, T'mar could never remember issuing any orders, but somehow he reoriented his wings upward and in an instant they were far above the Istan riders, dragon flames reaching even higher to sear the steady line of Thread that could just be discerned against the glare of the sun.

Have them get above us! T'mar told Zirenth, who relayed the order to the recovering Istan riders. They went *between*, returning almost immediately above and behind the Telgar riders. A moment later he issued the same order to his dragons and the two Weyrs leapfrogged until they were as high as they could fly and T'mar could feel his lungs straining for air, his cheeks tingling with the lack, and the color in his eyes wavering, threatening to turn gray.

High enough, T'mar said. He gazed at the Thread in front of them and grunted as he saw it falling in steady, predictable streams.

Some must have gotten through, he reminded himself. We'll have to send sweepriders later.

But for the moment they could fight Thread, teetering at the very heights at which a man could breathe, every moment wary of going too high or straying too low.

T'mar could sense Zirenth's concern and felt an echo come in from H'nez through Ginirth, *It's hard to fly this high.*

T'mar chuckled at the understatement and then laughed aloud as he saw the Wings tearing into Thread, flaming it into nothingness.

At least we're on top of the Thread, T'mar said, patting Zirenth lightly on the neck and peering around him to assure himself that the fight was now firmly in hand.

"They're flying high," Fiona remarked absently as she and Lorana found a moment alone together. "It will wear the riders out even more."

Lorana nodded lightly and Fiona narrowed her eyes speculatively. She gestured to Shaneese. "Lorana needs to sit."

The headwoman nodded and sent a weyrgirl sprinting off with a wave of her finger. The girl came back just as quickly, puffing under the load of one of the canvas chairs, but she smiled brightly as she set it up and conscientiously guided Lorana into it.

"How are the eggs, my lady?" the girl asked, greatly daring.

"They're doing well," Fiona told her with a smile. "Perhaps after this Fall is over, we'll let you have a look."

"I'm only a girl," the youngster replied, deflated. "I can't imagine a queen will want me."

"It still doesn't hurt to look, does it?" Fiona asked.

The girl thought it over and shrugged. "It'd be better if I was a boy," she said after a moment, frowning. "And even if I were, I'd be too young yet."

"Dragons pick who they will," Fiona said, gesturing to herself with a grin and then glancing significantly toward Lorana.

"Yes, Weyrwoman," the girl agreed dutifully.

Fiona snorted at the response and the girl gave her a startled look. "I'll tell you this: It'd be hard to imagine a dragon Impressing someone who's so certain she won't."

The youngster pondered upon that for moment and then nodded solemnly. "Yes, Weyrwoman."

"So stop with the long face, and come find me tomorrow, and we'll see if the queens are ready yet to accept visitors!"

A shriek broke quiet of the Weyr and Fiona glanced up as the first casualty returned to the Weyr.

"I never imagined I could be so tired!" H'nez said as Jeila hauled him into bed later that day. "It's not even evening and I can—" he yawned widely "—hardly keep my eyes open."

"The air, timing it, and the stress of fighting," Jeila said in terse explanation as she drew the covers over him.

"Three days," H'nez said, fighting back another yawn. "Three and we fight again. How can we be ready?"

Jeila shushed him, leaning down to brush his lips with her own. "Sleep. Rest and we'll talk later."

She straightened up, giving her mate an expectant look, surprised that he didn't have some martial retort ready, but instead the soft, jagged sound of his snores rose up in response. She smiled lovingly, then her expression changed as she asked herself, how *could* they fight again in just three days?

"I don't feel as bad as some of the others," T'mar said the next morning at breakfast, as if in answer to Fiona's unspoken question of the night before. Fiona quirked an eyebrow questioningly and the Weyrleader shrugged.

"I think it's because I've felt so exhausted these past several Turns that the stress of timing it and flying in thin air didn't affect me as much as the others," he said, with a jerk of his head toward H'nez's empty place.

Fiona reached for the *klah* and topped off both their mugs with a grin, saying, "Well, if it's only *that* bad . . .

"They'll be ready enough for the next Fall."

"Only if we don't have to time it beforehand," T'mar cautioned.

"On the other hand, if you *do* have to time it, you might want to tap those who are suffering from this exhaustion," Fiona said, "if they too prove as unaffected as yourself."

T'mar raised his hands and spread them wide in a warding gesture, saying, "I wouldn't consider myself all *that* well-rested."

"But you could fight again, if you had the need."

T'mar accepted her notion with a grimace, saying, "I'd prefer to leave it to another Weyr."

"True," Fiona said and was silent for a moment as she spoke with her dragon. "I've had Talenth relay the news to Melirth at Fort and Lyrinth at High Reaches."

"Good thought," T'mar said. "We should have done that last night."

Fiona's eyebrows rose in agreement, adding dryly, "So Sonia has just told me."

"They know about M'tal, don't they?"

"Of course," Fiona said. The loss of a Weyrleader was the sort of news that traveled instantly through all the Weyrs. She shook her head sadly, saying, "It must be a double blow for Dalia, on top of losing C'rion."

T'mar nodded, his lips pursed tightly. "At least she's got S'maj," he said a moment later. "He's a seasoned rider; that should be some help."

"But Bidenth won't rise until after her clutch has Hatched, so there could be a lot of friction beforehand," Fiona said. She frowned, adding, "I can't recall all that many bronzes at Ista, come to think of it."

T'mar thought for a moment. "S'maj's Capith isn't much younger than M'tal's Gaminth."

"Age has nothing to do with a mating flight."

"But it *can* affect the size of the clutch," T'mar said, "particularly if both dragons are elderly."

"You know," Fiona said, shifting abruptly in her chair, "I hadn't realized how few bronze dragons we now have."

T'mar bit off a quick retort, instead cupping his chin in his hand thoughtfully. "Not all that many more than the queens themselves," he agreed after a moment.

"There are more bronzes at Fort, Benden, and High Reaches," Fiona said.

"Particularly true for Fort, but not so much now with a queen egg," T'mar said. "Benden probably has the most bronzes per queen, Ista has the least with just the two bronzes and two queens."

"And we've lost quite a number of bronzes in the past half-Turn," Fiona said, raising her eyes to catch T'mar's. "We're likely to go on losing them, as they're usually wingleaders, too." She shivered. "What if we lose them all?"

"I suppose you'd have to make do with a brown."

"Even if a queen would let a brown catch her, wouldn't the clutch just naturally be smaller because the mating flight would be shorter?"

"Probably," T'mar agreed with a grim look of his own. "Although, if we keep losing bronze dragons at this rate, we—rather, you—may find out before too long."

"Perhaps we should consider conserving our bronzes," Fiona suggested. T'mar shot her a look that she shrugged off, saying, "Just as we do with our queens."

"So if a Weyr's strength in bronzes falls to just one, you'd recommend keeping that bronze out of a Fall?" T'mar asked, adding, "I'd like to see you explain that to someone like S'maj."

"They need someone at Ista to cheer them up," Fiona said, clearly having reached this conclusion without reference to the rest of the conversation. "Someone like M'kurry."

"So, are you now going to tell K'lior how to arrange his Weyr?" T'mar asked giving the younger woman a glowering look.

"No, I'll leave that to Cisca," Fiona said. She rose from her chair.

"Where are you going?" T'mar asked, anxious at the implications of Fiona's actions.

"I'm going to talk with Lorana and Kindan if they're awake," Fiona said with a victorious smile at his discomfiture.

"And if not?"

"I promised one young girl a chance to view the eggs on the Hatching Grounds," Fiona replied easily. Her eyes twinkled as she caught the quick turning of heads at her words.

"I expect she'll have lots of company," T'mar said in agreement, glancing around at the eager weyrfolk.

"We'll start small," Fiona said to him as the girl who'd spoken with her yesterday came scampering up and curtsied, eyes shining with delight and anticipation. "And with small groups, too." She looked down at the youngster. "Ready?"

"Now, Weyrwoman?" the little girl squeaked in surprise.

"Right now," Fiona told her crisply, turning toward the Weyr Bowl in the direction of the Hatching Grounds. She glanced down at the girl's feet. "You've sandals on, so you shouldn't be bothered by the heat of the sands."

"And I'm wearing white, my lady," the girl chirped, pulling at the edges of her dress in emphasis.

"It's a bit early for that," Fiona said. "The eggs won't hatch for a while yet."

"And I'm too young," the girl added by way of agreement.

"I wouldn't know as I've no more idea of your age than I do of your name," Fiona told her, smiling to remove any sting from her words.

The youngster blushed mightily. "I'm sorry, my lady! I'm Darri, and I've nearly eight Turns."

"Do you know Xhinna and Taria?"

The youngster nodded mutely.

"Well, can you run and get them?" Fiona asked. "Bring them to the Hatching Grounds when you come back."

Shaneese, who had moved closer to get an ear on the conversation, spoke up warningly. "They're in one of the back playrooms."

"Tell them to bring whoever's with them," Fiona told Darri, adding to Shaneese, "It will be all right."

The young girl gave the headwoman a questioning look. Shaneese shrugged and waved her off. After the youngster had scampered away, Shaneese said to Fiona, "Just remember, my lady, that the behavior you encourage is what will persist."

Fiona smiled. "I'm counting on it," she said. "I won't be at all surprised if I'm shortly deluged with all sorts of requests."

Shaneese's eyebrows rose in surprise.

"Which," Fiona continued, her smile growing broader, "I will soon delegate to Xhinna and Taria."

"Oh!" Shaneese said. She smiled, adding, "I can see how that will work on many levels."

Fiona gave her a quick nod and grinned. "I rather thought you might."

"But what if the queens get too bothered?"

"Then they'll let Xhinna—or Taria—know," Fiona said. Anticipating Shaneese's next question, she added, "I've already spoken with Jeila about this and she agrees."

"So those two young ladies will be hearing directly from the queens?" Shaneese asked, mulling the notion over. Fiona nodded. "It will add to their duties."

"It will," Fiona agreed. "I'm sure they'll manage just fine."

"I can imagine some riders might complain about letting anyone wander the Hatching Grounds with only the by-your-leave of those two," Shaneese said.

"Yes, I suppose that's possible," Fiona said. "Besides, the queens are agreeable."

Shaneese raised an eyebrow as she asked, "And H'nez has no problem with this?"

"Wingleader H'nez wasn't asked," Fiona retorted crisply. After a moment, she relented under the older woman's gaze and added, "But, to be honest, I don't think he'll mind at all."

"And I'm certain that Xhinna and Taria will be fair about it," Shaneese said to herself.

"Oh," Fiona said with a grin, "I wouldn't be at all surprised if some of their least favorite duties were . . . relinquished."

"You're not expecting them to get some of the weyrlads to watch the little ones?" Shaneese asked in wonder.

Fiona shrugged. "I imagine they'd even agree to diaper duty if the demand's high enough." She gave Shaneese a measured look, adding, "I think that Xhinna's already well-proven she's able to do a lad's work, so why shouldn't they have to show they can do a lass's?"

Shaneese snorted loudly at the notion.

"And," Fiona added a bit more seriously, "I think that those who are willing to undertake some of those more demanding duties are exactly the sort who will appeal most to a new-hatched dragonet."

Shaneese pursed her lips for a moment, then nodded decisively. "You could well be right there, Weyrwoman."

"Which is exactly what T'mar said when I mentioned the notion to him."

Grinning, Shaneese asked, "And did he, before he Impressed, have to do diaper duty at Fort Weyr?"

"I certainly hope so," Fiona replied tartly. "I have warned him that he'll definitely be obliged when the time comes."

Shaneese's eyebrows rose high in surprise. "I thought—" she cut herself off. Fiona gestured for her to continue. Shaneese cleared her throat, choosing her words carefully. "I mean, and is this a duty he will be expected to perform soon?"

"Perhaps not for me," Fiona said, surprised both at her own tone and her own feelings in the manner, "but I've told him that he can expect to be aiding Kindan as much as I'm aiding Lorana when her first baby comes."

"I see," Shaneese said. She screwed up her nerve for another question. "And this is what he wants?"

Fiona shook her head. "I'm not sure," she admitted. "I think that he still doesn't know himself." Then she grinned, saying, "Not that I plan to give him any chance to object, regardless."

Shaneese hesitated once more, then moved closer to Fiona. "Not that it's my place," she told the younger woman, "but there aren't many who don't get jealous over time."

"I know," Fiona agreed with a sigh. "I'm not one of them, nor is Lorana." She allowed a wary look to cross her face. "I'm not quite sure what T'mar wants. I think Kindan is still grappling with his feelings."

"He probably always will be," Shaneese said. Fiona looked up at her, trying to keep her worries from showing. "You look like the woman he first loved, you aren't the woman he learned to love next, and yet . . ."

"And yet he loves me in spite of all that," Fiona said, hoping that the words made the truth.

Shaneese nodded. "I think that's so." A moment later she added, "But T'mar?"

"He thinks he's too old for me, even though he's not much older than Kindan," Fiona said. "And he worries that his place is with me only because his bronze flew my gold."

"But isn't that so?"

"I can't say for certain, but I don't think so," Fiona said. She met the older woman's eyes squarely. "He was my first, I chose him. But I think more than that, I love him because he's honest with me and will tell me truths I don't want to hear and trusts that I'll listen to him and respect his words."

"He is quite a man," Shaneese said in agreement. She gave the young Weyrwoman a calculating look and raised her hand to wiggle a finger warningly under Fiona's nose. "And if you *do* decide that he doesn't suit you, don't be surprised to find him with me instead."

Fiona chuckled at the thought. "You are quite an attractive person," she said. "And I believe that the two of you would make a good pair." Then she chuckled mischievously.

"What?"

"Why don't you find out, then?" Fiona said. The headwoman's surprise was total, so with another chuckle Fiona turned away from her and started out to the Weyr Bowl, pausing only long enough to call back over her shoulder, "I see nothing wrong with sharing."

"She should take you up on that," Lorana said as they stood inside the Hatching Grounds; when she'd met Fiona she'd asked her what was so funny. Fiona had relayed the entire conversation.

"She'd be good for him," Fiona said. "She's closer to his age and she'd bolster his confidence."

"Whereas you," Lorana said with a twinkle in her eyes, "have entirely too much!"

"Maybe," Fiona said, shrugging one shoulder. "Sometimes I think it's all an act and perhaps when I get older I'll regret all the decisions I've made"—she paused, hugging Lorana closer to her—"except this one."

"Which one?" Lorana asked. "The decision to save Zirenth was mine and the mating flight was a natural result of that first decision." She pursed her lips. "Unless you're trying to claim you influenced Talenth in her choice of mate?"

"Not as much as she influenced me," Fiona said. "But we worked as a team that day, as you and I work as a team now."

"Do you suppose we could choose to break our bond?"

"I hope not," Fiona said. "But I suppose it's possible." She frowned, adding, "There's nothing like this in the Records and no guarantee that it will last." She glanced down to Lorana's belly. "Perhaps when your baby is born the bond will break."

"I hope not," Lorana said softly, surprising Fiona. She caught the young woman's reaction and patted her on the arm, admitting softly, "I *need* someone to share this all with—"

"What about Kindan?"

"With him I share what he can't feel," Lorana said. "With you, I share what we *can* feel."

"We complete each other, don't we?" Fiona asked, hoping that Lorana would agree and worried that she might not.

"The three of us."

"Four, I think," Fiona said. "I think T'mar is part of it." Lorana furrowed her brows questioningly. "If it had been another bronze injured and you and Kindan had bonded with it, I'm not sure I would have reacted the same way; I'm not sure Talenth would have mated with him."

"And if it had been another man with me than Kindan . . . ?"

"I'm not sure."

"So what happened required four people to be in love and committed to their best interests," Lorana said.

"Yes," Fiona agreed. "I doubt it would happen any other way." She smiled at Lorana. "And not just any people but four very special people."

"Each with their own pain and their own need," Lorana added in agreement. Fiona said nothing; she hugged her tighter.

"So, are we rested?" T'mar asked H'nez, his lips quirked teasingly as the tall, lanky bronze rider and he strode out to their dragons shortly after lunch two days later.

"As much as we can be," H'nez allowed grimly. He leaned closer to the Weyrleader, lowering his pitch for his ears alone. "I'm still concerned about the Wings."

"With the split?" T'mar asked, glancing up at the taller man's troubled brown eyes. "We need a reserve group, riders to get more firestone."

"That's exactly what M'tal thought."

"His reasoning was sound," T'mar said. "And B'nik reports light winds aloft . . . as do our watch riders."

One of the reasons T'mar had decided to keep the twenty-five dragons of Telgar's fifth Wing in reserve was that it allowed him to send out watch riders who would, after the Fall, be immediately available to sweep for Thread burrows. After the disastrous Fall over Keroon, T'mar's exhausted riders had discovered no less than three well-established burrows. Fortunately, all were quickly dispatched, aided in particular by the flamethrowers that Fiona had inspired the Smithhall to develop ten Turns ago when they were back in time at Igen Weyr.

T'mar shook his head and slapped the lanky rider on the arm affectionately. "Don't worry."

H'nez glanced down at him, frowning. He let out a deep sigh, releasing his worries with it. "We'll do our duty."

T'mar mounted Zirenth quickly, waving back at Fiona, who very ostentatiously blew him kisses while, standing next to her, Jeila did the same with H'nez—causing the swarthy rider to color noticeably. T'mar smiled, wagging an admonishing finger at his Weyrwoman and totally spoiled the effort immediately afterward by blowing a kiss back at her.

"Fly safe!" Fiona called loudly.

T'mar grinned, surprised at the warmth of his feelings for the difficult young woman who chose her own ways to love and, with one final glance into her eyes, raised his arm in the ages-old signal for the dragons to fly.

Fiona's grin faded the instant the last of the dragons winked *between*. Grimly she turned to Jeila. "Help Shaneese finish setting up, would you?"

Jeila accepted the request with a nod, adding, "Where will you be?"

"I'm going to check on Lorana and the Hatching Grounds," Fiona said, trying to keep her tone light. But, as she turned to leave, Jeila reached out with a hand to restrain her. Fiona turned back, worry plain in her eyes.

"What is it?" Jeila asked softly.

"I don't know," Fiona said. "I just feel that something is going to happen."

"Something bad?"

"Maybe," Fiona said. Then, with a shrug, "Probably." She shook Jeila's hand off her arm and strode off purposely toward the Hatching Grounds.

Kindan caught up with her just as she arrived. "Have you seen Lorana?"

Fiona shook her head. Kindan's eyes narrowed as he sensed the stress in her motions and followed her.

"Weyrwoman!" a voice called out excitedly as soon as she was visible.

"It's the Weyrwoman!" another young girl's voice piped up in excitement.

In a moment, Fiona and Kindan were surrounded by a small cluster of wide-eyed, excited, happy, weyrchildren who all seemed intent on telling their particular story with all the excitement of the very young. Fiona noticed that even though they all wanted to be heard, they were all very careful to keep their voices down, not wanting to disturb the two queens indulgently watching the proceedings from their respective nests on the warm sands of the Hatching Grounds.

Xhinna appeared and walked briskly toward the cluster, looking anxiously around for Taria.

"I'm sorry, Fiona, I was—"

"—just looking at the eggs," Fiona finished for her, smiling. "That's what you're here for."

"Taria and I are supposed to be watching—"

Fiona cut her off with an upraised hand. "Have you seen Lorana?"

Xhinna's brows rose in surprise and she shook her head. "I think she was here earlier," she said, glancing around.

"She left," Taria said, approaching with a gaggle of youngsters trailing behind. "She was here earlier."

"Where?" Xhinna asked abruptly.

"I don't know," Taria replied, sounding cross herself.

Fiona sensed Kindan glancing at her pointedly, but she didn't need the harper's presence to guess that the two had been quarreling. She'd heard some rumblings through Mekiar and Shaneese already; apparently Taria was convinced that Xhinna would Impress a queen and leave her, while Xhinna feared exactly the same of Taria.

Fiona searched for something to say to defuse their fears, but gave up with a shrug: Finding Lorana was more important to her at the moment. With an arch look, she turned and strode out of the Hatching Grounds, heading for her quarters.

Thread! Zirenth called as they entered the air over Crom, diving suddenly to avoid the menace, then turning and twisting back up while at the same time flaming, charring and burning the threatening Thread with sinuous grace.

T'mar had only a moment to wonder at the speed of the assault before he was completely engaged in the instant-to-instant fight against the streams of falling Thread that threatened his life and his planet.

He heard and grunted in surprise at each injured bellow, keeping a half-count in his head as dragon after dragon went *between* to freeze off tenacious Thread, trying to count back all who returned to the fray, but he was too overwhelmed by his own efforts and those of his bronze to keep any more than a vague number in his head.

Dive, rise, turn, twist, bend, flame. Reach down, grab a bag of firestone, haul it up, toss the stones into Zirenth's open maw, turn back to scan the skies overhead and flame again.

Too much, too quick, T'mar thought in a sudden, grim, chilling realization. He peered from side to side and then over his shoulder, craning to count the dragons of his wing and the wings on either side of him.

Call in the others!

A new group of dragons suddenly appeared, the reserves. With an eager bellow, the twenty fresh dragons joined the fray and for a moment, T'mar felt safe. And then—

"They're too heavy with firestone," T'mar growled to himself as first one, then two and finally three dragons screamed in pain and blinked *between*. Only two returned.

A bronze dragon suddenly appeared beside him: H'nez. One quick look at H'nez's expression was enough to confirm T'mar's worst fears.

We must get help, T'mar thought, wondering which Weyr to ask, and how soon help could arrive. Another dragon screamed in pain, its bellow cut off midway as it sought the safety of *between*.

"We're getting destroyed!" H'nez's voice carried across the dragon-length's distance.

T'mar nodded in grim agreement.

"I'm going to ask for help," T'mar yelled back.

"Who?"

But before T'mar could respond, a bellow from above caused him to glance up and he saw a Wing of dragons burst into existence above him.

"Benden!" H'nez shouted. "We're saved!" Even as he said it, he urged

Ginirth down into a tight dive to circle back and up to the head of his own Wing in flight on T'mar's right.

T'mar glanced up, a big grin of relief on his face as he picked out the brilliant red diamond with the Benden "II" in the center—B'nik himself had come to their aid!

T'mar waved enthusiastically, and then, as he saw the sudden peril, waved frantically to the Weyrleader hoping to alert him to his peril just as—

—the clump of Thread landed on the rider's back and, in one instant obliterated the red and diamond of Benden Weyr, engulfed the rider in a haze of blood and death. With one horrible scream, rider and dragon disappeared *between* forever.

A lone bronze dragon burst into the early evening air above Benden Weyr and dropped quickly into the Weyr Bowl, the rider ignoring Minith's warbled challenge and racing across the grounds, eyes wide, searching desperately for something.

"What is it? What are you doing?" Tullea shouted to the frantic man. She recognized the shoulder knots of a Weyrleader and the white and black fields of wheat—T'mar of Telgar.

T'mar skidded to a halt in front of her, tears streaming from his eyes, and he fell on his knees in front of her, clasping her around the waist.

"I'm so sorry, so sorry," T'mar cried, his voice muffled against the folds of her pants.

Tullea raised a hand to her cheek, eyes wide with fright. "B'nik?"

T'mar glanced up at her, his face tear-streaked. "He flew to our aid. Flew to save us and . . ."

"No!" Tullea cried, herself collapsing to the ground with him. "No, it can't be!"

Inside the Hatching Grounds, Minith bugled in concern and horror.

"It can't be!" Tullea repeated, tears starting down her cheeks as she shook her head in the vain hope of shaking off the Telgar Weyrleader's words.

A rush of air above them and a roar of dragons startled everyone. From within the Hatching Ground, Minith bugled again, this time sounding defiant and proud.

Tullea glanced up at the returning dragons and then over accusingly to T'mar, "You lie! How dare you!"

She threw off his hands and stood up abruptly, reaching down to drag him up beside her.

"There he is! There's B'nik! And Caranth, safe as can be!" She turned and slapped him hard across the face, palm wide with all the force she could muster. "What sort of a sick trick is this? Did Lorana set you up for this?"

T'mar shook his head, looking from her to B'nik, confusion written in his eyes.

"What's going on?" B'nik asked, closing the gap between them quickly while pulling off his riding gloves. He recognized the bronze rider. "T'mar! How are you? How was the Fall?"

"B'nik?" T'mar repeated in blank surprise. He turned to Tullea in apology and surprise. "But I saw . . ."

"Saw what?" Tullea demanded. "This is just some sick joke—" She cut herself off, grabbing B'nik tightly in her arms and growling, "*He* told me you were dead!"

"Dead?" B'nik said, pushing her away from him, careful to keep a hand on her as he looked over to T'mar.

"We were overwhelmed in the Threadfall, it was falling in clumps and our strength was too little," T'mar said, his eyes smoldering with the memory, "and then you came with a Wing and—but you're here!"

"I didn't come," B'nik told him. "We never flew to your aid."

"There was a rider wearing your jacket—the Benden Weyrleader's jacket," T'mar said. "He flew with a Wing until—"

"Until what?" Tullea demanded.

"Until he was engulfed in Thread," T'mar finished in a whisper. He looked imploringly to B'nik. "But if it wasn't you—" T'mar broke off, his confusion evident.

"Yet," B'nik said.

"Yet?" Tullea repeated, glancing at her mate demandingly.

"Have Minith talk with Zirenth," B'nik said in a flat, chill voice.

"Talk with Zirenth?" Tullea repeated dully. "Why would—"

"Because Zirenth saw it, too," B'nik told her, his expression wooden, his eyes bleak with pain. "T'mar tells the truth."

"Yet," T'mar repeated to himself, hissing in a horrified breath as he looked sharply at the Benden Weyrleader. "This is yet to be?"

"Clearly."

"What?" Tullea cried as she absorbed his meaning. "B'nik, you can't die!"

"I can't see how I *can't*," B'nik told her sadly. He waved a hand to T'mar. "It's already happened."

NINETEEN

Smither, tanner, crafter know
Where and how your work must go.
As prospers thus the dragon weyr
So will Pern be kept Thread clear.

Telgar Weyr, evening, AL 508.5.26

"We can't fight with just three Wings again," H'nez said, controlling his temper with difficulty as he and the other wingleaders discussed their tactics for the next day's Fall.

"We can't fight without firestone," F'jian replied, wearily wiping a hand across his face. They had been arguing for the better part of two hours, ever since their evening meal just after another grueling day of drilling. C'tov sat silently between them, clearly not happy at the issue set before them.

"So the only choice is to time it," T'mar repeated, glancing first at his oldest and then at his youngest wingleader. "And because of that, I'm elected."

"Trying to emulate B'nik?" Fiona asked sourly from where she sat in solitude at the end of the long table. Her sense of doom had only increased with the news of B'nik's impending loss. She kept the worry to herself, lying to both Kindan and Lorana, pleading duty or distraction when she couldn't otherwise avoid them. She sensed that Lorana had an inkling of her fears, but Fiona was desperate to keep any stress from the older woman and her growing baby.

T'mar gave her a sour look. "Not particularly," he said. "But we have to face our needs."

"And the Weyr needs its Weyrleader," Fiona shot back. She regretted her words even before she caught the look of disappointment in T'mar's eyes. She knew that he was doing his best, just as they all were. It just wasn't enough.

T'mar's lips twitched as he suppressed his retort and Fiona, realizing the effort he was making, gave him an apologetic shrug.

"We're all under stress," T'mar said, cutting his gaze to the other wingleaders, a gesture that caused Fiona's spirits to sink even further at the implied rebuke. "But as you know, Weyrwoman, I and those who share your fatigue seem to be less sensitive to the extra strain of timing it." Fiona grimaced at his words. "So it would seem that we are the best choice for the job."

"So you're going to provide our reserves *and* bring firestone?" H'nez asked again, his incredulity unalloyed.

"No," Fiona replied, before T'mar could draw breath. "They're going to ferry firestone and provide relief *only* if needed." She nodded toward T'mar. "So you'll only time it if absolutely necessary?"

"That wasn't my plan," T'mar admitted, choosing his words carefully. "But I think there's sense in that."

"Let me get this clear," F'jian said. "You'll fly the Fall with firestone and then, only if we need it, you and your Wing will time it—after the Fall— to give us additional strength."

"Makes sense," H'nez muttered, reluctantly approving. Then he frowned. "But won't it be a bit unnerving to supply yourself with firestone?"

"I suppose that's possible," T'mar said. He spread his hands open above the table. "But it's the best plan we've got."

"So it's agreed," Fiona declared, glancing down the table challengingly.

▼ ▼ ▼

It was late the next evening when T'mar collected his weary Wing and urged them back into the skies—and back in time to fight the Threadfall they'd already fought.

"At least we know the worst," B'len, T'mar's latest wingsecond allowed with a grim look as they mounted their dragons once more.

"Are you sure you want to do this?" T'mar asked the brown rider.

"We know that I already did," B'len said. He straightened as he looked toward Lareth, his brown. "I've had time to say good-bye, and that's more than J'lantir had."

B'len had come to Telgar as J'lantir's wingsecond; they'd flown together for many long Turns.

"You know," B'len said philosophically, "it's really true that knowing you're going to die gives you a greater appreciation for all that's good in life."

"I'm sorry."

"Don't be," B'len told him. "I've had a good life and I know that I'll die the way I wanted—taking Thread with me."

"And saving Pern," T'mar said. "If I had known, B'len, I wouldn't—"

"Don't say it, Weyrleader!" B'len cut him off, clapping him on the shoulder. "You would have done it, because it was needed. And still is needed."

T'mar groped for words, found none, and shook his head in mute sympathy for the brown rider who would shortly go back in time to his death.

"B'len!" Fiona cried, running up to him and wrapping her arms around the brown rider's waist, enveloping him—as best she could—in a tight hug.

"Weyrwoman," B'len said, returning the hug. After a moment, he pushed away from her. "It has been a pleasure knowing you."

"And you," Fiona said, tears suddenly welling in her eyes. "Somewhere, somewhen, if there is something beyond *between*, we'll meet again."

"It will be a merry meeting," the brown rider replied with a weary grin.

"I'm looking forward to it."

"Not too soon, I hope, Weyrwoman," B'len told her. He caressed her cheek softly and she leaned into it. "You have Turns yet, and more, before your time." He grinned, adding, "Not to mention children of your own to raise."

Fiona could say nothing in reply, nodding mutely. B'len turned away and climbed up to his mount on brown Lareth.

"I'll see you later," Fiona said to T'mar, embracing him fiercely. T'mar hugged her back but was unable to suppress a weary yawn and Fiona called, "I'll have *klah* ready!"

Later, in the dark night as she lay awake, worried, Fiona felt the warm, wet tears of the Weyrleader who had led his men back in time to death.

She moved slowly and softly against him, shushing any protests he made as she gave him all the comfort she could.

In the morning T'mar woke to see her young, freckled face grinning up at him. He arched an eyebrow questioningly and she chuckled. "There are *always* things to live for!"

T'mar frowned, perplexed, until the young Weyrwoman proceeded to demonstrate.

At breakfast, Fiona noted the weary, wary look on H'nez's face, saw the way that Jeila cautiously caressed his hand, and guessed that the other weyrwoman had herself demonstrated to her mate one of the fruits of life. Jeila caught her look and gave her a half-smile in response, confirming Fiona's suspicion. The dark-skinned weyrwoman's smile flared briefly across her face as the two shared a quiet flash of understanding. Fiona reached a hand across to Jeila, who grabbed it and clenched it firmly before releasing it. Men might fly the Falls, Fiona thought, but it was the women who kept the Weyrs whole.

Kindan and Lorana approached and sat beside her. Fiona gave the harper a quick glance, saw his troubled look, and raised an eyebrow inquiringly.

"Benden lost six," Kindan told her softly, his expression grim.

"Six dead, seven mauled, three injured," Lorana said in a quiet voice, a shiver of pain running down her body.

"And?" Fiona prompted, aware that that older woman had more news to impart.

"Ciaday's Sadenth clutched," Lorana said. Ciaday was the younger weyrwoman at High Reaches.

"Twenty-one or twenty-two?" Jeila asked, guessing that Lorana was distressed over the paltry number of eggs.

"Twenty-two."

"One queen egg," Kindan added, his tone upbeat.

"So that's good news," Fiona said brightly. Lorana glowered in her direction. Fiona knew that the older woman was convinced otherwise. "We'll have weyrlings soon and that always cheers a Weyr. We'll have them everywhere on Pern."

"Weyrlings aren't fighting dragons," H'nez said. He jerked as Jeila pinched him under the table, but he was not to be deterred. "It takes three Turns to make a fighting dragon."

"Two, if need be," T'mar said, dropping his tray onto the table beside Fiona and glancing over in the older bronze rider's direction in greeting. "I'm sure we'll hold off as long as we can, but I imagine they'll be fighting before we would like."

"Lorana has news from Benden," Fiona told the Weyrleader and then groaned inwardly as he winced in anticipation. "They lost six and ten injured."

T'mar's expression cleared; this wasn't the news he'd feared.

"They don't fly again for a while," Kindan said.

"Nor do we," Fiona said. "The rest will do us good and we'll have two more ready to fly again before the month's end."

"But only three and a half Wings," H'nez remarked sourly. He glanced over to T'mar. "And we'll have to time it again, almost certainly."

"We'll be well-rested," T'mar said, not disagreeing with the grim bronze rider.

"We can't keep taking these losses."

"We'll do what we must," T'mar responded in a tone more acerbic than he'd meant. H'nez jerked in reply, his eyes glowering. In an effort to restore the mood, T'mar turned to Jeila. "And how is your Tolarth today, Weyrwoman?"

"She's doing well, thank you, Weyrleader," Jeila said, her tone almost as frosty as H'nez's. Fiona shot her a surprised expression, which the other weyrwoman ignored.

"She can hardly sleep with all the little ones crawling over her," H'nez growled. He glanced at Fiona, then turned back to T'mar. "I don't see why you allow it; none of those will Impress."

T'mar flushed at the heat in the other man's words.

"Xhinna and Taria will stand on the Hatching Grounds," Fiona said. "It's right that they get to see the eggs early."

"And it's good for the rest of the Weyr," Kindan said. At H'nez's look, he continued, "Children are the future of the Weyr, we all know that."

Jeila gave the harper a warm smile and turned to H'nez, her hand caressing his possessively. The lanky rider looked down at her hand and covered it with his other hand, his mood lifting.

Fiona gave the weyrwoman a quick, probing glance and leaned back in her seat, her eyes glowing brightly. Jeila was definitely pregnant; her previous fears had clearly vanished.

The dark-eyed weyrwoman noticed her expression and gave just the slightest shake of her head, imploring Fiona to keep the revelation to herself. Fiona nodded.

"We'll have weyrlings soon enough to teach," Fiona said, raising her voice and casting about for Shaneese even as she rose from her chair. "I doubt I'll need to ask Shaneese, but it *is* a Weyrwoman's duty to see to such things as preparations for the weyrling quarters." With a nod toward T'mar, she added jokingly, "And, O Weyrleader, whom will you entrust with the care and rearing of our future flock of flamers?"

"Kindan," T'mar replied immediately. The harper, who was eyeing

Jeila with an abstracted, thoughtful air, startled at the mention of his name.

"Weyrleader?" Kindan asked, bemused.

"He's no rider!" H'nez said.

"He knows the lore!" C'tov shouted back, having paid closer attention to the conversation than Fiona had expected, given his unusually morose look.

"It's all moot until they're older, anyway," F'jian said in Kindan's defense. "It's not as though he doesn't know the drills, and he'd be teaching them the ballads regardless."

Kindan's eyes widened as he caught up with the import of the conversation and he turned to T'mar in surprise. "You want me to be Weyrlingmaster?"

"I can't think of anyone better," T'mar told him. "You've raised watch-whers and fire-lizards, you know all the dragon lore, and"—he frowned as honesty compelled him to admit—"we can't easily spare any fighting pair for the duty."

"He's flown Threadfall, too!" F'jian declaimed loudly with a challenging look in H'nez's direction. The older bronze rider snorted derisively.

"Actually," Jeila spoke up, her tone conciliatory, "he has more experience than anyone else." She smiled at Kindan as she ticked off her fingers, "Raising a watch-wher, and a fire-lizard."

"It won't be forever," T'mar told Kindan, with a half-glance in H'nez's direction. "But . . ."

"Weyrleader, I . . ." Kindan groped for the right words and trailed off as he realized he didn't know what he wanted to say. He glanced at Lorana, his eyebrows arched questioningly.

Lorana met his eyes for a long moment, then turned to T'mar. "What if *he* Impresses on the Hatching Ground himself?"

H'nez snorted in surprise at the question. A moment later, he admitted, "I suppose it might happen."

"I think he should still take the duty," Jeila said. "His age would make him steadier than any other rider and his understanding of dragons would make him a natural choice as senior."

"And it'd be about time!" C'tov agreed heartily, pounding the table before him emphatically. Kindan found himself grinning broadly at the man who had been his boyhood enemy. C'tov grinned back, then wagged a pointed finger toward him. "Although you may find your age makes your aches all the greater."

"I think we're counting our eggs too quickly," T'mar said, bringing the conversation back to the ground. He rose and leaned on the table, looking down at the harper, his expression firm, hand outstretched. "Will you accept the position?"

"I will, Weyrleader," Kindan said, taking T'mar's hand.

"Heard and witnessed!" C'tov and F'jian roared in approbation.

"You do realize that you've agreed to take on a *third* job, don't you?" Fiona asked Kindan later that evening as they prepared for bed. Lorana, who was already curled up in a comfortable spot, chuckled wickedly.

"Three?" Kindan repeated blankly.

"Harper, Weyrlingmaster, *and* father," Fiona said, ticking the duties off on her fingers.

"Four, if you count mate and lover," Lorana murmured from the bed.

"Not to mention comforter and caresser," Fiona agreed, turning to Kindan and tugging him toward the bed. The older man gave her a startled look, but before he could make any protest, Fiona giggled and shook her head, gesturing toward Lorana.

"It's her that needs the comforting and caressing," she assured him, turning toward Talenth's unoccupied weyr. "I'll see that T'mar gets some rest."

Kindan nodded vaguely, relieved that he hadn't been required to ask the Weyrwoman to leave; particularly as it would have required him to ask her to leave her *own* quarters. Still, he felt awkward: She was so gracious in her behavior that he wanted to dash her off her feet and wrap her in his arms, yet at the same time he was pleased that she didn't expect it.

"She offered," Lorana said, looking up from the bed and gesturing for him to climb in. A smile played on her lips. "She is a remarkable person; you're lucky she loves you."

"I'm lucky *you* love me," Kindan replied emphatically.

"I suppose," Lorana said, her tone uncertain.

Fiona's voice from the entrance startled them. "Hey! There are warming stones at the side of the bed, Kindan! You're supposed to comfort her, not talk her ear off!"

She made a gesture of someone rubbing with their hands, then shook her head in exasperation and trotted off into the darkness of the Weyr.

"Oil, too," Kindan observed as he turned in the bed and found the small basket of warming stones. He poured some oil over them, inhaled deeply of their soothing scent, carefully wrapped his hand around one, and turned back to Lorana. "Roll over, and we'll ease those sore muscles."

Kindan ignored her feeble protests and, as the warm stones and his oily fingers sought out the tense and tired muscles of her lower back, was rewarded with her soft contented sighs. When he was done he placed the used stones back in their basket with warm feelings for Fiona's foresight: *He* would never have thought of such things!

The soft noise of a woman clearing her throat alerted T'mar to Fiona's presence and he looked up from the slates he was poring over as he stretched out on the table in the back room of his quarters.

"You should be sleeping," she said to him as she approached and peered down at his work. "Reorganizing?"

T'mar agreed with a frazzled nod, and bent back over the table.

"You've two sets of slates here, enough for two Flights but we've barely one," Fiona remarked. Her eyes narrowed as she peered at the marks he'd chalked. "Timing?" When T'mar nodded, she cried, "You're planning on timing it with the full Weyr?"

"I think it's our best choice."

"Are you hoping to imitate B'nik and die in a blaze of glory?"

"I'm hoping to save the Weyr and do our duty until we have enough weyrlings," T'mar countered, running a weary hand through his hair and rubbing the back of his neck. Fiona batted his hand aside and replaced it with both her own.

"I'm sorry," she apologized, as she found a knotted muscle and started gently kneading it. "I know you're under a lot of stress."

T'mar stood up straighter, easing the tight muscles Fiona was working, and grunted, "What if they're right?"

"They, who?" Fiona dropped one hand from its work and ducked around under his shoulder to peer up at him inquiringly while still working on his neck with her other hand.

"Everyone," T'mar said. She quirked an eyebrow and frowned, so he expounded, "The ones who say that the cure caused the small clutches and that all we'll get are small clutches."

"And that they won't be enough and that we'll die out and lose Pern?" Fiona asked softly. T'mar dipped his head in agreement. Fiona took a deep breath and met T'mar's eyes frankly. "I don't think it's so. But even if it is, I won't stop, and you won't stop, either." T'mar frowned, unconvinced. Fiona continued, "If worse comes to worst, then I'll feed Talenth firestone and you and I will fly together, with Lorana and Kindan flying any uninjured dragon and Nuella and all the watch-whers of Pern flaming at everything we can." She paused, pursing her lips grimly. "And if *that* doesn't work, then we'll go together, you, I, our dragons, everyone— we won't stop until the last of us falls or is charred beyond life."

"You," T'mar said in voice choked with emotion, even as he wrapped his hands around her and dragged her tight against him, "are a gift."

Fiona's eyes welled with tears; she could find no words. A moment later she pushed back against T'mar and he looked down at her as she told him in a soft, firm voice, "You have to share me, you know."

"I know," T'mar said, his voice both soft and tender. His lips quirked up as he added, "You're far too much for one man alone!"

Fiona joined him in a smile and he crushed her in another hug that he only broke when she gasped, "And you've got to let me breathe!"

TWENTY

Sands heat,
Dragons hum.
Shells crack,
Mates become.

Telgar Weyr, early morning, AL 508.6.19

Xhinna blearily rubbed her eyes as one of the youngsters whimpered beside her, clearly disturbed by a bad dream. She saw that it was little Darri
and moved herself close enough to touch the youngster's head, crooning, "It's all right, it's all right."

Darri rolled her head away from Xhinna's hand with a soft sigh as the
dream lost its grip on her.

Xhinna spared a fond look for the little girl and then her expression
darkened into a frown as she wished that events of the past twelve days
could be as easily forgotten.

Sixty-six! That was the total fighting strength of the Weyr at this moment. There were nearly as many injured, but only the thirty-five least
wounded could be expected to fight again in the next thirty days.

In the past two Falls, the strength of the Weyr had fallen by more than
a full Wing.

Xhinna heard others muttering darkly that Telgar was unlucky, that it was taking a far greater strain than the other Weyrs, that timing it was killing dragon and rider. There was a certain truth in that last moan; it was evident that timing it left both dragon and rider more exhausted and less able to fight a Fall than those who didn't time it.

The second Fall, the last one over Igen, had been the worse of the two last Falls, causing twenty-one casualties, including ten lost—the majority of the losses occurring when the fighting dragons timed it back to fight again.

Xhinna wondered how anyone could force themselves to jump back in time knowing already that it would mean their death. But the brave words of B'len were echoed time and again by dragonriders, bright-eyed with repressed sorrow as they assured themselves and their lovers that it was for the best; that they were glad to actually *know* it was their time, that they were glad to have a chance to give a proper farewell.

Xhinna wasn't sure if T'mar's practice of allowing enough time between the original fight and the timed return to the Fall made it easier or harder for the riders. Clearly, resting up from a Fall was important, but she wondered if it really helped the riders who knew that they were leaping back in time to their death.

Darri stirred again and Xhinna absently hummed a little melody to ease the child back to sleep even as her eyes darted to the entrance of the darkened Hatching Grounds; she could just make out the first gloaming of morning. She would have to get up soon. Carefully she schooled her worries away, knowing that the little ones would be looking to her for guidance.

She heard Taria stir beside her and smiled; perhaps there would be time for a quick, heartening cuddle before the work of the day overtook them. But Taria was in no cuddling mood, her eyes suddenly going wide as she sprang up, crying, "Get up! Get up! They're Hatching!"

"Quickly, quickly, put this on!" Fiona urged as she threw the white robes toward Kindan and immediately busied herself dressing him.

"We can manage," Lorana called from the bed, rolling over and sitting upright with some difficulty. At just over twenty weeks, Lorana's belly was only beginning to show a bulge with her pregnancy, but she was careful not to jostle the baby and handled her movements protectively. "You go on!"

Fiona needed no further encouragement and tore out of her quarters, through the Weyr Bowl, and into the Hatching Grounds, telling Talenth, *I'm coming!*

T'mar met her at the entrance, reaching up a hand to point at the cluster of white robes she still had thrown over her shoulder. "What are these for?"

"I'm not sure that Xhinna or Taria got theirs," Fiona said. She looked around hastily, licking her lips. "And if I can snatch Bekka, I'll set her out there, too."

"So you've—what?—five girls on the grounds for twenty-one eggs?"

"And thirty boys," Fiona corrected him archly.

"What about Kindan?"

"That's including him," she said as he reached over and grabbed the robes off her shoulder, shifting them from one hand to the other so that he could guide her toward the stands.

"No," Fiona said, shaking him off, "I want to be down here."

T'mar gave her a surprised look. "Breaking more Traditions?"

"I'm going to be with Talenth," she said, snatching the robes back out of his hand. "You head up to the stands and talk nicely to the Holders."

A roar from Talenth affirmed Fiona's choice, so T'mar, still shaking his head ruefully, made his way up to the stands even as his Weyrwoman moved toward the clump of eggs nearest her queen.

Fiona reached Talenth's side as soon as she'd handed out the last of the robes and turned back to stare out across the clutch of eggs toward the light of the Weyr Bowl with an air of fierce possessiveness.

"You were great," Fiona said aloud as she patted Talenth and felt herself glow with pride as the first cracks appeared in the nearest egg.

A dragonet burst forth, creeling anxiously, and looked in Fiona's direction.

"That way!" Fiona called, pointing to the waiting Candidates. Talenth bugled in agreement. With another cry, the dragonet awkwardly scrambled out of its shell and wobbled off, skirting the other eggs and searching, neck craning one way and then the other, searching for its mate.

Fiona felt the dragons' hum grow to a higher pitch as the little dragonet and her new rider found each other with an exclamation of joy. Another egg cracked, and another, and suddenly the Hatching Grounds were filled with creeling, red-eyed, anxious dragonets searching for their mates.

Fiona shouted encouragement to each and every one, lost in the thrill of the moment, and cheered with each Impression.

One green stood in front of Taria creeling anxiously while the youngster waved her away.

"She's yours!" Fiona shouted. "What's her name?"

Taria looked toward the Weyrwoman, straightened her shoulders and looked back at the green in front of her, gingerly reaching out a hand to touch the green's snout even as her own face burst with a look of pure joy. She cried back, "Coranth!"

Finally there were only two eggs left. One was rocking, the other seemed quiescent. Talenth craned her neck over to the still one and wailed.

"Maybe . . ." Fiona began, wondering how to gently tell her queen her fear that the egg was stillborn.

He needs help! Talenth leaped forward, her jaws agape. She bit at the egg gingerly with her fangs, just breaking the surface. From inside, a creel erupted and then a beak could be seen tearing away at the inner membrane.

Meanwhile, the other shell had torn open and a brown dragonet squirmed out of it, frantically searching for its mate.

"Help him!" Fiona cried, rushing forward to join her queen in freeing the still-struggling blue. Her words were unheard over the din of the creeling brown and the remaining Candidates were distracted by the din.

"He needs help!" Fiona shouted again, looking around frantically even as she reached the egg and bunched her hands into fists to pummel at the hard shell. She spied someone in the distance and shouted, "Xhinna!"

Startled, the girl looked her way and then raced over as Fiona beckoned urgently with one hand while still working away with the other. The blue, eager to escape his shell, nipped her and Fiona snarled back, "I'm trying to *help* you!"

Xhinna appeared opposite, her eyes darting fretfully to the gash on Fiona's hand and back to the sharp teeth of the dragonet. She hesitated only an instant, even in the knowledge that he might deal her the same injury, before diving in and pounding and kicking the shell to release the trapped dragonet.

"Come on, come on, you can do it!" Xhinna cried as sweat burst forth from her brow from the speed and strength of her exertions.

Fiona paused, eyes widening as she looked at the desperate girl and the desperate blue . . .

Xhinna must have felt her gaze for she stopped in her efforts and lifted her eyes to the Weyrwoman in surprise. "But blues are for boys!"

"What's his name?" Fiona asked her softly, even as she moved forward to gently stroke the wings and back of the dragonet.

Xhinna dodged the answer, looking around frantically for any free Candidate. The blue creeled in a tone mixed with urgency and despair. Xhinna stopped her head in its frantic arc and slowly looked back at the blue.

"But I'm a girl!"

"I don't think he cares," Fiona said softly. Xhinna looked up at her, her expression a mix of horror and hope as Fiona repeated the ancient question, "What's his name, blue rider?"

"Tazith," Xhinna replied quietly, raising her arms once more to tear apart the shell. She took a deep breath and started smashing the shell open with all the fierceness of a mother protecting her child—or a rider fighting for her dragon.

"Louder," Fiona called back, gesturing to the great expanse beyond them.

"His name is Tazith!" Xhinna shouted, turning her head back so that her words could echo strongly across the sands.

"Good, blue rider," Fiona said, grinning at her friend. "Now let's get him out of this shell."

"No, you're not!" Fiona declared firmly. She glanced from Lorana toward Kindan. "I completely understand your desire, Kindan, but Lorana will stay here. She needs her rest and *you* aren't going to be getting any for the first fortnight at the least, probably the first two months."

"Well, you're too small to keep her warm," Kindan returned hotly. "And who's going to help her sore back?"

"T'mar," Fiona told him simply. She raised a hand imperiously as both partners drew breath for hot retorts. "He's large enough to keep us both warm and he's got good hands—" a smile flicked across her face "—I can assure you."

Kindan gave her a mulish look and opened his mouth to argue, but she beat him to it. "It's settled, Weyrlingmaster."

From his look, however, it was clear that it was *not* settled and Fiona's choice of title was inappropriate. She held up both hands placatingly. "T'mar's honorable, Kindan," she told him in a softer tone. "Let him honor Lorana and help your child grow in a calm environment."

Kindan snorted, his eyebrows twitching with humor. "If I was hoping for a calm environment, I couldn't imagine you as part of it."

Fiona gave him a hurt look which was compounded by defensive noises from Lorana.

"All right, all right!" Kindan declared, raising his own hands in capitulation. "I'll grant that T'mar is honorable and that my place is with the weyrlings although, to be honest, with Xhinna on hand, I'm not at all certain that they've any need of me."

"Xhinna is good with children, not dragonets."

"But still," and Kindan raised a hand to indicate that he hadn't finished making his point, "I don't see why Jeila couldn't stay with you, after all—"

"She's smaller than I am, Kindan," Fiona said, stamping a foot impatiently. "And she'll soon need all the cosseting *she* can get." Fiona regretted her choice of words and went on quickly to cover her gaffe. "Tolarth's clutch will hatch next week, after all."

Kindan gave her a dubious look.

"It's too early to say for certain," Fiona told him, remembering that "nothing is ever kept long from a harper's hearing" and guessing that he'd already heard rumors of Jeila's pregnancy.

"Even so," Fiona persisted, "Lorana's going to need strong arms to help her up morning and evening."

"And while we both expect and hope those arms will be yours," Lorana added smoothly, "I think we all have to recognize that you might not always be available."

"This is my child we're talking about," Kindan said, still not entirely pleased.

"This is *our* child," Fiona corrected. "We will raise him together, all three—four—of us."

"You've mentioned this to T'mar?" Kindan asked, eyebrows arched high.

"Not . . . officially," Fiona temporized. Kindan's expression deepened. "I told him that he was to expect to provide lots of aid and support as he would need the practice."

"Wouldn't it simply be easier for you to stay with T'mar and Lorana with me, then?" Kindan asked in a reasonable tone.

"No," Fiona said in a small voice. "T'mar will have duties that keep him out at all hours, and so will you and I *can't* sleep alone!"

A smile played across Kindan's lips. "I remember that," he said softly, turning toward Lorana to explain. "She used to invent every excuse to crawl in with me when she was little."

"And if not you, then someone," Fiona said. She gave them a troubled look as if weighing whether to relay a deep confidence and then admitted, "I've always wanted a large family."

Kindan nodded slowly, glancing quickly to Lorana who was herself nodding in agreement. He had come from a large family himself and while he never recalled the times he shared his bed with two brothers fondly, he could understand how a young survivor of the Plague that had swept through Pern twelve Turns back would feel the need of the comforting warmth of others. How was it, he wondered even as he realized that once again he would relent to Fiona's whims, that such a young person could possess such a forceful personality?

"And lots of kids," Lorana added, her eyes reflecting Fiona's quiet fervor.

"I'm a good sharer," Fiona said to Lorana hopefully. Lorana nodded and smiled back at the younger woman.

"You are at that."

"Good," Fiona said with a firm nod, grinning up at Kindan. "Because now I'm going to share with you two the joy of explaining the new arrangements to T'mar!"

"Look at this shell," T'mar said, tossing a chunk of egg to Kindan as he, Fiona, and Lorana entered his quarters minutes later. Kindan made the catch easily and glanced down at the proffered shard for a long moment before looking back up again to the Weyrleader. At a gesture from Lorana, the harper passed the piece over.

"It's thick," Lorana said after a moment, glancing up to Kindan and T'mar to see if they agreed. She passed the piece to Fiona. "This was from Tazith's egg?"

"No," T'mar said, reaching for another, even thicker shard of egg. "This is."

Kindan cocked his head thoughtfully, gesturing for T'mar to pass him the piece. "Mmm, much thicker."

Fiona peered up from her inspection of the first piece and craned her head over the piece the harper held. "I can see why he had such a hard time breaking out."

"I'm surprised more didn't have trouble," T'mar said, his lips pursed tautly. Lorana and Kindan exchanged a troubled look.

"You think this might have something to do with the cure?" Fiona asked.

"It certainly seems the case," Kindan said reluctantly. Beside him, Lorana nodded, her face bearing a glum expression.

"You two!" Fiona snorted. "It's as well you've agreed to be separated or you'd take responsibility for all of Pern's woes!"

"She's right," T'mar said, raising a hand to forestall Kindan's protests. "Oh, it could well be an unwanted effect from the cure, but it could also be a desired effect or even a result of merely *having* the cure."

"How so?" Lorana asked.

"I could see that Wind Blossom might have decided that the shells would need extra protection," T'mar said, hefting the thicker shell. "I imagine this would be proof against most Thread."

Something in his words caused Fiona's eyes to light with interest but they dimmed again as he continued, "Of course, it's also possible that Talenth had eaten enough shell material to make thicker shells or that, as a result of her recovering from the sickness, she had extra shell material."

"If that were the case, queens who weren't sick would make normal eggs," Kindan said.

"And as Talenth is the first queen to clutch, we won't know one way or another for the next sevenday," T'mar said. He glanced at the other three, brows narrowing as he added, "It *is* certain that the clutches will hatch next week, isn't it?"

"The Records all agree," Fiona said. "The time from mating to clutching is variable, but the time from clutching to Hatching is always five weeks."

"I imagine if the sands were colder it might be longer," Kindan said.

"Or shorter if hotter," Fiona agreed with a shrug.

"I wouldn't be so sure," Lorana said, cocking her head at Kindan and intoning:

> *"Count three months and more,*
> *And five heated weeks,*

A day of glory and
In a month, who seeks?"

"That *is* what the Teaching Ballads say," Kindan agreed.

T'mar frowned, saying, "I'm not sure I understand them, even now."

Kindan gave him an expectant look, so the Weyrleader continued, "Well, it seems that the three months and more is the time from mating to clutching, correct?"

"That's how I learned it," Kindan said.

"And so the five heated weeks would be the time the eggs are on the Hatching Grounds," T'mar said.

"All the Records I've read agree on that," Fiona told him, clearly wondering what he was getting at.

"And, 'A day of glory' refers to Impression, doesn't it?" T'mar asked, keeping his attention on Kindan. The harper nodded. "So then, what's the last part mean: 'And in a month, who seeks?'"

"I've always thought that referred to the time when a queen could rise again," Fiona said quietly, not surprised to feel heat rising from her cheeks.

"It seems out of place, though, doesn't it?" T'mar persisted. "Why bring that up when the rest of the verse is about eggs and Impression?"

Kindan thought it over and nodded. "I hadn't really thought on it too much, as no one's ever questioned it before."

"It all seemed to make sense," T'mar said. "And," he added with an apologetic grin, "we're all used to the way harpers take license with the truth."

"Anything to keep a rhyme," Fiona said with a sardonic look at Kindan.

"But what else could it mean?" Lorana asked, recalling her own memories of Arith. "Unless that it refers to the time a weyrling can fly."

"Perhaps," T'mar said, not sounding convinced. He dismissed the matter with a wave of his hand, saying, "Well, I was just wondering. It's not something that should concern us at the moment."

"Nor should thick shells," Fiona asserted, "especially when we've only the one clutch—and Talenth's first, at that—to gauge by."

"If Tolarth's clutch is the same, then we'll have to reconsider," T'mar said.

"In the meantime," Fiona said, "what are you going to do about the next Fall?"

T'mar's face darkened and he shook his head.

"Fort's the strongest, they could loan us a Wing," Fiona suggested.

"They've less than five Wings."

"And we have little more than two," Fiona said. She cocked her head at him consideringly. "You're *not* thinking of timing it with just two Wings, are you?"

"It may come to that."

"But not now!"

"It might be better to find out now, rather than later," T'mar said.

"Only if you've got support arranged beforehand," Fiona retorted quickly. She gave him another suspicious look, then declared, "You've talked with K'lior!"

"I have," T'mar admitted, nodding. "I've discussed it with H'nez as well."

"So that explains the strange looks he was giving you this evening!"

"Partly," T'mar said. Fiona eyed him again and shook her head in exasperated admiration, saying, "He had some suggestions regarding our casualties, did he?"

T'mar's expression betrayed him and Fiona's temper flared up and she shouted, "As if he could do any better!"

T'mar raised a hand in a calming gesture but it was pointless.

"Telgar's going to take more casualties than the other Weyrs because Telgar is fighting over a greater area than the other Weyrs."

"Not that much," T'mar said.

"Enough," Fiona said, glancing at Kindan for agreement. Reluctant to be drawn into the argument, Kindan cleared his throat before saying, "Telgar and Benden tie at six Falls each cycle for the greatest number of Falls."

"Things would be different if Igen were flying."

"There are still not enough dragons, no matter how many Weyrs you put them in," Fiona said.

"It doesn't matter," T'mar said, giving Fiona a quelling look. "I'm the Weyrleader—"

"Until Talenth rises again!" Fiona snorted angrily.

"—and I've made the best decision I can," T'mar finished, acknowledging her interjection with a sad nod. "As it stands, Telgar has the greatest experience in timing it and our dragons and riders are trained the best in coping with it.

"I felt that it would be more dangerous to introduce a new wing into our ranks, given that we would probably have to time it even with their numbers, so I decided we would perform the experiment."

"And how many will die in this experiment?" Fiona demanded hotly, then quickly brought her hand up to her face in horror, her eyes wide with guilt and sorrow. "T'mar, I'm sorry! That was uncalled for!"

"Fewer perhaps than would die the other way," T'mar responded, his voice cold with anger. "Although, as we'll be certainly fighting twice, the chances of your needing a new Weyrleader are clearly doubled."

"Stupid, stupid, stupid!" Fiona growled, then offhandedly said to T'mar, "Not you, me. I should never have said anything of the like; it's only that I am worried about you." She caught his eyes with hers and added in a softer voice, "I'm afraid that you'll make the mistake B'nik made."

"He hasn't made the mistake yet," T'mar said, reaching up a hand to accept her apology. His eyes narrowed as he continued half to himself, "In fact, it might not even be him."

"I thought you said you recognized him?"

"Not him," T'mar replied with a quick shake of his head, "his jacket." He took a breath and continued, "I saw the Benden Weyrleader's jacket quite clearly before the Thread consumed it."

"Well, I couldn't imagine B'nik just giving *that* away!"

"No, I couldn't, either," T'mar admitted. "But it could be possible that a different person inherited it."

"Not as long as Tullea's senior!" Kindan said, chuckling.

"Indeed," T'mar said. "But until it happens, we won't really know *who* wore the Benden Weyrleader's jacket when it did happen."

"But it seems fair to guess that whoever was wearing it was the Benden Weyrleader," Kindan said. "Even if this Weyrleader is from the distant future, he was still destroyed by Thread."

"And just as true if it really was B'nik," T'mar said. "But my point is that we don't know when this will happen, when some future B'nik jumps *between* to save us—after saving M'tal beforehand."

"Although, with our numbers so low, it could be soon," Fiona said with a grim look.

"It could be," T'mar said. "But it gives me hope that perhaps we can survive longer before that day comes to hand."

"Long enough for our weyrlings to grow to fighting strength?"

T'mar shrugged at the notion but Fiona could tell he was hopeful.

"So . . ." Fiona began slowly, "because B'nik's not dead yet, you're hoping that this will somehow mean that you won't die when you fly the same Fall twice, am I right?"

T'mar's hopeful look faded as he stammered, "I wasn't quite looking at it *that* way."

T'mar was not completely surprised when Fiona arranged for Kindan to stay with Lorana that night with only the thin excuse, "Xhinna needs a chance to prove herself."

Nor was he surprised to be awoken by her quietly slipping into his bed not much later.

"If you are going to get yourself killed, bronze rider, then I'm going to need something to remember you by," Fiona told him firmly. As his lips quirked up in a smile, she added severely, "And more than just one good night."

She put actions to her words and gave herself so completely and demanded so much of him that neither was in doubt afterward of the nature of the gift, the willingness with which it had been given, nor the love with which it had been received.

Later, in the afterglow, Fiona propped her head on one arm and told him, "And when you come back, you're to make more time for Shaneese." She smiled as she plumbed the depths of his expression. "As I told Lorana, I share. And I plan to get all the help raising children I can."

Wisely, Telgar's Weyrleader said nothing.

"You came back, you came back!" Fiona cried flinging herself into T'mar's arms two days later as they returned from their first round of flying the Fall.

"We still have to fly again," T'mar warned her.

"But you'll come back from that, too," Fiona said, gesturing toward Lorana in the distance, before burying herself once more against his chest. "She knows."

"I see," T'mar said, hugging her back tightly. He pushed her away gently, his eyes filled with pain as he asked, "And does she know how many we've lost?"

"Yes," Fiona replied, equally grim, casting her eyes upward to avoid meeting his. "Seven lost—two now, five more when you go back. Three severely injured and five moderately injured in addition to more than the usual number of scrapes, cuts, and near-misses."

"How did she take it?"

Fiona raised a hand, gesturing toward the distant figures of Lorana and Kindan as they went from rider to rider.

"She's taking it well," Fiona said. She moved away from the Weyrleader, adding, "I'm going to make my farewells."

T'mar let her go with a solemn nod; he needed to rest a moment before he went to speak with those riders he knew wouldn't be returning.

"Here, drink this!" a voice piped up beside him. He looked toward it and saw Shaneese proferring a large mug of steaming *klah*. "Fiona said you'd need it."

"She's right," T'mar agreed wholeheartedly, taking a long draught of the warming liquid. He gave Shaneese a quizzical look as he swallowed. When he found his breath, he said, "You've added something."

"A bit of spice," Shaneese agreed. "Nutmeg, it gives it a special kick."

"It's very good," T'mar said and, recalling Fiona's words, gave the headwoman a very grateful smile. "It's clear that you show proper respect for a Weyrleader!"

"I certainly try," Shaneese replied, a smile dimpling her face. She glanced around to distant throngs of riders and dragons, adding, "I know that the Weyrwoman sometimes gets too . . . involved to notice such matters."

"Usually she's very good," T'mar said in agreement, "but sometimes she lets her youth carry her away." He smiled down at the dusky-skinned headwoman. "I'm pleased to see that you are so able to alleviate her deficiencies."

"She and I try to work as a team," Shaneese said, glancing up shyly at the Weyrleader.

"Together, I'm sure you're more than the sum of your parts," T'mar said, draining his mug and holding it apologetically to the headwoman. "I'm afraid it's all gone."

"Oh, there's plenty more where it came from," Shaneese said, turning toward the Kitchen Caverns. "Shall I get you some?"

"Maybe later," T'mar said. "We've another Fall—rather the same one again—to ride." He smiled. "And when I get back, I fear I shall be too weary to do much more than crawl into bed."

"I'll see to it that hot stones are ready for you," Shaneese offered.

"I'm sure you'll be just as busy and weary as I will," T'mar allowed, his senses not so dull that he couldn't detect the double meaning. "I'd hate to think of delaying you from your bed just for that."

"It would be no trouble."

"I could ask Fiona to bring them with her to bed," T'mar said, wondering how far to push this exchange.

"That would be difficult for her, as I understand she's decided to sleep in the Hatching Grounds to keep Tolarth and Jeila company," Shaneese said. "She suggested you would be too tired to put up with her this evening."

"She did, did she?" T'mar said. "And she thought I'd appreciate a cold bed by myself?"

"No," Shaneese said, her lips curving upward in a smile.

"Well, if she's not going to be there and you're going to bring the hot stones, I see no reason for you to have to traipse across the cold Weyr Bowl back to your quarters by yourself."

"I really couldn't ask you to escort me back after flying two Falls," Shaneese demurred.

"And I," T'mar confessed, "couldn't imagine myself capable." He paused as if in thought. "But if you'll be so kind as to bring the hot stones, then—if you don't mind—you could just as easily rest with me." He added quickly, "Not that I'll be much company, with two Falls flown." He held up a cautioning hand as he added, "I'll probably snore."

"Fiona says that your snores are cute," Shaneese said, grinning. Her grin faded as she added, "I'd like to hear them."

"Then, if you wish, you shall," T'mar told her, placing a hand on her shoulder companionably.

"I'll look forward to it," the headwoman said, her face blossoming with a grin that again showed her marvelous dimples.

"Now, I'd best be about my duties," she said, turning away and gently removing the hand he'd placed on her shoulder, her own grasp lingering for a moment before she let him go. "I'd hate for people to say I was monopolizing you."

"Of course," T'mar allowed with a smile of his own. Much refreshed, he turned to survey the rest of the group in the Weyr Bowl. The riders and dragons were a small knot nearly lost in the growing dusk.

Small, T'mar thought grimly, and soon to be smaller. His eyes sought out the slim form of Fiona. He spotted her and saw that she was looking in his direction. He waved at her, smiling.

That girl takes on entirely too much to herself, he mused. And yet, he had to admit that now he was looking forward to his return from the Fall in a way he would not have expected—and he owed it to her forethought and caring. He raised his hand to his mouth and expansively blew her a kiss. Fiona theatrically caught the kiss, clasped it to her breast, held her hand there while raising her other hand to her lips and returning the gesture to him in the grandest style.

If anything were to happen to her, I don't know what I'd do, T'mar thought grimly.

You'd survive, Zirenth responded, surprising T'mar, who'd believed that he'd kept his thought to himself. He got a glimmer of feeling from his bronze and the chord resonated with him: She'll see to that.

Is that why, T'mar mused, his heart suddenly going cold, she arranged this evening with Shaneese?

True to his word, T'mar practically stumbled into his bed that evening when he returned from the Fall. He was extremely grateful that Shaneese was there and quickly demolished all her attempts to leave him alone. He was glad that he did; the headwoman was older and more mature in the ways of people than Fiona, but she was nearly the same size while more pleasantly rounded. Her brilliant eyes and bright teeth shown in her dark face with an intensity that Fiona's blue eyes and tanned skin would never realize, but there was a similarity between the two that T'mar couldn't identify in his exhaustion.

"Thank you," he said a moment later as Shaneese rubbed his back with a warm oiled stone. "I didn't think about that."

"Fiona suggested it," Shaneese murmured quietly.

"She suggested the whole evening," T'mar grumbled. He felt Shaneese stiffen for a moment and then she continued moving the oiled stone over his sore muscles. She sighed, and T'mar turned his head back to cast her an inquiring glance.

"Can you love more than one person?" she asked him softly, her hands not pausing in their work.

"Yes," T'mar said. He thought for a moment, choosing his words carefully. "It takes time and effort and caring but it can be done. Fiona does it."

"Fiona is a world unto herself."

"No," T'mar replied slowly, "not really." He felt the headwoman's surprise and added, "She doesn't even want to be her own world; she wants all of us in it and she'll do whatever is required to *make* that so."

Shaneese thought on that, moving the oiled stone to another tight spot and rubbing.

"She snares people in her delusions," she suggested at last.

"No, honestly, I think she inspires them to share her dreams."

"Even now?" Shaneese asked, her question encompassing all the pain and loss that Telgar and every Weyr had endured since the beginning of the Third Pass.

"Particularly now," T'mar replied. He thought for a moment, adding, "She is not without limits. I know that she's afraid and that she hurts—"

"I've seen that, too."

"—but as long as she can keep her spirits up, she'll keep our spirits up," T'mar finished. "She knows that if we lose hope, we'll lose everything."

"And so she arranged for me to be here tonight to keep up your hopes?" Shaneese asked with a trace of irritation creeping into her voice.

"No," T'mar replied, "I think she expects that to come in the morning." He turned over and grabbed the stone from her hand, dropping it back into the basket at the side of his bed as he gestured for her to lie down, telling her with a mischievous grin, "And for that, you'll need your rest."

Shaneese closed her eyes for a while and then opened them when she was certain he was asleep. She could see his eyelids flutter and his mouth work in silent pain as his dreams replayed the events of the last Fall. A feeling of tenderness overwhelmed her and she ran her hand across his cheek, stroking him out of his nightmare and back into relaxed slumber.

She looked at him as he slipped into a deeper sleep and then laid her head beside his.

Weyrwoman, I accept, she thought as his slow breathing turned into gentle snores.

"What are you doing here?" Kindan's voice betrayed his surprise as he spied Fiona curled up on the warm sands of the Hatching Grounds.

"Waiting for you," Fiona replied with a smile, taking great enjoyment in the harper's increased surprise.

"I was just shooing—"

"—the shell-seekers," Fiona finished for him, her brows furrowing in confusion. "I've never quite understood the logic . . ."

"It's complicated," Kindan agreed, turning back to herd the last of the weyrling riders out of the Hatching Grounds and back to their beds. Fiona waited patiently, carefully settling the most disturbed knot of youngsters who were camped out near Tolarth's clutch. She was satisfied with them pretending to sleep, knowing that they would soon bubble up again, their excitement overwhelming their fatigue. Fiona smiled; she hadn't guessed that the *first* Hatching would increase the interest the younglings had in the *second* clutch. She suspected that Shaneese or any of the older weyrfolk could have told her but Shaneese—Fiona's face lit with a wicked grin—was otherwise indisposed at the moment, or at least so she hoped, and all the other weyrfolk were probably too busy with their anticipated joy at the Weyrwoman's discomfort. That they were wrong in their assessment pleased Fiona even more; she liked children and enjoyed their wide-eyed excitement, breathless babbling, and the sheer joy they brought to every activity.

"Complicated, you said?" Fiona murmured to Kindan several minutes later as he, having finally seen off the last of the weyrlings, made ready to head back to the weyrling barracks himself.

"Complicated," Kindan agreed, willing to put off his next duty for a moment. He frowned, gesturing toward the children. "And why is it, Weyrwoman, that you are in charge of this brood?"

"It's part of a deal with Xhinna and Taria," Fiona said, adding quickly, "So what about this seeking egg shards is complicated?"

Kindan shrugged. "First, it depends upon the seeker."

Fiona raised an eyebrow politely and Kindan's lips curved upward as he acknowledged her restrained response.

"For those who've Impressed, the purpose is obvious: The shard represents a memento, a good luck piece," he explained. Fiona nodded in understanding, then flicked her eyes for him to continue. "For those who didn't Impress, it's more like a promise, a token of a future possibility."

"So did you take a piece?"

"No," Kindan replied, shaking his head. Fiona gave him an inquiring look. "I have pieces of Kisk's egg and pieces of Valla's egg; I think I've got all the tokens I need."

Fiona reached into her vest pocket and pulled out a shard, grabbing one of his hands with her other and placing the shard in his hand, clasping both hands around his and forcing his fingers to close.

"Then this is for you," she said. Kindan's brows twitched and he pulled his hand out of her grasp, holding up the piece to the light.

"It's a blue shard, from Tazith's shell," Kindan said as he examined it. His blue eyes looked down to meet hers. "Are you saying that I should set my hopes on a blue?"

Fiona chuckled, shaking her head. "No, I'm saying that you should consider that some shells are harder than others." She took a quick darting step toward him and stood on her tiptoes to rap him gently on the skull. "But that doesn't mean there won't be a hatchling coming forth."

Kindan met her twinkling eyes with a dour expression. "It's also possible that not all eggs hatch."

"That's an old saying," Fiona agreed. "But it refers to chickens and other fowl, not dragons."

Kindan snorted softly at the correction. He glanced around, noticing Talenth curled up in the distance for the first time, and glanced meaningfully in her direction.

"Talenth decided to keep Tolarth company," Fiona explained. In a whisper she added, "I think it might have more to do with the hot sands, personally." Fiona turned to Talenth and, impulsively, back to Kindan, grabbing his hand and tugging him after her. "Maybe you should try it, it's good for muscles."

"But—"

"Xhinna will take care of the weyrlings," Fiona told him, carefully keeping her face away from him lest her expression reveal that that was part of her plan.

Much later, as they lay in a quiet sheltered spot that had, Kindan noted, been both carefully chosen and carefully prepared, he muttered to himself, "Good for the muscles!"

"I didn't say which," Fiona purred in response, nuzzling up close against him.

A short while later, as Kindan was still trying to decide whether he was glad, angry, or bemused over the whole thing, Fiona rolled over and sat up, staring down at him sleepy-eyed. "You've got to go," she told him, her tone half-sad, half-firm.

"Go?"

"Lorana needs someone to be with her, too, you know," Fiona said, her eyes losing focus as they peered unseeing into the distance. She glanced back at Kindan and turned to the pile of clothes nearby, pulling out his trousers and sliding them toward him.

"Lorana—" Kindan began in protest but Fiona cut him off.

"—she needs someone to *be* with her, Kindan, nothing more," she said chidingly. "I've got to watch the weyrfolk here."

Fiona pulled on a night tunic and snaked a pair of sandals—neither of which Kindan had seen her wearing previously, he noted with some amusement—and then hustled him into getting dressed.

"I'll walk you to the exit," she told him, adding a quick kiss and intertwining the fingers of one hand with his.

"What if some of the children see us?"

"Well, those who are old enough to know probably don't care—and they're not here, most likely—and the rest are too interested in the eggs to notice us," Fiona decided with an easy twinkle in her eyes. "Besides, I like children and I've discovered I'm pretty good at distracting them when they ask awkward questions."

"That's only because there's not so much difference between you and them," Kindan said gruffly.

"It may be," Fiona said easily. "But I like to be prepared, so I think it's wise to spend time with children, don't you?"

"So this"—Kindan waved a hand around the Hatching Grounds with a firm nod toward their cozy quiet place—"is all for the children?"

"Yes," Fiona replied, her eyes twinkling with mischief. "Either about keeping them or"—she lowered her voice suggestively—"getting them."

Kindan groaned.

"Really, Kindan," Fiona said, her brows arching downward disapprovingly, "you would think, being a harper and all, that you'd understand that at the end of things it's all about children."

Kindan gave her an inquiring look.

"Without children there is no future and no reason for living," Fiona told him. Her mood lifted as she added with a giggle, "Besides, they're too incredibly cute!"

"You were cute," Kindan blurted out suddenly.

"I hope I still am," Fiona said, batting her eyelashes at him outrageously.

Kindan chuckled. "You still are."

"Then I'll say good night to you, Harper Kindan, and please give my best to Lady Lorana."

Kindan waved and took off briskly across the cold Weyr Bowl toward the Weyrwoman's quarters, wondering how it was that Fiona always seemed to get exactly what she wanted.

It was, he decided as he increased his pace up the ramp toward the weyr and sleeping Lorana, because she quickly decided on her goals and never wavered from them.

Something I learned from you, Kindan heard her saying in his head.

He shook himself, wondering whether he had really heard her or if he was just imagining her response.

"Kindan?" Lorana called from the bed.

"You're supposed to be asleep," Kindan called back softly, a smile curving his lips as he crossed the last of the distance between the entrance and the bed.

"Fiona's been tormenting you again, hasn't she?" Lorana asked in sympathetic humor.

"How—did Talenth—?"

"No," Lorana replied with a laugh, "it's just that I understand her."

"How so?"

"She's frightened," Lorana told him sadly. "She's afraid she'll lose everything and she's doing her best to grab what she can."

"A child?" Kindan asked in surprise. "From me?"

"From you, from T'mar, as many as she can get," Lorana said.

"She said that children are the future," Kindan said musingly.

"Without children there is no future," Lorana corrected in oblique agreement. Kindan could see her glance down in the dim of the glows to her own belly. He threw off his clothes, pulled on a night tunic—not at all surprised to see it ready to hand, draped over the back of a chair—and quickly dove into the bed.

"I love you," he told Lorana feelingly, wrapping hands around her back and gently kneading the tight muscles he found there.

"I know," Lorana replied. She exhaled blissfully as Kindan found a knotted muscle and teased it out. She leaned herself against him, her head resting on his shoulder. "I know."

"Yes, Weyrwoman, five more fighting dragons have recovered," H'nez said heatedly to Fiona two days later as the wingleaders met in the Council Room, "but that's no cause for cheer. We've still got nearly two full Wings of injured dragons and less than that of fighting dragons."

"In these days we need to find cheer where we can," F'jian said.

"We'll fly in four Wings," T'mar repeated, firmly reiterating what he'd first said to start the discussion. "That way we'll have bronzes leading each Wing and we'll have a reserve to haul firestone."

"And fourteen dragons in each Wing," H'nez growled darkly. Fiona shot him a glare and then a beseeching look toward Jeila who, instead of backing her authority, lowered her eyes and glanced away. H'nez saw the exchange and raised a hand placatingly. "Oh, I'm not saying it's a bad plan! In fact, T'mar, I think it's the best plan we have, given our circumstances."

Fiona gave him a surprised look, and glanced at Jeila, who raised her eyes to meet hers again, her lips quirked in a lopsided grin. Fiona smiled and shook her head: She should never have doubted the petite weyr-woman.

"The question is, T'mar, when are we going to be too weak?" H'nez asked him seriously. "And what will we do then?" He paused and glanced around the table. "For, like as not, the day is coming."

"And soon," C'tov said in agreement.

"There'll be another Hatching soon—" Fiona began hopefully.

"And three Turns from now we'll be grateful for the extra strength," H'nez said dismissively.

"Two Turns," C'tov protested. H'nez shot him a look but the scarred bronze rider persisted, "We can get them ready in two Turns."

"But it won't solve our problems *now*."

"No, it won't," T'mar agreed with a sigh. "And I plan on talking with the other Weyrleaders about this—after this Fall." He glanced at H'nez before continuing, "But for the moment, we've a Fall to ride in less than two hours."

"The ground crews are ready," Kindan said, glancing at Fiona, who nodded in agreement. This Fall would be over both Telgar Hold and the Weyr itself, and Weyrwoman Fiona was responsible both for the care of the injured and the Weyr's ground crews. Kindan, as Weyrlingmaster, had been tasked with detailing weyrlings to ground crews—part of the revised training that he, T'mar, and H'nez had all unanimously agreed upon.

"We're going to have the reserve Wing deposit crews and equipment up with the herds and the other outliers," Fiona said, nodding toward C'tov, who'd been elected to lead the reserves.

"So," T'mar said, rising from his chair, "I think we've covered everything we can. Wingleaders, prepare your Wings."

The others nodded, rose, and filed out of the room. After a moment, Kindan shuffled off after them, nodding to both weyrwomen as he departed.

Fiona sat for a long while, her eyes darting toward Jeila, who kept her head bowed and remained silent.

Fiona waited patiently.

"This baby will have a father," Jeila said.

"Of course."

The other weyrwoman glanced up to her, glaring, challenging, dark eyes brooding. "Can you guarantee that?"

"No," Fiona told her softly, rising from her chair and coming around to where Jeila sat. She crouched down behind her, placing her arms on the petite woman's shoulders. "I can't guarantee anything except that as long as I draw breath I will do everything to protect you, your children, and your loves."

Silently, tears started down Jeila's face and the weyrwoman leaned her head on Fiona's right hand where it rested on her shoulder. "I'm not like you, I can't live without him."

"Yes you can," Fiona told her encouragingly. "You can because you'll have the baby. If you lose him, you'll still have that part of him."

After a moment, Fiona stood and, grabbing Jeila's arms, forced the weyrwoman to rise out of her chair.

"You have the strength of the desert in you, Jeila," Fiona told the dark-haired woman quietly. "You'll not succumb to a drought, or to sorrow."

Jeila's eyes brightened as she looked up into Fiona's blue eyes. She wiped her tears away and smiled tentatively, telling the taller Weyrwoman, "You do realize that you are every bit as difficult as my relatives said you were?"

"Did they say that?"

"They did," Jeila declared with a nod. "Stubborn, prideful, cheerful, indomitable, and"—she paused to gather breath, her lips curving up in a tentative smile—"the best hope of Pern."

"By the First Egg, I certainly hope not!" Fiona chuckled, feeling the discomfort of the weight of all those expectations bearing down on her shoulders.

"You and Lorana."

"We can't do it on our own," Fiona said, marveling again at the other woman's thin bones and petite frame. She grinned at Jeila, adding, "I'd like to think we'll get help."

"If I lose him . . ."

"It's never wise to take sorrow before its time," Fiona said, wondering where she had first heard the phrase . . . Kindan? She wrapped her arms around the other woman and hugged her tightly.

"So you're pregnant," Fiona murmured after a while. "When's the date?"

Jeila drew in a sharp breath and stepped back so that she could look up, incredulously, into Fiona's eyes. "You, too?"

"We were incredibly lucky," T'mar said when he returned from the Fall for the first time, "we only lost three."

He frowned as he glanced at two disconsolate riders and those grouped mournfully around them. "Rather, we lost one now and we'll lose two more when we go back in time to fly again."

"I know," Fiona said, gearing herself up for the renewed loss. "How many were injured from those that timed it?"

T'mar pursed his lips thoughtfully. "Two, three?"

"We've one mauled and two injured now," Fiona said, nodding toward the weyrfolk who were working to patch up one badly scored green dragon and her rider. She wrinkled her nose distastefully. "Why does it always have to be greens and blues?"

"Because there are so many of them," T'mar said, glancing around the shadows of the night darkened Bowl. "When we return, it'll be the middle of the night."

"We'll be ready," Fiona said. She shrugged, adding, "Although it'd be nicer if I knew how many injuries I had to deal with, then I could let helpers get more sleep."

"Doesn't Lorana know?"

"She can talk to any dragon, but she can't talk into the future," Fiona said. "Imagine how awful *that* would be, if she could!"

T'mar, too tired from Threadfall, merely nodded. He turned to the others, then back to Fiona. "Have Lorana let them know that we fly again in two hours' time."

"Go to your quarters, take a break," Fiona suggested. "I'll come along later."

T'mar gave her a guarded look and Fiona smiled. "You'll have enough time to let me work on some of those knotted muscles! I won't do anything to put you to sleep, but there's no point in having you fight the same Thread twice if you're too sore to move!"

"I wish someone could do the same for Zirenth," T'mar said feelingly, as he and the bronze trotted off to their weyr.

When Fiona found him later, he was seated at his desk, his legs stretched out under the table, a tray with a pitcher of *klah* and a mug before him, the steam still rising from the mug.

"Shaneese brought it," he said as he gestured for her to sit down. He smiled as he added, "And *someone* must have mentioned my whining to her as Zirenth had a whole wing of weyrfolk oiling him not much later."

Fiona went around behind him, laying her hands on his shoulders. They were as hard as stone. Silently she began kneading the muscles, working her hands up to his neck, particularly at the base.

"Get up," she told him after a few minutes.

T'mar rose as instructed, eyebrows raised. "Should I lie down on the bed?"

"No, just sit backward in your chair," Fiona said, reaching around him to turn the chair around and shoving him toward it. "If you're not too cold, you might lift your tunic, so I can get to your muscles directly."

Smiling, T'mar pulled off his shirt, draped it over the back of the chair, and then sat down in reverse position, with his chest pressing against the shirt.

"This is something I learned from Bekka," Fiona said as she crouched down and began working her hands over his hips.

"From Bekka?"

"She learned it from her mother, to ease knots out of expectant mothers," she said as she leaned into her work. A moment later, just when she expected to get the greatest rise, she added, "I expect you to take careful note; you'll need it."

However, instead of even twitching at her revelation, T'mar said nothing.

"T'mar?" Fiona asked, irritated that he hadn't responded as she'd hoped. She peered around to look him in the eyes: They were closed. The Weyrleader was snoring gently, asleep, his head bowed.

"That's the last of them," Fiona told Terin as she and the youngster stood, bathed in the green dragon ichor that they'd been drenched in while sewing up the worst of the injured dragons.

Fiona reached for a towel, threw it to Terin, and grabbed another for herself, wiping off her hands, arms, face, and then what was left of her clothes. She had sensibly dressed in older clothes: a tunic and trousers with soft shoes. Her feet hurt from standing so long, her back hurt, her shoulders and hands felt cramped, but she smiled at the younger woman. "That wasn't so bad."

"It could have been worse," Terin agreed, stifling a yawn.

"Get to bed!" Fiona ordered, jerking her head in the direction of F'jian's weyr.

"Bath first, I think," Terin said, sniffing herself reflectively.

"Then come with me," Fiona said. "If you bathe alone you're likely to fall asleep and drown."

Terin's eyes flashed but another yawn stifled her retort and with a sheepish look she gestured for the Weyrwoman to precede her.

As they made their way through Talenth's empty weyr and into Fiona's quarters, she whispered, "We'll need to be quiet, I don't want to disturb Lorana."

"I can't sleep anyway," a voice from the bed startled them. The room grew lighter as Lorana turned over a glow. She gave the two others a quizzical smile as she explained, "The baby's kicking."

"We're going to wash off all this muck," Fiona said, gesturing to the remnants of the dragon ichor, "why don't you join us?"

"A warm bath might help," Lorana agreed. Fiona moved quickly to her side, gesturing for Terin to help. Solicitously they helped Lorana out of bed, ignoring her protests—"I'm not *that* big!"

Somewhere along the way, Fiona dozed off to be woken by a dig from a giggling Terin.

"I was *saying*," Terin told her making it clear that she'd spoken before she'd noticed Fiona's slumber, "that this is the first time that the three of us, recipients of Tenniz's gifts, have been together for months." She frowned at Fiona thoughtfully as she added, "Have you gotten any closer to figuring out his meaning?"

"Well," Fiona began slowly, "as there's a queen egg on the sands, I suspect we know what your gift means."

Terin sniffed wistfully. "I wouldn't presume that egg is meant for me." She turned to Lorana. "Wouldn't it be for you instead?"

Lorana gave her a questioning look and Terin responded, "I mean, your prophecy implies that you'll have another queen, doesn't it?"

Lorana flicked her eyes away, expression grim.

"Well, mine makes it clear enough," Fiona said cheerfully, "Tenniz said it would all work out." She glanced Lorana's way, adding, "And in many respects, I think it already has." She caught Lorana's dubious look and continued, "We've weyrlings and eggs on the ground, we've dragons that can fly when just months before we feared we'd have none— and new life on the way. I think things will only go on getting better."

Even if she didn't quite believe it herself, Fiona knew that she had a duty to appear unworried, cheerful. And, maybe there was more truth than hope in what she'd said. Perhaps things *were* getting better.

They finished quickly and Fiona made certain that Terin made it back to her weyr before turning in. By the time she got into bed, Lorana already looked to be asleep. Fiona pursed her lips as she wondered whether to continue their earlier discussion, but, with a weary sigh, decided to leave it for morning.

When she woke the next morning, the demands of the day and injured dragons and riders drove the issue completely from her mind. Kindan arrived early with a pitcher of steaming *klah* and a smile on his face; Fiona took a mug for herself and bustled off to the Dining Cavern for a proper breakfast, leaving Kindan and Lorana time alone together.

She found T'mar and the wingleaders already in deep discussion, breaking their fast almost as an afterthought.

"Make them eat or they'll be useless," Shaneese said urgently as she came by to place a basket of fresh steaming rolls temptingly in front of the Weyrleader. She gave Fiona a probing look and added, "And make sure you eat your share; don't forget the juice."

Fiona looked at her in surprise and the headwoman continued brusquely, "You're eating for two now; even if you thought you had no need, you've got to consider the other."

The other? Fiona glanced around furtively to see if any of the wingleaders had noted the exchange and was surprised at her sense of disappointment when she realized they hadn't. Men, she snorted disgustedly before glancing back up to the headwoman, her eyebrows raised in inquiry.

"Think Tenniz was the only one with gifts?" Shaneese asked. "You're the right age and you've been trying so hard—wouldn't be surprised if you had two."

"That'd be a good start," Fiona said.

Shaneese smiled, saying, "I suppose it would, for you, at that." She reached over, grabbed a moisture-beaded pitcher, snagged a clear glass, and deftly poured a large helping of the juice, placing it near Fiona's right hand and the pitcher just above it. "Be sure you drink at least two glasses, then," Shaneese ordered. "Every meal."

"But you've never . . . ?" Fiona uttered, trailing off in surprise. She judged Shaneese to be within ten Turns of her own age and not yet a mother.

"I've a mother and sisters," Shaneese replied. She glanced openly toward T'mar and added in a poorly concealed tone of joy and surprise, "After L'rat, I never thought the right one would come along for me."

Fiona hefted her juice glass, half-turned and raised it high in salute to the headwoman before draining it in one go. She put the glass back down on the table, her brows raised in surprise as she exclaimed, "Tart but sweet!"

"Good for you, too," Shaneese said, reaching over to refill her glass pointedly. Dutifully Fiona emptied the second glass. As she reached for the pitcher of *klah*, Shaneese warned, "You might want to be careful with that, I've heard it said that some babies'll keep their parents awake at night if they've had too much."

"It's better to be awake at night than asleep in the day," Fiona said, punctuating her words with a wide yawn. She poured the *klah* and gratefully downed a portion before adding, "I don't know how I'd survive without this."

"Talk to Bekka and Birentir before you get too far along," Shaneese said, resting a comforting hand on the Weyrwoman's shoulder.

Fiona turned again to look up at her questioningly.

Shaneese responded with a troubled look, then leaned down close to Fiona's ear to confide worriedly, "This may not be the best time for you." Fiona's eyes widened but she said nothing. "If that's so, there's ways—"

"Ways?"

"'Seven breaths *between* keeps a body flat and lean' is what I've heard," Shaneese said, her tone devoid of any emotion.

"I'd heard eleven," Fiona said. "Are you saying that I should be careful going *between*?"

"At least you should know your choices," Shaneese said. She gestured toward the pitcher of *klah*. "You've still no understanding of why you're so tired—"

"Nor does T'mar!"

"But he's not growing a baby, is he?"

"No, just flying Thread," Fiona reminded her, surprised at her own clashing emotions. She was irritated at the headwoman's suggestion; she *knew* what she was doing and why, but she hadn't considered that her weariness might provide complications. Come to think of it, was there a correlation between the tired riders and injuries? She glanced at the wingleaders, saw T'mar and F'jian both stifle yawns—which, Fiona conceded, could just as easily be from their ongoing fatigue as from their exertions flying Thread. She made a note to herself to follow the issue up later.

"I'll support you either way, Fiona," Shaneese said, grasping some of the younger woman's feelings better than the Weyrwoman did herself, "but I'd be remiss if I didn't make you aware of your options and your risks."

"Thank you," Fiona said, aware that her tone was stiff but unable to control it. The thought of terminating the pregnancy was nearly as frightening as the thought of losing it to her fatigue.

Shaneese rubbed her shoulder affectionately. "Talk to Bekka and Birentir, they'll know better."

"I will."

Shaneese moved away, not without a worried glance back over her shoulder as she left. Fiona returned to her breakfast, switching partway through her mug of *klah* to another glass of the juice, somewhat surprised that the smell of the *klah* wasn't as pleasant this morning as it usually was.

As she self-consciously chewed on a roll, Fiona found herself paying more attention to the wingleaders' discussion. It was a moment before she realized that they had stopped and were staring at her.

"I asked, Weyrwoman," T'mar told her with a smile, "if you knew the strength of High Reaches?"

"Ninety-two," she replied quickly to disprove any notion that she might not be fully alert. A moment later she added, "Ninety-four later, when two of their wounded are cleared back to flying."

"And don't forget that five of our own injured should be cleared tomorrow," F'jian said, glancing pointedly toward H'nez. "We'll have fifty-five then."

"Less than two Wings."

"Benden will have another five as well tomorrow," Fiona said. "So that'll give them over three Wings—three and a half."

There was a moment of polite silence before T'mar cleared his throat, saying, "Yes, we'd already mentioned that."

"Oh," Fiona said, sitting back in her chair, feeling heat rise in her cheeks even as she explained, "I was talking with Shaneese."

H'nez glanced pointedly away from her and back toward T'mar. "So the fighting strength of all Pern"—he cast a glance quickly in Fiona's direction—"*tomorrow* will be four hundred and seventy-nine."

"That's over five Flights," C'tov pointed out.

"And yet we should expect at this moment to have better than eighteen Flights with all six Weyrs," T'mar said with a sigh and an acknowledging look toward H'nez. "We know the situation is grave, but it is less than it was when the sickness was taking dragons every day."

H'nez turned to Fiona. "Was there ever a time, in all the Records that you read, that a Weyr's fighting strength was less than a Flight?"

Fiona shook her head. "Igen had a time in the Interval when it was down to two Flights, but that's the worst I recall."

"And their solution was to merge with Telgar," T'mar said, grimacing.

H'nez nodded, returning his gaze to Fiona as he asked, "And so, even given that we survive the next Fall, on what do you base your hopes that Pern will find the missing Flights—more than four Weyrs' worth—before we are all annihilated?"

Fiona shook her head in painful admission of her ignorance. The other bronze riders shot angry glances at H'nez, but there was no dodging the question. "I don't have anything," Fiona told him slowly, "beyond a feeling, a determination that somehow we will prevail." She paused before reminding him, "Just as we prevailed against the sickness."

"I, for one, will go on fighting with my very last breath," C'tov told the older rider firmly.

"He knows that," Fiona told him sadly. H'nez raised his eyebrows in surprise. She nodded at the other riders, adding, "He knows that you'll all give your lives to protect Pern."

"That's not the question," H'nez said in confirmation.

Fiona locked eyes with him. "The question you want answered is: Who will watch over your child when you are no longer. The answer is: I will."

Mutters went around the table. "Child?" "H'nez?"

The bronze rider broke away from Fiona's gaze, his face flushing as he met the eyes of his fellow wingleaders and nodded mutely.

"Congratulations, man!" C'tov said, rising from his chair and patting the older rider hard on the shoulder, his face split ear to ear with a huge smile. "I can see why you're concerned!"

"But it also means you've got something to live for," F'jian added, trying to puzzle out why the wingleader was so glum.

"I think our ancestors, back when the first Threads destroyed their crops and their dwellings, must have felt the same way," Fiona said to H'nez. "And they found a way to overcome the menace."

H'nez turned back to look at her. "Dragons."

"And watch-whers," a new voice spoke up, closing in from the exit to the Weyr Bowl. It was Kindan. He nodded toward Fiona and H'nez and pulled up a seat opposite the wiry bronze rider. "You know what killed Lorana's queen, H'nez?"

The bronze rider shook his head.

"She didn't know it at the time," he went on, his expression bleak, "but one of the four vials was meant to be kept separate." A sour look crossed his face, which he schooled away with effort. "The vials were mixed up and we didn't know . . ."

He shook himself out of his grim reverie. "The fourth vial was meant to make a watch-wher into a dragon."

"So if we lose all our dragons, we could start over?" C'tov asked.

"Only if there were still watch-whers," H'nez muttered.

"Does Nuella know?" Fiona asked.

Kindan nodded.

"Good," Fiona said to herself. She glanced back to H'nez. "So there is still reason to hope, as much or more than our ancestors had."

"How are the weyrlings?" T'mar asked of Kindan, to change the subject.

"They're doing well," the harper said. Adding, with a grin, "Xhinna is showing her mettle."

"A woman riding a blue," H'nez muttered darkly.

"The dragon chooses its rider," Fiona reminded him.

"Strange dragon," the wiry rider said.

"We'll see," T'mar said, turning back to Kindan. "But we've Turns yet."

"If we sent them back in time—" F'jian began.

"Igen was the only unused Weyr and we filled it with our injured," T'mar said.

"Well," F'jian said, groping for a solution and looking up, eyes bright with sudden inspiration, "why not send them forward in time, to after the Fall?"

H'nez's dark look made it clear to Fiona what he was thinking: assuming anyone lives.

"How?" C'tov asked the younger bronze rider.

"It's too far a jump," T'mar said. "It was dangerous enough"—he shot Fiona an accusing look—"to go back ten Turns in time; but to go forward fifty?" He shook his head at the impossibility of it.

"I suppose so," F'jian agreed, his shoulders slumping.

"But don't stop thinking," Fiona told him encouragingly. "There may be something we haven't yet considered that could help."

"I'm not sure it would be a good idea to send the weyrlings away," T'mar said. "It was far too great a risk the last time."

"We needed them," Fiona said. "If we hadn't done it, imagine where we'd be now."

"And it was K'lior's idea," F'jian said, partly in the Weyrwoman's defense.

"It was K'lior's suggestion that the least *injured* go back in time," T'mar replied quellingly. He glanced toward Fiona, adding, "*Someone* decided to lead the weyrlings and the most injured back in time as well."

"Which only emphasizes the need of them," Fiona responded tartly. "Besides, Weyrleader, we know that it wasn't *my* idea, so you can stop with the accusing glares!"

T'mar pursed his lips sourly and sat back in his chair, flipping open a hand in a gesture of defeat.

"Anyway," C'tov went on, returning to the original subject, "with all the eggs on the sands at all the Weyrs we've only got—what?—another three Wings?"

"Twenty-two eggs, one queen in each of the five clutches," Kindan said, glancing meaningfully toward first T'mar and then Fiona. "One hundred and five fighting dragons and five queens."

"Well, five queens would be a help," F'jian said. Fiona caught his eyes and the bronze rider flushed—it was an open secret that he was hoping Terin would Impress the queen from Tolarth's clutch.

"In three Turns, when they rise," H'nez remarked sourly.

"But with the Hatching, our queens will soon rise again," Fiona said. The others looked at her. "The Records show that the queens usually rise twice a Turn, sometimes as many as three."

"All of which might"—H'nez began and corrected himself when he caught Fiona's arch look—"will help us in the Turns to come but . . ." He shrugged.

"It's not wise to count your eggs before they hatch," T'mar told F'jian in a reproving tone whose sting was softened by his grin.

The younger bronze rider accepted the rebuke with an easy shrug.

T'mar sat forward decisively, glancing toward Fiona. "The Hatchings will be soon?"

"Probably tomorrow," Fiona said. She glanced toward Kindan for confirmation as she added, "The Records are very firm that Hatching occurs five weeks after clutching."

"It's very consistent," Kindan agreed.

"I remember, from the Teaching Ballads," C'tov said, frowning as he recited:

"Count three months and more,
And five heated weeks,
A day of glory and
In a month, who seeks?"

He glanced toward Kindan, asking, "I've always wondered about the last two lines—what do they mean?"

C'tov's question sent a chill through Fiona; she'd heard this only days before from Lorana—and read it in the Records even earlier. What *did* it mean? Clearly it meant something special, that she, Lorana, and now C'tov remarked upon it. She sat back and let the rest of the conversation spill over her, engrossed in thought.

"A day of glory—that's the Hatching," H'nez told him chidingly.

"I figured that," C'tov said with a dismissive glower for the older rider before returning his attention to Kindan, "but what about the last bit: 'In a month, who seeks?'"

"Well," Kindan said with a wry look toward Fiona, "the current thinking is that the last line is merely a harper's twiddle said to make the whole verse rhyme."

"And how many of the Teaching Ballads are riddled with such twiddles?" H'nez asked archly.

"It's easier to remember that which rhymes and trips off the tongue, H'nez," Kindan said without any hint of apology in his tone. "As far as I can recall, though, all the other Teaching Ballads are without embellishments."

"So what makes this an embellishment?" C'tov asked.

Kindan shrugged. "If it's not, I can't decipher its meaning."

"Maybe that's when dragons can go *between*," Fiona spoke up into the uneasy silence that had fallen. The others turned to her incredulously.

"I suppose it's possible," T'mar said. He glanced toward Kindan with a warning look as he added, "But I wouldn't recommend it."

"We had Impressed not much more than two months before we went back in *time* to Igen," F'jian said.

"And I still wouldn't recommend it," T'mar reminded him with a quelling look.

"Anyway, even if they were old enough to go *between*," C'tov said thoughtfully, "they'd be too small to fight Thread."

"Too small to carry firestone!" F'jian snorted in agreement.

"Two Turns at least," H'nez agreed tersely, looking toward T'mar. "Three is better."

"Two in a pinch," T'mar said.

"And we're in a pinch, there's no doubt!" F'jian exclaimed.

T'mar nodded, then glanced at Fiona with a sad look. The Weyrwoman needed no dragon to interpret it: Two Turns or three—either was too long for Pern.

TWENTY-ONE

▼▼▼▼▼▼▼▼▼▼▼▼▼▼▼▼▼▼▼▼▼▼▼▼▼▼▼▼▼▼▼▼▼▼▼▼▼▼

Eyes faceted,
Eyes fearful.
Hearts beating:
Beat as one.

Telgar Weyr, evening, AL 508.6.25

Fiona smiled as she spied a glint off the red-blond hair of the figure walking through the entrance into the Hatching Grounds as the last rays of sun filtered through the Weyr Bowl that night.

"I figured you'd be here," she called out, waving Terin over to her, not worried about disturbing the group of weyrchildren clustered nearby—they were not sleeping, too excited at the prospect of the Hatching the next day; most likely, in the morning.

"F'jian sent me," Terin said, her tone mixed with anger and fear. She gave Fiona an anxious look. "But I'm too young!"

"You're not much younger than I was when I Impressed Talenth," Fiona said. "And you're older than both Xhinna *and* Taria."

"But they didn't Impress a queen."

"I don't think *age* chooses color," Fiona replied, chuckling.

Terin glanced around nervously, even as baskets of glows were turned over to add their illumination to the dimming light. "There are a lot of girls here!"

"I'm not sure that all of them are hoping for queens," Fiona said.

"Why not?"

Fiona laughed. "You'd think every girl would wish to ride a gold, but I think, with Xhinna's example, some have realized that they could actually fight Thread."

"Queens fight Thread."

"In the queens' wing," Fiona agreed. "When there are enough of them, and at a relatively safe level."

Terin frowned at her. "I read the Records at Igen—"

"You did?" Fiona asked. "When?"

"When you were off gallivanting around or stuck in exile as watchqueen," Terin snapped in reply. "And I read enough to know that those queens in the queens' wing, while not chewing firestone, weren't exempt from scoring and injury."

Fiona nodded, surprised that the youngster had taken note—it was not something often mentioned. Fiona suspected that part of that was because the Werywomen traditionally kept the Records—they certainly edited them!—and did not want to make the dangers of the queens' wing too apparent to any nervous Weyrleader.

"Still," Fiona said, conceding Terin's point with a shrug, "it's not the same as flying in a fighting Wing."

"Yes, I can see that," Terin said, swiveling her head to gaze at the ranks of smaller eggs set not so close to Tolarth's watchful gaze. Fiona could follow her thinking, her indecision as the temptation of flying firestone together with F'jian formed in her mind, and could see the slight shake of her head when Terin decided that she'd prefer to be a queen rider.

"You'll make a great weyrwoman, Terin," Fiona told her.

"You act as if the eggs've already hatched!"

Fiona shrugged, reached closer, and patted the younger woman on the shoulder. "If not this time, then certainly sometime."

"It would be perfect if it were now," Terin said, turning back to Fiona as she continued softly, "but I was really hoping it'd be one of yours."

"Well, if the egg hatches and the queen comes toward you, don't tell her!" Fiona teased.

Sleep came with difficulty, for the youngsters and the Candidates were all too anxious to do more than toss and turn, causing Fiona to reconsider her decision of allowing weyrfolk to sleep on the Hatching Grounds. What she got was fits and starts and even giggles and mutterings from the youngsters, until she finally lost her temper and shouted at them. She regretted it instantly, but she was too out of sorts to show any contrition.

Apparently her outrage worked. The gathering quieted down enough for her to get some moments of sleep before she woke up again, later, grumbling.

"What makes you think they'd sleep any more in their own rooms?" Terin asked, stifling a yawn even as her bright eyes flicked toward the queen egg, straining for any signs of motion.

Dawn had come and light was creeping into the Hatching Grounds, changing the eggs from indistinct grayish blobs into blurs of various colors, some greenish blue, some bluish green, some brownish bronze, others copper brown—none, save the queen egg, identifying with any certainty the color of the dragonet still slumbering inside.

From the distance of Talenth's weyr, Fiona heard her queen rumble cheerfully, a noise returned with both greater volume and greater enthusiasm by Tolarth where she lay curled up, the queen egg protectively within her grasp.

"You have done marvelously!" Fiona called to the queen. Tolarth regarded her with complacent green-swirling eyes.

They will do, Tolarth said in an agreement tinged with some hidden certainty, as though these dragonets were destined to save all Pern.

As will ours, Talenth added with the same sort of smugness that made Fiona agitatedly wonder how the dragons could be so certain—they barely remembered yesterday, how could they predict tomorrow?

The bronzes started humming and Fiona felt, on a level below her own senses, an exchange between Tolarth and Talenth that resulted in her own queen suddenly bursting into the air above them, startling all the weyrfolk and the bronzes as she winged her way in deftly to take a place close to Tolarth—nearly exactly where she'd lain before with her own clutch.

Careful! Fiona called warningly.

I always know where I am, Talenth assured her, her smug tone still quite evident.

She gets it from you, Fiona heard Lorana say with a mixture of amusement and affection.

I suppose she does, Fiona said, turning to wave and smile at her queen. She looked at the gathered weyrfolk, saw the youngsters stream off to the viewing stands, spotted the Candidates quickly donning their white robes, tossing their nightclothes to those passing up to the stands—it all looked terribly well managed. Fiona turned toward Terin and gave her a calculating look.

"What?" Terin asked innocently, her own white robes neatly tied with a belt.

"Still the headwoman," Fiona said, shaking her head and smirking. Terin returned the smirk with a grin.

"Well, it wouldn't do for Tolarth's first Hatching to be marred by confusion and disarray."

"Not to mention that I probably wouldn't allow anyone to sleep on the sands again," Fiona said.

"Not to mention that!"

Fiona waved Terin away. "Go! You're supposed to be there!" She spotted T'mar as he broached the Hatching Grounds' entrance and waved to him.

Who's with you? Fiona asked Lorana as she spied Kindan and a knot of weyrlings entering, taking positions so quickly that Fiona was certain that Kindan had given them all assigned positions and duties. She waved at Xhinna as she climbed up to the group of youngsters in the stands, even as she plotted a route back to the weyr and Lorana; she wouldn't leave her on her own.

Bekka is here, Lorana replied. *Though, even without you and this, I've got every dragon in the Weyr ready to answer my slightest call.*

And well they should! Fiona said. It was clear from Lorana's response that she was not feeling left out of the proceedings and any concerns about Bekka she thrust from her mind, recalling that that youngster had grown up attending birthings with her midwife mother.

Fiona's previous declaration that Bekka should stand on the Hatching Grounds had been charred by the girl herself. "As if I don't have enough to do already!" Bekka had declared.

As for Lorana, the question of her returning to the Hatching Grounds as a Candidate had evaporated with the news of her pregnancy.

Someone stepped close to her and Fiona reached her hand out without turning, knowing that T'mar's rough fingers would twine over hers. She could see Kindan in the distance, noted that he had not put on Candidate robes and snorted to herself.

"He can't possibly believe that a lack of robes will deter his dragon!" she exclaimed to T'mar. The Weyrleader shot her a sidelong glance, but said nothing.

A crack suddenly hushed all other noise. Eyes searched for the hatching egg, ears heard the second crack and zeroed in—a brownish egg in the center.

Fiona tensed, wondering if she should move forward to help, but T'mar's hand tightened on hers.

"They know what to do," he said, nodding in the general direction of the Candidates. Among them, Fiona noted with approval, stood H'nez and Jeila; surrogate for the hatching eggs' larger parents.

Moving separately, circling back and forth behind the Candidates, the wingleader and weyrwoman ensured that the hatchlings found their partners, guiding human and dragon alike as they made their way to Impression.

Fiona cried with delight as Terin stood boldly in front of the queen egg, her eyes intent, her expression determined. The queen egg burst into shards under the pounding blows of the dragonet inside. The movements were so quick that it was hard to know who was more eager—queenling or headwoman—but in the instant the gold was free from her shell, she was thrusting her head toward Terin's outstretched arms and creeling in delight as the green-eyed girl became her one and only partner forever.

Fiona heard T'mar beside her make an indeterminate noise and elbowed him sharply just on principle. He dodged the worst of it, giving her a grin before turning toward Terin and shouting, "What's her name?"

"Her name is Kurinth!"

"It was over too soon," Fiona lamented as she recounted the details to Bekka and Lorana later.

"And Kindan didn't Impress?" Bekka asked, still shocked at the revelation.

"Kindan didn't Impress," Fiona said. She noticed that Lorana kept her expression carefully neutral.

"Well, at least we've got twenty-one more weyrlings," Bekka said. "And another queen." She rushed on, "And soon Talenth and Tolarth will rise again and there'll be more eggs on the Hatching Grounds."

"There will," Lorana agreed. Fiona flashed her a concerned look, for Lorana's tone was on the chilly side of neutral, but she decided not to make an issue of it.

"And you," Bekka said, turning back to the ex–queen rider, "will be having your baby at nearly the same time."

"So you're hoping Kindan will become a father and a dragonrider at the same time?" Lorana asked the youngster in surprise.

"It's been done before," Fiona told her, adding with a grin, "Besides, it's not as if he won't have plenty of help with either!"

Lorana allowed a smile to play across her lips but said nothing and, not long after, feigned fatigue to send her companions away.

"'Rest, eat, pee'—that's what my mother said pregnant mothers do," Bekka prattled on confidently as she and Fiona made their way back to the Kitchen Cavern. Bekka swiped a fresh roll from one of the bakers with an impudent grin before darting away to find Birentir and update the Weyr Healer with her reports.

Fiona lingered, looking for Shaneese or Mekiar, feeling a growing unease even as the sounds of the weyrlings drilling outside in the Weyr Bowl provided a comforting distraction to her cares. She found herself a seat near the hearth and looked wistfully toward those working there until one took pity on her and brought her a pitcher of juice—juice!—and fresh rolls.

At least in her time with Lorana and Bekka she'd managed to fill in some of the gaps of her knowledge of pregnancy and could now safely ascribe some of her current feelings to the changes going on in her body.

The catalog of strange pains and feelings was growing, and she found Lorana's half-gloating commiserations completely understandable, given the other's more advanced pregnancy. She made a note to herself once again, and forgot it just as quickly, to pin Bekka down and track down the meaning of the few raised eyebrows the young healer had made when Fiona had been describing her physical state. Clearly there was nothing that concerned her or Bekka would have immediately contacted Birentir—or probably her own midwife mother—but still . . . there was something that caused the younger girl to take note.

"Make sure you drink a lot," Bekka piped up suddenly, rushing on her way through to some new errand. "And, if you can, cut down on the *klah*."

She was gone before Fiona could question her and the distraction was enough to drive her other worries from her mind.

TWENTY-TWO

▼▼▼▼▼▼▼▼▼▼▼▼▼▼▼▼▼▼▼▼▼▼▼▼▼▼▼▼▼▼▼▼▼▼▼

Dragons soar,
Dragons thrive,
Dragons flame—
Keep Pern alive.

Telgar Weyr, morning, AL 508.6.28

The early-morning air was broken by the bellow of the watch dragon's challenge and a resounding reply, causing Fiona to startle to wakefulness.

Tullea? she wondered. What's she doing here?

Trying not to disturb the others, she crawled out of her bed and threw on a robe, sliding her feet into slippers before she rose as quietly as she could. But it was no use.

"Wait," Lorana called quietly from the bed, "I'll come with you."

"I was hoping to let you sleep," Fiona said.

"Tullea's come to see me," Lorana said. Fiona found her slippers and helped her into them.

"What does she want with you?"

"Maybe it's Ketan," Lorana said as they made their way past Talenth and down the queens' ledge to the Weyr below.

They were only halfway down the ledge when Tullea reached them. She was obviously in a hurry.

"Tullea, how may we help you?" Lorana asked.

"Let's get someplace warm, first," Fiona said, gesturing toward the Kitchen Cavern. "The cold of *between* must be in your bones, and it's still early for us."

Tullea snorted but allowed herself to be led away, even as she said, "I didn't come to see you, Weyrwoman. I came to see Lorana."

"What is it?" Lorana asked. "Ketan? Is he all right?"

"Him!" Tullea said. "He's crawled into a wineskin and never comes out. He still thinks it's the Hatching!"

They entered the Cavern and Fiona directed them toward a table close to the night fire while she helped the cook prepare a fresh pitcher of *klah* and some rolls still hot from the morning baking.

"Here, get some warm in you," Fiona said, recalling Neesa's peculiar turn of phrase as she pushed a mug to each of the seated women and poured the rich warm brew.

Tullea scarcely noticed her mug, wrapping her hands around it but not drinking. Lorana shot Fiona an imploring look and the Weyrwoman sat next to her, filling a mug for herself.

"So, Tullea, what can we do for you?" Lorana asked.

"Your Hatching went well enough, didn't it?" Fiona asked, trying to find the source of the Benden woman's visible distress.

"That's not it," Tullea said. She glanced at Lorana. "It's B'nik—you need to save him."

Fiona and Lorana exchanged a glance: They had seen too many riders knowingly go back in time to their deaths not to understand the Benden Weyrwoman's dread. T'mar himself had seen the Benden Weyrleader die. It was only a matter of time before, one day, B'nik would go back in time to save T'mar—and die himself.

"I don't see how, Tullea," Lorana said slowly when the Weyrwoman had explained her problem.

"I can't lose him," Tullea said. "I'll give you anything—I'll give you Minith—just find a way to save him!"

"You can't break time," Lorana reminded her. "If it's happened, then it will happen."

"If he dies, I'll take Minith *between* forever," Tullea swore. "I'll go with him, by the First Egg, I swear I will!"

"You weren't there," Fiona pointed out. "Just the Wing."

"I've already told them they're not to go with him," Tullea snapped. "If they won't go, then it can't happen, can it?"

"I'm sorry," Lorana said. "It did happen." She let out a deep sigh and closed her eyes against the pain. So many things had happened, so much pain.

"There has to be a way!" Tullea said, pleading.

"I'm the wrong person to ask," Lorana told her, opening her eyes once more and shaking her head. The Weyrwoman glanced up at her sharply and Lorana continued, "If I could have found a way, do you think I would have ever given up Arith?"

Tullea held her eyes for a long moment before lowering her head and shaking it slowly. "No. I suppose not." A moment later she looked up again. "But you have Kindan."

Lorana returned her gaze wordlessly.

"What can I give you?" Tullea begged. "I can't live without him."

Lorana shook her head sadly. "Nothing," she told the Weyrwoman. "I would do it willingly if I could, but no one can break time."

"So B'nik will die, and so will I, so will Minith," Tullea said. "And Caranth."

"I cannot help you," Lorana repeated. "I would if I could but no one has ever been able to alter time."

"There *must* be a way!"

"Let me check with Kindan," Lorana said, seeing the desperation in the other woman's eyes.

"If you need Minith, just send for her," Tullea told her. "She'll go with you, she already has."

Lorana nodded mutely, marveling that the other woman was too distraught to see how that could defeat her own suicidal threat.

Tullea rose then, looking back to Lorana as she added, "I never knew, never until I knew that I would lose him, how much I loved him."

"I understand."

"I don't know how you manage, half-alive without your dragon," Tullea said with pity. She frowned. "It's tearing Ketan apart, that's for certain."

"Ketan," Lorana repeated sadly. "I should see him."

"Last I saw him, he was drunk, head down on a table in a pool of his own spittle."

"We can go, right?" Fiona asked as she glanced down at Bekka. She had no problem deferring to the girl's expertise.

"The older midwives all agree that neither of you are in great danger," Bekka said, looking up to Fiona where she sat, perched on Talenth. "But don't stay *between* too long and be certain to bundle up—what might give you a cold could terminate a pregnancy."

"We'll be careful," Lorana promised as she started to climb up toward Fiona.

"And I'll make certain they do," Kindan said, as he helped her reach Fiona's outstretched hand and then followed her up Talenth's foreleg into a position behind the Weyrwoman. He'd been furious when he'd heard how Tullea had dismissed the older healer's troubled drinking and had insisted on accompanying Lorana and Fiona on their visit to Benden Weyr.

"And not too much *klah*, either of you!" Bekka called as she stepped back.

Talenth moved away from her, took a leap, and beat her way into the midday air.

"Look!" Fiona called, pointing down. "There's Xhinna!" The dark-haired girl waved at them, while her blue dragonet butted his head against her leg.

"Will she be all right?" Lorana asked, craning back to Kindan.

"She'll do fine," he promised. "She has a gift with young ones."

As soon as they reached the level of the Star Stones, Fiona gave her queen the image and they went *between*.

▼ ▼ ▼

"I'm sorry, I—" Ketan apologized in a slow, dead voice as he sat up at his desk, drinking from a mug of *klah* placed in his hand by Kindan, who had arrived at the healer's quarters before them. "I thought I could manage," he croaked, glancing furtively at Lorana before returning his eyes to the mug in his trembling hands. "I thought perhaps with enough drink, I could . . ."

Lorana shot Kindan a desperate look, but the harper could only shake his head; he had no suggestions.

"You've got to concentrate on what you have to live for," Fiona said softly.

"Live for?" Ketan barked a laugh. He waved a mug in her direction. "I've nothing to live for!" He raised his other hand and made a sweeping gesture. "Face it, Weyrwoman, *we've* nothing to live for."

"What do you mean?"

"The Weyrs are dying," Ketan said.

"But the Hatchings! There are weyrlings now—"

"Who'll not reach fighting age before burrows of Thread bury us all," Ketan cut across her sharply. He grimaced in apology for his harsh words. "You've patched them up—you know." He glanced at Lorana. "We patch them up, they fly, they die." He dropped his mug onto his desk with a loud thump and followed shortly with his head which he cradled in his hands. "Drith, my Drith! Why wouldn't you let me go with you?"

"He said that you had to stay, had to find a cure," Lorana reminded him softly.

"And now that we've found a cure, what?" Ketan barked, turning his head so that his eyes raked her. "What now? And how, if we only hatch twenty-two eggs, are we supposed to repopulate the Weyrs?" He shook his head and closed his eyes. "No, Weyrwoman, we tried and we came up with a cure." He let out a deep sigh and screwed his eyes tighter. "And the cure's killing Pern."

Fiona glanced at the other two who sat in stunned silence and jerked her head toward the exit. They followed slowly, with backward glances for the ailing healer.

"What do we do?" Lorana asked as soon as they were out of earshot.

"There's not much we can do," Fiona said. Kindan looked surprised. "My father said it happened after the Plague, that there were those who chose death over life no matter how hard those around them tried."

Kindan nodded grimly; he had seen it himself.

Fiona reached out to stroke Lorana's arm comfortingly, knowing that the older woman was distraught over the healer's collapse. "You have something to live for," she told her firmly, nodding toward her growing belly. "And you hear every dragon, that's not something Ketan has."

Lorana nodded. Fiona recognized that the ex–queen rider was merely humoring her. She was not convinced.

"I just wish there was something we could do for him," Lorana said.

"He wants his dragon back," Fiona said. "I don't see how you can do that."

Lorana said nothing.

"Come on, we need to get back before T'mar misses me."

"Lorana will think of something," Tullea predicted confidently as she and B'nik prepared to meet the other Weyrleaders and Weyrwoman in their Council Room later that afternoon.

B'nik grunted noncommittally. It had been over a month since T'mar had brought news of his impending doom and the Weyrleader had grown almost anxious to get to the end. He had said his good-byes, had set his affairs in order as best he could—he was lucky in that he had no less than seven bronze riders all capable of running the Weyr after his˙ death. Although, he admitted to himself, only a few would be his first choice, and he was worried about their ages.

S'liran was by far the most confident and poised, he brought order out of chaos in any situation—doubtless, B'nik ruefully admitted, the result of his superlative training by D'vin when he was a weyrling at High

Reaches Weyr. That S'liran's Kmuth was one of the first bronzes born with resistance to the dragon sickness—and the largest bronze he'd ever seen—only added to the young man's prowess.

W'ner, on the other hand, was an old rider. Experienced, yet prone to rely perhaps too much on others; he loved to hear the sound of his own voice. It was a pleasant voice and what he said with it usually made sense, if it often seemed to B'nik that he could have easily used fewer words to convey the same meaning.

In an odd way, it was somewhat refreshing to realize that the problems of who would lead the Weyr were soon going to be out of his hands. He found himself spending more time relaxing, more time enjoying each new dawn, more time bouncing children on his knee when he visited the Lower Caverns—even despite Tullea's pointed remarks about their parentage, parentage he didn't dispute much to her annoyance and his amusement.

In a way, B'nik mused, *what I'll miss most is how I've changed.* Knowing that he was going to die, B'nik no longer had a reason to put up with Tullea's antics or demands and Tullea had dropped them as soon as she'd accepted that he was going to die. Their relationship had grown steadily stronger, more intimate, restful.

If he had one regret, it was that he could not live long enough to see how their new relationship would unfold.

"B'nik?" Tullea said, impatient at his lack of a response. "Did you hear what I said?"

"So now we have two full Wings," T'mar remarked bitterly as he and Fiona ate quietly together in the Records Room. She'd sent Terin to relieve Bekka in her watch of Lorana. Fiona wondered if anyone guessed at the growing sense of unease the Weyrwoman had about the ex–queen rider. Bekka had assured her repeatedly that Lorana's pregnancy was advancing normally—the young healer was rather tart in her choice of words: "You worry too much!" Still, Fiona worried.

Bekka's hints that Fiona's worries were prompted by her own pregnancy were ones that she couldn't dismiss—that she was merely projecting her own fears onto the other woman was a distinct possibility.

"Two full wings with more to come," Fiona reminded him, catching and holding his eyes until the Weyrleader nodded, however glumly. "And we've more than a fortnight before the next Fall." She glanced over at the chalk tally board she kept of the Weyr's injuries, pointing to it as she added, "And we'll have another thirteen return to the fight in the next sevenday, so we'll have those to haul firestone and fly in reserve."

"We've seen worse," T'mar agreed. He glanced up again to catch Fiona's eyes as he admitted, "It's just that, lately, I've been feeling like something is going to happen."

"Something worse?" Fiona asked in a matching tone of dread.

T'mar nodded.

"That's why I've had someone with Lorana," Fiona said. "She hasn't been quite the same since we returned from Benden."

"Because of Tullea—"

"No," Fiona interrupted, "I think because of Ketan."

"The healer?"

"He lost his dragon not long after hers," Fiona said. "I think his collapse has caused her to question her own feelings."

"The pregnancy—"

"Oh, it could be the pregnancy," Fiona agreed quickly. "In fact, some of it must be." She pursed her lips. "But it seems like there's more, like she's all ready to give up hope."

"She's got Kindan—"

"Whose presence as Weyrlingmaster merely reminds her of the dangers we all face," Fiona cut him off.

"She's got you," T'mar tried again.

"And I've got a queen, and I've got you, and I've got Kindan," Fiona said. "Sometimes I think that she might not be so happy to have me."

T'mar eyed her thoughtfully for a moment before saying, "So you are worried, too?"

Fiona bit her lip. She knew what the Weyrleader meant—that she was not just worried about Lorana, but also worried about their situation: the losses, the slim numbers, the lack of hope.

"I'll never admit that," Fiona said after a moment, shaking her head firmly. She lowered her head for a moment, avoiding his eyes and then raised it again, her expression set. "I'm worried about Lorana."

T'mar suppressed a chuckle. It was clear that Fiona was sublimating all her other fears into this one.

"Well, I think she'll be fine," he told her cheerfully.

"You take care of yourself," Tullea told B'nik feelingly as the bronze rider sat astride Caranth as he prepared to lead three full Wings of fighting dragons—with two half-wings ready to haul firestone and provide reserves—into the first combined fight of Benden and High Reaches Weyrs eleven days later.

"We'll be fine," B'nik assured her with a grin, gesturing to include all the fighting dragons. "D'vin's a fine leader and his Weyr is the best-trained of us all."

"But you're fighting the rising sun!" Tullea wailed. Around them, dragons and riders were just becoming visible as dark night gave way to the predawn half-light.

"We'll do fine, don't worry."

"Oh?" Tullea demanded, her brows arched. "So I suppose I should tell Mikkala and Ketan to stand down, that you won't be needing their services?"

"Tullea!" B'nik's tone was one of exasperation mixed with understanding. He leaned down toward her to bring his face closer to hers. "We'll be all right."

"You'd better!"

B'nik smiled and waved at her before straightening up once more and turning to the dragons nearby, making the ancient signal to fly.

Caranth was up first, followed in rapid succession by the rest of his Wing, then S'liran's Wing, followed by L'moy's Wing and then by the two half-wings led by D'kel and J'han.

Tullea waited until the last of them blinked out, just visible in the gloom. She sighed, her shoulders slumped, before turning around to survey the injured riders, weyrlings, and weyrfolk left behind.

"What are you waiting for? Get to work!" Tullea bellowed and was glad to see them all scampering off.

"One thing, my lady," a voice spoke up in the darkness. Tullea turned and found herself looking at a small dark blob: Lin, the new queen rider.

"What?"

"If he's flying with the Weyr, he can't go back in time," Lin said.

"Of course," Mikkala called out quickly from her position at the aid station nearest the kitchen, "if he gets injured then he certainly can't go back in time."

"Why not?"

"Because there were no reports of his being injured," Ketan spoke up from the darkness. He snorted. "So I wonder if we should be hoping that he gets injured now?"

Tullea snorted in disgust at the notion. "What a thing to say!"

A little injury wouldn't stop him, she thought, wondering if she could survive seeing him scored or his Caranth horribly injured. She shook her head; no she couldn't.

"Lorana will think of something," she told herself. "She saved us all before."

"She didn't save her dragon," a voice grated in the darkness: Ketan.

B′nik swiveled in his seat to look left and right, surveying the formation of his Wing and the other two Wings arrayed on either side. They looked good.

He turned and peered behind him, trying to pick out the two half-wings trailing behind, ready to provide more firestone or enter the fight as reserves. If he committed one half-wing, they would release their extra firestone—they'd need the extra speed they'd get without the weight of the firestone. He couldn't make them out against the brilliance of the rising sun, especially with the added glare of the icy snow below them.

This Fall started in the Snowy Wastes and slanted down through the mountains above Benden and Bitra. Once below the snow, the high mountain peaks were mostly inaccessible to humans, except where special roads had been made to get at the hardy timber that grew there. Burrows were especially difficult to find in this area and B'nik suppressed a shudder at how well-established a burrow might get before it became apparent to a sweeprider. Few lived in those tree-covered mountain ranges, so there would be no ground crews—and a burrow would be just as deadly.

I hope D'vin gets here soon, B'nik thought, worried about getting their formations straightened with the brilliant glare of the sun in the same place as the falling Thread.

Caranth, have Doohanth take his Wing up high to scan for Thread, B'nik told his bronze. He scanned behind him and grunted in satisfaction as, a moment later, he dimly made out shapes moving upward in the air.

J'han's half-wing had just barely gained position when a bellow announced the arrival of the High Reaches dragons.

B'nik's elation was dashed with the cry of: *Thread!*

J'han's half-wing bellowed and bucked, diving away from the menace—as reserve forces, they had not yet chewed enough firestone to flame.

Rise up! B'nik ordered his riders even as he grimaced at the first wails of injured dragons. A sudden commotion from behind him startled him and he turned in time to catch one of the half-wings dumping its extra firestone even as its dragons were chewing their own firestone, ready to join the fray.

A sinking feeling came to B'nik as he belatedly realized that the Weyr now had only half the firestone it needed for the first part of the Fall.

Caranth suddenly veered right, falling.

Sorry, the bronze dragon apologized as he fought to regain his position. *It's the wind.*

B'nik's position on Caranth's neck was scarcely more protected, but he hadn't felt the gust that had thrown Caranth's left Wing high into the air. He twisted around, looking to the left and the right—as he expected, the gusts had unsettled his formations. Behind him, higher in the sky, the dragons of High Reaches had fared no better. Among them, in the glare of the sun, he spotted gouts of fire as they found Thread to destroy.

Ask D'vin if we should support them, B'nik said. No sooner had he made the offer than one of his wingseconds let out a bellow and he spotted a flurry of Thread coming their way.

In an instant everything was chaos, a constant blend of motion, of sight, of glaring sun and snow-capped mountains while' B'nik fought to keep himself and his dragon free of Thread, flaming into char all that could be found.

Order collapsed, and B'nik was too overwhelmed with his own immediate survival to reestablish it.

From the sounds above him, neither could D'vin.

Fiona was with Lorana when she gave her first tortured cry.

"What is it?" Fiona asked, rushing from her place beside Talenth toward the ex–queen rider. "Is it the baby?"

It was too early, far too early for the baby, Fiona thought desperately even as she had Talenth order Birentir and Bekka to their aid.

"No, it's the dragons!"

It took a moment for Fiona to grasp her meaning. "Benden?"

"The sun, the glare, the winds," Lorana gasped in response. She looked up and met Fiona's eyes. "They've lost ten already."

"We should go help."

"I'm not sure Tullea would—"

"I'll send Jeila to her, along with Birentir," Fiona said, sending the orders to Talenth. She glanced at Lorana, her lips pursed in thought. "You can't come, it wouldn't be good for the baby."

"We wouldn't be *between* that long."

"No, we wouldn't," Fiona agreed. "But I don't want you to have the added stress of tending the injured while also growing a baby." She smiled wryly, adding, "Besides, you'd be too tired."

Lorana sighed in agreement.

"What happened?" T'mar demanded as he rushed into the room, flanked by Bekka and Birentir.

"Benden," Fiona responded tersely. "I'm going to send Birentir and Jeila to help."

"Should we send someone to High Reaches as well?" Jeila asked, glancing toward Fiona.

Fiona hesitated.

"Go on, if you want to help," Lorana told her.

T'mar, sensing her distress, added, "I'll stay here."

"I'll leave Bekka," Fiona said, turning quickly to her closets and quickly flinging on riding clothes. She paused long enough to be certain that Jeila was getting her Tolarth ready, before shouting to Talenth, who was already waiting below the ledge.

In a moment, queen and rider were airborne and then, gone *between*.

"What are you doing here, Weyrwoman?" Sonia asked in startlement as she recognized Telgar's senior queen rider. For a moment, suspecting the worst, Sonia paled, but Fiona's words revived her, "I'm here to help, Weyrwoman. You've got injuries."

"Not many," Sonia said, gesturing to the two dragons being tended in the distance. "We've more lost than hurt."

Fiona glanced around and nodded in surprise.

"Lorana says that the wind and the morning sun have made it worse," Fiona said even as another dragon bellowed in the sky above the Weyr and descended swiftly to the Weyr Bowl. Fiona started, instinctively, toward the dragonpair.

She nodded quickly at the attendants who rushed to aid the scored dragon and rider, hovering just far enough from them to avoid interfering while close enough to be able to examine the wounds.

"If you stay too close, you'll get them all worried," Sonia's voice startled her as the Weyrwoman spoke at her side. Fiona turned to see that the older woman with her startling white forelock was watching her with no small amount of amusement.

"They know what they're doing," Fiona said, loud enough for the weyrfolk to hear her. "I just like being close to hand if there's anything I can do to help."

"I understand," Sonia said. "It's a different way from my own; I tend to wait until someone asks."

"Your father was a healer, wasn't he?" Fiona said, recalling a chance comment from C'tov months back.

Sonia nodded.

"I'm still learning," Fiona said. "Sometimes I can help, sometimes I can learn something new."

"I see." Sonia noticed the way Fiona started to raise her hands, the way the younger woman tensed to speak or move forward, and the way she restrained herself. "It's hard not to help."

"It's not that," Fiona said even as she clenched her fists once more to restrain her impulse to dart forward, "it's not knowing when it's help or hindrance."

"You are young, you worry too much."

Fiona turned to meet her eyes. "In these times, can anyone worry *too* much?"

"The Weyrwoman sets the mood of the Weyr," Sonia said in answer.

"Yes, I know." Fiona frowned. "There's a fine line between trying anything and trying nothing. They can both be signs of despair."

Sonia's eyes narrowed as she examined the girl in front of her. "You won't give in to despair."

"Ever," Fiona agreed. "I grew up with the example of Kindan."

"What about Lorana, then?" Sonia asked, careful to keep her tone casual.

"I think she's still learning from Kindan," Fiona said after a moment. "I understand that the Plague was very hard for her."

Sonia nodded.

"And with Tullea's demands on top of her feeling all the dragons, it's a wonder she's managed to keep her baby," Fiona added in a rush.

"Tullea's demands?"

"She wants Lorana to find a way to save B'nik," Fiona said, quickly re-counting Tullea's conversation with Lorana before adding, "And on top of that, there's Tenniz's 'gift.'"

Sonia gave her a questioning look.

"Tenniz is one of the desert traders I met when I was at Igen," Fiona said. "When I arrived at Telgar, he had left gifts."

"He did?"

Fiona nodded. "Well, actually, Mother Karina left the gifts; Tenniz left his words. He was one of the traders who could sometimes see into the future. He knew that I would come to Telgar." She frowned as she added, "And he left a gift for Terin, a gold fitting for a riding harness with the words: *This is yours and no other's.*"

"She's the one who Impressed Tolarth's queen?" Sonia asked. Fiona nodded. "So what did he leave Lorana?"

"It looked like a brooch but, if so, it was unfinished," Fiona said, describing the gold staff with twined serpents that marked the symbol of a healer. She mentioned the odd small holes on either side.

"And what did his note say to her?"

"'The way forward is dark and long. A dragon gold is only the first price you'll pay for Pern.'"

Sonia glanced away, staring at nothing as she mulled over those words.

"And what did he say to you?" Sonia asked as she looked back at the Weyrwoman once more after she finished her musings.

"My note was from Mother Karina," Fiona said. "Tenniz had her tell me that 'it will all turn out right.'"

"That seems to leave a great burden on you!"

"Pardon?"

"Well, doesn't that make it your responsibility to determine what 'all turn out right' actually means?"

Fiona gave her a confused look.

"Would it be all right for you if Lorana's price was her life?" Sonia asked by way of example.

"No," Fiona said. "I would sooner lose Talenth than her."

From up on the watch heights, Talenth bellowed in agreement.

"She saved Pern," Fiona said, gesturing up toward Talenth, "she saved my dragon."

"Sometimes, as Tenniz seems to know, the price of a job well done is the payment of a higher price," Sonia told her softly.

"Then she won't pay the price alone," Fiona declared, her eyes flashing angrily.

"I wish I could agree with you," Sonia said. "But whatever pain you're willing to suffer for her will only add to her pain, not replace it."

"She's been through too much already!" Fiona said, the pain in her voice wrenching at Sonia's heart. "It's time for someone else to take over."

Another dragon burst into the sky above them, creeling with pain, her left wing hanging limply as she plunged through the sky.

Silently, Sonia's Lyrinth rose from the Weyr Bowl as Fiona's Talenth dove from her position on the watch heights, working together to position themselves under the falling green, catching her and lowering her gently to the ground.

"I think they need us now," Fiona said, as she started racing toward the injured green.

Sonia was an instant behind her, shocked at how well her Lyrinth had worked with the younger Talenth. She eyed the back of the blond Weyrwoman thoughtfully as she raced to catch up.

Hours later, covered in ichor, exhausted, cold from the afternoon winds that had picked up, Sonia turned from the younger Weyrwoman in time to be wrapped warmly in D'vin's arms.

"Her," Sonia said, as she struggled to breathe in the bronze rider's tight embrace, "her too."

D'vin raised an eyebrow in surprise but reached out and dragged Fiona into his embrace. He was surprised to see Sonia wrap an arm around the other woman, surprised to see Fiona return the embrace, and surprised by how tightly the younger Weyrwoman squeezed him back. Most of all, he was surprised by one thought: Sonia doesn't share. Apparently, that had changed.

▼ ▼ ▼

"You are going to stay here the night, they'll manage without you," Sonia said as she eyed a nightgown thoughtfully and threw it toward the younger Weyrwoman. It would be big but it would do, she decided. "Put that on."

"But—"

"The correct answer is: 'Yes, Weyrwoman,'" D'vin called out drolly. "In fact, the only answer is—"

"Yes, Weyrwoman," Fiona dutifully finished, chuckling. She'd drunk too much wine, she could feel her cheeks heating and tingling with the effects as she added superfluously, "That's the answer at my Weyr, too."

"So you've got them well-trained," Sonia said. She canted her head appraisingly as Fiona slipped on her nightgown. "As I thought: big but not too big." She gestured toward the sleeping quarters beyond. "D'vin's not the warmest man but between the three of us, we'll keep you from getting too cold, even in that."

Fiona's thoughts of further protests were eliminated by a yawn.

Stay there! Lorana's voice told her adamantly.

You should be sleeping, Fiona said, secretly glad to have the contact with the ex–queen rider.

"What was that?" Sonia demanded of her suddenly.

"What?" Fiona asked, startled by the words spoken out loud.

"You weren't talking with your dragon," Sonia said, eyeing her thoughtfully.

"Lorana," Fiona confessed. Her cheeks flushed hotter: She wanted to keep that a secret.

"You can *talk* to her?"

Fiona nodded mutely, going pale.

Sonia eyed her for a long moment before asking, "And what did she say?"

"'Stay there,'" Fiona repeated. She gave Sonia a beseeching look. "I don't want anyone else to know."

"Why?"

Fiona shook her head, unable to come up with a quick answer. "It's special. We don't know if it will last—"

"How long have you had it?"

"Since the mating flight," Fiona said. "She and Kindan—well, Kindan and she—I don't know, they were with Zirenth when he rose."

"And T'mar?"

"Still unconscious," Fiona said, adding, "If Lorana hadn't held Zirenth when T'mar was injured, he would have gone *between*."

"And so you and Lorana . . . ?"

Fiona shook her head, blushing furiously again. "Kindan," she said in a small voice.

"Whom you've always wanted," Sonia said.

"Yes," Fiona agreed in a whisper, eyes lowered in shame. She raised them again to meet Sonia's. "But I want Lorana, too. Like a sister, only more." She paused, groping for words and then shook her head when she couldn't find them, saying desperately, "I never realized that love is so different."

Sonia quirked an eyebrow upward in question.

"I love Kindan," Fiona said slowly, trying to make her meaning clear, "and I always will. I want children with him." She paused. "But I want to help Lorana *raise* her children."

Fiona hadn't heard D'vin's quiet footsteps approaching behind her so she started when he spoke up softly, "If she's cut, you bleed?"

"Yes," she said. "But not like with Kindan or T'mar."

"A heart grows when you love," D'vin said, carefully keeping his eyes on Fiona. "The more you love, the more you can love."

"As a Holder, I was expected to marry," Fiona said. She shook her head slowly. "I was expected to have only one man."

"A queen rider doesn't have that choice," Sonia said.

"Her queen chooses in the mating flight," Fiona said in partial agreement. "But she chooses all other times."

"A good Weyrwoman—"

"—has the Weyr's best interests at heart," Fiona cut in, smiling at the older woman. "I know that."

Sonia gave her a wicked look, as she said, "But a Weyrwoman doesn't have to be good all the time!"

Fiona's face took on a sober look. "I'm only beginning to understand love," she said slowly. "I'm beginning to see that there are many types." She turned to face D'vin. "There are two men in my life right now, Weyrleader."

D'vin nodded, understanding the unsaid part of her words. He smiled, gesturing toward Sonia. "I'm glad because there's only *one* woman in my life!"

"And that woman is cold and wants to get warm," Sonia declared, grabbing Fiona's hand and tugging her along. "So let's stop chattering out here and get under the blankets!"

In the middle of the night, Fiona woke, startled by the breathing of the two people next to her.

Lorana! she called out drowsily.

I'm here, the woman's thoughts came back to her quickly, unperturbed. *Kindan's with me.*

Good, Fiona thought with relief. She added a quick mental caress, an apology for disturbing the other woman and received a comforting thought in return: a feeling that Lorana appreciated the contact, the warmth of the mental touch. Satisfied and relieved, Fiona rolled over into a dreamless sleep.

Even so, when she woke the next morning, she was still sore and tired, more tired than she had felt for a long while. She was also eager to get back to her Weyr.

Sonia sensed this and let her go after they'd finished seeing to the worst of the injured.

"Remember: 'Five coughs *between,* keeps the figure lean,'" Sonia told her warningly as Fiona sat astride Talenth and prepared to leave.

"At Telgar, they say 'seven,'" Fiona said. "But I'll be careful."

"So you want the baby?" Sonia asked, not able to keep the surprise out of her voice.

"Of course!"

"Who is the father, then?"

Fiona smiled and shook her head. "Does it matter?"

"Perhaps to the father."

"Well, there's a choice of two, and even if I knew for certain, I wouldn't tell them," Fiona said. She caught Sonia's look and explained, "My child is going to have two fathers, two mothers, and a whole Weyr for parents." She paused and added, "As will Lorana's."

Sonia cocked her head sideways at the younger woman thoughtfully. "Well, whatever you wish." She stood back from Talenth and gestured in the time-honored signal. "Fly safe!"

Fiona was greeted with glee by T'mar and Birentir when she returned to the Weyr. After the Weyrleader let her out of his embrace, he invited her to join him and the wingleaders in the Council Room.

"*My* Council Room?" Fiona teased, as the Council Room was off the senior Weyrwoman's quarters.

"I hope you don't mind," T'mar said. Fiona waved his apology away, grinning and shaking her head. Her mood evaporated when she entered the Council Room and saw the expressions of the other wingleaders.

"How bad was it?" H'nez asked the question that was on all their lips.

"The injuries were the worst," Fiona said, "the losses, less so." She grimaced. "I don't know if it will help that they've only three days before they ride again."

"Probably," T'mar said. "D'vin will work them hard, as he must, and that will distract them."

"So where are we now?" H'nez asked, frowning. He glanced down at a tally slate set between the riders on the table.

Fiona glanced at it, spoke with Talenth, and reached for the tablet, quickly wiping away old numbers and replacing them with the current strengths of all the Weyrs.

"It's better than you think," she said as she put the slates before them once more. "High Reaches has eighty-nine, Ista has ninety, Benden has one hundred and eight, Fort has ninety-six."

"So against the two Falls, the one over Benden Weyr will have over two full Flights, as will the Fall at Keroon," T'mar said. The other wing-leaders around the table relaxed visibly.

"What about burrows?" H'nez asked. "That Fall over Upper Bitra was all in mountains."

"I've volunteered to help with the sweeps," T'mar said. "We'll bring in ground crews where needed."

"Makes sense," C'tov said. "We need training, we don't have a Fall for another six days—"

"Five," H'nez corrected.

"—five days," C'tov said with a nod toward the older rider, "so we can help and train at the same time."

T'mar nodded. "How soon can you be ready?"

"Give us a quarter of an hour," C'tov said, rising from his seat, "and we'll be over Bitra's mountains."

"Talenth and Tolarth will come, too," Fiona said, sending a silent order to the two queens. The other riders looked at her in surprise, so she explained, "Well, you can't expect Terin's Kurinth to fly with us, can you? She's a little young yet!"

F'jian nodded emphatically even as he looked a little wistful. Fiona laughed at his expression. "Just give them time, F'jian, give them time!"

The remaining bronze riders joined in with her until the youngest bronze rider raised his hands in surrender and rose from his chair with all the dignity he could still muster.

T'mar caught up with her after the others had filed out. "That was a good idea, to have the queens along."

Fiona nodded. "And we need the exercise," she said in agreement, spearing him with a look as she added, "I don't want to get *fat* after all!"

T'mar grimaced as the barb struck home but a moment later his expression changed. "You will be careful, won't you?"

"As will Jeila," Fiona said. "We're not going that far and we're not going to time it, so we'll only get three coughs *between*."

T'mar's eyes took on a troubled look as he digested her words but he, wisely, merely nodded in agreement.

"We're both early enough, as far as the Records indicate, that even a longer jump poses no threat," Fiona assured him. "It's the end of the first trimester and the beginning of the third that are the most susceptible." She paused for a long moment, then added sweetly, "And, by the way, how did you know I was pregnant?"

T'mar blushed bright red, unable to speak.

"Really, it's too early to tell," Fiona said when she decided that she'd had enough enjoyment at his expense. "And Bekka says that nothing's really certain until about the twelfth week." She gave him a challenging look, quirking her eyes upward questioningly.

"I was hoping," T'mar said.

Fiona burst into a bright grin. "Good! Don't forget that when it comes time for diapers."

Telgar's Weyrleader snorted in amusement, his eyes dancing.

Fiona and Jeila were very careful going *between*, even going so far as to obey H'nez's admonition to wait until the fighting dragons had arrived over Upper Bitra and could give them a sense of the winds before setting out.

The cold of *between* seemed harsher and longer to Fiona, even as bundled up as she was in the extra wher-hide vest that Bekka had insisted upon for both the weyrwomen.

Immediately upon their arrival in the air over the Bitran mountains, Fiona regretted her submission to the young healer's demands: The vest made her very warm, almost hot, and Fiona loosened her wher-hide jacket to let some of the cold Bitran air cool her off but decided not to, for fear of losing the flamethrower strapped on her back.

She and Jeila took positions close to the mountains, veering left and right to scan into tree-lined valleys, looking for any sign of burrowed Thread.

They had been looking for scarcely an hour when Jeila paused and Tolarth whirled in the air, making a tight circle over one spot. Fiona and Talenth circled around long enough to get a look at the drooping trees, the dark center, and confirmed the burrow.

We'll land there, Fiona said, giving Talenth an image close to the burrow.

As the queen started a slow, almost lazy, swirl to descend to the location, T'mar's Zirenth burst above them bellowing loudly.

What are you doing? Zirenth demanded.

Going for the burrow, Talenth responded reasonably.

You're a queen! the bronze declared, and that was an end to the discussion.

Fiona glowered as the bronze rider and two blues made their way to the ground. She watched as they flamed the burrow into crisp char.

Tell T'mar to send in a ground crew, Fiona said acerbically to her dragon, *we've only one Weyrleader.*

To her surprise, the bronze rider looked up and waved agreement, turning back to his bronze and soon he and Zirenth were aloft and then *between,* gone, doubtless, to Bitra Hold for a suitable ground crew.

They seemed to take forever to get back; she and Jeila had spotted three more burrows and H'nez had dispatched the smaller greens and blues to flame the worst of the infestations, but it was clear that only flamethrowers working directly on the ground would completely eradicate the tougher of the burrows.

When T'mar returned, Fiona could tell just by the way Zirenth flew that the Weyrleader was furious.

T'mar says you and Jeila may fight on the ground, Zirenth relayed in a resigned tone.

Why?

He says that if we wait on Bitra, all Pern will be Threaded, Zirenth responded.

Fiona grunted in response. She'd heard about Bitra when she'd been at Benden; this merely confirmed her worst impressions of the Hold and its Lord Holder. She instructed Jeila to take the first burrow, aided by two blues, while she and Talenth descended toward the third burrow with a green and a blue at her side.

What would it be like, she mused, to have greens and blues as escorts for the queens' Wing all the time? Queens' Wings, perhaps? She had never read of such things in the Records, but Igen's deserts were so dry and barren that they never had many burrows. The lush plains of Telgar presented a different possibility.

The work was hot and straining. After her third burrow, Fiona relegated most of the work to the sturdy riders, taking time to divest herself of her wher-hide vest and, later, even of her wher-hide jacket as she labored to support those fighting the burrows.

It was late morning before they had finished. Eleven burrows had been destroyed. Even so, still wary, T'mar left a dozen dragons behind to ride another final sweep.

"You idiot!" Bekka roared as she caught sight of Fiona when the queen landed back at the Weyr Bowl later that day. Bekka squatted and retrieved the vest and jacket that had fallen as Fiona had started to scramble down Talenth's side.

"What?" Fiona asked, surprised at how sore she felt. Her head felt odd, too.

Bekka ignored her question, pulling on the sleeve of her tunic to drag Fiona down to her height and placing a hand on her forehead quickly.

"Into bed, right now!" Bekka growled, sending the Weyrwoman off to her quarters.

"But Lorana—" Fiona's protest was cut short.

"Right, tell her she'll need to move," Bekka said quickly. "You get into the bath, make it as hot as you can take it, and don't come out until I get you."

"I've got to use the necessary!" Fiona complained.

"Then the bath, and hot!" Bekka said. Fiona looked at her mulishly. "Do you want to lose the baby?"

Fiona was shocked.

"You've got a chill, now get into a bath while I sort things out," Bekka said, turning to head toward Jeila, ready to perform the same treatment.

Fortunately the other queen rider had remembered to put on her vest and jacket before returning *between* from the Bitran mountains.

Fiona managed to make it to her quarters without any more fuss even as she realized how her head ached.

"Idiot!" she said to herself as she made her way into her rooms.

"What?" Lorana asked sleepily from the bed where she'd been napping. She glanced more closely at Fiona and sat up. "What is it?"

"I was an idiot and I forgot to put my vest and jacket on when I came back here *between*," Fiona said. She started toward the bathroom. "Bekka says I'm to have a hot bath while she figures where to put you."

"Nonsense," Lorana said peremptorily. "Come here."

Fiona grimaced but approached the bed. Lorana lifted a hand to her head, repeated Bekka's examination and frowned. "Well, you've got a fever, there's no doubt," Lorana said, her lips pursed tightly. She thought for a moment, then slid farther to the back of the bed. "Get out of your gown and get in here with me."

"But Bekka—"

"Bekka's not the only one healer trained," Lorana said. "Get Talenth to have Shaneese send us some chicken broth and in the meantime, you get in here."

Fiona was tired and not at all disposed to argue. In a short while she was cuddled in tight against Lorana, who had thrown on extra blankets. Not long after, she was fast asleep.

She awoke much later, in a muck sweat.

"Fiona!" Lorana called urgently. "Fiona, wake up!"

"Mmm," Fiona murmured, thrashing about in search of a place in the sheets that wasn't soaked with her sweat.

"You were dreaming, it's all right, you're all right now," Lorana told her soothingly. Fiona felt her hand stroking her head. She made a pleasant sound, and turned her head closer to the comforting fingers. Slowly she drifted off again, even as she recalled the horrors of her dream: *Can't lose the baby! Can't lose the baby! Can't lose the baby!*

TWENTY-THREE

Cold between
Freezes harm.
Wear jacket,
Keep warm.

Telgar Weyr, early evening, AL 508.7.17

"Your fever's broke, you're lucky," a voice told her softly as Fiona opened her eyes. The glows that lit the room seemed overly bright and she closed her eyes again.

"The baby?"

"Fine as far as we can tell," the voice replied. Terin; it was Terin's voice.

"Lorana's?" Fiona asked, her stomach knotting in some unreasonable dread.

"Fine, that we know for sure," Terin told her. "She's in the bath now, you'll see her soon."

"They didn't move her?" .

"She wouldn't move," Terin said, adding with a snort, "You can open · your eyes, you know. You haven't got the Plague, just the sort of fever you pick up when you're overdoing things and go *between* while wet with sweat."

"Igen's a dry heat," Fiona said in response to the editorial undertone in the other girl's voice.

"Still, you should have known," Terin said. Fiona heard her friend stretch and felt her hand touch her forehead in a soft, gentle caress. "You've got the whole Weyr on edge."

Fiona groaned, and rolled over, raising herself on one arm and making to sit up.

"No you don't, lie back down!" Terin ordered. "Lorana's still in the bath and I want her to take her time."

Fiona made a face as she ruefully absorbed her friend's words.

"I stink," Fiona said sourly.

"You've been in bed for four days, of course you do," Terin said. "You can have a bath when Lorana's all done and ready."

"She should be sleeping."

"Not the least because it's nighttime," Terin said in agreement.

"Four days?" Fiona repeated, her mind picking the number over. "Threadfall tomorrow."

"That's right," Terin agreed. "K'lior's been here, and Seban was here whenever Bekka was; they've all looked in on you." She paused, adding, "I even have a note from Weyrwoman Sonia."

"Sonia?" Fiona asked. "What did she say?"

"One word," Terin said, her voice sounding chipper.

"'Idiot,'" Fiona said, beating the other girl to the punch.

"How'd you know?"

Fiona snorted, glad to be right. "It's what I would have said to her under the same circumstances."

"And you'd be right, too."

"We all make mistakes," Lorana spoke up from the entrance to the bathroom.

"Some more than others," Fiona amended glumly.

"Well, after T'mar's head, your fever is nothing, really," Terin told her. She stood up briskly, giving Fiona a quick smile before she turned toward the exit into Talenth's weyr. "And now, if you'll excuse me, I've a dragon of my own to tend."

"Oh, I doubt if you're tending it all on your own," Fiona teased and was delighted at the expression on Terin's face. "I'm sure that even at this moment there's either a gaggle of goggle-eyed weyrkids tending her every need or at least one *very* attentive bronze rider at her beck and call."

"Both, actually," Terin agreed with a grin. With a final wave, she strode off, out of sight.

"F'jian's keeping an eye on the weyrlings," Kindan explained as he escorted Fiona and Lorana back to the queen's weyr that evening after dinner.

Fiona had insisted that as she was "fully recovered," she was more than able to sit at the high table and mingle with her Weyr.

She was glad she had. The relief visible on the faces of some of the weyrwomen was more than ample vindication of her decision.

"You rest up, now, Weyrwoman!" one of the most sour of them had called as Fiona departed. She was joined by a chorus of agreeing voices, the most heartening of which was one who said: "We don't want anything to happen to our Weyrwoman!"

Our Weyrwoman. The phrase resonated in Fiona's mind and cheered her. It had not been all that long since the old Telgar weyrfolk had looked on her with stern faces. Now she was theirs—and they worried about her. It wasn't just that this was her Weyr, now they were her weyrfolk, too. The realization brought a smile to her lips.

Still, she had to admit that the walk to the Dining Cavern and back was as much exercise as she was good for that evening.

She suspected that her visible fragility was the strongest reason that she and Lorana had for Kindan's comforting presence. Idly she thought of suggesting that she spend time with T'mar, but she dismissed the thought almost as soon as she had it—she didn't doubt that Shaneese was with T'mar on this evening before Threadfall. Fiona grinned as she mused that T'mar was probably so tense that Shaneese was there more for her skills as masseuse than as lover.

Lorana was in a mothering mood, demanding that Fiona get in the bed first, then herself, then Kindan.

"I suppose we could fit four," Fiona mused as they found themselves close, but not without room of their own under the blankets.

"Children are smaller," Lorana said. "We could fit five."

"Should I take up with the woodsmith about a new bed?" Kindan asked as he turned the last of the glows and the room went dark.

"Perhaps," Fiona said. "I'm sure if he made a bed and we didn't need it, someone would find a place for it."

"Xhinna's brood would doubtless love to romp on it, at the very least," Kindan said in agreement.

Something about his tone alerted Fiona. "And who is handling her brood now that she's Impressed?"

"She is, for the most part," Kindan said, his tone going grave.

"I can talk with Shaneese," Fiona said.

"No," Kindan said. "I think we should see how this works out."

Fiona's agitation prompted him to explain, "If we are to have more women riders, we're going to have issues like this." He paused consideringly. "Xhinna and Taria have been handling it well, so far."

"But what about when they start flying?" Fiona asked.

"That's two or more Turns in the future and the children of her brood will all be that much older," Kindan said.

Fiona made a note to herself to spend more time with the weyrlings. She admitted that the reason she hadn't done so earlier was partly that she didn't want to monopolize Kindan's time and partly that she didn't want to become embroiled in any issues regarding the women riders; she'd heard enough mutterings from H'nez.

Perhaps, though, she had put her worries in front of her duties as a Weyrwoman.

"How are they working out?"

"Well, actually," Kindan said, sounding pleased, "there are only four girls, Xhinna with her blue, the rest with greens."

"I wonder if that will change, in future Hatchings," Lorana mused.

"It takes a particular sort of woman to be a blue rider," Kindan said.

"It takes a particular sort of *person* to be a blue rider," Fiona corrected drowsily. "I can understand greens far more easily."

Kindan made no reply and slowly Fiona drifted off to sleep with Lorana's warm presence beside her and the distant susurrations of Kindan's breathing to comfort her.

"N o, no, no! Cold! Cold!" Fiona awoke, startled, to find Lorana thrashing beside her, her words quick and frantic.

"Lorana, wake up!" Fiona said, reaching to push the older woman on the shoulder.

"What is it?" Kindan asked. "What's up with her?"

"Cold, no cold!" Lorana wailed.

"Lorana, wake up!" Fiona persisted.

"Lorana, shush now, it's all right," Kindan added soothingly.

With a start, Lorana woke up, her breath coming in gasps. Fiona could smell her fear and feel the heat coming off of her.

"You had a nightmare," Fiona told her quietly. "It's all right."

"Not a nightmare," Lorana said, shuddering. "A memory."

"Do you want to talk about it?" Kindan asked in a gentle tone that sounded well-practiced to Fiona's ears. She closed her own eyes in thought and remembered—it was the tone he'd used to talk to those with nightmares from the Plague.

"You're both so cold," Lorana said, shivering. She twitched as Fiona laid a hand on her forehead.

"No, you're very hot," the Weyrwoman said. "Kindan, feel her head."

Kindan's hand was little warmer than Fiona's and Lorana gasped once more.

"So we felt cold," Kindan said as he removed his hand. "Was that it?"

"Yes," Lorana said quietly.

"You were in bed with two others who were cold?" Fiona guessed.

"My brother and sister."

"I'm *not* going to die on you," Fiona assured her fervently.

"Sometimes," Lorana said in a pained voice, "you remind me exactly of my sister."

"And she said the same thing," Fiona guessed.

"Yes."

"I'm still here, my heart's still beating," Fiona said, moving closer to Lorana, grabbing a resisting hand in her own and dragging it to her heart. "See? Feel it?"

"No one can predict the future," Lorana said in protest, pulling her hand free.

"Not unless you go there and look," Fiona agreed. "But, by the First Egg, I'll never abandon you: as long as I draw breath, I'll be there for you."

"That's all anyone can ask." Lorana took a deep, calming breath.

"Well, that and some more blankets," Fiona said. "Kindan, could you pull the spare ones up?"

The harper complied and moments later, Lorana felt Fiona turn on her side, the length of her warm back closest to her. Kindan reciprocated not long after and Lorana found the heat she'd been missing in her nightmare.

"Everything's ready here," Fiona assured T'mar as she steadied him on his climb up to his perch on Zirenth. "Just make sure we don't need it, okay?"

T'mar swung his right leg over Zirenth's neck and adjusted his seat, tying himself to the riding straps and checking, once more, the straps that held the sacks of firestone on the harness close to hand.

"We'll try, Weyrwoman."

"You come back in one piece, with no nicks or cuts," Shaneese told him fiercely from where she stood next behind Fiona.

"Of course, headwoman," T'mar agreed, a broad grin on his face. "I wouldn't dare disappoint either of you!"

"Just as long as that's understood," Fiona said, moving back to grab Shaneese by the hand. Her own mood slipped and she strained upward, using her hold on the headwoman to aid her as she added, "Fly safe."

T'mar nodded, his grin slipping into a steady look. He took a deep breath, then turned to the rest of his Wing and gave the arm-pumping gesture for them to fly.

Fiona guided Shaneese back as the downdraft from Zirenth's great wings blew up dirt and pebbles, while behind them more circles of dust rose in the early afternoon air under the other dragons of his Wing.

The Wing itself was half the size of a normal, full-strength Wing, as were the other three Wings that rose with it. Telgar Weyr could count only seventy-three fighting dragons as its strength now.

Fortunately, they would be joined by the eighty-nine dragons of High Reaches Weyr, forming almost two full Flights of dragons. Almost.

Less, really, when the reserve Wing of thirteen dragons was counted. Those thirteen, under C'tov's leadership, still waited on the ground, ready to fly to aid or to replenish those low on firestone.

Still, Fiona thought with relief, it was much better than the notion of flying with only three short Wings.

She glanced around at the first-aid stations being set up without any real concerns; time and practice had drilled the weyrfolk to a fine pitch. Her eyes narrowed as she caught sight of Lorana arranging bandages near the Hatching Grounds and, suppressing an irritated growl, Fiona sprinted over toward her.

"Don't say anything!" Lorana said, a hand raised to forestall Fiona's incipient scolding. "I'm going to sit down as soon as this is arranged and I won't get up again until I'm needed."

"You should be getting your rest."

"No," Lorana retorted, her lips curving upward in a slight smile, "you should be getting *your* rest."

"She's right," Shaneese chimed in, having caught up with her peripatetic Weyrwoman. She shook her head at the Weyrwoman in exasperation as she added, "If anyone should be resting, it's you."

Fiona glanced back and forth between the two women, caught sight of Bekka and Terin bearing down out of the corner of her eyes, and surrendered sweetly, saying, "How about if I just sit here?"

Lorana examined her carefully, suspicious at her sudden acceptance. "Well . . ."

"Don't!" Bekka's voice cut across hers even as the youngster raced up and halted, nearly breathless, to stand bent over with her hands resting on her knees in front of the table. "Don't let her get away with anything!"

"I was just—" Fiona began in protest.

Terin caught up with Bekka, her face split in a big grin: She'd heard the whole exchange. She glanced at the young healer, saying facetiously, "So, you've heard about our Weyrwoman, have you?"

Bekka ignored her, catching her breath enough to push herself upright once more and tell Fiona, "You get to bed and rest."

"The Weyrwoman—"

"—has more than enough help and will show that she can follow orders," Lorana cut across Fiona's protests. Fiona glared at her, but the older woman was unrelenting. "Didn't you mention something about setting an example?"

"But—" Fiona spluttered.

"Rest," Bekka ordered, jerking a thumb toward Fiona's quarters. She glanced up. "It's too hot to argue out here and we'll need our strength for later."

"Come on, Fiona, I'll get you settled in," Terin told her kindly. "You've been going nonstop since you woke up this morning, don't think we haven't noticed."

"Do you really *want* to be in bed with that fever for another four days?" Bekka asked menacingly, her arms on her hips.

"Sometimes," Fiona said phlegmatically as she allowed Terin to escort her away, "I think it was a mistake to let Bekka come back here."

"Only sometimes," Terin said, smiling. "But that's just a sign that you're still feverish, you know."

Fretfully, Fiona allowed herself to be settled in to her quarters, but she stoutly refused to get into her bed.

"I'll sit here with Talenth," she said with a pout. "You can bring me some blankets."

"I'll bring you a chair," Terin said. "You can't get comfortable on all that stone and dirt, not if you're going to sleep by yourself."

"I can't sleep by myself," Fiona said. "I can never sleep by myself."

Despite her words, propped up in a comfortable chair with cushions cheerfully plumped up by Terin, Fiona found herself dozing as the heat of the midday sun warmed the Weyr and the susurrus of Talenth's steady breathing seemed to lull her into a daze.

She reached out with her mind, hazily, toward Lorana and felt a comforting, humorous response; not quite a rebuff but a gentle pushing away, kind and amused. She heard Kindan's voice in the distance and opened her eyes long enough to pick him out of the group of weyrlings busily bagging more firestone and stacking it in readiness for the reserve Wing.

Soon, she thought. The Wings would meet Thread, be joined by the High Reaches riders, and the battle would commence.

It was odd, she mused; once before High Reaches had come to Telgar's aid. Only then—and a chill ran through her—there were no Telgar dragons to fly with. Her eyes snapped open in fright at the thought and she reached out desperately for T'mar, for Zirenth—she couldn't find them!

They're fine! Lorana's voice came to her quickly, soothingly. *They've just come out of* between.

Chagrined, Fiona felt her cheeks burn with shame and sent an apology toward Lorana. The older woman certainly didn't need such reminders of the grim past.

Still, Fiona couldn't quite shake off her unease. She took a slow, calming breath and carefully pushed the thought deep inside herself: The last thing she wanted was to worry Lorana with her own fears. She could tell that she was successful because she felt no resonance from the ex–queen rider but, even so, she couldn't shake off the nagging feeling that something would go horribly wrong.

Memories of her fevered chanting came back to her: *Can't lose the baby, can't lose the baby, can't lose the baby!* It mixed with Lorana's nightmare cry, her sweaty, gasping breaths and as Fiona fought to quench her fears she had raked over one horrifying thought—whose baby? Or babies?

▼ ▼ ▼

That's it? T'mar thought in surprise as they came to the end of the Fall. Like the Upper Bitra Fall, this one had started way up north in the Snowy Wastes, where Thread could only freeze and die—a pleasant thought— and had crossed into the mountains above Crom, ending a good half hour's flight from the Hold itself.

The air had been steady if mildly turbulent and the Weyrs had no trouble picking up the Thread and following it as it crossed into the higher mountains and then ended at the foothills and high plains above Crom.

An easy Fall. T'mar snorted derisively. Easy enough: Telgar and High Reaches had each lost two dragons, and both had the same number of injuries. High Reaches had only two dragons badly mauled against Telgar's three, but while Telgar had the same number of slighter injuries, High Reaches had four dragons and riders who would not fly again for the next month or more.

Zirenth, have C'tov— T'mar cut himself short: C'tov had been one of the injured with another score on his left side. This time, fortunately, it had been his left thigh that had borne the brunt of it, even as Sereth's neck had been lightly nicked just below—protected by the extra bulk of his rider's leg. *Have C'tov's wing fly sweep.*

Very well, the bronze said. *Winurth leads.*

J'gerd? T'mar thought in surprise. He hadn't realized that the brown rider was C'tov's wingsecond; he'd been injured not all that long ago. T'mar snorted to himself; it was hard to keep track of who flew where these days.

Let's go back, T'mar thought even as he waved farewell to D'vin and the High Reaches riders.

Even with C'tov's injuries and the other five injured dragonpairs, the mood at the Weyr that night was one of relief, almost festive.

"Not bad," F'jian said, sounding very pleased with himself as he raised his glass to Terin for a refill. "If I do say so myself, not bad at all."

"Well, at least you didn't come home too battered," Terin said with a sweet smile to take most of the sting out of her words. F'jian gave her a hurt look, but she shook it off saying, "Don't let your head get too big for your helmet!"

"I won't, I won't," F'jian protested even as the laughter around the table brought red spots to his cheeks. He glanced at T'mar and raised his glass toward him. "You trained us well."

"To fly, perhaps," T'mar said with a grin, adding as he shook his head, "But in drinking . . . not at all."

"Flying's what's important," F'jian said merrily, glancing at his riders and raising his glass to them once more. He drained it and held it out to Terin, who cocked her head thoughtfully. "Another glass and you'll be asleep before the party starts."

"What?" F'jian roared, waving his free hand around to the folk gathered in the cavern. "This *is* the party!"

"Well, it's one party," Terin agreed, her eyes twinkling suggestively.

F'jian blinked at her in his confusion and Terin sighed.

"I think one party will be enough for him tonight," Fiona said, coming up behind her. "They fight again in three days."

Terin turned in her chair to peer up at the Weyrwoman, her expression bleak. "I know."

Fiona smiled down at her. "If you'd like, I'll wait with you."

"No, you're still supposed to be resting," Terin said. She turned back to F'jian, gave him a quick peck on the cheek, and then pushed back her chair. "Let me escort you to your quarters."

"Kindan can—"

"Kindan will be pouring the wine all night long," Terin said, watching the way the harper was pacing back and forth among the revelers. "And then he'll be up early in the morning, drilling the weyrlings."

"Are we working him too hard?" Fiona asked, even as Terin linked arms with her and started off toward the exit to the Weyr Bowl.

"No more than any other," Terin said. "Of course, with C'tov grounded, I'm sure he'll find himself with more help."

"Weyrwoman!" T'mar's voice called across the distance and Fiona stopped and turned back to face the throng. T'mar raised his glass in toast and she waved back happily in response.

"To the best Weyrwoman on Pern!" F'jian said suddenly, lurching upward and raising his glass high.

"Fiona! Fiona! Fiona!" the rest of the riders cheered in agreement. They quickly drained their glasses and held them out for more.

Fiona waved and cheered them in return before turning back with Terin to the cold night outside. "They'll feel it in the morning."

"Good morning!" Fiona called cheerfully as she entered T'mar's quarters carrying a tray on which she'd perched a pitcher of warm *klah,* three mugs, two plates, and a basket of fresh, warm rolls.

"Unh!" T'mar groaned in response. Fiona's smile grew broader as she placed the tray on his day table. She quickly filled a mug and made her way over to him, humming loudly, off-key. "Unh!"

"Did you sleep well?" Fiona asked loudly, as the bronze rider sat up in his bed, wincing at the cold stone beneath his feet and cupping his forehead feebly in his hands. She relented enough to waft the warm mug in front of his nose and say quietly, "Fresh *klah* for the weary Weyrleader."

"Mnh," T'mar said, lowering one hand to grasp the mug and bring it to his lips. He drank slowly, lowered the mug, raised it again and took another sip.

"F'jian is apparently not feeling too well this morning," Fiona went on with a quick smile. "Terin served him his breakfast about an hour ago."

"Unh," T'mar grunted once more, bringing his mug up for another swallow. He raised his head enough to give her a bleary-eyed look. "And to what do I owe my extra rest?"

"I'm not as mad at you as Terin is with him," Fiona told him simply. She shrugged, adding, "Anyway, I know you drank less than most and needed more sleep than others."

She craned her head around toward the bathroom and called out loudly, "I've *klah* and rolls, Shaneese!"

"Thank you!" the headwoman called back softly. A moment later the

dusky woman appeared, wrapped in a robe. She clucked sympathetically at T'mar and gratefully accepted the mug Fiona poured for her.

"I let you sleep in," Fiona told the headwoman, smirking at T'mar's
expression. She went to the tray at the table, filled the last mug and, peering over the edge, told the other two, "I'll leave you to it; just know that
Kindan's going to be drilling the weyrlings in another half an hour
or so."

Shaneese smiled at her and blew a kiss in her direction. "Thank you
for the warning!"

Fiona nodded and spun about, mug cradled in one hand as she made
her way briskly out onto the queens' ledge beyond. As she made her way
into Talenth's weyr and saw Kurinth peer curiously into one of the still
vacant weyrs, she thought: Pretty soon we'll have to rearrange things.

Telgar was laid out differently than some Weyrs, with the senior
queen's and junior queens' quarters all on one side. She wondered at that
as there was room available on the other side of the Weyr Bowl for another queen's weyr. Fiona guessed that D'gan must have decided to leave
Lina on the side of the Weyr closest to the kitchens while he quartered on
the farther side. It made some sense to have all the queens together, but
only when the Weyrwoman was not actively fighting Thread.

As it was now, T'mar was quartered in one of the junior queens'
weyrs, close to Fiona. She made a note to talk the arrangements over
with Shaneese—two more queens and they would have the decision
taken out of their hands.

Not, she mused as Kurinth snorted in surprise at something inside the
empty weyr, that it was much of a problem now—Kurinth was quite
willing to share a weyr with Ladirth, doubtless encouraged by her rider.
All the same, as was easy to see from the young queen's curiosity, it was
probably time she settled in her own weyr.

Fiona furrowed her brows as she looked around, wondering why the
young queen was so far from her normal weyr. Her eyes widened as a
whirl of dust whisked through the air and Kurinth just barely dodged it,
snorting, eyes whirling red, craning her neck back in surprise.

"There!" Fiona heard Terin exclaim grumpily. She continued on to herself, "Thinks *he* can stay up all night!" She snorted. "Expects me to carry him back to his weyr!" Another cloud of dust erupted. "Wants me to bring him breakfast!"

"Can I help?" Fiona asked, brushing past Kurinth and suddenly sneezing as another cloud of dust filled the air.

"You can—oh!" Terin looked up, saw the dust settling over Fiona and stopped, her expression halfway between contrition and mirth.

"It's high time you had your own weyr," Fiona said, glancing at the pile of clothes strewn in one corner. "If you'll wait a moment, I'm sure that Shaneese can find you some help to straighten it out." She glanced back at Kurinth who blinked up at her. "And Kurinth is getting big enough that she'll need a proper weyr of her own."

"You *know* that's not it!" Terin growled, eyes flashing.

"And in your own weyr," Fiona continued smoothly, ignoring the young weyrwoman's response, "you can entertain as you see fit."

"Oh!" Terin's brow puckered as Fiona's words registered. Her anger evaporated. "Oh, I suppose I can."

"And people who get too much into their cups will have to find their own weyr, without disturbing you or—" Fiona paused, glancing around in surprise "—where *are* your usual helpers?"

"I don't know if I'll have them anymore," Terin said. "Most of them were taken away last night by their mothers."

Fiona thought that that was probably just as well. She could also imagine how the older, Thread-seasoned bronze rider might find it difficult to maintain his best behavior surrounded by small ones who viewed him with awe.

"I'll have Kindan send some food over for Kurinth," Fiona said. She paused and met Terin's green eyes frankly. "And how was his head this morning?"

Terin straightened and her eyes danced as she reported gladly, "F'jian was not feeling at *all* well this morning!"

"Hmm," Fiona said. "Well, perhaps you should consider that in"—she glanced outside—"a few minutes, Kindan will start exercising the weyrlings."

Terin gave her a blank look and then comprehension dawned and her face took on a wicked smile. "Oh!"

After she'd got Terin settled in and they'd both gleefully watched as Kindan drilled the weyrlings—who shouted quite loudly—Fiona left to check on Lorana. She found her in the Records Room with a basket of glows near at hand.

"It can't be done," Fiona said as she peered over Lorana's shoulder, looking down at the contents of the slates spread in front of the ex–queen rider.

"There's no mention of timing it in any of the Records I've found," Lorana said.

"That's because it's not a wise thing to do," Fiona said. "Too many accidents, too much confusion." She shrugged. "You know."

"Like B'nik," Lorana agreed.

"Like all those who got to see their own deaths hours before they went to them," Fiona said. She sighed, eyes downcast as a litany of faces came to her mind: faces sad but resigned—those of the riders; faces fearful and forlorn—those of the bereaved. "He can no more escape his fate than they." She sighed, walked around the table and dropped into the seat opposite. Lorana looked up at her. "You know, T'mar told me that some of the riders—the ones who had timed it—actually waved at themselves in farewell, tried to comfort their past selves."

Lorana gazed at her, shaking her head.

Fiona tried a different tack, saying, "Tullea's no different from any of those who get this bad news." She shook her head sadly. "She'll recover in time."

"I don't know," Lorana said. "I think she's so desperate, so . . . hurt—in pain—that she really would follow him *between*."

"And there's only that one new queen at Benden," Fiona said by way of agreement. She grimaced, adding, "I don't see her binding the wounds that would leave."

"No, Lin needs seasoning before she'd be able," Lorana agreed. The new junior weyrwoman at Benden was far too unsure of herself to take charge in Tullea's stead.

Fiona shrugged. "Well, there are mature queens in the other Weyrs, if it comes to that."

"I'd be happier if there were another way."

"Another way," Fiona said half to herself. "Another way."

"M'tal saw him and then T'mar . . ." Lorana began thoughtfully.

"With a whole Wing, no less," Fiona pointed out.

Lorana nodded then glanced up at Fiona, lips curved up in a thin smile as she added, "And Tullea's forbidden his Wing to go with him."

"So he found another Wing, how hard would that be?" Fiona tossed back with a shrug. She frowned again, adding, "And anyway, we don't know *when* he timed it—"

"What?" Lorana asked, sitting upright in her chair.

"We don't know *when* he timed it," Fiona repeated, scarcely hiding her exasperation.

"We don't even know *if* he timed it."

"If?"

"We know that someone did," Lorana said, "but all that anyone saw was a man wearing the Benden Weyrleader's jacket."

"So maybe it was a different Weyrleader?" Fiona asked. "From a different time?" She frowned, shaking her head. "It could be but we won't know until it happens." She smiled wanly at Lorana and said with a sniff, "For all we know, it could just as easily have been someone who stole B'nik's jacket."

"It was just a thought," Lorana said with a quick shrug. She looked down at the slates once more, sighed, and stood up, swaying slightly with the awkward weight of the baby. She gave Fiona a pleading look, saying, "Would you clean up here? I'm not—I must—"

"Go!" Fiona said, waving her away. She'd heard enough about "peeing for two" to understand. I'll probably know about it firsthand soon enough, she mused as she reached for the scattered slates and started to put them away. A smile crossed her lips and she started humming happily.

▼ ▼ ▼

"**W**ell, as of this evening, you've seventy-two fighting dragons," Fiona said proudly to T'mar as they gathered together for dinner. She quirked a quick grin, adding, "C'tov *tried* to get back to flying, but I sent him to his quarters."

"Well, I'm glad to hear that he's eager," T'mar said, glancing at the wingleader, who was seated glumly at the end of the table. He raised his voice to carry, saying to him, "I'm sure that Kindan appreciates your help with the weyrlings."

"I've learned a great deal," Kindan said, sending a thankful nod in the bronze rider's direction. C'tov waved a hand in acknowledgment.

"Seventy-two is a good deal less than I'd like," T'mar said to Fiona.

"I'd prefer three hundred and, if wishes were dragons, that's what we'd have," Fiona said.

T'mar pursed his lips grimly, nodding. He glanced at Lorana, telling her, "If it weren't for you, we'd have none."

"I know," Lorana said quietly, looking no happier. T'mar shot a look at Fiona, to which the Weyrwoman responded with a quick shake of her head.

"Well," T'mar continued, "with Fort's eighty-six and our seventy-two, we'll be close to two full Flights in strength."

H'nez raised his eyebrows at that appraisal: The total number was a full Wing short of two Flights. Beside him, Jeila shook her head quickly, and he grimaced, and resumed his meal without comment.

"Where's Terin?" T'mar asked, peering down the table and spying F'jian eating glumly by himself.

"She's in her new quarters," Fiona said casually. She tilted her head toward the Weyrleader. "Actually, that brings up a good point: We should reconsider the disposition of the lower-level weyrs."

T'mar raised an eyebrow and motioned for her to continue.

"Traditionally," Fiona continued, putting a tone of disdain on that word, "the Weyrwoman and Weyrleader have lodged in the weyrs to the north of the Bowl nearest the Hatching Grounds."

T'mar nodded.

"The junior weyrwomen have all lodged on the opposite side, where we've now got you quartered."

"But your quarters are there, too," T'mar said.

"True, as is the Records Room that we're also using as the Council Room," Fiona said. "But to the north there's a perfectly good room for the Council to meet in, and another large room with access from both the Weyr Bowl and the Weyrwoman's quarters for the Records." She made a face. "I think the current arrangements are a holdover from when Igen integrated with Telgar.

"But with Terin in her quarters, we've now got all four of the junior weyrwomen's quarters filled, and the senior Weyrwoman's and Weyr-leader's quarters remain empty."

"So what do you propose?" T'mar asked. He quite liked being close to the Kitchen and Living Caverns—the life of the Weyr centered there—but he could see how crowded they were getting and understood Fiona's hidden hope that they would soon have enough queens to fill all queen weyrs.

"I don't know," Fiona admitted. "Obviously the traditional thing to do would be to move you and me out into the quarters on the north side of the Weyr."

T'mar chuckled: It was obvious that Fiona was no more enamored of that prospect than he.

"I suppose we could do with the extra exercise," Fiona said thoughtfully, adding with a flash of her eyes, "after all, no one would want us to get *fat*, would they?"

"No, I suppose not," T'mar replied diplomatically. "And I suppose the weyrs are large enough, maybe even larger than our current quarters."

"But I'll miss the ease with which I can talk with Jeila and Terin," Fiona said.

"I'm sure that *they* will need exercise, too," T'mar quipped, working to control his smirk. His expression slipped as a new thought came to him. "Of course, that will put us near the weyrlings."

"Yes," Fiona agreed blandly.

T'mar gave her a probing look, for rarely was the Weyrwoman bland, and thought on the implications. Being nearer the weyrlings would mean being nearer to Kindan, the Weyrlingmaster. That would put Lorana closer. In fact, the only one who would stand to lose from it would be Shaneese—the headwoman was in no danger of getting fat, having barely a spare gram on her. Still, T'mar admitted privately to himself, the same could be said of Fiona, although in her case she tended more toward wiry strength than even the dusky-toned headwoman.

"If you're thinking of offering to stay in your weyr for a while longer," Fiona said, guessing all too accurately at the thrust of his thoughts, "consider that that would put you near Terin and Jeila and ask yourself how that might impact their partners."

"I've no—" T'mar started in protest. He cut himself short as he saw Fiona's eyes dance once more in amusement. It was true that he was not so foolish as to attempt to dally with the other weyrwomen—Jeila was far too attached and both were far younger than he preferred.

His attachment to Fiona was still something of a mystery to him. What had started as a simple act of kindness had solidified into something that caused him much pain, but which he knew would cause him even more pain to finish. He met her eyes frankly and peered deeply into them, once again amazed at their depths. She was, in far too many ways, still a child and yet . . . she was Weyrwoman to her core, more so even than Cisca or Sonia.

"I wouldn't want to be that far from you," T'mar said. He caught Fiona's shudder of joy and she reached for his hand, grabbed it tight in hers. She let it go a moment later, glancing around to be sure that no one had noticed.

"Good," she said. "Then it's decided."

"Can we wait until we aren't so pressed for time?"

"I wasn't thinking of starting until after this Fall," Fiona said. "I merely wanted your decision on the matter."

"Thank you," T'mar said, warmly surprised that she'd wanted his decision and not his approval.

Fiona accepted his words with a nod, continuing, "And now that we've decided, when we're done we'll have two empty weyrs there, at least temporarily."

T'mar cocked an eyebrow at her wonderingly. What was she getting at?

"I think, as we're moving around, we should arrange it so that your wing lodges above us—they can come down the central stairs," Fiona told him. T'mar nodded, that much seemed reasonable, but he was certain that Fiona had more and he motioned for her to continue. "That will leave us free then to move H'nez's wing above the queens' weyrs," Fiona continued. "And, as we'll have two empty weyrs there, if he wants, he could take the one nearest to Jeila."

T'mar's eyes widened as he caught on to her plan.

"I'm sure that would make the weyrwoman happy," T'mar agreed with a twinkle in his eyes; it would hardly make H'nez *unhappy*. "And F'jian?"

"Well, I think it best if we consider putting his wing over the Caverns," Fiona said, her tone losing some of its levity. T'mar gave her a startled look and she continued, "We could perhaps change that later, but for the time being, that's a good location for him—I mean, for his wing."

"Around the back, toward the lake?" T'mar asked. He knew full well that there were choice locations in the Weyr and places no one wanted— being located just above the lake and the feeding pens was one of the least desired locations: noisy and noisome both. It was, traditionally, the place where irate Weyrleaders or Weyrwomen placed those who had earned their wrath.

"Perhaps not quite there," Fiona said, pursing her lips. "Although that might not be a bad idea."

"It's far from the wine," T'mar said.

"Then, by all means, whatever you think best, Weyrleader," Fiona said in the blandest of tones.

T'mar glanced down toward F'jian and wondered what, exactly, the young bronze rider had done to annoy his lady so much that the Weyrwoman wanted revenge.

"I'll have to think about it," T'mar said after a long pause.

"Don't think too long," Fiona told him warningly. "Or if you must, talk with Shaneese first."

"Shaneese?" T'mar asked in surprise. From the sound of it, Fiona had already conveyed her impressions to the headwoman and, to T'mar's surprise, it was clear that Shaneese had emphatically agreed with her.

"I think it's important that the lesson be well and truly learned," Fiona said with a sour look.

"Should we do more?"

Fiona sighed and shook her head, leaning closer to T'mar to tell him, "No, it was a foolish mistake. I just want to make sure that he doesn't consider repeating it."

"I'll talk to Shaneese then," T'mar said making it clear in his tone that he considered that only a formality.

"Best do it before you come to bed," Fiona said. T'mar gave her another surprised look. She pushed back from her chair, having finished her meal a while back, and called out to the group, "Dragonriders, Thread falls tomorrow and I must rest!"

The riders all rose dutifully and nodded to her, eyeing the Weyrleader warily. T'mar rose, too, giving his half-eaten dessert a quick, rueful glance before adding, "A good night's sleep would serve us all well!"

The others needed no more hints and slowly the dragonriders finished eating and, in small groups, made their way from the Dining Cavern to their weyrs, some accompanied by other riders, some by werymates and family.

Fiona was waiting for him in his quarters.

"Kindan is spending the night with Lorana," Fiona told him. "Xhinna and the others know to call Talenth or Tolarth if they've need."

"And you?" T'mar asked, gesturing to his room.

Fiona smiled and cocked her head up at him. "I'd like to stay with you tonight."

T'mar smiled. "I've learned that it's never good to disappoint the Weyrwoman."

▼ ▼ ▼

Later, much later, as Fiona rested her head on his shoulder, she asked, "What are we going to do?"

"Do?"

"Every Fall we lose two more," Fiona said with a sigh. "Sometimes more, sometimes less but, on average, two. And with seventy-two fighting dragons, that gives us less than thirty-six Falls."

"Much less," T'mar said. "Really, we can't hope to fight with less than a full Flight."

"You could time it," Fiona said, nuzzling deeper into his shoulder.

"The casualties would increase."

"So we don't have the time," Fiona said.

T'mar was silent: He had no answer for her.

"It can't be like this," Fiona said. "Our children should grow up in the Weyr, strong, happy, and healthy—"

"And be dragonriders?"

"If they wish," Fiona said. "But we shouldn't have to face the end of everything, the last dragon, the last rider, the last Weyr." She shook her head. "That shouldn't happen."

"No, it shouldn't," T'mar said. Which didn't change the fact that it would. Thirty-six Falls would come in little more than four months—five at the most. It would take the weyrlings just hatched another twenty-three months at the least to mature and grow strong enough to join the Weyrs. "We could send them back in time."

"The weyrlings?" Fiona guessed. "Where to? We can't send them back to Igen, all the time there was used."

"Southern?"

"We sent the fire-lizards there," Fiona reminded him. "The dragons are cured now, but I don't know if they couldn't get sick again." She paused in silent thought for a long while. When she moved again it was to prop herself up on one arm. She leaned forward and kissed T'mar gently on the lips.

"You've a Fall tomorrow, you shouldn't be worrying," she said before bending back down to tease his lips once more.

▼ ▼ ▼

Fiona woke early, eyes narrowed, inhaling deeply of the morning air: Something disturbed her. With a tender glance at T'mar, she shifted the blankets and quickly rose out of bed. She slid her feet into her slippers, found the robe she'd left at the end of the bed, shrugged it over her shoulders, and felt around for the small glowbasket at the front of the bed. Its light was weak and in need of recharging, which suited her as she only needed it to provide her with a clear view of her path into Zirenth's lair.

The big bronze was sleeping, his breath coming in slow, steady waves. Clearly he was no more disturbed than T'mar. Fiona crept quietly past him, leaving the unnecessary glow at the weyr's exit.

She stood there in silence, her senses stretched, trying to locate the cause of her worry. Frowning, she turned her head toward her own weyr, and listened. Her eyebrows rose in surprise as she recognized a noise closer, coming from Terin's new weyr.

The sound was an odd mix and it was only when she ducked away from a sudden gust of dust that Fiona could make sense of it: Terin was sweeping Kurinth's lair and muttering—no, crying—to herself.

"Terin?" Fiona called softly, having stepped away to avoid another cloud of dust.

The younger weyrwoman stopped sweeping and muttering abruptly. A moment later she spoke, sounding miserable. "Fiona?"

Fiona entered the lair and saw that poor Kurinth was huddled in one far corner, her eyes whirling a distressed red as she eyed her mate with alarm. Fiona stepped forward briskly and grabbed the broom from Terin's hands. The youngster looked up at her in surprise, her lower lip quivering. Even in the dim light, Fiona could tell that she'd been crying: Her eyes were red-rimmed and her cheeks tear-streaked.

"I couldn't sleep," Terin confessed miserably. She gave Fiona an anxious look as she added, "I didn't wake you, did I?"

"Come here," Fiona said, turning toward Terin's darkened quarters as she reached for the younger girl's hand. She led them to Terin's bed and sat down, pulling the young weyrwoman down beside her. She pulled Terin's head onto her shoulder and held it, stroking the young dragon-rider's soft red-blond hair soothingly. "Talk."

"I couldn't sleep," Terin repeated. When Fiona remained patiently silent, she added, "I kept thinking of him." She lifted her head off Fiona's shoulder and turned her head up to face her, her eyes flashing dimly in the low light. "He got drunk because he's afraid," she said, her voice miserable. She choked back a sob before continuing, "He's afraid he's going to die. Or worse."

"Worse: See all those around him die first," Fiona guessed.

Terin's eyes widened in surprise even as she breathed, "Yes."

"Well, we've over four Wings' worth of weyrlings between the five Weyrs and more to come," Fiona reminded her in a light voice. "That'll—"

"I'm sorry Fiona, but that won't be enough," Terin interrupted firmly. "I can do the sums, and even if somehow we could bring them all back in time and have them grow up, that would still be nearly two thousand dragons too few to save Pern."

"Well," Fiona said, turning to a different tack, "with *your* queen and the pair we've got already, we'll have easily another four Wings from them in a Turn."

"And in two Turns, they'll be able to fight Thread," Terin replied, shaking her head.

"We'll think of something."

"What?" Terin demanded. "And will it be soon enough to save F'jian?"

"Or T'mar," Fiona added, allowing a bitter tone to creep into her voice. "Or H'nez. Or C'tov, even."

Terin was surprised at her tone.

"Go find him, go talk to him," Fiona said, rising from the bed and dragging the younger girl with her. "There are never any guarantees in life, Terin. The only things we can hold are the memories we're given."

"I'm not ready to—"

"I'm not saying that!" Fiona cut her off with a snort. "But if you're hurting this much just worrying about him, then you at least owe it to him to let him know that."

"Okay," Terin said reluctantly. She paused as they entered Kurinth's lair and turned to her queen, kneeling down and stroking the dragonet lovingly. "I'd better feed her first."

"No!" Fiona said. "Don't dawdle! I'll feed her, if she's willing." She paused, smiling down at the pretty little queen. "Or I'll ask Lorana, if she prefers." She turned back to the entrance and jerked a thumb toward it. "Go! Go now."

"What if he's asleep?" Terin asked, temporizing.

"You'll figure it out," Fiona said, turning back to Kurinth and putting the young queen rider out of her sight. She remained in that position, assuming Terin's squatting position to rub the young queen's eye ridges until she heard Terin scamper away. To the young queenling she apologized, "She's really a good choice, you know."

Yes, Kurinth agreed, angling her neck so that Fiona could reach the itchiest patch.

"You'll be big before you know it," Fiona promised, surprised at how small the recently hatched queen seemed to her own Talenth.

Yes, I know, Kurinth said. Fiona wondered at the dragon's certainty and shrugged; it was probably just youth and an intense desire to have that particular itch scratched.

How long they remained like that, exchanging words for caresses, Fiona didn't know or care. She only turned away from the young queen when she heard sounds behind her outside the weyr.

"Well?" Fiona asked as she turned, expecting to see Terin return with a broad grin on her face.

It wasn't Terin she saw. It was Lorana. The older woman was looking out over the Weyr Bowl, looking up into the air with a quizzical expression.

"Lorana?" Fiona asked, making her way quickly to the ex–queen rider, unable to keep a tinge of worry from her voice.

"Mmm?" Lorana murmured, her eyes still focused skyward.

Fiona followed her gaze but could see nothing but the Weyr—brighter now in the morning sun. Dust, probably left over from Terin's exertions hung in the air, flickering in the morning light.

"Are you all right?"

"Just looking," Lorana returned dreamily. Fiona cocked her head in worry but said nothing, standing beside the older woman, ready if she needed help. She half-expected Lorana to collapse or something by the way she was staring so intently at the dust motes.

"What color are they?" Lorana asked suddenly.

"Color?"

"The specks," Lorana said, half-raising a hand.

"It's just dust, Lorana," Fiona said, trying to keep her voice normal.

"Dust is usually brown, isn't it?"

"On the ground, maybe," Fiona said, wondering why Lorana found the topic so fascinating. "It sparkles like gold in the air, though."

"Gold?" Lorana asked, cocking her head to one side critically.

"Well, goldy, I suppose," Fiona allowed. "Or bronzy, maybe."

"Mmm, bronze," Lorana agreed. She dropped her head suddenly and turned to face Fiona, catching her eyes. There was no sign of any strangeness in them. "Could you and Talenth bring me to Benden? I want to talk with Ketan."

"Ketan?" Fiona asked. "There's a Fall today, Lorana, we've got to get ready soon." She paused, adding, "And Benden's got a Fall, too."

"I know," Lorana said. "If you could take me now, that would work, wouldn't it?"

"Right now?"

"We could be changed in ten minutes," Lorana said, glancing down at her robe and slippers with some surprise. "I really need to talk with Ketan."

"Well . . ." Fiona temporized then said decisively, "All right. But we have to be careful." She pointed to Lorana's midriff.

"Three coughs only," Lorana swore.

Kindan was already gone. Lorana explained that he had gone to rouse the weyrlings early and she'd escorted him as far as the weyr ledge. They dressed quickly even though Lorana found that, to her embarrassment, she had to have Fiona's help.

"I expect I'll be asking *you* to help *me* soon enough!" Fiona said as she laughed off the older woman's discomfort.

Even so, they were ready in less than the ten minutes Lorana had promised. Fiona spent longer working with Talenth's riding straps, partly because she still felt some misgivings over Lorana's state of mind. She waved at T'mar, but the Weyrleader was busy with the preparations for the Fall.

Finally, she could delay no more. Talenth took up a position below the queens' ledge, her forewing raised so that Lorana could climb aboard without difficulty. And then Fiona was on and Talenth stepped away from the ledge, bugled a challenge to the whole Weyr, took one leap and was *between*.

They appeared again over Benden Weyr moments later even as Fiona was still berating herself for letting the queen set such a bad example by going *between* so close to the ground. Her worries and shame vanished as the Benden watch dragon challenged them and Talenth roared in response. Her bellow was greeted by a rousing chorus from the Weyr Bowl even as she wheeled sharply and spun her way down to the ground, Fiona crying in pure joy at her queen's wild maneuver.

"What are you doing here?" Tullea demanded as soon as she got within earshot. She made out the form of Lorana and her expression changed, rushing forward she cried, "Have you found it?"

Fiona shot the older Weyrwoman an irritated look as she gingerly guided Lorana down to the ground below. Couldn't Tullea at least wait until they were safe?

"I need to talk with Ketan, if he's available," Lorana said, her soft contralto voice sounding calm and collected; focused in a way that she had not been with Fiona on the ledge earlier. Lorana turned back to Fiona, who was starting to dismount and held up a hand. "You should get back," she told her with a grateful smile. "I'm sure Tullea will give me a lift, when I need it."

"If you're going to help, you can take Minith yourself," Tullea offered, glancing around the Weyr, her eyes full of dread. "Anything to save B'nik."

"Where's Ketan?" Lorana asked, looking around. When she didn't find him, she turned back to Fiona. The young Weyrwoman made no attempt to disguise her concern. Lorana smiled up at her. *Go on, Kindan will be worried.*

Relieved at hearing Lorana's words, Fiona smiled and nodded. *I'm here if you need me.* Aloud she said, "Come on Talenth, Thread's coming soon!"

She nodded toward Tullea and this time instructed Talenth to climb up to the proper spot above the watch dragon before departing once more *between* for Telgar and home.

"**Y**ou'll probably find him in his quarters, drunk," Tullea said as she watched the Telgar queen climb up toward the heights. Her eyes narrowed as she added, "What does he have to do with B'nik?"

"I don't know," Lorana said. "I want to talk with him first."

"Very well," Tullea said sourly. "If you need me, come find me. We've got Thread to fight today."

"And if I need to borrow Minith?" Lorana asked.

"Take her," Tullea said with a wave as she trotted off toward a knot of dragonriders. "Do what you must."

"Very well," Lorana said, turning toward the healer's quarters. "I'm going to have to go to High Reaches later."

Tullea made no response beyond another wave of her arm and then she was lost in the throng of riders.

Lorana found him in the healer's quarters, head down on his arm, snoring loudly.

"Ketan," she called. He stirred then resumed his snores. Lorana's eyes narrowed and she sighed, moving forward to grab his shoulders.

"Ketan!" she shouted, shaking him roughly.

"Wh-what?" the ex-dragonrider said muzzily, lifting his head up and waving his hands. "Go 'way!"

"It's me, Lorana!"

"Lorana?" Ketan pried one eye open and peered at her. He jerked back in surprise and pulled himself upright, his neck craning around to peer at her. "What are you doin' here? You're at Telgar."

"I wanted to talk with you," Lorana told him, her expression softening. "I wanted to talk with you about Drith."

"Drith!" Ketan's voice was a thready wail. "My beautiful, beautiful Drith!"

Lorana gave the healer a long, thoughtful look, took a deep breath, and said quietly, "Do remember the last words you had with him?"

"Why?" Ketan demanded angrily. "He's gone and I'm here and—oh, Drith! How I *hurt* without you!"

"Ketan," Lorana began again softly, "I'm not trying to hurt you."

"Go 'way!" the healer replied, turning back to his table and dropping his head on it, eyes closed firmly as if by not seeing Lorana he could make her disappear.

"Didn't he say: 'I must do this while I still can'?" Lorana asked quietly.

"Yes, to die!" Ketan growled, his eyes snapping open in anger and then closing again in hopes that his tormenter would leave him.

"T'mar saw the Benden Weyrleader die," Lorana said. "He saw him come back in time, he saved him just as he saved M'tal."

"So?" Ketan demanded. "He dies, they die, we all die." He paused. "And then I'll be with Drith."

"I think you can be with Drith before that," Lorana said, her heart beating loudly in her chest. "I think you can save three lives."

Ketan had opened his eyes again at her words. He lifted his head off the table and craned it up so that he could see her from the corner of his wide-open eyes.

"Would you be willing to steal B'nik's jacket?"

"Steal his—" the healer jerked upright and jumped out of his chair. "Steal his jacket? But I've no dragon!"

"No dragon *now*."

The healer's expression slowly changed from one of surprise and despair to one of hope.

"I'm not offering you much," Lorana cautioned. "A chance to ride Drith again, and to make a difference—"

"My lady, to be a dragonrider again, just once!" Ketan shook his head, his eyes brimming with tears. "For that, I'd do anything."

"First, the jacket."

"And then?"

"We go to High Reaches."

"High Reaches?" Ketan looked perplexed and then illumination struck. "Oh! And then the wherhold, no doubt."

"We'll see Nuella," Lorana agreed. "But not until after."

"And then?"

"And then, K'tan, you'll get your last ride."

TWENTY-FOUR

▼▼▼

The way forward is dark and long.
A dragon gold is only the first price you'll pay for Pern.

Fort Weyr, second hour, AL 507.11.18, Second Interval

Lorana sighed wearily as she glided silently down into the Fort Weyr
Bowl in the dark of night.

Four coughs *between*. The same as when she'd brought Ketan back to
Drith to make their offer and again when Drith had accepted. And again
when Lorana and K'tan had arrived at the wherhold with the vial she'd
retrieved from High Reaches Weyr. While she'd explained in private to
Nuella the purpose of the vial and had sworn the half-sighted woman to
secrecy, K'tan and Drith had rolled in the gold-flecked waters of the
miner's river. In the distance, with the sun in the right position, anyone
who had merely a brief glimpse of brown Drith would easily take him
for a bronze, particularly when the rider was wearing the Benden Weyrleader's distinctive jacket.

It had taken only Lorana's word to recruit a ready wing of Istan dragons willing to follow K'tan unquestioningly: J'lian had more volunteers
than they needed, even though all were sworn to secrecy. She watched,

from a distance low to the ground where she wouldn't be seen as K'tan first saved M'tal and then again, with the Istan wing, had saved T'mar—and sacrificed himself.

And now, there was one thing more to do.

First though, she had to say good-bye. She couldn't do it in person, so she chose a different way, going back in time—here, to Fort Weyr, a little less than nine months before. On the day after the Hatching, after Fiona had Impressed Talenth.

In the distance, a dragonet creeled.

Lorana stretched her senses to the quarters where Kindan had just woken, startled by something he couldn't identify. She sent him a warm thought and turned her attention toward the queen's quarters.

Fiona, she thought quietly. A touch of a smile played across her lips. She shook her head, I'm sorry. I know what I must do, I understand now:

The way forward is dark and long. A dragon gold is only the first price you'll pay for Pern.

Beneath her, Minith trembled, as if sensing her fears.

Lorana pursed her lips tightly and shook her head in determination.

We've been here long enough, Lorana told the queen beneath her, *let's go.*

As you wish, the dragon responded. With a great heave of hind legs, the dragon leaped into the air and went *between.*

EPILOGUE

It will all turn out right.

Telgar Weyr, evening, AL 508.7.21

Fiona only started looking for Lorana after the worst of the injured dragons and riders had been tended. The casualties were bad, but the numbers were reassuring. Even though the Weyr had lost another two dragons
and it would be months before all six injured would be able to fly again,
the Fall had been easier than she'd feared.

It was her memory of that fear that brought her to wonder about Lorana, because the fear had started that morning when she had seen the
ex–queen rider looking up at the flecks of dust.

"Bekka," Fiona called as she spotted the smaller girl bustling about,
"have you seen Lorana?"

The youngster shrugged and hurried on about her duties.

Fiona berated herself, realizing that she could have Talenth ask
Minith.

I cannot find her, Talenth replied a moment later, her tone tense.

Fiona felt panic well in her heart. She turned on her heel in a great circle, scanning the Weyr for any sign of the taller woman. She did not find her.

"Kindan!" she shouted as she spotted the harper. Kindan waved toward her but, somehow alerted by her stance, stopped what he was doing and raced over to her. "Have you seen Lorana?"

"No," he said, shaking his head.

"I brought her to Benden," Fiona said. "Tullea said that she might take Minith." Kindan arched an eyebrow in surprise but Fiona rushed on, "And I can't find Minith."

"What about Lorana?" Kindan asked and Fiona flushed in surprise that she'd forgotten her strange link with the older woman.

Lorana! she called loudly. She waited. Her face fell and she glanced worriedly at Kindan as she shook his head. She was about to say more when the air above erupted with a bronze dragon from *between*.

"Where is she?" a voice bellowed from above. It was Tullea. She was riding behind B'nik. "Where is that dragon-stealer?"

The two scampered down the moment Caranth had touched the ground, racing over to Fiona and Kindan. T'mar, alerted by the shout, rushed to their side, giving Fiona a questioning look.

"We can't find Lorana," Fiona told him in chill tones.

"She had that healer steal B'nik's jacket!" Tullea began angrily. "He stole it, Lin saw him!"

"Your Weyrleader jacket?" T'mar asked, turning to B'nik.

The Benden Weyrleader nodded, running a hand wearily through his hair from front to back. "I thought it was a poor joke, but I didn't have the time to track it down before Threadfall."

T'mar grunted in understanding. "And now?"

"D'vin told me that Lorana and Ketan had come to High Reaches, they went to the Records Room—and that's the last they've been seen," B'nik said.

Fiona and Kindan exchanged looks at the mention of High Reaches' Records Room. Tullea saw it and cried, "What? What were they doing there?"

"I don't know," Kindan admitted. "But when we went there last, Lorana and I put the fourth vial in the Records Room."

"The fourth vial?" B'nik repeated, his eyes narrowing thoughtfully.

"The one that killed Arith?" Fiona asked, her voice heavy with emotion.

"The one that can turn a watch-wher into a dragon," Kindan explained. "We put it at High Reaches where it would be safe."

"Why would Lorana want that?" T'mar mused. With a sad frown he added, "I can see why she would want B'nik's jacket, but not that."

"What?" Tullea demanded. "Why would she steal that?"

"For K'tan," Fiona said, turning to T'mar for confirmation.

"Ketan?" Tullea repeated. "What would he need with—"

"But a brown's not a bronze!" Kindan exclaimed.

B'nik's eyes widened and he mouthed the words "a brown" to himself.

"The dust!" Fiona said, turning to the others. "That's what she meant with the dust."

"What dust?" Kindan asked.

Fiona took a deep breath and said slowly, "This morning, before we went to Benden, I found her looking up at the dust above the Weyr Bowl."

The others looked at her in confusion.

"She asked me what color it was," Fiona continued. "I told her it was brown on the ground but in the air it shimmered."

"Like gold dust," Kindan breathed in surprise, fingering the brooch on his tunic. He turned to Fiona and commanded, "Check with Nuella, I'll bet they were there."

"Why?" Tullea demanded.

"Because, if the gold dust was on his skin, in the sunlight—for an instant—a brown could pass as a bronze," T'mar said, his eyes wide in sudden enlightenment. He turned to B'nik. "That's why he stole your jacket."

"But—a brown!" B'nik protested.

"Drith," Kindan said.

"Drith's dead," Tullea said flatly.

"Drith is certainly dead *now*."

"But he wasn't *then*!" Fiona declared, turning glowing eyes toward Kindan. She shook her head admiringly. "That's brilliant!"

"What?" Tullea demanded, still lost.

"Kindan and Fiona think that Lorana went back in time with Ketan to when Drith went *between*," T'mar said slowly, his eyes sliding toward the harper and Weyrwoman for confirmation.

"But he was sick, dying!" Tullea declared.

"Yes," Fiona agreed. "But apparently he could still fly."

"Long enough to save M'tal, me, and . . ." T'mar turned to B'nik, ". . . you."

"If that's so, then where's Lorana?" Tullea demanded. "Where's Minith?"

"You can't hear her?" Fiona asked in surprise.

Tullea shook her head.

"Then she's gone," Kindan declared in a flat, dead voice. The others looked up at him. "She went with Drith and K'tan." He pursed his lips grimly. "That's why she gave the vial to Nuella. She knew there is no hope, so she went as best she could."

"No!" Fiona's word was loud, clear and defiant. "She didn't do that."

Kindan frowned at her and shook his head. "Your problem, Fiona, is that you don't know when to quit."

"Of course I don't," Fiona agreed, her eyes flashing angrily. "*You* taught me that!"

"Me?"

"'Step by step, moment by moment,'" Fiona said, repeating the words of Kindan's song from the Plague. "Vaxoram said those words to you. You remembered them; you didn't give in when the Plague threatened to kill us all." She jabbed a finger at him, her eyes welling with tears. "*You* saved my life when even my father had given in to despair." She reached out and grabbed his chin in her hand, forcing him to meet her eyes. "I *won't* let you give in."

"She's dead, Fiona!" Kindan shouted, jerking out of her grasp. "She's gone *between*, her grief too great, and she's left us. She knows we're doomed and she couldn't bear to keep watching us all die slowly, dragon by dragon." He turned to Tullea. "So she kept her word to you and then she left." He turned back to Fiona. "She's gone. You can't hear her, can you?"

Fiona shook her head, lips quivering. "No, I can't." She looked up at him again, declaring stoutly, "But just because I can't doesn't mean she isn't alive, Kindan.

"She won't give up, she loves you too much."

"She's left me you," Kindan said bitterly. "She could leave me knowing that you're still here. In fact, she probably left because of you."

Fiona's eyes flashed and her hand leaped up, the sound of her slap startling everyone.

"Don't ever say that," Fiona told him savagely. "Don't ever think that."

"Because the truth hurts too much?" Kindan asked, raising a hand to massage his stinging cheek.

"It's not the truth," Fiona said quietly. "The truth is that she loves us both."

"She loved her brother and sister, too, Fiona," Kindan replied, his anger suddenly gone, his voice matching hers. "She couldn't save them, either."

"She wouldn't give up," Fiona declared. She looked up at him. "She learned it from you, just as I did." Kindan's eyes widened and his head jerked up at her words, as though stung once again. Fiona shook her head. "She'll pay any price, Kindan, she's *already*—oh!"

"What?"

"Oh, no!" Fiona sobbed, her legs sagging. Kindan and T'mar rushed to grab her and she wrapped her arms around them feebly for support.

"What is it?" Tullea asked. She moved closer and gently touched Fiona. "Fiona, what is it?"

"Any price," the young Weyrwoman sobbed. "Any price."

"Oh, no!" Kindan sighed, his eyes misting. "Fiona, you don't think—"

"Tenniz said it," Fiona said, lifting her head long enough to look toward Tullea. "He said that Terin would get her queen and he said this to Lorana: *The way forward is dark and long. A dragon gold is only the first price you'll pay for Pern.*"

Beside her, T'mar gasped. "She's gone ahead!"

"Turns ahead," Fiona said. "More than nine or even eleven coughs."

She pushed herself upright, unaware of Terin and Bekka rushing toward the commotion, not seeing Shaneese appear suddenly beside T'mar. Her eyes were only on Kindan.

"She paid the price," she said. "She paid the price with her child."

Kindan gasped in understanding. If Lorana had gone so far in time that Fiona could no longer hear her, Lorana had gone too far for her pregnancy to survive.

"'Step by step, moment by moment,'" Fiona repeated. She held his eyes with hers. "She paid the price. *We*"—and she turned to catch everyone in her gaze—"will do no less."

She drew herself up to her full height and, regal Weyrwoman, declared fiercely, "*We* will be here with all our love when she returns!"

Anne McCaffrey's Pern books are some of the most beloved science fiction novels in the world. Over the past few years, though, she has allowed her son Todd to take over the reins of Pern—molding the world and its stories with his own vision, while always maintaining the spirit and caring Anne has imbued into her novels.

Upon reading *Dragonsblood, Dragonheart,* and the book in your hands, *Dragongirl,* though, Anne was so enchanted by the story Todd was crafting and the characters he was bringing to life that she asked his permission to join in the final drama of his tale of Pern.

We are extremely pleased that the follow-up to *Dragongirl* is once again going to feature a collaboration between mother and son, as Anne and Todd McCaffrey work together to bring you the next exciting book in the Pern series:

DRAGONRIDER

On sale May 2011

ABOUT THE AUTHOR

TODD MCCAFFREY is the bestselling author of the Pern novels *Dragonsblood* and *Dragonheart*, and the co-author, with his mother, Anne McCaffrey, of *Dragon's Kin, Dragon's Fire,* and *Dragon Harper*. A computer engineer, he currently lives in Los Angeles. Having grown up in Ireland with the epic of the Dragonriders of Pern,® he is bursting with ideas for new stories of that world, its people, and its dragons.

www.toddmccaffrey.org

ABOUT THE TYPE

This book is set in Palatino, designed by Hermann Zapf for the Stempel foundry in 1950. It is one of the most widely used typefaces in the world today. Classical Italian Renaissance letterforms blend with the crispness of line needed for twentieth-century printing processes, and Palatino's generous width aids readability at small sizes. Although Zapf originally intended it to be a display face, the graceful and highly legible Palatino is a frequent choice for setting text.